FEATHERS THAT BLEED

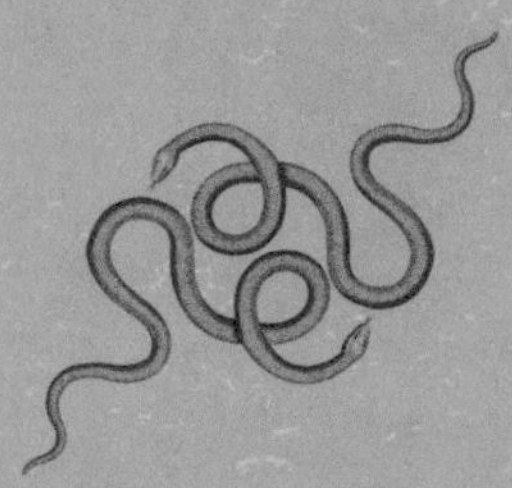

SANA KHATRI

WELCOME TO

Riverside, California

Feathers That Bleed

Cover illustration & background by Daniel Toro (DannoTC)

Cover Design by Sana Khatri

ISBN: 978-93-340-0920-0

DISCLAIMER

NOTE: *Check the **trigger warnings** on the next page.*

Feathers That Bleed is a dark romance. I repeat: this book is a **DARK** romance. A lot of the themes, events, or words mentioned in this book may be triggering to some, so please, *please* consider your comfort before diving into this story. But, if you *have* decided to venture ahead, then I'm ever so grateful to you! This is my first dark romance project, and I really hope I've done at least an okay enough job of giving you a wild story to read, and even wilder characters to fall in love with.

– Sana Khatri

Trigger Warnings

This book consists of **detailed mentions** of child abuse, child SA, murder, gore, mutilation, torture, suicide, knife play, blood play, blood consumption, breath play, mild degradation; child, women, and organ trafficking, rape, physical abuse, and cheating (FYI: The main characters **do not** cheat on each other after having met each other).

Also by Sana Khatri

Those Chance Encounters

Can We Pretend?

Presuming You

Unturned Rubbles

When Words Waver

To those who thought I could never touch the dark side, let alone dive into it. This one's for you, love. Thank you for doubting me; thank you for making my will so fucking ironclad that I not only stepped foot into the dark, but I think I even stole a piece of it for myself.

Pronunciations

- Dorran: *Door – rah – un*
- Cignette: *Sig – net*

Search for 'Feathers That Bleed' on Spotify

- Like A Villain – Bad Omens
- What It Cost – Bad Omens
- CONCRETE JUNGLE – Bad Omens
- ARTIFICIAL SUICIDE – Bad Omens
- Mercy – Bad Omens
- Your Time Has Come – Tribal Blood
- Silent Killer – KXLLYXU
- Monster – Mustafa Atarer
- Reaper – Glaceo, RIELL
- Wicked as They Come – CRMNL
- Losing Control – JPB, Mendum, Marvin Divine
- MACHINE – Neoni
- Good to Be Bad – CRMNL
- BOUNCE! – Zack Merci, Nieko
- The Chase – Zack Merci, Nieko
- Rhapsody In Pink – Stela Cole
- Kingdom – Royale
- Way Down We Go – KALEO

- Puppet (Demo Version) – Faouzia
- Animal – Jim Yosef, RIELL
- DARKSIDE – Neoni
- Overthinking – Zoe Wees
- Born Without a Heart – Faouzia
- Control – Zoe Wees
- The Dark – ARCANA
- Live Wire – Meghan Kabir
- Holy Water – Freya Ridings
- Villain – ARCANA, Zack Merci
- Ultraviolet – Freya Ridings
- Free – BROODS
- SANCTUARY – Neoni
- End It – RIELL
- Game of Survival – Ruelle
- Bottom Of The Deep Blue Sea – MISSIO
- Poison – Freya Ridings
- Wolves – James Arthur
- Body on Me – Rita Ora, Chris Brown
- Broken Pieces Shine – Evanescence
- Ghost – Zoe Wees
- Kiss or Kill – Stela Cole
- Still Alive – Demi Lovato
- Conscious – BROODS
- Not Afraid Anymore – Halsey

ABOUT THE AUTHOR

Sana Khatri is an International Bestselling author, an IT (Information Technology) graduate, a bunny momma, and a makeup junkie. She resides with her aunts, mother, and her younger brother in Mumbai, India. Because her dad is the one who initially motivated her to keep writing, she makes sure to ask him for book-related opinions and suggestions whenever she needs them. She is an unwavering reader, dreamer, and believer, and prefers to have a speck of reality in her fictitious stories.

Twitter & Instagram:

@isanakhatri

Part One

THE *Beginning*

1. DORRAN

My cock slides in and out of her ass as I pound into her from behind. Tightening my grip on her raven-black hair, I press the side of her face further against the filthy cobble wall and continue to fuck her.

That's how she wanted it – from the back, rough and hard. And so, that's exactly what I'm giving her.

She rubs her clit with one hand, while the other is braced on the dumpster next to her. She tries to push against my grip on her hair so that she can move her face, but I apply more pressure on it, making her cry out. She's saying something, but the words fizzle out as she goes from moaning, to trying to be coherent. Either way, I couldn't give a shit.

My balls slap against her cunt as I quicken my pace. I feel myself draw up, so I close my eyes and tip my head back, relishing the rush of my orgasm. My shoulders stiffen, and with a jerk, I come inside her tight little ass, groaning as I do.

Fuck, that was hot.

"Dorran?"

I open my eyes and look to my right. "What?" I grit out.

Jayce purses his lips as he assesses me for a brief moment – cock still buried inside the chick whose name I didn't care to ask – then lets go of a soft exhale. His towering presence conceals the streetlights behind him, making him appear muted against the night.

"We've got him," he tells me.

I pull out of the girl's ass, and watch as my cum starts dripping down her hole, then lift my boxers and jeans up before buttoning and zipping the latter.

She turns around and fixes her skirt, followed by the rest of herself. "My name's Sylvia," she says to me.

I give her a quick head-to-toe scan as I click my belt back on, then walk away from her, leaving her dumbfounded.

I don't care who she is, as long as she gives me what I want. Which she *did*, of course.

Quick fucks in darkened alleys don't require association or one-on-one conversations, so when chicks try doing just that, it confuses and irks me.

"You just *had* to get your dick wet, didn't you?" Jayce comments the second I've reached him.

"Had to get the edge off," I snark with a grin. "Besides, she readily offered herself to me. I couldn't have said no even if I wanted to."

He scoffs. "Let's just fucking go; we've got a job to do," he says, then turns around and starts heading towards the main street.

I stretch my neck side-to-side and follow after him, itching to get my hands dirty.

The real fun is about to begin, and I'll be in the front-fucking-seat, making it all happen.

2.
DORRAN

Blood – thick and warm – gushes out of his freshly punctured skin. It deftly flows down to my white-knuckled fingers that are wrapped around my switchblade's black handle, then slithers onto the porcelain floor beneath us like a living art waking itself from a slumber.

Upbeat music, muted by the closed bathroom door, flits in, and the ground vibrates faintly against its impact.

The man jerks under me – a vain, pathetic effort, really – and tries to scream around the wad of cash I'd shoved in his mouth after having successfully thrown his scrawny ass off his feet with a single punch in the face a couple minutes ago.

I lean in, bringing my face close to his, and am immediately hit with a smell that's a blend of sweat, luxe cologne, and my absolute favorite: *blood.*

The man – Devon Summers – pants unsteadily, so I push my blade a bit further into the side of his open neck.

He gasps; his eyes bulge out – sockets marred with red veins – and then, after a few painstaking seconds, he stills. *Completely.*

Mission accomplished.

I pull my switchblade out and get to my feet, just as Jayce stops the recording on his phone. I sidestep the now dead Devon, walk past Alex and Varsha, and make my way over to one of the sinks in the men's bathroom.

It wasn't hard to find Devon at *Indulgence*, a VIP-only club in the heart of upper-side Riverside. He *screamed* money – from his *Armani* three-piece to his shiny *Berluti* shoes. And, not to forget, with the number of half-naked chicks he had fawning over him, he was pretty much an easy scout, even in a crowd full of drunk, lust-driven elites.

When my long-term client, Edgar 'Eddie' Hank, had ordered Summers' kill a week ago, I'd almost turned him down. Elites like Summers always have a fuck load of enemies anyway, and I don't take on a kill unless the reason behind it stands for something.

I've executed meaningless kills in the past, and they've never given me the thrill I so madly crave. The sense of fulfillment, that hunger for rising over someone's demise, the feel of a fading pulse against my blade – those are the things that drive me, that make me who I am.

And killing Devon – the man responsible for abducting and killing 34 suburb children for their organs just to further broaden his pockets – did just that; it made me feel liberated, fucking dizzy with adrenaline.

I stop in front of the massive, gold-rimmed mirror, and look at myself. There's blood splattered on the right side of my face, and on my yellow vest. More of it inks my hand and forearm, as if it's attempting to claw its way up. My dark blue eyes shine against the white lights above me, and when my crew's gazes meet mine in the mirror's reflection, we grin at each other.

"Just sent the video to Eddie," Jayce tells me, then chuckles. "It's like he was waiting for it, because he transferred the cash to your account after less than a minute of receiving my text."

Varsha leans against one of the empty stalls and scoffs before folding her arms across her tiny frame. "Typical."

Alex steps on Devon's stomach and crosses the way to where Jayce is standing behind me. "You think our little Eddie's gonna jerk off to the sound of Devon's last breath tonight?" he asks around a sharp smile.

Jayce bends and presses a kiss on Alex's lips. "I love it when you talk dirty, babe."

Varsha pretends to gag, while I simply shake my head, which causes my dark curls to sway a bit.

"Did you confirm the cleanup with Hank?" I question Jayce, who pulls away from his husband long enough to say, "Yup. His people should be here in ten, tops."

Oh, and did I mention that Edgar owns *Indulgence*? Well, he does, and he takes it upon himself to keep track of all the sins its members have committed, before assigning said members' deaths to me. Me and the crew get to do what we love, earn a motherfucking load of cash out of it, and we don't even have to worry about the mess we leave behind after doing our jobs.

Win-fucking-win, huh?

"Good," I say, then drag my bloody right thumb over my jaw before bringing it to my mouth. I part my lips while looking at myself in the mirror, then wrap them around my thumb before sucking off the blood around it. Goosebumps rise throughout my body when the similar yet potent taste hits me in full force, and I refrain from moaning as I swallow and pull my hand back.

"Fuck," Alex mutters as he looks at me, his grey pupils all but dilated.

It's more about the act for him, rather than the person performing it. A 70-year-old could be doing what I just did, and Alex would still get a boner. That's just how he is, and honestly, me and the rest of the crew wouldn't have him any other way.

'Fucked-up and proud' is my team and I's sole motto, after all.

Jayce quirks a brow at me. "How's it taste?" he asks, referring to the blood I've consumed.

Varsha smirks, because she already knows what my answer's gonna be, while Alex looks on with intent.

I grin at Jayce's reflection. "Like victory," I answer, then run the tip of my tongue over my bottom lip.

"Hell yeah," Alex chimes, and I can't help but laugh at his enthusiasm.

He's the youngest among us – just 23 – so he usually gets away with behaving however the fuck he wants.

"Time for the *Bloody Prince* and his band to make an exit, brother," Varsha says to me.

I turn, wink at her, and twist my switchblade between my hands. "Well, let's give em' a show, then, shall we?"

3.
CIGNETTE

Hands – calloused and firm – travel down my bare shoulders and arms. They circle my waist, then slowly move to my belt buckle.

The room smells too clean, too…*dry*, I guess – making my nostrils burn a little. But, given that it's a tattoo parlor, I can't really expect it to smell like a damn spa, now can I?

The mauve curtains in the room are pulled back, making the early-morning sunlight stream through the glass window and cast warm shadows on the wallpapered wall and worktable. It's kind of a laughable contrast to the tattoo guns, inks, gloves, gauzes and various other items that fill up the area, but I think that's exactly what makes it mundane.

"How ready are you for me, huh, Princess?" Gavin asks from behind. He unbuckles my belt and unzips my denim shorts, then brushes his long fingers over my panties.

Oh, how my mother and uncle would react if they saw me like this. 28-year-old daughter of the county's most fashionable woman, niece of Riverside's County Administrator himself, getting ready for a quick fuck in one of the private rooms of a tattoo shop on the Main Street in the suburbs.

There's a sound of something falling outside, followed by a muffled curse.

I move my long, flamingo-pink hair over a shoulder. "You really wanna do this here, with your girlfriend just outside at the reception desk?" I say, then arch against Gavin's chest when he cups my pussy in a rough grip.

"I'm sure she's too busy schmoozing with the customers to care about what I'm doing with my cock right now," he whispers in my ear.

I grab his wrist so that I can pull his hand away from between my legs, then turn around and raise a brow at him. "It's 9 in the morning, Gav," I tell him. "It's safe to assume that Nicole is most likely busy waiting for you to leave this room than she is chatting up your *customers*." I click my tongue. "I don't think people wake up and decide to just walk into a tattoo shop on a regular basis. Doesn't seem very logical to me."

Gavin scowls. "Well, *you're* here, though, aren't you?"

I run my eyes over his shoulder-length blond hair, piercing jade eyes, clean-shaven jaw, tattooed forearms, and broad shoulders that are concealed behind his fitted black t-shirt. "Hmm," I start, then glance at the bulge straining his dark jeans. "But I'm here for the *lovely* view, and nothing else."

Gavin continues to scowl. "You're a fucking menace, Cigs."

I chuckle and hop onto the worktable behind me. "And that's exactly what makes me so special, doesn't it?"

Him and I don't fuck in his shop; the first time had been the only exception. It's always in his jeep, in his apartment, or in the bathroom of a grocery store. We like it convenient, quick, and filthy, but we also don't want Nicole walking in on us. I prefer Gavin's balls exactly where they are, thank you very much.

I'd met him three months ago, when I'd first visited his shop, *Radical Ink*. I'd had a craving to get a tattoo, both to have something that would define me in a way nothing else ever would, and to spite my mom whilst also living up to my colorful reputation in Riverside. You know, the 'fucking and drinking around' kinda reputation. Pure classic.

They don't call me the *Flawed Princess* for nothing, after all.

So, back to the tattoo. A quick Google search had shown me that the best place to get inked was Gavin's shop, and so, one random afternoon, I'd lied to my bodyguard, Maverick, about having to meet a "friend" for brunch – unchaperoned, of course – before driving over to Main Street.

The moment I'd seen Gavin, I'd known that he'd be something to look forward to. We'd fucked on the recliner in his private workroom twenty minutes after having met each other – unbeknownst to Nicole, obviously – and let me tell ya: he didn't disappoint *at all*.

The tattoo he'd inked on my upper-back that day – a massive swan with her feathers disbanded around her – is a true piece of art, and the exact reflection of how I feel. I'd merely given him a vague idea of what I wanted, and he'd done nothing short of an outstanding job of defining the essence of me through ink on flesh.

Because it really *is* an essence of me – a cygnet. A *swan*.

That's what my name is taken from, modified by my uncle to make it sound more…*posh*.

But, as much as *I* love my tattoo, my mother despises it twice as much. That afternoon, when I'd gotten home from *Radical Ink*, she'd left more bruises on my body than she has in a while.

Her beating me is a usual feat, but sometimes, she crosses the line; makes me see exactly what I mean to her, which is absolutely *nothing*. Because really, I don't mean shit to her. I'm the product of a drunken one-night-stand, for Christ's sake. I'm as neglected as they come. All I'm good for is managing the social media accounts of her fashion brand, *Lure*, and on several occasions, being a toy for her to manhandle and mark.

Gavin doesn't care about said marks, though. He sees them, but he doesn't ask, doesn't offer anything in regards to them. And I don't exactly care that he doesn't, to be honest. I love each and every one of my bruises, because they remind me that I'm real. They're temporary stamps of victory that come and go – victory against the hate my own mother has for me.

"Cigs?"

I look up and meet Gavin's eyes.

"Are we doing this, or what?" he asks a bit impatiently. For a man so talented at his job, he sure is a dense motherfucker.

I pull up a fallen strap of my white tank top. "I can't," I say simply. "I just…not right now."

The anger on his face is almost comical. "Then why the fuck did you come here anyway?" he all but spits the words at me.

Wow, *seriously*?

I clench my jaw and get off the table. "Watch your tone, Gav," I hiss. "I don't live on your damn commands, you get it? I'm Cignette Adler, and I don't take shit from rock-bottom *assholes* like you." I snatch my phone from the table, slide it into my back-pocket, and march out of the room.

"Oh, hey, Cig–" Nicole starts, but immediately stops when I walk right past the reception desk.

I briefly hear Gavin and her exchanging a few words as I push open the shop's door and step out, but I don't stop, even as I feel his presence behind me.

"Cigs," he says helplessly. "Cigs, come on." He tries to grab my hand, but I sidestep him and finally reach my pink Cadillac.

"Look, I'm sorry, okay? I'm fucking *sorry*."

I take my keys out of my shorts and swivel around. "I'm *this* close," I begin, then emphasize my point by bringing my forefinger and thumb close, "to stabbing my key into your skull, so don't even *try* to test me right now."

"Gee." He scratches the side of his jaw. "Talk about anger issues."

"Funny, especially because I don't remember turning red in the face when I said no to having sex with you just now. It was *you* who almost lost it, not *me*."

His lips part in surprise. "I did not–"

"Don't even try to deny it."

"I'm pretty sure I didn't."

"And I'm a 100% sure you *did*."

He huffs and steps closer. "Look–"

"Stop it." I realize we're behaving less like adults and more like confused teenagers. "Just stop," I say, then sigh and turn around. I unlock my car, get in, and put the key into the ignition before twisting it.

Nothing happens.

I try again, and there's a weak clicking noise, but then that, too, is gone.

"No," I breathe. "No, no, *no*." This can*not* be happening right now.

A shadow falls over my car's open window. "Oh, look; the little Princess's fancy carriage broke down on her," Gavin muses, then pouts.

I grit my teeth, pull my keys out, and make to shove one of them into his eye, but he quickly grabs my wrist around a chuckle, then kisses the back of my fingers before saying, "Lemme help."

"*Fuck you*."

He winks. "Maybe later – if you're lucky."

"You–"

He stops me by leaning in and pressing a chaste kiss on my lips. "Shut the fuck up, Cigs," he whispers. "For once in your uptight life, just shut up and listen to me."

I glare at him when he moves back and looks at me, but don't say anything.

He takes the keys from me and tries starting the car again, but it doesn't work. After several attempts, he exhales loudly and rests his forearms on the car's hood. "We'll need to get it checked."

I roll my eyes. "No shit, Sherlock."

He grins. "There's a garage at the end of the street," he tells me. "The best one in the entire county."

I look ahead, as if I'll be able to see said garage.

"I'm sure you've passed by it the couple of times you've visited my shop," Gavin adds.

I shake my head. "I don't think I've paid any attention to it."

He laughs. "*Anyways…*"

I glare at him again, which makes him laugh harder.

"I'll push your car over to the garage," he says. "We'll see what they say is wrong with it, and if they wanna keep it in, that's fine. I'll bring it over to your place once they're done fixing it."

I work my jaw as I glance between him and the steering wheel. I kinda feel like a jerk for saying the shit that I said to him, but I also feel like he deserved some of it, if not all.

I lick my lips and put the car in neutral. "Okay," I tell him, then meet his gaze. "Thanks for doing this for me."

He smiles. "Don't mention it." He then knocks the driver's side door twice, so I pop it open for him.

"Work the wheel and brakes while I push, yeah?" he says.

I nod, then clutch the steering wheel tighter.

Instead of getting ready to push ahead, though, he bends and looks at me again. "Listen…" He curls his hair behind his ear. "Just…just be careful while we're there, okay?"

Confused, I shift in my seat and furrow my brows at him. "Why?"

An unmistakable shadow passes over his beautiful features, and his bright eyes seem to dim a little as he says, "Because, Cigs, the owner of the garage we're going to, is Dorran motherfucking Ledger."

4.
DORRAN

"Yo, Ledge," comes Jayce's voice from ahead of me.

I move out from under the hood of the Ford Fiesta I've been working on, then wipe my grease-stained palms over the front of my faded jeans as I straighten. "Yeah?"

He grins darkly, and his brown eyes all but twinkle as he says, "There's a special customer out front. I think you should take this one yourself."

I arch a brow and pull a cigarette out of my back pocket. "Don't fuck with me, Jay; I've got shit to do."

"I'm not. Just indulge me for a second, will ya?" Christ, he looks almost giddy with joy.

He's 35 to my 32, and yet, right now, he's clearly not acting his age.

I place the cigarette between my lips, then light it up before taking a long drag of it. "Who is it?" I ask through the smoke, then fix the straps of my green ribbed vest.

"Like hell I'm telling you."

I kick him in the shin, to which he chuckles.

"Real mature, asshat," I mumble around the cigarette, then point a finger at him. "Finish working on the Fiesta. I'll go handle this *special customer* of yours."

He gives me a mock salute. "You got it."

I roll my eyes and step away from the car, then glance around the garage as I exhale a puff of smoke.

Alex is busy fixing a Jr. Scout, and Varsha is working on the Corvette that came in last evening.

My garage, *Finesse*, is my pride. It's the result of years of blood and sweat – both literal – and hours upon hours of trial-and-errors turned into success. Jayce and I built this place from the ground up 5 years ago, and despite the fact that almost everyone in Riverside knows who I am, they still bring their trusty-ass vehicles to my garage to get 'em fixed.

Finesse isn't extravagant by any means. With a concrete-made interior, it's as simple as it gets. There's a main counter right in front of the entrance, with a bathroom on its left and a small workstation for two-wheelers on its right. Alex has a mini fridge in there, and all that's inside it, is booze.

There're two massive bays on both sides of the wide area, each one with its own tool box. The metal platforms lining the space around the garage's entrance, home the necessary spare parts we need for the everyday fixes. And then finally, there's a short wooden staircase – just behind the main counter – that leads to my loft.

But this place – it wouldn't be what it is, not without my crew. Without Jayce, who's my fucking rock. Without Alex, whose enthusiasm is a drug the 4 of us need in abundance, especially on days where shit feels too heavy. And without Varsha, who makes me stronger than I am.

We may not share blood, but me and my crew are made from the same thread of immorality; from scars that are rooted within similar grounds. And that, in my opinion, is the best kinda bond there is in this world.

I sigh and tap the cigarette with a finger, resulting in ashes to fall next to my work boots. I then turn around and walk outside the garage.

A muffled conversation suddenly halts – most probably due to my presence. I lift my head as I come to a stop, and that's exactly when I see her.

Her hair's so fucking pink that it all but demands a person's attention, but I guess it goes really well with the vibe she's got going 'round for herself. Her olive skin is a physical sin wrapped around her willowy body; the way she shifts against my perusal makes my veins burn. She's got a mole just below her slightly hollowed left cheek, and a noticeable indent just above her top lip.

I meet her eyes – so dark they threaten to suck me into their abyss – and realize that I've never been more gravitated towards anything in my life than I am to her.

Cignette Adler exudes wild beauty, and I'll be damned to the pits of hell if I even *try* to convince myself otherwise.

She smirks when I push my curls away from my forehead, then runs the tip of her tongue over her bottom lip when I take a quick drag of my cigarette before smirking right back at her.

I know *of* her, of course, but I don't exactly *know* her. And I'm sure with the way she's looking at me – with intrigue and something else I can't really put a finger on – she's on the same page in context to me.

A movement on the left catches my eye, and when I glance at it, I feel my back stiffen. I clench my jaw as I stare at the man next to Cignette.

Gavin Langford.

He regards me coolly, as if he holds some kind of power over me, which is hysterical, to be quite honest.

What a gullible little fuck.

I glance at Cignette again, and find that she's studying me with apt interest.

What the hell are you doing with this dumpster rat? I wanna question. *Why the fuck are you here with* him*?*

But it's not my place to ask any of those things to her. It's none of my damn business.

My right hand itches to touch my switchblade that's in the front pocket of my jeans, but I refrain the urge and face Cignette again. "How can I help ya?" I ask her clinically, as if I'm not thinking of all the ways I wanna cause physical harm to the man next to her.

"Her car won't start," Gavin responds.

I clench and unclench my free hand to release some of my anger upon hearing his voice, then take one last drag of my cigarette before killing it under my boot.

Both Gavin and Cignette watch my every move, and when I take a few steps in the latter's direction, Gavin instinctively shifts closer to her.

I laugh, then – *actually* laugh – because I can't help it. Man, he's so damn stupid.

Cignette presses her lips together as she glances between Gavin and I, then clears her throat and says, "He's right; my car won't start." I realize that this close, I can easily smell her citrusy perfume, see her unblemished skin better, and look closely into those depthless eyes of hers.

I nod, then glance over her shoulders – at the car in question – and run a hand over my mouth to hide a grin.

A fucking *pink* Cadillac.

Accurate, I suppose, given her status.

I look down at her. "Keys."

She straightens, which brings her even closer to me.

I watch, helplessly transfixed, as her eyelids flutter, her lashes brush against her slightly flushed cheeks, and her chest rises and falls at a hypnotic rhythm as she pulls her keys out of her shorts and offers them to me.

"I can show y–" Gavin interrupts, but I cut him off with a glare.

"Don't fucking talk," I tell him.

He tries to do just that, but I step back and make my way over to the Cadillac.

I get into the plush driver's seat, put the key into the ignition, and turn it, but that does absolutely nothing. There's no lights, no radio, no nothing. I repeat the process, and hear a barely audible clicking sound.

Gotcha.

"The battery's dead," I announce, then get out of the car.

Cignette purses her lips. "So…that means you'll have to…"

"I'll have to replace it, yeah," I say.

"How long's that gonna take?" Gavin asks, just to further grate at my nerves. "We can leave the car here and come back for it later."

I ignore him, naturally, then turn towards the garage. "*Jay?*" I holler.

"Yeah?" he's wiping his face with a towel as he walks over, then puts his *Witcher* cap on backwards, which effectively hides his buzzed hair.

"We got any 534s on hand or somethin'?" I ask him. When he reaches close enough, I discreetly grab him by the collar of his grey t-shirt and hiss, "Couldn't you have warned me beforehand about the chimp being here?"

"What, and miss the Oscar-worthy look you have on your face right now?" He winks when I tug at his collar. "I just wanted to see how you reacted to him in little miss Adler's presence, okay? Jeez, dude; relax."

I glower at him. "Well, fuck you very much for *that*," I say, then add, "Make sure Varsha stays inside while he's here."

Varsha and Gavin had dated for a year, right before the asshole had decided to up and cheat on her with one of his customers. Varsha had visited *Radical Ink* to get a tattoo, had chickened out at the end moment, and had instead fallen for Gavin's charms. Shit was great between them, I guess, but then she'd one day found him ass-fucking a random chick in his shop, and she'd broken down completely. Closed herself off, in a way.

Gavin had tried to weasel his way back into her life weeks after their breakup, but when I'd put my blade to his throat and asked him to back off, he had. He knew better than to act against my warning.

But that was 11 months ago; that's when we'd last seen him. The dipshit takes the long way home every single day just to avoid passing by *Finesse*, so I don't know why he has chosen to show up here today.

Trying to figure out how men like him work, isn't my job, but if he's here with ulterior motives, then he sure as fuck isn't walking out alive.

Jayce nods at my request, then says, "Why's he here anyway? What's a piece of trash like him doing with *her*?"

I sigh and let go of his collar. "That's exactly what I'm trying to figure out."

He raises a brow. "Are you now?" he muses.

I ignore the hint of surprise in his question. It is, after all, doing absolutely nothing to push aside my own confusion over my sudden interest in this woman.

"Find me that fucking battery, Jay," I order.

He raises his hands in surrender and starts back-walking. "You got it, boss."

Alex appears behind him, and when Jayce sees him, he turns fully, kisses him senseless, then whispers something in his ear before jerking his head towards Gavin.

Alex nods, then joins me outside. He gives Gavin a dismissive once-over. "Fuck you," he tells him, so casually that I have to bite the inside of my cheek in order to stifle my smile.

"Thanks, man," Gavin deadpans.

I cough, and Cignette looks thoroughly amused.

Alex's brown hair ruffles chaotically with the warm wind as he faces her. "You wanna come inside and have a drink with Varsha and I while Ledge gets your car fixed up?" he asks.

"It's barely 10 in the morning, Alex," Gavin provides his two cents.

Alex looks appalled. "Please keep your irrelevancy in your pants. It's really not needed here."

Cignette is trying so hard not to laugh, whereas Gavin looks like he might fucking detonate in shame.

"I–" he starts, but Cignette cuts him off.

"I'm down," she chimes with a grin, and my God, I feel something inside my stomach twist at that simple action of hers.

Dammit all to hell.

"Perfect; follow me."

"Cigs, stop–" Gavin tries to grab her arm, but she's already reached Alex's side and is striking up a conversation with him.

I wait until they've gone inside, then slide my hands into the back pockets of my jeans before making my way over to a nervous-looking Gavin.

I widen my stance just a little as I come to a stop in front of him, and when a muscle jumps in his jaw, I narrow my eyes at him. "Why are you here?" I question.

"I told you why." He's trying to act bored, but I notice the constant bob of his Adam's apple as he keeps glancing around us.

I smirk. "I feel like we're way past third-grade lies, Gav, don't you think?" I tell him. "So, I'm going to ask again: *why are you here?*"

He scoffs. "I don't know what you expect me to say, Dorran," he states, then meets my eyes. "I'm here because Cignette's car broke down, and your garage is the closest one in the area. That's it; that's the *only* reason why I'm here."

I search his face, and realize he isn't lying. "So you're not here to manipulate Varsha into getting back with you?"

He laughs and shakes his head. "Fuck no, man; I'm over her. For real."

His watered-down tone makes me grit my teeth, but I try not to lose my cool over it.

"You're dating the County Administrator's niece, then? Trying to get it on with the elites, or some shit?"

He chuckles. "Not really." He runs his fingers through his hair. "She's way outta my league, and you and I both know that."

I relax my stance and fold my arms across my chest. "So what, you brought her here out of the kindness of your heart?"

He lets go of a breath and runs a hand over his jaw. "We're fucking, okay?" he says. "I'm dating someone else, but Cigs and I – we're…" he trails, then swallows.

I don't know why I was expecting a different kind of answer from him. It's always the same pattern with him, no matter what.

"Does Cignette know you're in a relationship?" I ask.

He nods. "Yup."

"And does your girlfriend know about Cignette?"

He shakes his head. "No."

I dig the heels of my boots into the ground. "So you're cheating on her."

He blinks in surprise. "What's it to *you*, man? Why're you so interested? It's not your *sister* this time, so my love and sex lives shouldn't be any of your damn business. Stay out of it, alright?"

Honestly, I couldn't care less about him or the woman he's dating, and I certainly don't give any number of shits about their feelings. But Cignette, on the other hand…

That woman is turning me into an open wound – fucking gaping and vulnerable. And, as much as I don't like what it's doing to me, I also wanna dive deeper and see where it takes me.

"I think you should go," I tell Gavin.

His brows pinch together as he stares at me. "Excuse me?"

"Get outta here, Gav," I say. "Are you suddenly hard on the ears or something?"

"And leave Cignette with *you*?" he asks incredulously. "I don't think so."

I lean in a little, and watch as he takes a step back. "I think she'll be *just* fine with me."

He sneers at me. "Well, what *I* think is that you're damn near *delusional*."

"Watch it, Gavin," Jayce warns. A second later, he's standing next to me, his gaze hard.

"Get. Outta. Here," I repeat, and this time, the fucker actually listens. He gives Jayce and I a pathetic excuse of a glare, pivots on his feet, and practically jogs back up the street.

"That was easy," Jayce observes.

I grin. "When has it *ever* been difficult with him?"

Jayce chuckles. "Touché." He then bumps his shoulder against mine. "I found the battery, by the way."

I nod at him. "Perfect."

He places said battery on the ground, next to a portable toolbox that he's already got set up for me, which makes me smile.

I really don't deserve this guy.

"If you need anything else, just lemme know," he tells me as he straightens.

I twist his cap around and briefly cup the side of his neck. "Thanks, man."

"I've got you." He squeezes my wrist, then goes back in to work on the Fiesta.

I follow him, grab my cap from the rack next to the entrance, and chance a glance to where Alex and Varsha are busy talking to a smiling Cignette.

She laughs, and I'm left standing there like a moron, staring at her.

It's an airy sound, her laughter. Almost weightless. And I realize, to my stupefaction, that I really like listening to it.

Her hair sways as she shifts and takes a drink from the beer bottle in her hand, and my lips twitch at the fact that she's *actually* following in on my crew and I's irregular routine of drinking at 10 in the fucking morning.

She lifts her head, and our eyes meet. She looks around as if searching for Gavin, but I shake my head subtly and mouth, "*Don't mention him.*"

She has no idea why I'm asking her to do that, yet she inclines her head at my request anyway.

I give her a quick wink, then head outside again.

I push my curls back, put my cap on, and pop open the Cadillac's hood. I grab a wrench from the toolbox and loosen the nuts holding the cables to the terminal. Beads of sweat trickle down my temples as I pull the negative cable off first, then proceed to do the same to the positive one. Once I'm done with that, I keep both the cables separated so that they don't end up touching each other.

I'm about to lift out the old battery when I feel a crunch of gravel behind me, followed by a flash of a shadow on my left. But, before I can turn toward it, though, Cignette appears in my line of view. Sans the beer bottle from earlier.

"Where is he?" she asks.

I lift the old battery and place it on the ground. "I asked him to leave."

"Why?" Pure curiosity laces her voice.

I sigh and wipe the sweat off my upper lip as I straighten. "Because he's Varsha's ex, and I didn't want her to see him, or him to see her."

Cignette sucks in a breath, and her brows rise a little. "I see." She shifts on her feet, and if I'm not mistaken, I notice a hint of anger on her face.

I purposefully brush by her to get to the new battery, and once I have it, I set it in and attach the cables to it – the negative one first, and then the positive.

I'm aware that she's tracking my movements, so I work slow; I let her see everything she wants to see. It only serves to feed my fascination towards her.

Once I'm done, I check to see if the nuts are tight enough, then step back and slam the Cadillac's hood shut. Placing a hand on it, I balance my weight sideways and say, "I'm assuming you're aware that he has a girlfriend." I know that she knows, but I still want her to admit it out loud.

Cignette swallows and leans against the car. "I am, yeah."

I hum. "Then I'm also assuming that you like him on quite a serious note." Like him to the point where you don't care about the chick he's seeing, or that him being in a relationship doesn't affect your decision to want to hook up with him, is what I mean.

"I like him enough to fuck him," she says, then lifts a shoulder. "Because that's all it really is – casual, meaningless sex."

I don't know why that confession riles me, but it does. The thought of Gavin fucking Cignette makes my skin crawl; makes me wanna reach for the strings of her memories that hold the stupid asshole in them, and pull them apart.

"Gotcha," I state, then jerk my head towards the car. "It's done. You should try starting it."

She gets in and does just that, then gives me a grin and a thumbs up when the engine roars to life.

Mission accomplished.

"How're you paying?" I ask her when she steps out and walks over to me again. "Cash or card?"

"Card." She reaches for the right back pocket of her shorts, frowns, then moves onto the other. She does that a few times – keeps searching all of her pockets – but all she manages to find is *nothing*.

"Fuck," she whispers, then pats her shorts once more. "Fuck-fuck-fuck." She looks at me with evident guilt on her face. "I can't find my card," she says.

I put my tongue to my cheek. "I can see that," I muse.

"Umm…" She sighs. "Look, if you gimme an hour, I can drive home and get you the cash. I don't have any on me at the moment, and I seem to have forgotten my card at the estate."

I pull off my cap and tousle my now-sweaty hair. "There's no need for that. You can come by tomorrow, if that's convenient for you."

She shakes her head. "No, that's not fair to you." She pauses, looks contemplative, then says, "Drop by the estate after you've closed shop. I can pay you then."

I hesitate at that.

I know every single one of the guards that's stationed by and in her mother, Miranda's, fancy house. Me and the crew do, after all, conduct all of the kills for her and her brother, Chase. I'm aware that every guard under his payroll has rotational shifts – ones that take them back-and-forth from his to his sister's estates. Cignette, of course, doesn't need to know that *I* know all of this shit, or that I kill for her uncle.

Still, none of it means that I can simply trot up to their house. But hey, when the fuck have I shied away from jumping right into a roaring inferno?

Never, as far as I can remember.

I scrub a hand under my jaw and say, "Sure." Why the hell not, right? I've already been acting deranged in the presence of this woman, so what's a little more madness to top it all off and damn me furthermore?

Besides, being alone with her might give me a chance to do the thing I've wanted to do since she got here: stake my goddamn claim on her. And yeah, it's very Neanderthal-like of me to say that, but this is who I am, and Cignette will have to get used to it, whether she likes it or not. Because one thing I know for sure is that she can't be with Gavin, not after *I've* laid eyes on her.

"Great." She smiles, and this time, I feel its impact straight to my cock.

We exchange numbers, and I can't help but think how Jayce is going to have my ass for this. But I guess it's too late for me to back out now, so eh, whatever.

"Oh hey, I forgot to tell you," Cignette begins. "You'll have to come over before 12a.m., because that's when our gates close, and they don't open for anyone until 8 in the morning."

Weird. I wasn't aware of *that* little tidbit.

I give her a nod. "Got it."

"Ledge!"

Cignette turns, and as she does, a gust of wind blows by us, pushing her hair sideways.

My eyes fall on her back, and there, inked on her skin, I see an untethered swan. I only get a brief glimpse of it before I have to avert my gaze from her and look in the direction of the voice.

"*What?*" I bark at Varsha, Jayce, and Alex. It's the former who'd called my name.

Alex and Varsha give me knowing looks, whereas Jayce simply shakes his head at me before saying, "Alex is hungry. We're headed to McDonald's for a quick bite. You coming?"

I glance at Cignette, then at my crew. "Yeah," I tell Jayce. "You guys go ahead; I'll catch up in a bit."

They nod and head out, and when I look down at her, I find Cignette gazing up at me.

I step close to her, and she inhales a sharp breath. "Are you gonna go back to Gavin now?" I ask, then cage her in by placing both of my hands on her Cadillac's hood.

She scans my face. "No," she answers in a rasp.

I tread closer, and when my hips brush her stomach, I stifle to urge to rock them against her.

"Good."

She smiles a little. "Good, huh?" she sasses.

I lean in – so close that I can breathe in every one of her sweet, beer-laced exhales. "Mm-hmm."

She pushes forward, and I feel her chest rising and falling in sync with mine.

I tilt my head and very gently run the tip of my nose over her cheek, her jaw, and then the side of her neck. My cock is straining against my zipper almost painfully, and I'm *so* damn close to stripping her down and fucking her raw that it's taking all my strength to hold myself in.

"Dorran…" she whispers, and Christ, my name on her lips is a vice of the darkest nature. It promises to feed my newly-found hunger for her, yet keeps me aching for what's to come.

"I…" she starts, then sighs. "Dorran, I have to go."

I move back just a little so that I can look at her.

She's completely flushed, and yet there's regret in her eyes as she again says, "I have to go."

I nod. "Okay."

"Yeah."

I chuckle, then push away from her before backtracking towards the garage so that I can lock it up before joining the crew at McDonald's.

"Go," I tell her, and run my gaze over her frame. "I'll see you at midnight, Little Swan."

5.
CIGNETTE

Little Swan. That's what he'd called me. Whether he knew what my name signified, or he'd seen my tattoo, I'm not sure. But what I *do* know is that the term sounded perfect coming from his lips.

And God, what lips they are. Titillating. Inviting.

Forbidden.

Earlier, when Gavin had told me who the garage we were going to, belonged to, I'd been thrilled – for lack of a better word – rather than scared. I understand now why *he* was hesitant about going to *Finesse*, but that's to be expected, because he's the kind of dipshit who'd rather die on a pile of his dust-collecting responsibilities than actually face them.

I sigh, pull my hair up in a half-assed bun, and spritz my mimosa-flavored body mist on my neck and shoulders.

A strong wave of ice-cold wind rushes into my bedroom from my open balcony doors, rustling the silk camisole and shorts I'm wearing. Seeing how hot the day was, it's kind of a relief to have a chilly weather tonight.

Thunder rumbles in the sky, and somehow, the sound makes me think of Dorran.

He's *beautiful* – in every logical way possible. From his curly hair to his defined jaw; from the long column of his neck to his broad shoulders and lean waist. And his eyes…

Fuck, his midnight-blue eyes are a storm waiting to pull me under. They are a direct gateway to my demise, and I am weak for the vice promises I see in them.

Dorran Ledger exudes danger, and I'll damn myself into hellfire before I even *try* to convince myself otherwise.

Until today, I'd only heard of him; seen a couple of photos here and there, maybe. But meeting him today, seeing the sheer power he emanates – it was exhilarating. I want more; I want it all.

My feet press against the plush black carpet as I pad over to my bed and grab my phone from my nightstand. It's 11:35p.m., and I've still not heard from him. The estate's gates will lock up in less than 20 minutes, and I know I probably shouldn't, but I was really hoping he'd show up, just so I could see him again.

It'd been a lucky coincidence that I'd forgotten to grab my card on the way out in the morning, and I guess, in a way, I have Gavin to thank for suggesting Dorran's garage for my car's repair.

Speaking of Gavin…

He's sent me dozens of texts throughout the day, asking if I'm okay. I'd responded to them with an '*I'm alright; I'm home*' message once I'd gotten to the estate, but he *still* hasn't let up. It's no wonder Dorran isn't keen on him, and it's endearing how he kept Varsha from meeting him today.

Spending time with Alex and Varsha had been a treat. We'd spoken about random gossips going around Riverside, street news, and weird fashion trends. It was positively mundane, yet it didn't, not even for a second, feel empty or hoaxed.

One thing I noticed while being at *Finesse* today was the sense of 'family' Dorran and his friends share. It's a concept so foreign to me that it should be painfully laughable, and yet, I couldn't help but envy the kind of ease the 4 of them have around each other. Their bond may be physically invisible, but it was right there in the air around them.

I'm about to make my way to the balcony, but stop when I hear the front door opening, and then closing a few seconds later. Staccato footsteps climb up the stairs and reach the hallway, and I wait, with bated breaths, to see if she'll stop by to ask why I wasn't at the HQ today.

But I know, even as I try to come up with plausible excuses in my head, that she won't knock on my door; that she wouldn't want to know why I didn't show up at work today, and it's because she simply doesn't care. I can bet everything I have that she must've not even noticed my absence during the day. She's just that ignorant, that cruel.

I have my own office and social media team at *Lure*. I'd messaged them to take over for me today, and they'd agreed without question. So, while they worked, I'd slept all afternoon in an attempt to pass the time until Dorran showed up to collect the money I owed him.

The smell of rain hits my nose, seconds before it starts drizzling outside.

Mom's footsteps start to fade, and it's clear that she's climbing up to her floor already. I don't know why, but I scoff and shake my head.

The only times she comes to me is when she wants to use me as her personal punching bag. Otherwise, she's either always bossing her employees around at the *Lure* HQ, or fucking random elites in her bed at ungodly hours.

I tighten my hold on my phone and hug myself as another bout of icy wind rushes by me. I look around my room – at the grey walls and white furniture and the mellow lights – and try not to let the screaming silence deafen me.

The estate stands two stories high, starting with the foyer, dining room, and living room at the bottom, my bedroom and personal library on the first floor, and ending with Mom's office and bedroom on the second floor.

With how extravagant it looks on the outside, the estate feels just as lonely and daunting on the inside. I've had nightmares about being pulled into the walls of the massive hallways, of being ripped to shreds by its long, unforgiving claws as pieces of me fall apart and bare me to the demons that lurk in them.

I reach the balcony, place my forearms on the slightly wet railing, and look out at the vast garden in front of me.

It's excessive, to be sure, but I'm still grateful for its presence because it gives me something to get lost into. I feel like the tall, grass-made figurines that surround the expanse hold more secrets than I'd care to list, and every time I walk through the gardens, I feel a sense of liberation that I only feel when I'm driving through the streets of Riverside.

The rain starts falling faster now. Thick droplets pelt the ground, and some even touch my face as the wind blows them in my direction.

I glance at the gates. I can't see them fully because of the direction my balcony is in, but I can still make out the 8 guards that are stationed in front of it, all of them clad in hooded black ponchos.

They're the night-shift team – far deadlier than the guards who man the gates during the day.

The rest of the morning shift guards – Mave's team – along with Mom's personal bodyguard, Steven, file out of the estate and head for the gates.

Time for them to go home.

The routine is pretty simple: guards are stationed both inside the estate, and at its gates, up until 11:30p.m., and then the night shift comes in, and they only manage the entrance gates. They are, after all, trained very differently than Mave and his team. They are ruthless and unforgiving, and can probably end a life with their eyes closed.

A soft, familiar knock sounds against my door.

I smile, turn toward it, and walk over to it before pulling the door open.

Mave is standing on the other side, and when he sees me, he grins, glances around the hallway once, then leans in and presses a long kiss on my forehead.

We'd had sex once – last year. It was after one of Mom's *Lure* parties. I was drunk; I was upset. She'd humiliated me in front of her "girlfriends" by making snark comments on my lack of work ethic. Mave had escorted me out of the club, into the limo, all the way to the estate, and up to my bedroom. I'd been crying, and all I'd wanted was to get lost in someone, and he'd just been…*there*.

But God, was he *good*. He was rough, brutal, all but painful, and that's exactly what I'd needed.

In the end, though, we'd agreed that as good as the experience was, continuing on that path would only get him fired, and I couldn't, for the life of me, lose him. He was kind of my constant; my '*I'll always be there for you*' in a world full of egocentric hostility.

Occasionally, when we're out alone, or when he's about to head home for the night, he'll kiss me till I lose every ounce of my breath, but that's as far as we go. For both of our sakes, of course.

When I'd returned to the estate earlier, he'd been more than upset with me for having left without informing him. I know he starts his shift at 9 in the morning, so I'd purposefully snuck out an hour prior to that.

We'd argued, he'd frowned, and I'd ended up slamming the door in his face. I realize now that I'd acted immaturely, but I'm a damn human being, and I'm allowed to behave irrationally whenever I want.

See? Now that statement *itself* is immature. Whatever, I guess.

"I'm clocking out," Mave says, then stealthily wraps an arm around my waist. "But I'm going to get here early tomorrow so that I can avoid failing at doing my job. *Again*."

Before Dorran, his touch would thrill the fuck out of me; make me so wet that I'd have to touch myself just to get the edge off. But now – after what happened today – I can't find it in me to lie to my body and mind.

That brief encounter with Dorran has left me mentally disheveled, and the only thing I can think of right now, is him. His eyes, his smell, his stupidly beautiful smile.

I try to keep my expression neutral as I slowly move out of Mave's grasp.

He notices that, of course, but doesn't say anything.

"Aren't you a bit old to be getting here earlier than your scheduled time?" I say. "Think of your bones, Mave; show them some mercy."

He laughs, and his grey eyes gleam under the moonlight streaming in through the hallway windows.

"What gave it away – my salt-and-pepper hair?" he muses.

"Your fading interest in wanting to stay alive, more like."

He scoffs. "I'm 41, Nettie," he tells me. "That's barely old."

I roll my eyes. "You're 9 years away from having a midlife crisis."

He laughs again, and it's kind of a hoarse sound. Warm and comforting.

Mave is way taller than me, and has the build of a damn wrestler or some shit. I used to fantasize about having all of that weight pressed against me, but not anymore.

"You're a fucking menace, Nettie," he says.

I give him a quick wink. "Funny. Someone else told me the exact same thing today."

He shakes his head. "You wanna tell me where you were?"

"No?"

"Come on, seriously?" he pushes.

I sigh and gesture at my body. "I'm alive and in one piece. Isn't that enough?"

His gaze darkens as he runs it over my frame, then brings it back to my face. "More than, but–"

"Nope, I'm not going to listen to your self-righteous speech again, not tonight."

He shifts on his feet and raises a brow at me. "*Self-righteous?*" he chuckles. "I'm *hurt*."

"You know how I roll," I tell him. "I ain't sugarcoating shit for you." I cover my mouth to hide a sudden yawn.

"Oh, I know." He smiles, then briefly touches my cheek before saying, "I'll let you rest." He sighs and scans my features again. "Good night, Nettie."

I squeeze his hand and return his smile. "Night, Mave." I watch as he crosses the hallway and jogs down the stairs, and once he's out of view, I close my bedroom door. I'm about to turn around when my phone vibrates in my hand.

I look down at it, and my chest all but tightens when I see his name flashing across the screen.

Dorran: *I'm here.*

Just two simple words from him, and I'm an absolute mess.

In my daze, though, I quickly realize that if Dorran is at the gates, then 1) The guards have seen him and have denied him access, and 2) Mave is about to walk out of those exact same gates, and if he sees Dorran, then shit will hit the fucking fan. In *very* unflattering ways.

And also that it's 11:55p.m.

Fuck.

I run to the balcony and look out. I'm out of breath, a little bewildered, and a whole lot of scared.

Mave high-fives one of the guards at the gates, and the two share a quick laugh.

I search the road outside, but I don't see him. He told me he's here, but where the fuck is he?

Mave says something to the guards, then finally leaves, and I watch as one of the poncho-wearing freaks glances at his watch, before making a 'shut it' gesture to the others.

Shit.

I check the time on my phone.

11:57p.m.

I look up again, and this time, I see a tall shadow in the trees just beyond the estate.

The guards are too busy working on the security panel to notice it – notice *him* – but not me. I track his every move.

I'm too stunned not to.

Jesus fucking *Christ*. What the fuck do you think you're doing, Dorran?

6.
CIGNETTE

I hear five consecutive beeps – a signal that the gates have been bolted. The guards turn their backs to it and start chatting amongst each other, and the shadow shifts again.

My mouth is dry as I stare at Dorran when he steps into the nightlight.

He's wearing a black vest and dark jeans, which camouflage him with ease and make it difficult to keep up with him.

He moves again, and it's with such deadly grace that I'm left speechless.

He's out of my line of view for a few aching seconds, but when I see him again, he's climbing up the concrete wall on the left side of the gates.

Ohmygod.

The rain has slowed down, which is going to serve as a disadvantage for whatever it is that he has planned.

At this point, I can only watch what he's doing, and pray that he succeeds, because if he's caught, then I'll have no way of justifying whatever this is, to Mave or to my mom, even if I try my hardest.

Dorran leaps, then lands effortlessly on the wet grass. The guards don't notice him, not even as he all but glides forward on sure, calculated treads.

The wind picks up again, ruffling his curls, but he continues to press forward – completely unaffected.

He takes cover behind the third figurine, just as one of the guards quickly sweeps his eyes over the garden, before looking away. They won't be able to see him once he reaches me. But the question is: how *will* he get to me?

If I open the estate doors right now, there's a strong chance that'll trigger the guards' attention, and I most definitely don't want that. I may not know Dorran well, but I sure as hell don't want the fucker dead for a few dollars.

He moves again – this time in front of the seventh figurine. That's a huge leap forward, but he manages to stay undetected, so I'm not complaining.

He shifts to his left first, then to his right, and keeps subtracting the space between us by moving under the cover of the scattered figurines.

Dorran is night incarnate – soundless, incalculable. Fucking fatal by nature.

A *thud* sounds from somewhere, and both Dorran and I look in its direction. One of the guards has dropped his backup pistol, and the rest of them are laughing at him. Why? I honestly do not know.

These men get paid to ensure Mom and I's safety, and here they are, cackling because one of them dropped a fucking weapon.

I've never felt more protected in my life.

I avert my gaze from them and look at Dorran again, and see that he's using the guards' distraction as an opportunity to rush forward. He crosses the garden and reaches the estate's ground, then finally gazes up at me. He grins, and Christ, it's so damn full of lunacy that it makes my pulse quicken.

He glances around. Then, in a movement too swift, he jumps and grabs the lowest concrete motif that's protruding from the right pillar of the estate's structure.

The guards are having a conversation now, but the words are unclear to me.

Dorran uses the motifs to climb higher, and the muscles of his bare arms stretch and flex as he pushes himself up without so much a grunt of struggle. He's so fluent, so mesmerizing to watch in his state of stealth.

I suck in a breath – the back of my throat icy, dry – when he clasps my balcony's granite railing. I take a few steps back when he swings one, and then the other leg over it, before turning inward and hopping down onto the floor.

Thunder rumbles the cloudy sky again, and it's followed by a zap of lightning that briefly illuminates Dorran's sharp features.

I swallow. "You're late," I tell him.

The bells on the antique clock in the foyer below, start ringing, and Dorran smirks.

"Am I?" he asks challengingly.

I push a fallen strand of my hair behind my ear. "I'll get your money." I turn and rush into my room, throw my phone on the bed, grab the cash from my nightstand's second drawer, and walk back to where he's waiting for me.

"You know," I start, then offer him the money, "you could've gotten yourself killed right now. The guards at the gates are merciless to a fault; they wouldn't have hesitated to end you. And, as savage as you might be, even the Bloody Prince can't take on more than half a dozen trained assassins on his own."

His lips spread into a manic smile as he takes the money from me and pockets it. "Don't tempt me, Little Swan," he says with a touch of levity in his voice. "Because I just might feel obligated to prove you wrong. I'm in a giving mood tonight, after all."

I laugh, and something in his expression changes. Before I can even blink, he's closed the space between us, pulled a switchblade out, and has wrapped a hand around my throat firmly.

He nudges me, and my back presses against the pillar behind me. He then leans in – so close that I can see every fleck of blue in his eyes.

"Now, Little Swan," he whispers, "what was so funny about what I just said?"

I stare up at him as my heart goes fucking insane in my chest.

He's beautiful.

He's brutal.

He's my key to salvation.

Dorran brings his blade to my cheek, and the cold metal all but bites my skin, resulting in goosebumps to rise on my scalp and neck.

"Tell me," he whispers again, then tightens his hold on my throat.

I try to gasp, but it's impossible. I can't breathe, and there's a slight ache in the middle of my chest that should be concerning, but it only excites me.

When I don't answer him, he drags the blade over my cheek and brings it to my lips. "Open your mouth," he commands.

I shift on my feet and continue to look at him, to which he chuckles and squeezes my throat even tighter.

I arch forward, and grab his wrist with both my hands when blackness creeps over the edges of my vision. I claw at his fingers because I really can't breathe now, and my chest feels too heavy and constricted.

Dorran simply smirks. "Open your damn mouth, Cignette," he orders.

Hell, the way he says my name – it's like dragon-fire on my chest. It sears through me; it thaws my damn rationality.

I relent and part my lips, and immediately, he loosens his grip on my throat.

"Good girl," he purrs. "Now, pull your tongue out."

I do, and feel myself get wet when he flattens the switchblade and runs it over my tongue. He starts from the tip, then pushes it up further, all the way to the inside of my mouth.

"You like that," he says. There's no question in his voice. "Who fucking knew." He pulls the blade out and flips it around, putting the weapon's black handle into my mouth. "Suck," he directs.

I wrap my lips around the metal, and it instantly warms against me. I then hollow my cheeks as I suck on it, and Dorran starts to slowly pull the handle in and out of my mouth.

"Harder, Little Swan," he orders. "I'm sure that mouth of yours can do better than this."

Thunder crackles, and a second later, it's pouring rain again.

I suck on the handle with as much pressure as I can, given how little space I have to move my head.

Dorran pushes the handle deep – to the back of my throat – and I gag. He pulls it out, and then pushes it in again. "That's right; suck it. Suck it like you would my cock. Take it all in and show me how bad you want it."

I moan, and he steps closer to me.

"You're going to be the end of me," he tells me, then scans my face. "And I promise you, if you take me down, I'm taking you to hell with me."

My pussy aches; my nipples harden. The things this man says drive me to the brink of insanity.

He tightens his fingers on my throat again, then all but shoves the handle to the very back of my mouth.

My eyes widen as I try to gasp, but end up gagging instead. My head presses against the pillar as I heave, but Dorran doesn't stop. He keeps shoving the switchblade's handle in and out of my mouth – faster and faster. There's spit dripping down my chin now, and a few tears fall down to my temples.

Suddenly, he pulls the handle out of my mouth, releases my throat, and takes a single step back. Then he watches me – slowly, deviously – and tilts his head to the side.

"Take off your shorts."

I swallow, and it hurts. "Why?" I ask. My voice sounds broken to my ears.

"Did you go to Gavin after you left *Finesse*?" he questions. He'd asked me earlier if I would, and I'd told him I wouldn't. I meant that.

"No," I say.

"Do you want him?" His eyes narrow just a little after he asks that.

I scoff. "Are you asking me this because you care, or because you're simply curious?"

He straightens his head. "Neither."

I swipe the back of my hand over my spit-covered chin. "Then why ask at all?"

"Because, Little Swan…" He leans in and braces both of his forearms on the pillar, above my head. "I don't share my shit with anyone, least of all with scums like him."

There's so much to unpack in that one sentence, that I take a moment and let it play in my head a second time.

The rain picks up further, and as gusts of wind blow by us, I can smell the sweat, cologne, and Earth on Dorran.

"So you *do* care, then," I say. "*Liar*."

He hesitates. "More like I'm undecided on it." He makes a soft *humph* kinda sound. "Yeah, let's go with undecided for now."

"Fine," I state.

"Fine," he repeats.

We stare at each other for a long beat or two, and then I cut through the silence by clicking my tongue.

"You called me a shit," I quip.

His lips quirk up. "Did I?"

"Uh huh."

"Well, I ain't apologizing for that."

I lift my left leg and gently nudge his cock with my knee.

His eyes darken to molten sapphire, and he rocks his hips against my leg, making me grin.

"You said I'm yours," I tell him. "But you barely even know me."

"You became mine the second our eyes met," he says. "But if you want that asshole instead, then I gotta know now, because if I find you with him after you've told me otherwise, then it won't end well." He smirks, and a piercing chill runs down my already cold spine. "Both for you, *and* for him."

I briefly run my eyes over his frame, then meet his gaze. "Well, Gavin has a cock that drives me *perfectly* mad with desire…" I muse, then brush the back of my fingers over his smooth jaw. "But he doesn't make me half as wet as you do, so I guess you have your answer."

He laughs, and the sound is so rich that it brings a smile to my face.

He notices it, and brings his arms down before sliding his fingers into my hair. He then tugs at it coarsely and roughly presses his lips to mine, and Christ, he feels so good when he pushes himself against me.

I fist his vest and pull him close as I open up for him. He tastes a little stale – like a blend of coffee and cigarette – but it's perfect; it works *just* fine for me.

His slightly chapped lips glide over mine, and he traces the tip of his tongue over my teeth, which makes me grin.

Our mouths close around each other's, and he sucks on my bottom lip before biting down hard on it.

I moan and pull him closer, and when his balmy breaths fan my right cheek as he exhales, I cup the sides of his neck and slide my tongue over his.

His hold on my hair tightens, and he pushes his groin against my stomach as our lips continue to move unabashedly, desperately.

Kissing Dorran is like walking on sea. There's an inevitable fear of drowning involved, along with a frantic hope for a torrent to all but consume you. It's a feeling so contradictory that it's naturally impossible not to get addicted to it.

And Lord, am I addicted to it.

He breaks the kiss, and every part of me aches at the small distance it creates between us. He then loosens his grip on my hair and pulls his hands away, and the sharp pricks that course through my scalp at that, make me shiver a little.

I drop my arms to my sides and try to clear the fog from my dizzy head, and that's when I realize we're both panting.

I have no fucking idea what this thing between us even is, but what I *do* know is that it's alive; that it's *breathing*.

And it's as real as the heart that's currently beating madly inside my chest.

God, I am *so* fucked.

Dorran gives me a once-over, then cants his head to the side. "You're so damn ethereal, Little Swan," he says. "Even the clouded darkness fails to hide your fierce beauty." He comes closer and begins to run the tip of his switchblade from my shoulder, all the way down to my arm, and then back up again. "Just look at you," he hisses, then meets my eyes. "Fucking *look* at you. So cruel…" He leans in and places an open-mouthed kiss on the space below my left ear. "So cruel," he repeats. "Stealing my breath like this; making me question my fucking morals." He sucks on the skin he'd kissed, and my eyes flutter shut.

"Dorran…"

He chuckles against my ear, then moves back to look down at me. "Take those shorts off – for real this time."

I slide my thumbs under my shorts' waistband and quickly push them down.

"Good," he says, then glances between my legs.

I squeeze my thighs together, but that doesn't help in dimming the ache I feel.

He briefly runs his fingers over the patch of dark hair above my pussy. "Straddle the railing, Cignette."

I blink as I process his words, but when he doesn't say anything else, and instead waits for me to obey his command, I frown and ask, "What?"

He gives me a slightly exasperated look. "The railing, Cignette – straddle it. *Now*." The way he emphasizes that last word, makes me swallow.

"But it's wet," I object. "And slippery."

Dorran leans sideways against the railing in question, and folds his arms across his chest.

"Not to sound absolutely juvenile right now," he begins, then grins, "but so are *you*."

He did *not* just say that…

"Fuck you," I sneer.

He laughs airily. "You just might; the night's still young."

I clench my jaw. "You're infuriating." The rain falls faster now, and gentle sprays of water hit the sides of Dorran and I's faces.

His eyes shine as they assess me. "And you don't know how to do what you're told to."

"That's only because you're setting me up to fall, asshole."

He's on me so quick, I barely have time to react. His switchblade is pressed against my throat, and one of his hands is cupping the back of my neck.

"Use that tone again," he says between gritted teeth, "and I won't hesitate for a second before slicing you open. You hear me?"

I don't answer him; I just keep staring up at him. He scares me. He entices me.

He makes me feel like I'm *real*, that I actually *exist*.

"*Do you hear me, Cignette?*" he repeats his question, but this time with a little more anger.

I nod.

"Words, Little Swan; use your voice."

"Yes," I whisper. "Yes."

He pulls away, and again, I ache at the space between us.

"Perfect," he tells me, then raises a brow. "Now, straddle the fucking railing."

I push the stray strands of my hair behind my ears and place both my hands on the slippery railing. I then slowly lift my left leg up and over it, shift a little so that I'm facing forward, and then sit my ass down on the chilly granite.

I'm shaking a little – not out of fear, I think to myself, but out of cold.

Ruthless rain assaults my left leg as it dangles loosely above the garden, and my pussy brushes against the granite when I once again shift a little.

If the guards can somehow see me through the onslaught of rain, they'll think that I'm finally ending my life. They probably won't even stop me – you know, one less human to protect and stay on-guard for, that kinda thing.

Dorran flicks open his switchblade, then folds it close.

Open.

Close.

Open.

Close.

He does that a few times as he watches me get comfortable, then clicks his tongue. "Press your back on the pillar behind you, move your hips forward, and spread your legs."

I swallow, lean back on the pillar, let go of air through pursed lips to calm myself down a bit, then push my hips forward before widening my legs.

Dorran's gaze immediately falls on my pussy, and he adjusts himself above his jeans.

I try not to smile at that, but end up failing.

He notices it, of course, and subtracts the distance between us by coming to stand impossibly close to me. He brings his lips over mine, and I'm positively engulfed in the warmth of him.

"Got something to say, Little Swan?" he asks softly.

I touch my nose to his. "Just that even the Bloody Prince has his weaknesses," I muse. "Affected by a simple *pussy*."

He smirks. "Oh, I don't get hard for just about any pussy, sweetheart." He flicks open his switchblade again and brings the blade over to my apex. He then drags it down to my clit, bites down on my bottom lip, and twists the weapon around before pushing its handle inside me in a single thrust.

I arch against the pillar when the cold metal enters my heated core, and grunt when Dorran begins to move the handle in and out of me.

"It's *your* pussy, Cignette, that's made me lose track of my mind," he tells me, then starts fucking me with the switchblade in earnest.

I arch further as the friction makes me wetter, then bring my arms behind me so that I can grab onto the pillar. My mouth falls open as I breathe heavily, and when Dorran twists the handle just so, creating an even intense rhythm, I grit my teeth and moan out loud.

"Uh-uh-uh." He stops, then looks down at me with amusement dancing in his gleaming eyes. "Unless you want everyone here to know what a slut you are for me, I'd suggest you keep it down a little." He slowly pushes the handle inside me again, but this time, he doesn't stop.

I gasp and try to move, but he shakes his head at me not to. I can feel the very end of the sharp blade against my entrance, and I shiver in fear instead of the cold.

"God, how good you'd look bleeding for me," he says darkly, then gives me a chaste kiss before pulling the handle out, and then thrusting it back inside me again. "I'd fall on my fucking knees in front of you, just to get a single taste of you." He continues to fuck me with the switchblade, and goddammit, his words, paired with his rough ministrations, make me clench around the handle as I get closer to my release.

Dorran brings his face next to the side of my neck again, and then inhales deeply. "You smell so fucking forbidden," he whispers against my skin, and I can hear the smile in his voice as he adds, "and…like oranges. You smell like fucking *oranges*."

I chuckle, and yelp when one of my hands slips, making me lose my balance a little.

Dorran quickly wraps his free arm around my waist and presses our bodies together, and when our eyes meet, he tilts his switchblade in a way that makes my orgasm practically shoot out of me.

My toes curl; my chest feels hot. My hips move upwards; my stomach contracts.

I open my mouth to moan, but he captures it with his own. I bring my hands up, fist his curls between my fingers, and fuck his mouth as he continues to help me ride out my all but blinding orgasm.

It's like I'm buzzing, like every inch of me has been set ablaze. My release fogs my brain, then clears it just as fast. I go slightly limp against Dorran's hold, and when we break the kiss, he slowly pulls his switchblade out of me and brings it between us. With his eyes on me, he takes the handle into his mouth and sucks, and I'm left motionless, because *fuck me*, that's the most erotic thing I've witnessed – ever.

His dark lashes flutter as he lets out a soft groan, then pulls the handle out before offering it to me.

I part my lips and suck on it once, but then he takes it away from me before kissing me again.

This little game we're playing – it's frustrating, aggravating. But I also love how it works, and because it's so beautifully impulsive, it keeps me thrilled enough to anticipate what's to come.

It's kind of electrifying, for lack of a better word.

"As if you weren't addicting enough," Dorran begins, then swallows, "you *have* to taste so fucking good. Damn you, woman; I can't even think straight at this point."

We're both breathing hard, and I've *never* wanted to have a man more than I do Dorran Ledger.

"I–" I start, but stop when his phone *pings* once, and then a second time.

He grunts in disapproval, moves back, slides his switchblade into his front pocket, lifts me in his arms, and sets me back on my feet. He then bends to pick my shorts off the ground. "I'm keeping these," he says around a grin before tucking them halfway into the back pocket of his jeans. "I'll need something to clean my cock with after I come under your name tonight."

I let go of a hiccupped breath, and his grin widens, but then he scowls when his phone *pings* again. He quickly pulls it out, reads the messages, then huffs before looking at me. "I gotta go." He then vaguely gestures at me. "Cover yourself. From now on, no one gets to see this pussy but me. That clear to you?"

"Not even my esthetician?" I quip.

"Well, unless they have a desire of having their bleeding guts shoved down their throats, Little Swan, then no; *no*, they cannot."

"Is this your way of staking your claim, then – using threat and pleasure to bind me to you?" I question.

Dorran smirks in a way that could make even Lucifer tremble. He grabs my chin and kisses me once, and then pockets his phone, walks over to the pillar opposite the one he'd climbed from, and gets onto the railing. Just like he had gotten up, he uses the rain as a cover, and the motifs to get down, and within seconds, he's crossed the garden and hiked the estate walls using the overgrown leaves covering it. He's out of sight before the guards can notice him, and it's then I realize that I've been holding my breath, so I close my eyes and exhale through my nose.

This man is going to get me brutally killed one of these days, and honestly, I can't wait to meet my end, especially because I know he'll be there with me – making me yearn for him, even in death.

7.
DORRAN

As I pull up my Harley and park it next to the curb, I see his silver SUV standing in front of *Finesse.*

The rain has finally let up, but the wind is still chilly, to the point where it actually bites into the skin on my face and arms as I make my way over to the man leaning against the side of his car.

Christopher Solo – former sheriff of Riverside County – is not only Jayce and I's mentor, but he's also the guy who saved our lives almost two decades ago. He pulled us out of the mud and made us who we are today, and honestly, I *love* who I am today. I'm content with the life I live, the things I do. And if it wasn't for the man standing before me, I'd be nothing but a stained memory against the countless others out there.

"I got your texts," I say by way of greeting as I come to a stop in front of him.

He's a polished motherfucker, that guy. With pressed black dress pants, a cream shirt tucked inside said black pants, grey hair slicked back, along with a thick stubble to match, he's as put-together as they come. But then again, he always dresses like this, so tonight shouldn't be an exception.

He straightens, then moves in to give me a one-armed hug, which I return.

"Christ, Dor," he mutters, then moves back to give me a scowl. "You smell like pussy."

I chuckle. "It's a hard one to resist, trust me," I tell him. "And so is the woman who owns it." My thoughts immediately go to Cignette, to the way she'd looked at me; the way she'd felt against me. To the way she'd kissed me, and the way she'd surrendered to me.

The little defiance she'd showed was strategic – because she wanted to see how far I'd push myself, and *her*, before she finally gave into me.

I like it – this little game of ours. It's maddeningly addicting, and it keeps me wanting more and more of it.

Solo rolls his eyes. "Don't tell me you're losing control over a *cunt*, Dor." His blue eyes narrow a little as he assesses me. "Because you and I both know you're way better than *that*." He glances down, then behind me, and clicks his tongue. "She gave you a souvenir as well, it seems," he muses, speaking of Cignette's shorts in one of my back pockets.

"Careful," I warn him, then grit my teeth. "You're still a man, Solo, even under all those lavish clothes – all flesh and blood and bones."

He laughs dryly around a shake of his head. "She's got you real good, hasn't she?"

I contemplate how to answer that, because truth be told, I don't know if I have a proper response to that question.

"That's a TBD kinda situation right now," I say.

Solo laughs again, and this time, I join him.

What Cignette is doing to me is confusing on multiple levels, but like I said: it is adherent enough that I wanna see where it leads me.

I never said I was mentally sane, did I?

I shove my hands into the front pockets of my jeans and jerk my head at Solo. "So, why'd you wanna meet this late?" I ask him.

"What, now I can't even meet with my favorite protégé whenever I feel like it?"

I scoff. "If Jayce hears that somehow, he'll end you before anyone else gets a shot."

He grins, and it's so fierce that it makes my veins hum. I know what he's about to say, and I'm all but high on the anticipation of it.

"We've been assigned 3 kills," he announces. "Maybe Jayce'll have a little mercy on me when he hears *that*."

Fuck yeah.

I match his grin. "You just gave my boner a fucking boost, man," I say.

His lips twitch. "Thought you'd have already scratched that itch with your…lady."

"Screw you."

He chuckles. "She left you to fend for yourself, then. Pity."

I fold my arms across my chest. "I don't appreciate you being so interested in her."

"That so?" He gives me a sharp smirk.

I shake my head. "Just tell me about the task, asswipe."

"You do realize that I'm quite older than you, don't you?"

"It hasn't put you out of business yet, so I don't think I quite care."

He snorts and leans back against the driver's side of his SUV. "Same-night kills," he begins, then folds his arms in front of himself. "All 3 of them have been accused of trafficking women to remote islands and high-pay buyers around the world for prostitution and slavery."

My hands clench inside my pockets after I hear that. "And the kidnapped women?"

Solo sighs. "Mostly of Asian descent. Their ages vary from anywhere between 16 to 35."

"Fucking dipshits," I hiss.

"I agree." Solo clicks his tongue again. "Locations for most of these trafficked women have been attained, so all you have to do is end the fuckers."

I nod. "Names?"

"Andres Salazar, Rizwana Hafeez, and Tomas Aetos."

All of them are elites, to no one's surprise.

I rub a hand over my jaw. "Place? I'm assuming there's a reason why it's a same-night kill."

Solo's eyes gleam as he hums. "Miranda Adler is hosting a charity ball at *Imperia* this Saturday, and all 3 of our kills have already RSVP'd for it."

I keep my expression neutral as I look at him, but the way *he's* looking back at me, it's like he's reading me; seeing right through me.

Imperia is a Michelin Star hotel that both Cignette's mom, and her uncle, own. It's just another show of power from those 2; the place could go up in flames and no one would care, not even them.

"A *charity* ball?" I muse. "Since when does Miranda do those?"

Solo laughs airily. "Since she was advised to do so." He lifts a shoulder. "It's basically a posh ploy to soft-launch her new clothing collection. She'd recently held an exclusive gathering to promote her casualwear crap, if you remember. Hosting another one so soon would only irate her peers, so she's masking this promotional shindig under the guise of charity. All the influencers and celebrities who are ambassadors for *Lure*, will be there, so you'll have quite an audience to evade."

"Interesting." I tilt my head to the right. "Who's ordered the kills anyway? For someone who wants not 1, but 3 elites dead, our client must be quite special."

"Oh, Dor," Solo says, then chuckles. "That's the best part of it all." He pushes away from his car and takes a step toward me. "Our client is Miranda's latest boy-toy, Waleed Najimi. And, before you ask: yes, he's paying enough for the kills *and* for the cleanup, and yes, him and his team were the ones who located the trafficked women and learnt of Andres, Rizwana, and Tomas's involvement in the act. And finally, yes, he decided to associate himself with Miranda merely to get close to our kills, and nothing more."

I whistle. "Bold."

"And rich as *fuck*," Solo adds. "He's 25, an heir to a petrol and oil company in Abu Dhabi, and respects women way too much to let this pass, not when he knows he can put an end to it."

"And yet, he's using a woman to get what he wants," I point out.

Solo waves a dismissive hand in front of his face. "Miranda Adler can hardly be labeled as a woman, let alone a dignified one."

"But she's got the money, the status, and the connections."

Solo gives me an exasperated look. "It shouldn't matter to us."

"I'm just trying to understand shit here."

He runs his fingers through his styled hair. "Do you have a plan, or what, kid? Because that's the only thing that matters."

I nod again. "Varsha'll get rid of Rizwana first. That way, we'll get the noisy fuss outta the way. I'll take on Andres, and Jayce and Alex can work on Tomas."

Solo looks impressed, as if he's never seen me device a plan so quickly before. "I like it; you distributed the kills precisely."

I give him a quick wink. "You've taught me well."

He grins. "That, I have." He points a finger at me. "Get that navy suit ready. I think you look very distinguished in it. When you're killing snobs, Dor, you gotta do it with a flair of formality."

"Don't I know that?" I quip.

"Doesn't hurt to refresh your memory, especially after seeing you so pussy-drunk earlier."

I tip my head back and laugh out loud. "You're such a dipshit," I tell him.

He gives me a two-finger salute. "Gotta maintain that reputation somehow."

"Just go before I clock you in the head, Chris."

He chuckles as he turns and gets into his car. He stops before shutting the driver's side door, though, and looks at me. "I'll see you on Saturday.

And, if you or the crew decide to alternate the plan, then shoot me a text. I need your A-game on this, Dor, you hear me?"

I incline my head at him as I start walking backwards. "Loud and clear, boss. I've got it." With that, I pivot on my feet and start walking towards *Finesse*, just as Solo revs up his engine and speeds away.

I'm not going to tell Cignette about the kills, obviously, but because I'm going to be undertaking them at her mom's party – I mean, *charity ball* – there's a strong chance that her and I will cross paths. It will definitely be interesting to see how my Little Swan reacts when she sees me in my element, or how my mind'll behave with her in such close proximity to me.

Either way, I'm fucked, and fucked for *good*.

8.
CIGNETTE

"I'm sorry, but why wasn't I told about this charity ball thing until *now*?" I ask, beyond baffled. When I'd walked into the HQ 15 minutes ago with Mave by my side, Mom's team of stylists had all but dragged me into the fitting room to get my measurements for an outfit for an apparent "charity ball" I was supposed to attend this Saturday.

"Umm, because you're literally Miranda's *daughter*," says Julian, one of Mom's stylists. "And also, you know, because the two of you live under the same roof and everything. You of all people, babe, would, and *should*, know about this." He fixes his blond ponytail and gets back to whatever it is he's drawing in his sketchbook.

I catch Mave's eyes in the mirror that's in front of me, then make a face.

He's standing next to the door, with his hands clasped behind his back, and gives me a look full of amusement before subtly shaking his head at me.

He'd been just as confused by the charity ball news as I'd been. It seems like Mom isn't going with the regular security team for this event; she's changing course. Because if she *was*, then Mave would have received an order to scout the venue, set up the guards' posts, and plan the exit routes at least two weeks before the actual ball. But we are only three days away from Saturday, so it's safe to assume that Mom's just doing whatever *she* thinks is right.

Again.

I lift my arms sideways when Julian's assistant, Melina, comes around to get measurements of my bust, arms, and shoulders.

"How long has she been planning this charity ball anyway?" I ask Julian, only because he now knows that my mom hasn't discussed shit with me about this event. So, it shouldn't exactly be a big deal if I get some information from him. And, because he works so closely with her, I'm pretty sure he knows just about everything pertaining this ball.

He looks up from his sketchbook and furrows his brows. "A month ago, I believe." He sets the pencil he's holding, behind his left ear. "She proposed the idea to me and the team, and said that it'd be a great opportunity for us to launch part of our newest collection as a teaser – sort of – to gauge the elites' reactions to it, get their feedbacks on it, etcetera."

This time when Mave and I lock gazes, it's *him* who makes a face.

How predictable of Mom to deceit people by finding ways to promote her brand whilst also appearing cool and generous in the process.

"And…" I bring my arms down, and touch my legs together when Melina crouches in front of me before wrapping the measuring tape around my hips. "What collection are we displaying at the event?"

"The winter-wear one," Julian says. "So, we're going to introduce the neutral colors for now, and keep the pastel ones for the full release promo."

"Gotcha." I sigh when Melina finally steps back and jots down the last of my measurements, then walks over to Julian and hands him the cream notepad.

I relax my stance and turn around, then settle into the white accent chair that's next to me. The soft fabric of my floral, flowy dress sighs against my skin as I cross my legs and place my elbows on my thighs, then look around the beige-themed room.

Three of the members of Julian's team are working on sewing machines that are stationed on the far left of the room. The furniture in here is elegantly muted, accented with rose gold to give it a chic appearance. There's a little coffee and snack area to the right, along with a trial cabin next to it.

Julian's worktable is a massive mess of papers, pencils, iPads, sketchpads, fabrics, and threads, exactly in the center of the room. The light in here is bright as shit, and kinda makes the ivory faux carpet appear washed out.

This fitting/designing room is one of the six workrooms in the HQ – each one of said rooms belonging to a head stylist. Julian is one of them, and has his own team, just like the others. But, because I've known him the longest and trust his sense of style, he's the only one who gets to design my dresses for events and such.

"So, sugar," he shifts in his plush chair and gives me a grin, "what are we thinking in terms of the vibes for this one?"

Mave looks bored as he glances between me and his watch every five seconds, and Melina once again has a notepad and a pen in her hands, probably so that she can write down my vision for this event's attire.

"Mom didn't set a theme or something?" I ask. She doesn't always do that, but occasionally, she'll go over-the-top with the dress code bullshit.

Julian shakes his head. "No, not this time. Remember: it's supposed to be a charity thing, so if there's a dress code of some sort, it might get a bit confusing for the guests."

"And here I thought she'd at least turn it into a masquerade," I quip.

Mave chuckles. "Announcing winter-wear during a masquerade ball would sure have been…*something*. I'm distressed we won't be witnessing history being made," he muses.

Julian scoffs. "You two are crazy; masquerade balls are cliché as fuck. What are we, a mafia circle or something?" He then claps his hands once –

loud enough to make me jerk a little in surprise. "Alright, back to your dress," he tells me, then pulls his pencil out from behind his ear. "Ideas? Notes? Requests? Throw them my way."

I hum as I lean back in my chair, and Mave tracks my every move as he tries, and fails, at not noticing the way my dress slides off my thighs as I shift.

I obviously didn't do it for him, so I try to ignore his stare, and instead, give Julian my complete attention.

"Yellow charmeuse, fitted, floor-length," I list, then click my tongue. "Spaghetti straps and…a super low-cut back so that my tattoo gets the spotlight it deserves."

Julian blinks at me for a few seconds, then clears his throat and says, "All of that sounds perf, but *yellow* charmeuse?" He blinks again. "*Yellow?*"

I try not to grin. "*Cyber* yellow," I specify, then purse my lips when Mave not-so-discreetly coughs behind a fist.

Julian looks like he's about to get on the table and jump headfirst into me. "I…" He runs a hand over his slender face in order to calm himself down. "Babe, Cigs, darling. *Honey…*" He slides forward in his chair. "I love your sense of fashion, I do. And you, like, *always* dress sexy, but…" He licks his lips. "Yellow? Fucking *yellow*?! That's the color of Homer Simpson's cock, the color of sun-vomit! It's *so* not the kind of color people wear dresses of on *formal events*!"

"But it's such a happy color," I object. "And I want people to know just how *ecstatic* I am to be a part of this…generous occasion."

"Ohmygod," Julian mumbles. "If you mention that color to me again, I swear on everything I hold dear, I'll jump out of the window."

I look at the window behind him, then click my tongue. "Not to be a downer, but that's too small a space for you to fit into. It'll be better if you just make me my yellow dress instead."

"*Cigs*," he says in warning.

"*Look at the stars, look how they shine for you. And everything you do, yeah, they were all yellow…*" I sing – or *try* to, anyway, and make sure to stretch the last word out a little too loudly.

Julian rubs both his hands over his face. "Jesus, take me now."

This time, I can't hold it in; I laugh.

Mave and Melina break down with me, and so do the rest of the stylists on the other side of the room.

"Please don't ever, and I mean *ever*, sing again," Mave tells me between bouts of laughter, then grabs a spare chair from his right before settling in it. "Jesus fucking Christ, Nettie; what the fuck?" He continues to laugh.

Julian looks baffled by the cackles that fill the room, then raises his hands in surrender. "You people are dicks," he states matter-of-factly. "Hairy, circumcised, herpes-infested dicks."

"You're really referencing that anatomy in abundance today," I tell him. "First with the Simpson, and now us. Is this going to be a thing now? Should I research dick jokes for our future interactions?"

He points a finger at me. "You little–" he stops when there's a knock on the door.

We all look in its direction, just as Mave gets to his feet, slides his chair away, and opens the door.

"Ma'am," he says civilly, no hint of a reaction on his face, and steps back.

My back straightens, and goosebumps rise throughout my body as my mother walks into the room with an air of unfiltered arrogance.

Her long blonde hair is tied into a high, no-bullshit bun. Her black, full-sleeved bodycon dress fits her like it's made specifically for her lithe figure – because it *is* made just for her. The classic gold jewelry she's wearing – ruby-studded teardrop earrings, a torque, a cuff bracelet, and a couple of cocktail rings on each of her index fingers – looks oddly prominent as the lights in the room reflect strongly against them.

Years of working in the fashion industry has kept Mom's standards for physical appearances and self-care intact, but fine lines and wrinkles still mar her pale skin, making her seem exactly her age.

Steven walks in a second later, gives Mave a curt nod, and stands next to him – his eyes focused solely on my mom.

His long, black hair is pulled up in a too-tight bun, and his clean-shaven jaw is set hard, while the expression on his face is basically poker.

Mom's nude pumps press onto the soft carpet as she comes to a stop, then glances around the room before locking those dark eyes with mine.

I get to my feet and take a step towards her, then give her a well-practiced plastic smile. "Mom," I say in greeting.

She leans in, and her and I share our usual *we're-in-public* air kiss routine.

What happens behind closed doors in Miranda Adler's estate, stays within the walls of said estate. No one needs to know about any of it, least of all *Lure's* employees.

When I move away from Mom, I see that Mave's jaw is clenched as he continues to stare at the back of her head, and that his posture is way too stiff to not come off as questionable. I know he despises her just as much as I do, but this – this just won't do. Especially when we have an audience.

I very subtly clear my throat, and his gaze jumps to mine. I raise my left brow just enough to show him that I've noticed his anger, and that he needs to calm the fuck down.

He sighs, gives me a quick nod, and relaxes a little.

As much as it stings to admit, it's true that Mave is powerless against my mom. If he wants to stay alive and make sure that I do, too, then he's gotta keep his head down and try not to get on her radar.

"Cignette," Mom says stoically, pulling me out of my thoughts.

I blink and look at her again, then send another one of my phony smiles her way.

Mom gives me a calculating once-over, then turns a little to face Julian. "I'm assuming you've finalized the croquis for my daughter's event attire," she tells him.

Julian's expression turns slightly ashen. "Actually–"

"We're still going over ideas," I cut in.

Mom returns her attention to me, and when I glance over her shoulder, Julian mouths, "*Thank you*," to me.

"What do you mean, you're still going over ideas?" Mom asks.

I rub my gloss-covered lips together and shift from one foot to the other.

I'm not scared of her, per se. I'm *used* to her, used to all of her expressions, reactions, and actions. She doesn't necessarily affect me the way she does Julian and the rest of the people who work at *Lure*, but that doesn't mean I don't have to think about everything I do and say, *twice*, while I'm in her presence.

"Umm." I chuckle clinically. "I've been giving him," I gesture vaguely at Julian, "a hard time with the color scheme. We were just discussing what shades we wanna play with for this one, so it's taking longer than expected."

"We will be done with it before lunch, I assure you," Julian adds.

Beside him, Melina makes a sound, but then quickly covers it up with a cough.

"See to it that you are," Mom all but orders without even looking at Julian. She then lets go of a breath and brings one of her hands up to my face.

I refrain from recoiling as her skin touches mine, and my toes curl inside my boots as I glance at Mave, who takes a step forward, but stops when I again raise a brow in warning.

Mom's hand travels down my face, and she then brings it over to the length of my hair before sliding it down to its very ends. She tangles her fingers in them and rubs them together, and I can hear the soft *scrunch* of my hair as it molds against her assault.

Her eyes bore into mine, and her features tighten as she just…stares at me.

I think one of the reasons why she behaves like this with me is because she's jealous of me; jealous of the liberty I have of doing whatever the fuck I want with my life. She's a popular face in the media, a woman of power and fame, so she's got to make sure she's perfectly poised and cautious, if only for when she's out in public – which, to her dismay, is most of the time.

It's been like this for her from a very young age. Her freedom was taken from her when she was a child, and she was forced to be what every woman in our family has always been: a bisque doll – meant only to attract, and not progress.

The Adler name is one that's been acclaimed for generations. My ancestors basically ran the county, and even now, my family is at the top of the food chain here. I don't know much about my grandparents, because they passed years before I was even born, but what I do know is that my grandfather was an only child, and also Riverside's Administrator, just like Uncle Chase now is. My grandma was a trophy wife, but she was also the one who'd built the original Adler estate, which is currently my uncle's residence.

Uncle Chase and Mom were homeschooled – as was I – and when my grandparents were killed in a rival's shootout almost 4 decades ago, my uncle was 21, whereas my mom was only 11. They were brought up by advisors and lawyers, and when Uncle Chase turned 25, he was named the county's new Administrator.

Because Mom didn't want to be like my grandma, or get married off to a nameless elite for further status and money, she started *Lure* at the age of 21. She had me when she was 24, and, well, the rest, as they say, is history.

There's a sharp knock on the door, which startles me a little.

Mom pulls her hand away from my hair, making sure to give it a rough tug as she does, and turns toward the door.

I grit my teeth as pain shoots through the side of my skull, and when I look down at her fingers, I see a couple of long, pink strands wrapped tightly around them.

I swallow my rage and try to breathe in and out at a steady pace.

I feel like despite everything she's been through, and everything that she has chosen to do in her life, she should at least *attempt* at being understanding towards my choices. Instead of hating me for wanting things that she, too, probably once wanted, but never received, she should be happy that *I* achieved them. Instead of hating me with her entire being for how I present myself and live my damn life, she should at least take pride in the fact that I haven't let society dictate their rules and regulations on me. That I've driven down my own road whilst also creating new paths for myself that only take me in directions I *wanna* go to.

But I guess expecting any of that from her would be like wishing for the sky to turn neon or some shit, so I've given up hope on that front.

Steven opens the door and steps back, and a young man – Waleed Najimi, I believe his name is – swaggers in and smiles at Mom.

He's wearing a greyish-blue suit with a white dress shirt, and brown Oxfords. And, with his dark hair coiffed, his facial hair trimmed way too precisely – along with the Patek Philippe Ref. 1518 around his left wrist, of course – he screams undeniably of wealth and status.

"Dearest," he says to Mom, then walks over to her. He gives me a brief nod of acknowledgment, then looks at Mom again.

“The new caterers are here,” he tells her in that very-hard-to-understand accent of his. Pair that with his flat voice, and you’ve got a recipe for an ear assault. “They have agreed to overtake buffet facilities for the ball, despite the lateness, and are also ready to accommodate our custom menu. If you can spare an hour of your time, I need you in the office with me so that we can go over the specifics and pricings with them.”

Everyone at the HQ knows that Mom’s banging Waleed. I mean, the two of them have done nothing short of a disastrous job of hiding their fling from Mom’s employees. At this point, there’re so many made-up, fanfic-like stories about their spontaneous sexcapades buzzing around every corner of the HQ, that it’s physically *impossible* to elude them.

And, it wouldn’t be such a zit in the ass if that was all I had to hear about the two of them. But, you see, it *is* a zit – a massive, painful one at that – because the #1 thing everyone at the *Lure* HQ can’t stop talking about is the age difference between Mom and Waleed. And to top it off, they keep adding *my* name into their gossip sessions.

Miss Adler’s new investor/fuckboy is younger than Cignette!

Oh dear, Miss Adler is getting railed by a 25-year-old petrol empire heir. Talk about being a stereotypical cougar.

Honestly, I wanna know what Cignette thinks of her mother having sex with a guy who’s half her age. Shouldn’t she *be the one getting some of that exotic dick instead of Miss Adler?*

I know, I know; it’s wrong to shame someone for their sexual preferences. But hey, it’s my *mom* these people are tattling about, so let’s not jump onto the defense boat here, alright?

Alright.

“Of course,” Mom says in regards to Waleed’s request of assisting him in finalizing the caterers.

He smiles again, and all but glides over to the door before pushing it open for her like the chivalrous man that he is.

Mom chuckles – yeah, she actually *chuckles* – before striding out of the room with him and Steven without so much as a glance in my direction.

"Typical," I mutter under my breath, careful not to let the others hear it.

9.
CIGNETTE

Utter silence has filled the room after Mom's exit. Julian is glancing at Melina, who in turn is glancing at me.

I glance at the stylists on the far end (I wish I remembered their names, but I really don't), and they glance right back in my direction.

It's intense; it's confusing.

It's kind of weird as well, come to think of it.

I'm in the middle of connecting visual stare-dots with Julian, when Mave suddenly clears his throat, making me jerk.

When I look at him, he arches a brow at me. It's basically his way of silently asking me if I'm okay.

I realize my body is rigid, so I relax a little and wink at him to let him know that I am, indeed, okay.

He sighs in evident relief. "We done here?" he asks Julian.

"*Almost*," Julian responds, then looks at me with slightly narrowed eyes. "Sooooo, yellow, then?"

I will my feet to move forward and start walking towards Mave. The first couple of steps are stiff, because I'd been holding myself too tight in my mom's presence, so any kind of movement I'm making now feels like a damn consolation of sorts. But my steps get more and more effortless and freeing as I keep going.

Mave opens the door for me, and I look over my shoulder at a still-waiting Julian.

"Silver," I tell him, then grin. "And make sure it's extra cool-toned so that it doesn't clash with my complexion. The rest of the details remain as is." I turn and head out of the room, with Mave right behind me.

"Are you *serious*?!" Julian hollers. "You can't just throw the silver card at me and walk out on me like you're Cruella de Vil or some shit!"

I chuckle. "You rock, Julian!" I call out. "I know you've got this." I head for the elevator, just as its doors open for me. We're on the 5th floor, which is practically the designing floor.

A few of the stylists smile at me and greet me good-morning, while the others wave my way and compliment my dress. And all of this is genuine, so I have no hesitation in reciprocating it.

The constant hustle and work enthusiasm here is addicting, but I can very clearly see a subtle dimness in everyone's eyes as they go about their business. They're happy to be working at *Lure*, that much is obvious, but they don't like *who* they're working for. It's visible in their drooped shoulders, occasional frowns, and, dare I say, their infrequent glances, which are full of fear.

I'm helpless when it comes to aiding their comfort. The only thing I *can* do is ignore and proceed.

Unfortunate, I know.

And, despite how much shit I give my mom and how much I complain about certain things, I really do have dreams of my own for *Lure* – a different vision, perhaps. There are things here I'd like to change, vibes that I would love to mend. But I've never really had the drive to let Mom know about any of that. It'll be a waste, really; she'll trash the idea even before I've finished proposing it to her.

Like I said before: unfortunate.

Mave and I get into the elevator, and I press the button to the 3rd floor.

The doors close with a smooth *swish*, and the overhead fan turns on, blowing my hair over my face.

"You okay?" Mave asks from next to me.

I give myself a mock once-over. "I mean, I haven't fallen in shambles at your feet just yet, so…"

"*Nettie*," he says in warning.

I sigh and push my hair away from my face. "I'll live," I tell him. "I just…" I cross my arms over my chest. "I just need a couple of espresso macchiatos to get my head on straight." When Mave lifts both of his brows at me, I click my tongue and say, "Fine, I'll need at least 3 of them to get through the morning. I'll let you know the afternoon and evening doses as per my recovery rate."

He laughs. "Don't you think you're being a bit overdramatic?"

"Have I *ever* joked about my caffeine intake?"

He puts his tongue to his cheek. "Not exactly, but–"

"Then I'm not being overdramatic, sir," I quip, just as the elevator *dings* and the doors slide open.

Mave and I step out, and I'm about to face him, but stop when my phone vibrates in my dress pocket.

I pull it out and glance at it, only to suck in a breath when I see Dorran's name on the screen, along with a text message.

Dorran: *You know, I just realized something.*

I swallow and lean sideways against the wall next to the elevator. I know Mave is watching me, and I also know that he has sensed my instant change in behavior, so I try to keep my expression neutral as I read Dorran's text again.

The 3rd floor is just as abuzz with activity as the others in the HQ are. But, being as it is the floor designated for both the IT and social media departments, you get to hear more keyboard taps and mouse clicks than you do the sound of fabrics being cut and sewing machines being worked.

I clear my throat and finally respond to Dorran.

Me: *Did you, now?*

He responds a few seconds later.

Dorran: *Uh-huh.*

I roll my eyes, and Mave shifts in front of me, making me look up at him.

"Who's that?" he asks.

"I thought you were going to go get me my macchiato."

He chuckles. "I'm not your errand boy."

"Of course not," I state, "but I still need my coffee."

He shakes his head at me. "Fine, but let me get you in safe first." He gestures ahead.

A few IT techs pass by us to get to the elevator, so I turn around and head for my office.

Mave's right behind me, of course, which makes me smile a little.

"Who's going to harm me here?" I ask, then glance around for emphasis. "It's not like these people have the balls, or the right tools, for that matter."

Mave groans in exasperation. "You're an obstinate little brat," he mutters.

I push open my office's glass door and step inside. "And you're a prickly asshole who doesn't have faith in my skills."

"And what skills are those, exactly?"

I pivot on my feet so fast, that he has to stop abruptly in order to avoid colliding with me.

"Morning, boss," Raj, Lexie, and Misty, say in unison when they see me, and then return to whatever it is that they are working on, on their computers.

Raj is in charge of creating and posting our social media posts, reels, stories, etc., whereas Lexie runs our website and YouTube channel, and

Misty answers, and solves, customer grievances via Twitter and Instagram DMs.

And I – well, *I* approve everything they do before they actually do it, and also look after *Lure's* official emails. Every collaboration, marketing, or sponsorship offer that comes *Lure's* way, is only sent forward to my mom if I give it the greenlight.

My office is a massive cubical area with separate worktables for every member of my team, and floor-to-ceiling windows behind a rectangular glass table, which is my personal workspace. There's a bathroom on the right and a small storage area on the left. That's it. Simple and spacious. Nothing over-the-top or too fancy to give me a pink eye.

I click my tongue. "Well, if I reveal all my skills to you," I tell Mave, "then I'll lose my element of surprise, won't I?"

"I'm pretty sure I can feel you out, though," he challenges.

I scoff. "That's a bit presumptuous, don't you think?"

He works his jaw as he scans my face. "Pepper spray," he says matter-of-factly. "Kick to the groin, heels to the head."

Fucker.

"You forgot fingernails to the eyeballs," I provide.

He grins. "Hmm, ballsy."

I roll my eyes. "Get your smug face out of my sight."

He grins further. "Fine." He laughs when I flip him off, then shakes his head again.

"I'll get your coffee, you brat," he says. "Just stay in here and don't leave the floor. But if you really *have* to, then text me before you do." With that, he turns around and heads out, still laughing.

I make my way to my desk and settle into my chair. I then turn on my laptop and get back to Dorran's message.

Me: *Sorry for the late response. Just got into work. So, you gonna tell me what you realized?*

Again, his reply is quick.

Dorran: *It's kind of anticlimactic when you take so long to get back to me.*

Me: *I gave you a reason, though xx*

Dorran: *I didn't get a chance to see your tits earlier – you know, when my switchblade was shoved deep inside your sweet little cunt.*

My neck and chest feel flush after reading that, and my breathing turns a bit erratic as I think back to what happened at midnight.

I gotta admit: it'd been tough getting proper sleep after Dorran had left. I could feel his hands on my skin, taste my cum, and his lips, in my mouth, late into the night. I'd touched myself to those very sensations, but the orgasm I'd given myself had been nothing compared to the one Dorran had given me.

How do you stop an addiction from shooting up your veins too fast?

How do you relish every second of it, and also not worry about it burning out before you even have the chance to get high on it?

"Boss?" comes Raj's voice.

I blink and look at him. "Yeah?"

He fixes his glasses and types something onto his computer. "I've just emailed you the graphics I created for the charity ball's social media announcement. Could you, like, give them a look? Because I gotta post them everywhere by noon."

I give him a nod. "Sure."

I open his email and download the attached files, then go over all three of them at length.

They look amazing, as expected, and anyone who saw these and didn't know my mom's actual motives, would think she's a damn saint for supporting the orphanages and women shelters that are listed in all three of the graphics.

"You're a *go* on these," I tell Raj, then get back on my phone.

"Thanks, boss," he says.

"Yup." I type in my response to Dorran.

Me: *Technically, it was your switchblade's* handle *that was inside me.*

Dorran: *Semantics.*

I chuckle.

I'm still thinking of what to say to that, when he sends in another text.

Dorran: *Did you touch yourself after I left?*

I press my thighs together as I reply.

Me: *I'm offended that that's even a question. Did* you*?*

Dorran: *I did borrow your shorts, didn't I?*

I swallow and push my hair behind my ears.

Fucking dipshit.

Dorran: *Is there a bathroom where you are?*

I shouldn't like what he's getting at, if only because I'm at work. But I'm too intrigued by this asshole to give a shit.

Me: *Yeah.*

Dorran: *Get in there.*

I stand and head towards the porcelain bathroom on the right side of my office. Once I'm inside, I lock the door and press my back against the tile wall next to the massive mirror.

I can feel my heartbeat at the base of my throat, and it's crazy because all I've done is walk into a damn bathroom, and I'm already spiked on adrenaline.

I guess this is what happens when you give into your impulses.

Or obey a guy's random command – someone you've barely known for a little over a day.

I work on maintaining my stupid breathing as I text Dorran back.

Me: *Alright, I'm inside.*

A second later, my phone vibrates in my hand with an incoming video call from him.

Good God, this guy is a walking, talking jeopardy to my existence. I've never felt more like a sneaky teenager than I do right now.

It's fucking insane how willingly I do things he wants me to. But then again, I'm too reckless not to, so there's that.

I answer the call, and Dorran's face immediately takes over my screen.

"Hello, Little Swan," he says in that scotch-smooth voice of his, and just like that, I'm sucked right back into the endless vortex of his allure.

10.
CIGNETTE

Dorran's in a dimly lit, brick-walled room. There're a couple of punching bags behind him, a few pairs of boxing gloves hung up on long nails that seem to be hammered into the wall, along with idle metal chairs strewn haphazardly around the area.

The overhead lights appear mostly fluorescent, and cast a subtle shadow over his side profile, making him look more beautiful than he already is.

His hair is slightly damp, and beads of sweat are running down the column of his strong neck. He's wearing a fitted black t-shirt that's all but clinging to his chest, and when I bring my gaze back to his face, I see the sharp contours of his features appear furthermore accentuated against the lights above him.

"I know you've got a reputation to uphold," I begin, "but you're taking the aesthetic game *way* too seriously right now."

His lips twitch. "And I know *you've* got one to maintain as well, but this…" He jerks his head forward. "This seems kinda extensive, don't you think?"

I move the phone around a bit so that I can show him the mirror and vanity area next to me. "What, the bathroom?"

He cocks his head to the side. "Is that really a bathroom, though?"

I chuckle. "Yeah, why?"

He places his right elbow on top of the back rail of his chair, then lifts a shoulder. "Looks too fucking pristine for it to be one."

"And bathrooms can't be pristine because…?"

He scoffs. "I don't know; maybe because all you do in there is shit and piss." He clicks his tongue. "I mean, an occasional quickie too, if you're feelin' like it, but that doesn't mean your bathroom needs to look like a fucking dollhouse or something."

I laugh. "I can't believe you're complaining about *this*," I tell him.

"It's an unnecessary show of wealth," he states. "I find it icky."

"I respect that." I smile at him. "But I didn't build this place; my mom did."

"Wouldn't expect anything less from her," he remarks.

"Have you met her, then?"

Dorran rolls his eyes. "I didn't ask you to sneak into your bathroom to talk about your *mom*, Cignette." He leans back in his chair. "Show me those tits of yours so that I can get a damn boner."

I can't help but laugh again, even though I know he just evaded my question, and very smoothly, at that. But I guess I'll have to let it slide. People don't willingly talk about my mom unless they absolutely have to, so I get it.

"Are you incapable of getting a boner without seeing me naked?" I ask Dorran.

He scowls. "Are you incapable of doing a single thing I ask you to do?"

"I did everything you wanted me to earlier," I remind him.

He grunts. "Dress – off. *Now*, Cignette."

Fuck, I love how he sounds, especially when he's riled up. It's fun to bring his edge out; it shows me just how easily I can affect him.

I press my teeth to my bottom lip as I gently push one, and then the other collar of my dress down my shoulders. The silk all but glides over my arms, and I quickly pull the front of it down to my waist before angling my phone far enough for Dorran to see what he wants to.

I'm not wearing a bra; I mostly never do. So, when I catch Dorran's eyes after putting myself on literal display for him, I see how dark yet heated they seem to look.

He swallows as he scans every inch of me that's visible to him through the screen, then runs the tip of his tongue over his lower lip.

My nipples harden to the point of pain; my breasts feel heavy. My chest warms against his stare, and my breaths turn shallow as I continue to watch him take me in.

"Dorran."

He meets my gaze. "Yeah."

I lean my head against the wall and grin at him. "Show me what I do to you."

He arches a brow. "Is that a command, Little Swan?"

I shrug. "Maybe."

He chuckles. "You're bad," he says. "So damn bad." He shifts in his chair, lowers his phone, and widens his thighs. He then brings his right hand over his crotch and cups the base of his very evident hard-on through his black, skintight tracks.

I suck in a breath when the veins on the back of his hand shift as he squeezes himself further.

"See?" he says, his voice a little raspy. "*This* is what you do to me, sweetheart. *This* is how much I want you; how much I want to ruin you, fucking worship every part of you." He squeezes himself again, and my God, I'm so close to bringing a hand between my legs and finger-fucking myself.

But I can't. I *won't*. Because I don't wanna miss a second of this – of him.

"Stroke yourself," I tell him.

His eyes blaze as they meet mine. "So demanding today," he muses.

"I like to think that I have just as much right to order you around as you do me."

He smirks. "Aye." He runs his hand over his length, and fuck me, he's big. "But if you were someone else, I'd have ended them before they even *thought* about asking me to do something."

"Noted," I quip, then raise a brow. "Now, stroke yourself proper, *dahling*; I don't have all day."

He laughs and shakes his head a little, then starts to really work himself. He squeezes his base, cups his cock from over his tracks, and strokes himself up and down. His chest is moving too fast, and with each rustle of fabric against his palm, his breathing grows more and more audible.

He thrusts his hips forward, increases his pace, and spreads his thighs further apart.

I'm hot – literally. I'm damn near burning up.

Watching Dorran touch himself because *I* commanded him to, is fucking empowering.

He's absolutely *stunning* like this – so disordered and blatant – and I simply can't take my eyes off him.

He tips his head back and moans, resulting in the muscles of his neck to stretch. It's a deep, slightly restrained sound, but it still makes me temporarily hold my breath.

He licks his lips, strokes himself one last time, and then moves his hand away from his cock before bringing his phone back up again. "If I continue doing that," he tells me, "I'll end up coming in my damn pants, and *that*, Little Swan, can't happen. Not right now, at least."

"But I didn't ask you to stop, did I?"

He chuckles. "No, you didn't. But if it were up to *you*, I'd be staining my pants with my cum, and that's way out of my style." He gives me a wink. "Just because I did what you wanted me to, doesn't mean I'll also give you complete satisfaction of it. I'm not that generous, sweetheart."

I work my jaw. "No, but you sure are a piece of shit," I tell him.

"Uh-uh." His features darken as he gives me a piercing look. "Watch that mouth, will you? Because I know just how to shut it."

"What, so you'll slit my throat for calling you out, then?" I ask.

He grins. "Oh, Little Swan." He laughs momentarily, and goosebumps prick my skin at the deliciously cold glint that takes over his eyes. "The only reason I'll ever spill your blood is if you ask me to. And trust me, with how much you've already affected me, it won't take a lot of persuasion from you for me to get a taste of what I so madly crave."

My throat tightens at his words, and a welcoming chill blankets me at the desire in his voice.

Is it nuts that I'm actually considering what he just said?

Am I crazy for wanting this – for wanting his blade to cut through my skin just so I can feel his mouth against it after?

Maybe; maybe not. What matters most, though, is that the idea itself makes me feel abuzz with something strong, something I've never felt before.

"The thought of your lips tainted with my blood – it makes me so fucking wild, Dorran," I tell him honestly.

He smirks. "Then ask me for it the next time you and I see each other, and I swear I'll give it to you."

"Only if I get a taste of you in return," I add.

That makes him grin again. "Without question," he says.

I'm so lost in this man that it's borderline insane. He's got a hold on me, and I don't want him to ever let go. And fuck me, I've only known him for a day.

But I guess an addiction doesn't really value time or purpose; it just attacks. It spreads and consumes you, because that's exactly what it's made for.

A knock sounds on the door, startling me a little.

I inhale sharply and straighten, then quickly fix my dress.

"Nettie, you alright?" comes Mave's voice from outside. "Raj told me you've been in there for a while. I'm just checking in."

Shit.

"I'm fine," I tell him, then curse under my breath. "I'll be out in two."

"Gotcha," he answers.

I look at Dorran and grimace. "*I have to go*," I mouth.

He chuckles. "*I know*," he mouths back, but it's more on the snarkier side, which makes me roll my eyes.

I flip him off, and then begrudgingly end the call before sliding my phone into my dress pocket. I turn and face the mirror, fix my hair, and gently clear my throat before pulling open the door and smiling at Mave.

"Hey," I say to him.

He looks me up and down, and I see that he's holding two cups of espresso macchiato in his hands.

"Ah, you got my coffee." I take both cups from him, brush past him, and head for my desk.

"You sure you're okay?" he asks.

I place the cups next to my laptop and slump into my chair, then stretch my legs and sigh before closing my eyes. "*Golden*."

"You look pretty damn red to me," Mave says.

I open my eyes. "Huh?"

He sighs. "Flushed, Nettie; you look kinda feverish."

If Dorran Ledger said the exact same things to you as he did to me, you'd be just as red in the face, Mave, I wanna tell him, but don't. For obvious reasons.

“Just a bit on edge,” I lie. “You know, with what happened earlier…”

His expression softens, and he nods. “Of course.”

I know he isn’t stupid enough to believe me entirely, but I also know that he trusts me enough to not doubt or question me unnecessarily.

I feel bad for not being honest with him, but how exactly am I supposed to tell my damn *bodyguard* that I’m into someone who’s the county’s most dangerous man; that he’s *literally* the Bloody Prince of Riverside?

Hiding it from Mave is the only option. The only *sane* one, at least.

And, as I smile at him again, I realize that the longer I keep Dorran a secret from him, the harder it’ll get for me to remove myself from the labyrinth of duplicity that I’ve created around the people in my life.

Things are bound to get messy, one way or another. But I guess I’ll have to wait and see how reality unfurls itself to me, even though all I wanna do is jump through time and see if I make it.

Or if wanting Dorran turns out to be the last thing I do before I meet my end.

11.
DORRAN

"Motherfucker!" I double over when Jayce punches me right in the gut. The tips of my fingers brush against the harsh concrete floor when my arms come forward, and my body bends downwards. And the pain I feel? Yeah, it's unendurable.

"Still distracted, I see," the asshole muses, which means that he knows.

I groan as I straighten, then press a hand over my stomach as I let go of a slow breath.

"Solo told you," I say to him.

Instead of answering me, Jayce goes in for another punch, but this time, he connects it straight to my cheekbone.

"*Fuck*," I hiss as razor-sharp pain shoots from the side of my face, all the way up to my damn skull.

We're blowing some steam after our work out at Solo's underground gym. Now, it's not a place people come to; it's just an *us* thing. Everything in here is for me, the crew, and Solo himself, and this place also happens to be where we usually plan our kills.

The gym is also stocked with weapons we might need to execute these kills, along with files and photos of the people we have taken down so far. It's kinda like our sacred ground, and for as long as Solo has owned it, it's been untouchable by the cops. No one dares to come near anything that belongs to Christopher Solo and his team, after all – even the new Riverside County sheriff and his deputies.

I touch my cheek, because it stings so fucking bad, and find the skin there to be tender.

The air conditioner in here is all but dead, so there's literally no way to avoid getting sweaty while working out or boxing.

"Solo did tell me," Jayce admits. "But what's fortunate is that he doesn't know who it is you're so pussy-whipped over. Because if he *did*, Ledge, then you'd be a dead fucking man." He pulls his right arm back and goes in for another punch, but I block it and jab him in the chin.

He grunts a curse, then wipes his mouth with the white strap that's wrapped around his hand.

"And it's fortunate that *you* do?" I say to him.

Jayce grits his teeth and takes a step toward me. "You really think messing with an Adler – let alone *Chase* fucking Adler's niece – is going to end well for you? Are you out of your goddamn mind or somethin'?"

"I'm sorry, *what*?" Varsha cuts in, then looks at me with wide, unbelieving eyes. "You're fucking that pink-haired Barbie?"

"Ledge," says Alex. "What the hell, bro?" He's surprised, which is an expression that's quite unlike him.

Him and Varsha are sitting on a bench a few feet away from me, enjoying protein bars that they didn't pay for, and watching me get my ass kicked by Jayce.

I swallow and run a hand over my sweaty face. "I didn't…" I sigh. "I didn't fuck her."

"So what, you just took a whiff of her cunt and wished her goodbye?" Varsha bites out.

"Careful," I warn her, and watch as shock takes over her features.

"Ledge, come on," Alex urges. "You can literally have *any* girl in Riverside – one who's way prettier than Cignette; one who comes with zero target signs aimed at your back. Have you even thought about that?"

I glare at him. "Fuck pretty," I tell him.

"We don't want your head served on a silver platter, asshole," Jayce says. "We fucking care about you. Unlike Cignette, who won't give a single shit if you disappear from her life, we can't lose you." He swallows. "Because we'll be damn near aimless without you."

"So you know her well enough to know what she does, and doesn't, give a shit about," I state.

"I don't," Jayce seethes, "but neither do *you*, Ledge. Where the hell's your commonsense?" He throws a punch at me, but I duck and pivot to the side.

"That woman is *known* for fucking around with random men," he adds. "We saw proof of it yesterday – with Gavin. She doesn't even care that he's in a relationship. Do you really wanna risk your neck for someone like her?" He goes in for another punch, and I lean back to avoid it. But, as I move forward again, he uses his other hand to clock me right in the nose.

I taste blood before I actually feel it dripping down my nostrils. I press the back of my wrist over it, and groan when that action results in pain to course through my septum.

Jayce smirks at me, which makes me clench my jaw.

I put my left foot forward and drive a punch in his direction, and it connects – quite perfectly, if I do say so myself – with his mouth.

I grin, then spit blood on the ground, just as Jayce does the same, hissing at the fresh cut on his bottom lip.

"Punch him in the dick, babe!" Alex calls out to Jayce, which makes him chuckle.

"Choke on your damn protein bar, Alex," I say to him.

"With pleasure," he chimes, then pretends to deep-throat his half-eaten protein bar.

Varsha rolls her eyes at him, whereas Jayce simply shakes his head.

I'm about to do the same, but end up stumbling when Jayce hits me again.

"Fucking *hell*, man." I cup my jaw when it throbs from the impact. "Are you trying to break my face or something?"

He shrugs, then moves again, but I parry his blow with a jab to his stomach.

He coughs, but doesn't stop to catch his breath. He's in my personal space so quick, that I have to get out of his way haphazardly in order to avoid getting hit by him again.

Back and forth we go – punch, duck, parry; jab, crouch, evade. But I'm out of breath, and so is Jayce. My body hurts, and I know for a fact that his does, too. So, when he comes at me again, I use what little strength I have to knock him in the face, which results in him to fall to the ground.

He's on his side, already trying to get up, but I slump onto the floor in front of him. "Don't even try," I all but pant, then close my eyes for a brief moment, take a slow breath, and then glance at Alex and Varsha.

The former is staring at his husband in concern, whereas the latter is looking at me with disappointment on her face.

Jayce sits up and brings his knees in front of him. He then places his forearms on them and shoots me a glare.

I mimic his position and wipe my bloody nose again. "I thought you guys, of all people, would get it – get *me*." I push my damp hair away from my forehead. "It's not like I go 'round chasing chicks on a daily. Hell, I wasn't even looking for any of this, but it just happened, and now I can't fucking stay away from her."

"We've got no issue with you chasing chicks, Ledge," Varsha tells me. "But what we *do* have a problem with is the fact that the one you're after, is a walking, talking death trap."

"And, need I remind you that Chase Adler is one of our clients – a top-tier one, at that. Fucking around with his family will cost you your life," Jayce adds.

I clench my fists and sneer at him. "My life, or *yours*?" I regret saying those words the second they leave my mouth, especially when I see the hurt on Jayce's face.

"Wow." Alex gives me an incredulous look. "She's fucking gotten into your head already, and you've known her for what, a *day*?" He scoffs. "Didn't expect you to fall so damn low, Ledge."

"*Alex*." There's so much anger in Jayce's voice as he addresses his husband, that it surprises us all.

"You met her last night, didn't you?" Varsha asks. "It's why you refused to hang out with us when I asked you to come over to my place."

I bite the inside of my cheek. "Technically, it was earlier today," I say.

Varsha, Alex, and Jayce live in the same building. Where Varsha owns an apartment on the 5th floor, Alex and Jayce own one on the 8th.

Their building's only a couple blocks away from my loft and *Finesse*, so we usually hang out and have dinner together. It's not a dedicated routine or anything, but we make sure to follow it as often as possible.

Until last night – when I was busy getting a taste of Cignette, and my crew had no fucking idea about how much trouble I was knowingly getting myself into just by seeing her.

Jayce raises a brow at me – a silent command for me to elaborate what I'd said to Varsha.

I scratch the back of my head and open my mouth to talk, but nothing comes out.

Dammit.

I glance at Varsha, then Jayce, and then Alex. They're all looking expectantly at me, like I'm about to recite an ancient folklore or some shit.

We stare.

We blink.

We stare again.

And I've perhaps shifted on my ass a few times, but I guess that's normal, given the environment.

"Well," Alex's voice cuts through the brief silence. "We're waiting, Ledge."

I swallow.

"She didn't have her card with her," I begin, then stop.

"What card?" Jayce asks.

"Her *credit* card, Jay," I tell him. "And she didn't have any cash, either." I loosen the strap tied around my left hand, and then start to unwrap it. "She said I could come over to her place when I had the time, and collect the money she owed us for the battery."

"Good God," Varsha mutters. "So you're telling me that you went to Miranda's *estate* last night?"

"I snuck in, actually," I clarify. "After the day-shift guards left their station."

"Fuck," Jayce whispers. He then closes his eyes and pinches the bridge of his nose. "Christ, Ledge."

"It wasn't a big deal, okay?" I say to them. "I'm fine; they didn't even know I was there."

"Yay you," Alex taunts, then scowls at me. "The guards could have killed you in a heartbeat, you fucking idiot," he adds.

"But they didn't – *because they didn't see me*." I lift a shoulder. "Are they even that good if they couldn't even catch me? We've only heard of how dangerous they are, but never exactly seen them do anything to prove that."

"I'm sorry," Jayce interjects, "but did you *want* them to catch you? Were you there to witness their skills or something? Are you *that* desperate to die?"

Varsha doesn't say anything; she's just watching us. And, because the whole situation is making me feel constricted, I decide to give myself some space from it. Throwing my bloody hand wrap on the ground, I stand and walk over to the table where my duffle bag is placed. I pull my water bottle out from inside it and take a few long swigs from it, then lean against the table to calm myself a bit.

I knew that when I told them about this, they'd be mad. But what I wasn't expecting was for them to be unreasonable about it; be so damn unwilling to understand.

I'm about to take another swig from my bottle, but stop when I hear Jayce's comment.

"She must really be something, then, if you've decided to be so fucking callous about things."

I close the bottle and place it on top of my duffel bag. "She is." I face Jayce. "You know I wouldn't have done any of this if she wasn't."

He glances at the rest of the crew as he sighs, then gets to his feet before sliding his hands into the pockets of his sweats. "Well, in that case, make sure to at least give us a damn heads up before you decide to infiltrate an elite's security again – you know, so that we can be there to watch you get shot in the ass for getting your dick hard over a pixie-looking chick."

I can't help but chuckle at that.

"Fuck you, man," I tell him.

He clicks his tongue. "Don't think Cignette will approve of that, unfortunately."

"And neither will I, you dumbass," Alex says to Jayce.

Varsha snorts. "My God, you guys are fucking *ridiculous*."

Alex already has a response for her, and he's about to voice it, but stops when Jayce's phone rings.

He pulls it out of his hoodie pocket and hands it to Jayce – who, after taking the phone from Alex, briefly touches his husband's jaw with a knuckle as a silent apology for having used an undeserved tone at him earlier.

Alex stifles a smile and acts unaffected, but I can clearly see that his shoulders have gone a little slack, and his overall posture, too, has relaxed a bit.

Jayce looks at me after having checked the caller's name, then answers the call before putting it on speaker.

"Solo," he greets.

"Jay." There's Sinatra playing in the background, and I already know that Solo is in his condo – probably with a bunch of naked people in their early twenties vowing over him.

"You guys feelin' ready for the party this Saturday?" he asks.

I walk over to Jayce and stand next to him, just as he answers Solo by saying, "You know we are."

"And Dor?"

I scoff. "I'm *fine*, Solo."

He chuckles. "Just making sure, kid."

I shake my head, even though he clearly can't see it, or *me*. "Go back to your orgy, boss; you don't have to worry about the kills," I tell him.

This time, he laughs, and the song in the background swells to a crackling crescendo – a little static through the line.

"This lot is quite…*efficient*, if I do say so myself," he provides.

"I'm going to pretend you didn't just say that," Alex says, then grimaces. "I know you're old, but you can't possibly be *that* old. *Efficient*, really? They're *people*, Solo, not your fucking life insurance policy. Because *that* is something you describe as efficient, not guys and girls who know how to have mind-blowing sex. Learn your praises before you end up using the wrong one and pissing one of those groupies into slitting your throat."

Varsha coughs, Jayce puts his tongue to his cheek, and I purse my lips in order to stop myself from losing my shit.

Solo bursts into a very unfiltered bout of laughter. "Oh, Alex…" He continues to laugh. "I hope you suck Jayce's cock just as well as you run that blunt mouth of yours."

Alex crosses his arms over his chest and shoots a quick wink at Jayce. "Much, *much* better, I'll have you know," he tells Solo. "Too bad your shriveled shrimp didn't get a chance to experience it before Jayce put a ring on my finger."

Jayce looks too close to losing it, whereas Varsha is trying really hard not to.

"And isn't that the biggest regret of my existence," muses Solo.

"There's always afterlife," I quip. "You've got a shred of hope to hold onto."

Jayce kicks me in the calf, which makes me grin.

Solo chuckles again, then clears his throat. "Anyway." His tone shifts to all-business. "We sticking to the same plan, then?" he asks.

"Yeah," Varsha answers. "Rizwana, Andres, and Tomas – that's the decided order."

"Copy." He pauses for a couple of seconds, and we then hear him talking to someone on the other side.

"Sorry about that," he says to us after a short while. "Alright, so where were we?"

"We confirmed the kill order," Jayce states.

"Ah, yes." There's a rustle of fabric against leather, footsteps clicking against hardwood floor, followed by the shutting of a door.

"Alright, so Waleed informed me earlier that he's got your names added to the event's invitees list," Solo informs us. "Mine was already in there, of course, so all he had to do was confirm my RSVP."

"Just making sure: he managed to get us in *without* freaking out the person responsible for the guest list?" Alex inquires.

"You underestimate the power our client holds over the entirety of this shindig, Alex," Solo says.

"Touché."

"So…" There's another rustle, followed by the groaning of leather. "I've acquired a softcopy of *Imperia's* blueprint," Solo tells us. "I'm emailing it to you as we speak. It's for reference only, by the way; you don't have to store it into memory or anything."

"Do we wanna know how you got your hands on it?" Varsha asks.

"Eat the damn mangoes and forget about the seeds, V," Solo answers.

"That's…hardly accurate." She clicks her tongue and pulls her phone out of her denim jacket. "Anyways… Password," she tells him, then taps on the latest notification she's gotten, which in turn opens the encrypted email Solo has sent her.

"The capital of Nauru, times ninety-four, times omega."

YAREN×94×OMEGA

Varsha types in the password, then flips her phone sideways before showing us the black-and-white blueprint.

"Give me a verbal rundown, Solo," I say, then take Varsha's phone from her.

Her and Alex come to stand next to me, and as I zoom into an area on the blueprint, I notice that they've moved the ballroom up to the first floor.

"Threat level is intermediate," he says. "The place may look like it was built to be some sort of a palace, but it's got none of the surprise factors of one. The layout is pretty standard, too – nothing we need to concern ourselves about. The security is top-notch, as it is to be expected, but they are quite easily persuadable if you've got the right words to say, the right tools on hand, and the perfect amount of status."

"Escape routes?" I ask.

"We've got 3 exits," Solo begins. "The first one, of course, is the entrance itself. The second one is on the ground floor as well – in the kitchen, northwest side. It's got a digital lock system and is supposed to stay shut unless an emergency hits, but the staff has disabled it for their random cigarette and coffee breaks, so you'll find it open at all times. It leads to 17th Ave, so you guys will have to take a bit of a turnaround to get to the parking lot – on foot – to reach your vehicles. Not the best bargain if, God forbid, you're being chased, but it's still a solid option. And then, finally, we've got the third exit…" He trails, and that's not exactly a good sign.

"What is it?" Jayce asks.

"Avoid it if you can, because the third exit is on the second floor – inside the manager's office. It's a massive glass window, basically, which opens to a metal platform, followed by a set of metal stairs that'll lead you directly to the hotel's parking lot."

"But we're to avoid it because the room itself is heavily guarded, I presume," I tell Solo.

"Bingo. The manager has a team of security that's always stationed outside the office. He's Chase and Miranda's puppet, and not only takes care of their illegal biddings, but also manages the hotel's finances. So yeah, he's kept well under protection."

"What's his name again?" Jayce asks.

"Manav Dheer," says Solo.

"You have any idea why they moved the ballroom to the first floor?" I ask him.

"It's because the area where it used to be before has now been turned into a seating room for international meetings or some shit. Chase wanted a room that's big enough, and also good enough to transform into a patriotic bullshit dungeon to cash in any foreign dignitary that visits Riverside and holds a meeting with him."

"Of course," I muse. "But this change *does* leave us at a disadvantage, doesn't it?"

Varsha studies the blueprint. "We'll be in the middle of it all," she says, then meets my eyes. "No matter what, we'll either have to ascend, or descend, an entire floor to get away once we're done."

"Exactly." I work my jaw as I look at the image again. "And the first floor has no exits, no shortcuts. It's got the ballroom, a very open hallway, a massive dining room, and a bathroom. Good places to perform the kills, but not close enough to our possible retreats."

"Then perform the kills on the ground floor," Solo tells us.

"Where, in the very-easily accessible foyer?" Jayce counters.

"It's got a bathroom and a dining area as well, you dumbass," Solo says.

"Right." Jayce rolls his eyes, and the rest of us chuckle.

"So it's settled, then," Alex states with a slightly manic gleam in his eyes. "We've got everything figured out?"

"Chill," I tell him. "We know the kill order and the layout of the place where we're to perform them, but the rest we'll have to figure out after observing the event. Making concrete plans restrains us within the lines we've drawn around the formulated idea. Let's not be completely decisive over anything unless we've studied the grounds and taken in every factor once we're actually there."

"Well said, Dor," Solo states. "Going into this with a tunnel vision won't help. You'll need to watch each other's backs *and* sides."

"Agreed," Varsha adds, just as Jayce says, "Copy."

Alex rolls his eyes. "*Fine*; kill my joy before it even has a chance to fucking *breathe*."

"But that's kind of our job, isn't it, babe?" Jayce tells him, to which Alex simply flips him off, making him laugh.

"Alright, guys; I've gotta go," Solo tells us. "I'll see you 4 on Saturday, yeah?"

"Yup," we say in unison.

"And Dor?"

"Yeah?"

"I want you focused – entirely, you hear me?"

I know what he means by that; he's indirectly asking me to keep my wits about me.

It's pretty obvious that Cignette will be attending the event, and despite being aware of that little factoid, I'll *have* to do my job; I'll *have* to perform those kills.

I gotta admit: I'm clueless as to what my state of mind will be then – with her being close – but what I *do* know is that I'll try my best not to fuck shit up, because if I do, then it's not just me who'll take the fall, but also Solo and my crew.

Easier said than done, though, especially when it comes to Cignette being my object of imperiling distraction.

I clear my throat and slide my hands into the pockets of my joggers. "*Adios*, boss; I'll see you in 3 days," I tell Solo, then give my crew a quick nod, turn around, and head for the gym's bathroom.

12.
CIGNETTE

The echoes of forgone calamity are the first thing she hears as she opens her eyes against the void. But, as she blinks to make sense of the situation she is in, walls begin to rise around her. Thick, slightly cracked, stone walls.

They open their eyes – milky-white and lifeless – and stare down at her kneeling form.

The ground beneath her moves. No, it slithers. It shifts like it's formless; unstoppable.

She looks down, and sees nothing but ink-black water under her. It swims past her – unaffected by the intrusion she's caused by being there.

"Come to me," a lithe voice, boundless of any direction, whispers to her. "Come to me…"

She lets go of a breath, and watches as puffs of air slip past her lips, and that's when she realizes that it's cold in here.

So very cold.

Chilly breezes blow over and around her, making her shiver. She attempts to stand, but stumbles against the stiffness in her body. The long, flimsy silk dress she's wearing, is doing nothing to aid her from the onslaught of cold. It bites into her skin and makes her teeth clatter.

The walls are still staring at her, as if expecting her to do something.

And so, she does. She gets to her feet.

Wobbling, grunting, yet successfully, she manages to stand, and feels the nebulous fingers of the still-flowing water brush her calves and ankles.

"Come closer..." The voice urges.

She takes a hesitant step forward, and the walls begin to shift. They hiss, as if upset, and start closing in on her.

She takes another step forward. One more. Then two.

Another.

And another.

She finally reaches the very edge of the path – where even the water seems to not flow – and glances below. At first, nothing but absolute darkness meets her gaze – bold and unrelenting – but as she peers deeper into the nameless abyss, a hand rises from within it.

An eerie, too-thick silence blankets the air around her, making her swallow.

A wave of icy wind brushes by her, rustling her long, rose-pink hair.

She shifts on her feet, which results in soft splashes of water to echo through the quiet.

The hand reaches out to her further, and curls its dainty fingers in a come-hither gesture. "Cignette..."

That voice...

She recognizes that voice.

It's a thing of calculating menace; a tune she knows just as well as she does the rhythm of her heart.

The walls rumble restlessly around her, resulting in goosebumps to mar her skin.

"Cignette..." that voice calls again. "Come to me."

She bends slowly and inspects the darkness, but can see nothing except for the eager hand calling out to her.

"You mustn't keep me waiting this long, dear," the voice says. "I yearn for you so..."

She blinks at the words; tries to understand the desperation they hold. She knows that voice, but…but why can't she put a name to it? Why can't she remember who it belongs to?

"Cignette!" There's an urgency in the voice now, one that makes her instinctively move forward and reach a hand out to the one that's waiting for her in the darkness.

The walls shake, as if enraged by her move, but as she turns her head to look at them, they begin to scream. They bellow in pain, more like.

The sound causes ripples in the water. It vibrates against her very bones with its intensity.

She gasps and straightens, and watches, with fear gripping her by the throat, as the walls open their toothless mouths and continue to scream. And then, as if something inside of them has snapped, they shriek, and blood begins to pour out of their mouths, followed by gore and rotten fungi. It flows in streams of revolting disarray, making her take a few steps back – away from the darkened edge.

Their eyes, lifeless only a few moments ago, now flash with a single, evidently clear emotion: pure agony.

She places the back of her left hand over her nose as an intolerable, decaying smell fills the air. It's unmistakably strong, so much so that it makes her eyes water.

She tries to breathe through her mouth, but ends up gagging when the smell heightens upon the walls' continuous state of duress. It's almost like she can taste the rancid and blood-dripping skin in her mouth with the way the stench hits her tongue, and it takes all her patience to not heave all over herself.

"Come to me!" that similar voice yells, but it's drowned out almost immediately by the constant howls of the walls. They clash against each other as if trying to push away the pain they're experiencing, but it's a

fruitless effort. They seem to be trapped in a maze of agony, and she has no idea what she can do to ease them out of it.

Because really, it was hurtful watching them struggle like this.

"Cignette!"

She swallows and returns her attention to the edge.

"Take my hand; let me get you out of this mess," says the voice. "You do not deserve this. You know you don't."

The screams get louder, and she has no other choice but to retract her hand from over her nose and bring it to her ear. It's too much… God, it's simply too much.

"Listen to me, Cignette," the voice urges. "Let me lead you out of here."

"Who are you?" she finally manages to speak, and even though her words are scratchy, they still hold firm against the havoc she's standing in the middle of. "I recognize your voice, but I…" She shakes her head a little. "I can't remember who you are."

"You know me," the voice answers. "More than anyone else in the world, you know me the most, Cignette."

"I–" She stops when she hears it – sharp, consistent flapping of wings.

The formless ground beneath her trembles, and the walls – still lost in their own demise – start falling apart in various forms of debris and ruin.

"Time runs short, Cignette," warns the voice. "You must hurry."

She brings her right arm forward, then second-guesses her move and pulls it back. But when she again glances around at the ongoing destruction, she reluctantly steps forward.

I may fall into yet another trap, but at least I'll get out of this one, *she thinks to herself.*

A probable risk to avoid watching the end of…of whatever this is.

She's about to place her hand over the one awaiting her in the darkness, but stops and turns around when a piercing cry cuts through the chaos.

The cry of a raven.

It flies over to her – majestic and fearless – before perching gracefully over a misshaped boulder a few feet away from her.

Cignette watches the raven with keen interest. She studies it.

It tilts its head and watches her back – more relaxed than alert, as if it knows exactly where it's supposed to be.

She's fascinated by it; drawn to its endless, midnight-blue eyes.

She runs her gaze over its obsidian feathers, and its strong talons that grip the stone to keep it standing.

Her lips twitch, right before she smiles a little, and the raven, in turn, widens its chest, while its gaze all but twinkles as it shifts in her direction.

She can't understand why she's so captivated by the bird, but somehow, she is; she simply can't help it.

She pushes a long strand of hair behind an ear, then moves toward the raven. Her feet are steady as she keeps reducing the space that separates her from the beautiful bird.

She moves closer, and the raven watches her in silent anticipation. She stops when she's in front of it, and then reaches out a hand before slowly, almost tentatively, running the backs of her fingers over the side of its neck.

The raven leans into her gentle touch, which makes her smile again.

Her knuckles graze its beak, and it all but croons in return. But, it's when she's about to kneel in front of it so that she can get a closer look at it, that it happens; that she's propelled backwards. She's pulled away from the bird with such force that a piercing scream rips its way out of her throat.

The raven screams with her, and she hears the agitated flaps of its massive wings as she starts to lose her footing. She falls, and is immediately hit in the face with the unforgiving stream of water she was standing amid. Frost-like droplets cut through her skin, and when she tries to stand, something grabs ahold of her ankles.

Claws.

Cold, calloused claws.

The grip they have on her ankles is awfully painful, and as she scrambles to get away from them, they yank at her again, making her slip further towards the edge behind her.

"No!" she cries, still slipping, and then looks at the raven, whose agony is clear in its now-watery eyes.

She's wet; she's shivering from the cold around her.

Her lips are dry; her tears, not so much.

Her hair – soaked and tangled – sticks to the sides of her face, and her neck.

She stretches an arm towards the raven, just as talon-like nails pierce the skin of her already bruised ankles.

She can feel the blood flowing through her punctured flesh, but she grits her teeth against the burn and tries to pull her upper body forward in an attempt to get away from whatever it is that is trying to pull her down.

"Let me go!" she yells, and her voice echoes aimlessly against the darkness that now surrounds her. "Fucking let me go!"

A sudden yank takes her off guard, bringing her further toward the danger – in such a way that her waist remains pressed against the edge, whereas her lower body dangles over it.

A flash of prismatic light catches her eyes, but she doesn't shift too much, so as to avoid falling completely. And then, a hand – strong, familiar, and inviting – reaches out to her.

The raven is nowhere to be seen, but this hand – it reminds her of someone. Who, she cannot recall.

She quickly places her right hand over the offering one, and sighs just a little at the warmth of the skin that meets hers.

She's being pulled forward, but then, that agonizing grip on her ankles returns. It's firmer now. More assertive.

Cignette tries to kick at it, but it's fruitless. She thrashes against it, but it only rewards her with more wounds.

Pain – there's so much of it; in such abundance. She's being stretched apart from different directions, and it's hard to say which one of the two is actually her saving grace.

Yank, pull.

Forward, backward.

A forceful jolt. A persistent tug.

It's too much.

She squeezes her eyes shut and prays that it'll stop. She doesn't want this anymore. She doesn't fucking deserve this.

Another pull. Another yank.

She's crying now. She's tired.

"Stop," she whispers through her sobs. "Please, just…just stop. It hurts."

But it doesn't stop. If anything, it grows in power.

She begs, she screams, and then she begs some more, but nothing works.

And in the end, there's only the cries of her agony as she's being ripped apart. And blood.

So much of it.

Warm, tasteful, and enticing.

She's drenched in it; she's made of it.

Until all that's left of her is her name.

Cignette.

Cignette…

Cignette.

Cig–

I gasp and sit up in bed. I'm shaking, sweating. My heart is racing so fast that I can actually hear each and every one of its beats.

I throw my blanket aside and touch my waist, and then my legs.

I'm fine, I think to myself. *I'm fucking fine*. It was just a nightmare.

I run both my hands over my face and push my trembling fingers into my damp hair. "Fuck," I all but exhale the word. "*Fuck*."

Fleeting sunlight shines through my curtained balcony slider, and I can hear the occasional chirps of the sparrows, along with the distant chatter of the guards below.

I'm about to lie down again so that I can close my eyes and work on calming my still-wired nerves, but turn when I hear a knock on my door. An almost authoritative and too-loud knock.

I glance at my bedside clock.

7:49a.m.

I swallow and let go of a jaded sigh, because I know damn well who's on the other side of the fucking door.

13.
CIGNETTE

I pull my tangled hair up in a bun, then reluctantly get to my feet. I stretch my legs a little, because God, they feel stiff as *fuck* right now.

She knocks on my bedroom door again, but this time, it comes across more as banging than actual knocking.

It's a little hard to decipher her motive and level of anger from this banging/knocking – because really, she only ever comes to me when she's pissed.

I admit that I'm less than willing to learn the reason behind her being here, but I'm also not in the mood to witness a tantrum from her if I do, in fact, ignore her right now and go back to bed.

My mother has never made it easy for me to come to concrete decisions without feeling guilty or partially unsure about them. And that, right there, is a talent – one she possesses in spades.

I reach my bedroom door, let go of a breath, and reluctantly wrap my fingers around the ice-cold doorknob. I swallow, and then finally open the door.

It happens so fast that it takes me a few seconds to realize it, and by the time I do, I'm on the floor, with my legs folded behind me, and my forearms pressed on the carpet under me.

I squeeze my eyes shut as the sting of her slap registers itself first, and covers the entire left side of my face. It's followed quickly by a wave of acute pain that starts at my left temple, and continues all the way to the back of my head.

"You *cunt*," my mother all but spits the words at me. "Did you really think you could overshadow me? *Me*?!"

I'm so disoriented that I can't even look at her, let alone grasp the meaning behind what she's just said. So, when she kicks me in the stomach and the breath is quite literally knocked out of me, my body weakly rolls a few paces away from hers.

"Did you suck Julian's cock in order to have him make you a dress that's better than mine?" she asks. "Was this your plan, then – to humiliate me at the charity ball by out-staging me in front of *my* guests and investors?"

I try to cough, but end up wheezing instead. My mouth, and the back of my throat, feel cold and dry, and every breath I take results in pinprick-like pain to shoot through my sides.

Julian had emailed me a digital copy of the sketch he'd made of my dress last night. As expected, it was absolutely gorgeous, and according to him, his team was confident that they'd have it sewed and perfected by Friday evening.

The dress doesn't even exist as of now, to be practical, so I don't know why my mother is behaving like this.

I blink my eyes open, but my left one immediately shuts itself again. I can feel the tears running down it, which tells me that it's either swollen, or my mother has accidentally hit the area around my pupil. Either way, it hurts so much, I can barely think.

"I don't…" I rise a little and attempt to move, but end up failing. "I don't know what you're…" I feel dizzy all of a sudden, and when I shake my head to get rid of it, it only intensifies. "I don't know what you're talking…about." I push myself away from her.

My mother bends and fists my hair, making me flinch. "I saw the rough draft of your finalized attire for the event," she says between gritted teeth, then yanks at my hair before bringing her face close to mine. "You have someone you wish to impress this Saturday, or are you simply looking to shame me?" She pulls at my hair further, which makes me groan, and for the pain in my head to multiply.

I can smell vodka on her breath, and when I glance at her with my one good eye, I notice that she's wearing the exact same bodycon dress which she had on at the HQ yesterday, which means that she was working late, and then most definitely went out for drinks with that Waleed guy after.

"You're overreacting," I rasp out, because that's all I'm capable of right now.

My mother – my own fucking flesh and blood – just injured me speechless because she thought I was trying to one-up her through an *unmade* dress for an event I didn't even wanna attend, to begin with.

At first notice, it does seem bizarre, doesn't it? But it shouldn't, not to me. Not when I've been beaten and bruised by her for far less in the past.

"I'm overreacting?" she hisses in my face, then all but throws me across the room.

I scream – I don't know how, given the fact that I can barely take a proper breath – and cry out as I crash against my dressing table chair. Something sharp cuts through my right cheek, and as I hit the ground, the chair falls next to me with a soft *thud*.

I don't even have time to recover before my mother is on me again. She turns me around and straddles me, but I grab her wrists before she can slap me again, and manage to push her off me.

She yelps and falls back, and I think her right arm connects dangerously with the fallen chair, because she shrieks and grabs her elbow.

I take that as an opportunity to drag myself away from her, but every bit of pain I'm feeling in my body right now, fails in comparison to the fear that's taken ahold of me.

I hit her.

Oh my God, I fucking *hit* her.

I don't have any sort of humanly compassion towards her, no; nor is my fear driven by the same. What I'm dreading is her kicking me out of the house for hurting her. Because she's done it before, and I've been subjected to my uncle's disappointment when I'd knocked on his door and asked him to let me stay with him instead.

"*She's your mother, Cignette*," Uncle Chase had said. "*Just because she hit you to put some sense into you, doesn't mean you should retaliate. That is very unbecoming of you, sweet pea.*"

My uncle loves me, but when it comes to his baby sister, he's blinded by love, and is willing to dismiss any and every wrongdoing written under her name.

If I'd somehow gathered the balls to get my own place after that little rejection of his all those months ago, then I'd have to face two very concrete consequences.

1) My credit cards getting blocked.

2) Becoming a constant target in not only my mother's eyes, but also on my uncle's hit-list.

And honestly, I wasn't exactly looking forward to either of those things.

It sucks, though. Despite her being an unmerciful human being, my mom has still got someone who she can always rely on for her safety and support.

Her own family.

And I? I don't have that; I've got no one.

I lose. I always do.

Why?

Because I'm alone.

"You bitch!" my mother hisses. "You fucking pushed me!" She charges at me, and slaps my right cheek before wrapping her fingers around my throat. "You worthless little cunt!" She squeezes my throat, and the madness I see in her glassy eyes would be terrifying to others, but it's nothing new to me. I know damn well the kind of darkness she hides behind them, and the kind of monster she really is.

I try to gasp for air when her fingers press on tighter, but it's useless. I kick and thrash under her; claw at her hands and lift my hips to get her off me, but she doesn't budge. She keeps squeezing, and squeezing – with a raw determination on her face – and soon, my vision turns hazy. My lips feel numb, and so does the rest of my body. My protests weaken, and I feel a leaden-like weight settle on the center of my chest.

She's saying something to me, but with the state I'm in, it's hard for me to focus on anything.

"Ma'am."

I'm about to close my eyes and succumb to the pressure, but blink when my mother suddenly lets go of my throat.

An unintelligible sound leaves me as I try to take in as much air as I can, and when I look toward the door, I notice Steven standing outside my room.

"Ma'am," he addresses my mother again, who seems enraged upon being interrupted.

She hastily turns to look at him. "*What?*" she spits.

"We have to go – *now*," Steven says, then taps his wrist watch to emphasize his point.

She gets off me, pushes me to the side, and struts over to him.

He opens the door further for her, and when she walks out of my room and into the hallway, Steven and I lock eyes. I'm not even remotely surprised when he gives me a poker, all but emotionless look, right before lowering his gaze, turning around, and following my mother up to her floor.

I wait until their footsteps have receded, then dig my nails into the carpet in order to pull myself forward.

I grunt against the pain, against the soreness in my limps, but continue to push. I take open-mouthed breaths because even the smallest effort I put into moving forward, makes me feel winded.

I know why Steven took my mother away, and why she let him. I know why he was here. It wasn't for me, no; it was because of…

I hear footsteps again, but this time, they are the approaching kind. They are sure and steady at first, but they slow down a little as they get closer.

There's a pause, so I take that time to draw myself forward one last time, and when I'm finally where I want to be, I place the side of my head on the foot of my bed, and lean my body against it for support.

I swallow against the lump in my throat, and keep my eyes trained on my wide-open bedroom door.

Any minute now…

Any damn minute.

The footsteps resume, but they sound rushed. I can feel their impact on the floor beneath me, just as a figure charges into my room and falls on his knees in front of me.

"Nettie…"

This is why Steven was here – to prevent a confrontation between my mother and the man in front of me.

I let go of a sigh, and choke on a sob as my eyes meet expressive grey ones.

"Mave…" I whisper.

The anger and concern on his face are palpable. "When?" He doesn't have to ask 'who', because him and I – we've been in this situation several times before.

"She…just left," I manage to speak. My head is spinning, and it's painful to get even a few words out.

Mave's gaze turns misty. He grits his teeth and makes to stand, but I quickly, albeit feebly, grab his hand, resulting in him to pause.

"Please…" I urge, then slowly shake my head. "Don't."

"I wanna hurt her, Nettie," he says darkly.

"I know."

"I wanna fucking…" He lets go of an audible breath. "I wanna–"

"Kill her," I finish for him, then give him a faint smile. "I…know that, too."

Mave knows what'll happen if he so much as *looked* in my mother's direction the wrong way. Uncle Chase wouldn't think twice before putting a bullet in his head. To him, he's just hired help, but to me, Mave is comfort. He's my safety; my shield against the hailstorm that is my life.

"Mave." I tug at his hand. "*Please*."

He sighs, stares at me while a look of contemplation plays across his features, and then, finally – *thankfully* – he decides to sit down next to me. He then cradles me in his arms and scans me entirely.

"God, look at what she's done to you," he whispers. "Fucking *bitch*."

"I'll…" I swallow. "I'll be fine."

His eyes flash as they meet mine. "You're *bleeding*, Nettie."

Am I? I can't feel it. It has to be the cut on my right cheek, I presume.

"It's just a wound," I say, then blink when my vision goes blurry momentarily.

"*I know*," he hisses. "But you shouldn't have to *be* wounded. You shouldn't have to be in a situation which requires you to recover, not like *this*." He gestures at my face.

"It is what it is," I tell him.

"But that's the thing, Nettie. It doesn't *have* to be."

"I know." I touch my fingers to his jaw. "I'm aware."

He frowns, and I don't think I've ever seen him this broken before. It brings an ache to my chest, and I feel so damn helpless. Not only for him, but also for myself.

I groan and rest my head on his shoulder when a wave of nausea takes over, and Mave instantly tightens his arms around me.

"You with me?" he asks, and I notice a crack in his voice at those words.

"Yes."

He sighs, then presses a soft kiss on my hairline. "Come on, then; let's fix you up. The longer I see you like this, the more tempted I'll be to punch a hole in your meritless mother's frigid heart."

I fist his jacket and inhale shakily, then nod and say, "Okay."

14.
CIGNETTE

There's water running in the background from the bath I've just started for myself. Apart from that, the only other sound I can hear is the elementary beating of my heart.

I stand in front of my bathroom mirror, wearing nothing but the scars my mother gave me this morning.

The left side of my face is a splendid shade of crimson, and is swollen – albeit a little less than it was a few hours ago. There's a gash on my right cheek – smaller than half an inch, Mave had said. It didn't require stitches, thankfully, but it still hurt like a bitch.

I swallow, and my gaze falls lower, to the untidy yet stark finger imprints on my neck. They don't hurt, per se, but they are so glaringly obvious that it makes my eyes sting.

They are jewels of my mother's rage, these scars. They are a warrior's proof of victory. *My* victory against her cruelty.

I take a step back, and then look at the bruise that covers most of my stomach. It's…*ugly*; deep to the point where it looks violet under my bathroom lights. My ribs still ache if I move too much, but it isn't anything a warm bath can't fix.

At least that's what I told Mave.

Mave…

My God, he's been heaven-sent. He spent the entire day by my side – like he always does after these…incidents. From disinfecting my gash, icing my face and stomach, giving me an ample dose of pain meds so that I could sleep most of the initial impact off, to quite literally feeding me lunch and dinner, he did it all. And, as embarrassed as I am to admit it, he also helped me take a dump and a few pisses throughout the day.

None of this is his job. Hell, none of this is even supposed to *happen*. But, even if it does – which it clearly does – he doesn't deserve to be the one to pick up my pieces and make me whole again. He's so much better than this; so much better than the mess he's gotten himself into. But I'm selfish. I can't ask him to walk away. I *need* him, even though it isn't fair to him. Still, I need him.

He wasn't ready to leave me, but I'd forced him out of my room; all but ordered him to go home and get some rest.

"*I can sleep here*," he'd argued.

"*On the floor, or on the bed?*" I'd asked.

His eyes had gone dark, then. He knew he couldn't share the same room with me, let alone the same bed. He knew what he'd end up doing if he decided to stay, and how it'd affect our rapport and friendship.

With me asleep and on painkillers, it was okay. But when I wasn't high on them, things could go very differently, especially with how much he cares and wants to be there for me.

"*I'll be back early, then*," he'd told me.

"*You'll be back at 8, like your new routine, and not a second before that*," I'd said firmly. "*You'll go home and get some much-needed sleep, Maverick Constance, or I swear to God I'll rain all my damn rage on you. Do you fucking hear me?*"

He'd pretended to appear pissed, but had eventually sighed and relented. He'd made me promise not to open my door for anyone, to which I'd had no issues in agreeing.

"*I'll text you as soon as I'm here*," he'd stated. "*And if you're up by then, just text me back so that I know you're okay.*"

"*Okay.*"

He'd given me his usual, assessing once-over, placed a kiss on my forehead, and then walked out of my room.

That was an hour ago, and I've spent every minute since then telling myself that I'll get into the bath and try to relax my sore muscles a little. But I haven't exactly done that yet. All I *have* done is get further acquainted with the bruises on my body.

I grip the white marble countertop and bow my head. The ridiculous excuse of a bun that I've tied my hair into, flops to the side, making me laugh. A little at first, but then I'm full-on shaking with laughter. I can't help it; I'm snickering senselessly.

The stretch of my mouth brings cutting pain to my entire face, but that doesn't stop me.

I look at myself in the mirror again, and then laugh harder. "This is who you are," I tell my reflection. "This is who you fucking *are*, Cignette."

Tears begin to run down my broken face as I bend forward when my hilarity grows in its intensity. I just…laugh, and laugh.

"*This is who she made you to be…*" I whisper, then snort in laughter. I try balancing myself as I straighten, but end up stumbling and falling backwards.

I'm on the floor now, cross-legged, and as the enormity of what I'm doing, of where I'm letting myself go, sets in, I place a hand over my mouth and start crying. I close my eyes, take in a loud breath, and continue to cry.

I cry, because it's so hard to numb the pain, yet so easy to let it take over.

I cry, because I hate my mother for being the way she is. For doing to me what no mother should do to her child.

And I cry, because I know I've won, and yet, I know that I've also lost.

15.
DORRAN

I tighten my grip on the pillar's topmost motif, then use my legs as a boost to haul myself upward. My palms burn at the impact, but the thrill that's coursing through me right now takes precedence over any strain I feel in my body.

There's something absolutely *delicious* about infringing the systematic cycle of things, isn't there? And I – I'm the kinda fucker who relishes being an oddity.

The weather is pretty brisk tonight, and I can kinda smell rain in the air. Not the most ideal condition, but eh, I've been here before, so I'm sure I'll be fine.

I eye the balcony on my right – merely an inch from my reach – and balance myself in such a way that I can lean in and grab the marble railing. Once I've done that, I take a couple of steps in a sideways fashion, and then carefully move one leg, followed by the other, over the railing. My boots make a soft *thump* sound when they touch the floor, and I let go of the breath I was holding before glancing behind me with a smirk.

"Assholes," I whisper when I see the nightshift guards – oblivious of my presence – chattering among themselves while stationed on the inside of the estate's main gates.

Perhaps my deep-green vest and dark jeans gave me ample leverage for blending in, but still, those guys didn't even *try* looking in my direction. I may or may not have pretended to be a bit lazy in the process, and even then, they didn't give any number of shits about the suspicious rustling in the garden.

I guess all one needs these days is a shiny exterior to fool people into thinking they're unbreakable, when, in fact, they're hollow and worthless – just like their claims and résumés.

I roll my eyes when a few of the guards laugh at something they were talking about, then turn my back to them. I take a step forward and look up, but stop when I notice her. I don't know how I missed it before – probably because I was focused on not falling on my ass whilst proving to myself that I can one-up the guards yet again – but I didn't see her until now.

Cignette's room is bathed in darkness; there's not a single light turned on. The silence in here is so heavy, it's almost like I can *feel* it brushing over my ears.

She's sitting on the side of her bed – the one that's facing the balcony – with her bare feet touching the carpet. She's wearing a pink-and-white letterman hoodie, and every other second, drops of water drip down her damp hair and fall soundlessly on her exposed thighs. Her head is bowed, so she hasn't seen me yet, but something about her posture heightens my attention.

I take another step forward, and that results in moonlight to stream into the otherwise unlit room. It reflects on her side profile, and a chill – one that has nothing to do with the weather – rakes over my spine.

Her face…

The left side looks slightly purplish, and there's a bit of swelling there. My hands clench into vise-gripped fists when I see the fresh scar on her right cheek. Immediately, the thought of Gavin having hit her crosses my mind, and my anger flares like a motherfucking fire.

I grit my teeth as my feet move forward on their own accord, and even though I'm slightly shocked by how strongly I'm reacting towards her, I don't dwell on the realization. I brush it aside as I keep erasing the distance between her and I.

She doesn't look up as I approach – not even when I fall on my knees in front of her.

"Cignette?" I say with caution, then place my hands on the mattress on either side of her, enclosing her.

She sits there motionless – still and silent – as if she's a sculpture made of the tatters of the incident she has endured.

"Cignette?" I try again, but she continues to stare downwards.

I work my jaw as I study her. She looks lost in her thoughts, probably revisiting what happened to her, or maybe even dealing with the mental impact it has left behind. Either way, it's making me restless seeing her this way, so I pull a hand away from the mattress and bring it to her face. With a swallow, I slowly, as gently as I can, cup the right side of her face and tilt her head up a little.

She parts her lips and sucks in an audible breath, but when our eyes meet, her brows pinch together in confusion.

"*Dorran*," she whispers my name with a rush of air, then shakes her head. "What are you doing here?" she asks.

"I tried calling you, but it kept saying that your phone was switched off," I tell her, as if that's a valid enough reason for me to breach the estate's security in order to see her.

Maybe it is. Maybe not. Fuck if it matters.

"Mave must've turned it off while I was asleep," Cignette says matter-of-factly.

I clench my jaw. "*Mave?*" I all but spit the word out. Whoever this fucker is, they must be someone Cignette trusts, because there's a familiarity and ease with which she says their name.

She blinks, sensing the slight change in my behavior. “My *bodyguard*,” she states, and the heavy emphasis she puts on the second word doesn’t go unnoticed by me.

I feel my shoulders relax, which frustrates me. I need to get a damn grip on my reactions.

“Who did this to you?” I ask her instead of acknowledging her answer. I know who her *Mave* is, but I wasn’t aware that Chase had assigned him to Cignette.

Maverick is a polished asshole, with skills so keen they could almost put Solo’s to shame. During the few times I’ve met him, he’s kept to himself and obeyed Chase’s orders to the T. He’s not necessarily the kinda guy who invites trouble, so that’s a relief, at least.

It’s comforting, but also unnerving, that he’s around Cignette most of the time, but he’s nothing I can’t handle. If he gets in the way, I’ll be forced to deal with him. Until then, he can continue breathing and stay in his fucking lane.

Cignette inhales in response to my question. “It’s–”

“If you’re about to lie to me, Little Swan,” I cut her off, “then make sure it’s a solid one, because I’m well-equipped in sniffing out bullshit.”

She lets go of the breath she’s holding, then shakes her head. “It’s nothing.”

My anger flares. She can’t possibly be defending the dipshit who hurt her.

I grit my teeth and move the hand I have on her cheek, to the back of her neck, before cupping it. I use my other hand to part her legs, then shift closer to her.

“*Bullshit*,” I hiss at her.

She looks pleadingly at me. “Dorran, please…”

“Was it Gavin?” I ask.

"What, no!" she says with enough incredulity that I'm assured it isn't the greasy bastard.

"Then who, Cignette?" I lean in and scan her face. "*Who* fucking did this to you?"

She swallows and places a hand on my chest. "Please…" Her voice breaks, and I watch as tears fall down her cheeks. She flinches when they touch the scar on her right one, then sniffs before saying, "Please," again.

I'm so fucking enraged at her stubbornness that I can barely control it. I slap the mattress with my free hand – hard enough to make Cignette gasp – and tighten my grip on the back of her neck before pressing her forehead to mine.

"Fucking *tell me*," I all but command. "Because if you don't, then I swear on everything I hold dear, I will rip through everyone who's in *and* around this damn house right now just to get you to name this person."

Cignette is fully crying now. "I can't," she says between her tears. "You don't get it; I can't."

"It's not that you *can't*," I tell her. "You simply *won't*. And why? Because you're scared of whoever is responsible for your state?" I'm not proud of provoking her like this, but I need to know what she's not telling me. And if I've gotta play dirty to get what I want, then I'll do it.

Cignette jerks her head back and glares at me with pure rage in her dark eyes. "*Fuck you*." She moves forward and pushes me in the chest, then groans and clutches her stomach.

What the hell?

I reach for her and grab her hoodie. She tries to shove my hands, but I don't let go, and instead, yank at her hem. "Lift your ass," I order.

She stares at me for a moment, and when she realizes I'm not giving up, she huffs and does what I've told her to.

"Good girl," I say to her, then raise her hoodie all the way to her collarbone, only to inhale a sharp breath when I see her stomach.

The bruise is purple – exactly like the one on her face – and starts just above the waistband of her underwear, covering almost her entire stomach. It's deeper at the bottom, but fades out completely along the underside of her breasts.

My chest tightens at the sight of it; I can't stop looking at it. My hands shake in anger, and heat rises in the back of my neck as I lift my gaze to Cignette.

"Did you get yourself checked out?" I inquire, then drop her hoodie back down.

She shakes her head. "Mave helped me ice it, and I've been taking painkillers." She pushes her hair behind her ears and gives me a hesitant look. "It...it usually heals in a few days."

I blink at her in absolute disbelief. "*Usually?*" I raise my arms by my sides. "How often does this fucking *happen*, Cignette? And who fucking *does* this to you?"

She swallows, and fresh tears start falling down her crestfallen face. She closes her eyes, lowers her head, and sniffs before saying, "I just…" She bows her head further. "It's…" She stops, then sniffs again. She brings her hands over her thighs and clenches them into fists. "It's my mom," she finally reveals.

I don't even know why I'm shocked, or why I didn't think it was Miranda who'd done this to Cignette. That woman is cunning in the most extreme of ways, and I don't think she possesses a single humble bone in her botoxed body. But even then, Cignette is her fucking *daughter*. What could she have possibly done to deserve any of this?

"Confused?" Cignette asks, then chuckles humorlessly. She lifts her head and looks at me. "You must think I live a perfectly uptight life, don't you?"

"Will you blame me if I say yes?" I counter.

"No," she answers. "I do keep up quite a visage, so it's only natural for people to be fooled by it."

I scan her face, then get to my feet before coming to sit next to her on the bed. "Why, though?" I question. "Why does she do it? And you said it happens often, too, so I'm beyond confused." I wanna skin Miranda alive, but first, I wanna know her motive; I need some intel.

I'm also trying not to bring back the memories of my past – ones I've done everything in my power to burn to ashes. Because really, it's useless going back in time and reliving the pain, the insults, and the hunger. It only affects my present and destabilizes my future.

Cignette sighs, pulling me out of my thoughts. She then goes on to tell me that her mother has been doing this to her since she was a kid, and that her uncle defends Miranda instead of siding with her. And, as she continues to list every incident from over the years, the reasons behind said incidents start to get more and more…ridiculous. *Especially* when she explains what happened a few hours ago.

"A *dress*?" I voice, and my resolve to skin Miranda Adler alive grows firmer as I try to let every detail set in.

"For the charity gala this Saturday," Cignette adds. "The dress isn't even ready yet – physically, I mean. It's merely a sketch on paper, but Mom must've seen it and thought I was planning on upstaging her during the event."

"But why?"

Cignette scoffs. "She's insecure, jealous. She clearly thinks my dress outshines whatever she's had made for herself for this gala, so she thought she'd do this," she gestures at her face, "to compensate for her lack of vision for fashion."

"But it's not a damn competition, is it? It's a charity event. Why does what one wear to such a thing, matter at all?"

Cignette blinks up at me. "Because it's always been like this with her," she says, then smiles ruefully. "She's always felt the need to compete, to rise above others. I think, in a way, she feels like if she doesn't, then she'll be left behind. Can't say she's wrong, especially given her status and profession, but most of the time, she forgets *who* she's competing with. In her craze to be on top of the chain, she's blinded herself to basic humanity and empathy." She clears her throat. "Even towards me."

I open my mouth, but literally *nothing* comes out.

Cignette senses it, and chuckles again – this time, in actual amusement. "It's okay; I wouldn't blame you if you're experiencing a brain freeze after hearing all that."

How thc fuck is she so damn calm about all of this?

I shake my head. "I'm not one to be at a loss for words, but right now, I can't think of *anything* to say," I admit.

"Then don't say anything," she tells me simply. "You're not obligated to, Dorran."

I pause to give her a once over, and watch as her lashes brush the top of her cheeks when she glances away from my inspection.

"Is she here right now?" I question after a while.

Cignette brings her eyes to me again. "What?"

"Is she here right now?" I repeat. "And you already know not to bullshit me, so don't even try."

Cignette lets go of a sharp breath. "Yes," she spits. "Yes, she is. But you can't do *shit* to her, Dorran. You absolutely cannot."

"And why's that?" I ask. "She's just as feasible as anyone else."

"Is she?" Cignette's gaze darkens. "With dozens of highly-trained guards at her command, does she really seem feasible to you?"

"I can take 'em."

"And risk your life in the process?"

"Yes," I answer easily. "Fucking *yes*."

Cignette fists my vest and pulls me closer to her. "Why?" she whispers against my lips.

"Because I can't see you like this," I admit. "Because it fucking *maims* me to see these bruises on you; to see you so tired of trying to be strong for yourself." I grit my teeth and cup her face again. "I wanna bring your mother tenfold the amount of pain she's caused you. I wanna *show* her what it's like to be marred. What it's like to be the one receiving what she's been so cruel to deliver – for years on end."

Cignette leans into my touch, and I erase the small space between us by pressing my lips to hers. She tastes like mint and tears, and it's fucking *everything*.

I push my fingers into her slightly damp hair and kiss her harder, but she makes a noise and pulls back, then places her cold fingers over my mouth before saying, "Gently. It…hurts." She points at the bruise on the left side of her face, and my chest contracts.

"Of course." I attempt at kissing her softly. "I'm sorry," I breathe, then part her lips before slowly running my tongue along hers.

She moans, then wraps her arms around my neck as she kisses me deeply, yet tenderly.

I'm not used to this. I always take what I want from a woman without being polite about it. But this – this very moment with Cignette – it's so damn *new* that it's hard not to get lost in it.

I drag my lips away from hers and bring them to the scar on her right cheek. I place a feather-light kiss there, then press sound, open-mouthed pecks on her chin and jaw.

I've only just reached her neck, though, when Cignette hisses and moves away again.

"What's wrong?" I look at her, and when she pulls the collar of her hoodie to the side to show me the finger marks on her neck, my heart hammers to the point where it fucking *hurts*.

I make to stand so that I can find the bitch and slit her throat, but Cignette grabs my arm and pulls me back down with surprising force.

"Fucking sit your ass down," she sneers. "You really think you'll survive the night if you march up to her floor and try to get to her?"

I snatch my arm away from her grasp and glare at her. "I don't care."

"But *I* do!" she yells, then pushes her hair back hastily. "I fucking *do*, you hear me?" She runs the sleeve of her hoodie under her nose and places her hands over mine. "Please, just…" She brings our joined hands up and kisses my knuckles, then looks pleadingly at me. "Stay with me for a while?"

I decide to relent – for now, of course – and give her a nod.

She smiles a little, and I pull her to me. Pressing my back against her headboard, I stretch my legs and help her sit between them.

She groans as she stretches her arms in order to tie her hair in a knot above her head, then gets comfortable against me by placing her back to my chest and settling her head on my shoulder.

"You need more room?" I ask.

"No," she says with a sigh, then closes her eyes. "This is perfect."

Moonlight is at its peak now, and casts crazy silhouettes on the walls that are on the opposite sides of the bed. They're subtle, but seem imposing regardless.

I gently wrap my arms around Cignette's waist, and make sure my hold is loose enough, in case she needs to shift.

All of this is so fucking domestic by my standards. If the crew saw me like this, I'd never hear the end of it. But then again, I haven't yet given any number of shits about what they think when it comes to Cignette, so it's only natural that I don't start doing it now. Being here with her is…nice, and I don't regret a second of it.

But, being here with her has also made me think of certain things I endured before stuff changed for me.

I bend and kiss Cignette's temple, then let my eyes fall shut as I inhale the smell of her hair, and her skin.

Oranges – she smells like fucking *oranges*.

"I was…sixteen when I killed her," I tell her. The words just tumble out of my fucking mouth, like they were aching to be set free or some shit.

Cignette stiffens against me, and momentary silence fills the air as I wait for her to say something. But then, mercifully, she starts turning around, and when our eyes meet, I'm relieved when I don't see any fear or uncertainty on her face.

"Who?" she asks, then tilts her head.

I swallow, and I don't know why, but my throat closes up a little as I say, "My mother."

16. Past

Year 2008

I dipped a makeup brush into the small blush palette – *Cheeky Glow*, it was called – then brought it over to my face before running it along my cheekbones. Using the pad of my index finger, I then applied a shimmery shadow over my lids, and finished off my look with a wine-red lipstick.

The crooked overhead light in my bathroom flickered, casting hideous shadows on some of the cracked and discolored tiles in the room, and when I stepped away from my messy counter, the light shut down completely, dousing me in darkness.

I reached for the switch next to the mirror, fiddled with it a few times, and then looked up when the light refused to turn on again.

I took another step back and pulled at the straps of the crimson A-line dress I was wearing. It was from Mom's old wardrobe, and she'd been nothing less than hostile when she'd given it to me earlier.

"*You better not fuck this up for me*," she'd told me. "*Marcus is a wealthy client. You will let him do whatever it is that he wants to you, and for however long he wishes to. By the end of it, you and I will have enough cash to last us at least the rest of the year.*"

I'd said nothing in return. I never did. I simply did as I was told, or the beating I received for my defiance kept me up several nights on end with harrowing pain and flashes of dreadful memories.

I didn't know where, or how, she found these clients. But she did, and they were always rich, middle-aged suburban men.

Marco was one of the many clients I'd had over the last two years – all of whom were fucked up to their very bones. I had three small suitcases full of costumes for them, because each and every one of them had different and very specific…tastes, for lack of a better word.

Someone wanted a nurse, while the other wanted a cop. Some wanted a barista, while the others wanted a schoolgirl. The list went on and on, and so did the nightmares I'd have after each of these encounters.

It wasn't like this two years ago – when my dad was still alive. It was easier to avoid Mom throughout the day because I'd be at school for most of it, and focus on my homework or assignments during the night. The only times I *had* to endure her presence was during the weekends, and even then, we barely spoke or looked at each other. She was always busy whining to my dad about how he didn't earn enough; how she had to work double-shifts at the salon just to "put food on the table every single day". He'd avoid her, she'd yell at him, and he'd walk out of the house, only to return the next day.

Things changed when he died two years ago. He was found dead at the end of the street where he worked as a mechanic. The cops said he'd had too much to drink, had probably passed out on the sidewalk, and had ended up choking on his own vomit, which in turn had led to his death. I'd cried for days – not because he was an amazing father, but because he was my only shield against my monster of a mother. When he died, I knew I only had hell to suffer. My dad may not have been the best, but he at least treated me like I was a damn human being.

Mom pulled me out of school after Dad's passing. At first, she started having men over as *her* clients, but when one of them saw me and decided to ditch her for *me*, she realized she could cater to fucked up men with fucked up fetishes with me as the scapegoat, and earn far more than she otherwise could.

When she'd proposed the idea to me all those months ago, I'd only been fourteen. I'd protested when she'd tried to force me to comply; I'd tried to run away, too. But she'd locked me in my room and had had random men come in and fuck me till I was screaming and bleeding. And, when I'd pleaded with her to help me with the bruises, she'd declined me and left me to fend for myself.

After a few times, though, I'd *had* to give up on my protests and oblige her, because otherwise, I'd either end up dead and forgotten like my dad, or worse.

I'd thought about those outcomes a few times. Compared to the life I lived – one *no one* should have to – death seemed like paradise. But dying would also mean that my mother would win, and I most certainly couldn't let that happen.

The overhead light flickered on, and I finally got a proper look at myself. My hair was slightly long, so I didn't exactly need a wig, and my makeup made me look more disheveled than put-together. I was sixteen, but it didn't feel like that to me. I felt weighed down and sullen, but I guess that was to be expected, given the life I led.

I fidgeted with the dress one more time – because the damn thing was itchy and uncomfortable – and when that did nothing, I sighed and decided to give up. I walked out of the bathroom and entered my disorganized bedroom, then looked up at the *Green Day* poster on the wall next to my bed. It's the only thing I had in my room as a "décor". Everything else in there was bland, impersonal.

It was after 11, so the street outside was eerily quiet. There was not a single light to be seen – neither from a house, nor from the streetlamps. One of the many norms of living in the suburb, I guess.

With one last glance at the window, I swallowed and headed out of my room.

The only reason I was able to walk straight was because it'd been a couple of weeks since I'd had a client. Usually, I could barely stand the first few days after one of these encounters, and it'd take me just as long, if not more, to be able to sit without screaming in pain, let alone take a shit without bawling my eyes out.

My bare feet pressed against the wooden stairs as I made my way down to the living room. I could smell cologne in the air, which meant that Marco had arrived already.

I stopped at the end of the stairway, and my heart hammered so fucking strongly against my chest when I saw my client.

Marco looked to be in his late forties. He was on the shorter side, and wore a lose grey shirt with black, ill-fitted trousers. With a head full of slicked-back blond-and-grey hair, a face marred with fine lines, and the little beer belly he was sporting, he seemed like a suburban broker or something. Mom, of course, hadn't given me any details regarding him or his profession, but she *had* mentioned that he was willing to pay a shit ton of money for me, so maybe I was right in my assumption. But who knows. These tedious tidbits wouldn't get me out of this situation, and neither would Marco – who was grinning at me as I walked further into the living room.

There was no escaping this; there was only enduring.

"Ah, *there* you are!" Mom all but sang when she saw me. She had an awfully theatrical smile on her face – one I've seen her use in the presence of every man that visited us. One that made my skin crawl in fucking disgust.

She'd glammed up for this, too. Her curly hair was tamed into a too-tight hairdo, and her face was packed with makeup. She was wearing a black-and-white sheath dress that did everything to complement her tall, lithe figure, but nothing against that cruel heart of hers – beating somewhere behind the confines of the dress's fabric. I sometimes wondered if she even had the organ inside her, or if she'd given it away in exchange for a few bucks.

I ignored her comment and kept my gaze downwards. When I was close enough to her, she roughly lifted my chin, gave me a quick, scrutinizing once-over, then grabbed my arm in a painful grip and all but shoved me toward Marco.

I stumbled a little – mostly because I wasn't expecting her to do that – and stiffened when Marco placed his hands on my shoulders in order to prevent my fall.

"Now, now, Delilah," he crooned at my mom in a smooth, almost velvet-like voice. "Be careful with my toy, will you? I hate it when they're rattled." He gave me a smile, and his eager eyes seared into mine. "I prefer to have their complete attention, after all. It makes it *so* much more pleasurable to fuck their wholeness out of them."

Ice rushed up my spine at his words. I was trying to keep my breathing in check, but I was fucking failing at it.

Marco took a step towards me, and every instinct in me was screaming at me to move back; to run away. But I couldn't. I simply couldn't.

He was slightly shorter than me, so he had to look up when he addressed me.

He brought a hand up and dragged a thick finger over my jaw, making me grimace a little.

"Aren't you a pretty little thing…" he mused, then leaned in before bringing his nose to the side of my neck. He inhaled deeply, and my body jerked in response to it.

He chuckled. "See? You're rattled – exactly like I'd predicted." He shifted, and his nose touched my cheek.

Goosebumps rose throughout my body, but I didn't dare move; didn't dare make a sound.

He inhaled again, and again, and then groaned as if in ecstasy. "*Exquisite*," he hissed against me, right before parting his lips and licking a slow line up to the right side of my face.

I wanted to gag, but instead, I just stood there and let him do what he wanted to. Why? Because I was helpless.

Marco grabbed my waist and pulled me to him. "You are delicious, toy," he said with a manic grin, and pressed a sloppy kiss on my mouth. He then pushed his hard-on against my stomach, and I imagined it mustn't take much for him to get a boner, given how he'd barely spent five minutes with me.

When I finally decided to lock eyes with his, he fisted the back of my hair and pulled my head back.

"You want my cock, don't you, toy?" he asked.

I swallowed, and my eyes stung as I lied by saying, "I do."

Marco's expression sharpened all of a sudden. He scowled at me, then slapped me with his free hand – hard enough that my head began to swim a little.

"*Master*," he spat, and slapped me again. "Call me your fucking *master*, you cunt."

I could feel tears on my cheeks. I don't know how they'd escaped, but they somehow had. Maybe it was because of how much my face hurt from his brief assault, or maybe it was because I felt sorry for myself. Either way, I had to make sure neither Mom nor Marco saw them.

"Master," I said in a dulcet tone, then licked my bottom lip. "Please, I need your cock. Now." My chest tightened when Marco's entire demeanor changed at my words, and fear rushed through me when he chuckled and let go of my hair.

"Good," he praised, then nodded around a smirk. "That's good, my toy." In one move, he turned me around and pushed my upper body over.

My breathing turned haggard, my palms turned cold, and I felt momentarily dizzy when the pain in my face multiplied upon my having bent forward.

I placed my hands on the living-room couch in front of me, and when I looked up, I found my mom standing on the other side of it. Her arms were crossed, and the grin she had on her face was nothing short of deranged.

She was going to watch me this time.

She wouldn't always stay in the same room as me once the client got his hands on me. But sometimes, she would, and she'd witness every single bit of what was done to me – all the while touching herself right before me.

It never came as a surprise to me that she took pleasure in watching me get fucked by random assholes. I knew she was an unstable human being, and that she was driven by everything questionable the world had to offer.

I broke eye contact with her when the sound of Marco unzipping his pants filled the otherwise silent room. My hands clenched over the couch's cushions as I braced myself for the inevitable pain, and my chest tightened in fear of what was about to happen.

It never gets old, this feeling. And I wasn't stupid enough to pretend that I was okay with it, or that I was so used to it that it didn't bother me anymore; that I was numb to it or something. Because I wasn't. I felt everything these men did to me, and I felt it in fucking *spades*.

"I forgot to compliment you on your dress, didn't I, my toy?" Marco said. "How inconsiderate of me." He ran his hands over the length of my dress, then yanked at it, making me suck in a breath. "Delightful…" He roughly pulled the dress up and above my lower back, exposing my ass. "*Yes*," he all but groaned. "What a sight you make, my little thing. Absolutely mouthwatering." He palmed my ass cheeks and spread them for his viewing, making me swallow.

"Marco."

I glanced up at Mom's voice, and saw as she grabbed a bottle of lube from the small table next to the couch. But as she straightened and threw the bottle over to Marco, something else on the table caught my eye.

A steel-made nail file.

My breathing quickened as I stared at it – lying there carelessly next to a couple of condoms Mom had set out for Marco.

It was there – right in front of me. A wordless beacon. A way.

A *possibility*.

And in that moment, I knew this was my only shot.

My fucking *moonshot*.

Marco shifted behind me, and the rustling of fabric indicated that he was pushing his pants down.

I couldn't stop looking at the nail file, though. It was the only thing I could see; the only thing I *wanted* to see.

I felt no fear with it so close to my grasp. I didn't feel remorse, didn't even have the desire to second-guess anything.

Something heavy pressed against my back, and a second later, I felt Marco's hot, stale breath over my ear as he whispered, "Are you ready, my little toy?"

For the first time in the last two years, I finally felt like I was.

I was *so* fucking ready.

17. Past

Year 2008

The loud crinkling of a plastic wrapper filled the air as Marco put a condom on. He then popped open the bottle of lube Mom had given him, and spread my cheeks further.

I gritted my teeth when he dripped a thin line of ice-cold lube over my hole, and closed my eyes when he circled the crown of his semi-hard cock over it.

Wait – I had to *wait* until I did something. I needed Marco to be taken off guard, because if he wasn't distracted enough, then there was a strong chance he'd take me down before I could do any proper damage.

And so, I had to endure a little – just enough to stay true to what I had in mind.

Marco hadn't even waited for me to say yes to his question before prepping me for himself. Again, I wasn't surprised. Men like him didn't really ask for permission; they simply took whatever they wanted.

"Ready or not, here I come, my toy," Marco announced, right before pushing his cock inside me in a single thrust.

My body jolted forward, and I clenched my jaw, along with my fists, when his action caused a burning pain in my hole.

"My God, you are so fucking *tight*," Marco hissed, then pulled out before thrusting into me again. "And you take my cock so well, my toy." He started a rough rhythm, and with each push and pull, the pain intensified, along with the sting in my eyes.

Fuck, it hurt. It hurt so damn much.

I glanced at my mom, and found her staring at Marco's movements with parted lips and dilated pupils.

She was turned on, that disgusting woman.

Marco grabbed my waist and started pounding into me, making my body jerk forward.

The pain increased – not only where he was fucking me, but also in my head from being slapped by him.

But still, I let him hurt me; I let Mom stay distracted. And, using his thrusts to my advantage, I kept shifting my body closer and closer to the side table. Every time he'd push into me, I'd slide my hands forward, and when I was finally close enough, I grabbed the couch's armrest and angled my body sideways. Just a little.

"*Harder*, Master," I managed to say, much to my mom's surprise. "Give me all you got."

"And you think I'm not?" Marco grunted, then doubled his efforts by quickening his pace.

Good.

But that also meant I had to move faster, because in provoking him like that, I'd reduced the time it would take for him to come.

I glanced at my mom again, and found her sneaking a hand under her dress in order to touch herself.

I swallowed and looked away, and when Marco moved inside me again, I stretched forward and grabbed the nail file that was merely a few inches away from me.

My heart was hammering, and the palm in which I held the nail file was starting to get sweaty.

I had to fucking *move*.

I gripped the metal object in a vise grip, and before I could second-guess my impulses, I twisted my upper body around and shoved the nail file into Marco's left cheek.

It didn't go all the way in, of course, and I had to withdraw it as a result, but I managed to puncture his skin nonetheless.

The feeling of flesh tearing open under my assault made a thrill run through my bones, making a smile creep up my face.

Marco screamed – a high-pitched shriek that rang violently in my ears – and pulled out of me before hastily stepping away from me. He covered his now-bleeding cheek with a shaky hand and stared at me in pure shock.

"What the fuck?" he whispered, then yelled, "*What the fuck?!*"

"You like that, *Master*?" I said to him – as calmly as I could – then took a step in his direction.

He almost fell in the process of getting away from me, and when I winked at him, he threw open the main door and practically ran out – naked from the waist down, and with his dick hanging limply between his legs.

"Dorran!" came Mom's voice from behind me, seconds before she grabbed my arm and turned me around to face her.

She was seething, trembling, and, dare I say, the latter reaction seemed to be coming out of fear. Her eyes, dilated only seconds ago, had lost their color and were wide as fucking saucers. Her complexion had paled, and her expression was one of complete horror.

She scanned my face, and what she found there must've scared her further, because she let go of my arm and put distance between us.

"Dorran…" My name left her lips in a barely-audible whisper. "What…what're you…"

I looked at her – *really* looked. The woman who gave birth to me. The woman who drove my father away. The woman who used me as a convenience to fill her pockets. The woman who hurt me.

The woman who scarred me.

My *mother*.

"I'll never forgive you for what you did to me," I said to her. "You took what little hope I had left in myself and my damn existence, and burned it on the fucking pier. You broke me in ways I can't even begin to list on hand." I swallowed. "You *repulse* me, Mom, and I thought that you should know as much."

"Dor–" She stopped, and her eyes widened further when I stabbed the nail file into her jugular.

A faint spray of blood splashed over my fingers, and its warmth drove something inside me. It ignited me, in a way.

Mom began clawing at my wrist, but her attempt was feeble, at best.

I pulled the filer out, relishing the slickness of blood coating its length, and swiftly pushed it into the wound again. She sucked in a breath and stumbled, so I pulled the nail file out and shoved her shoulder. She fell to the floor, but not before the back of her head knocked against the small table, resulting in condoms and a couple bottles of lube to fall over.

I tilted my head and watched her as she writhed in pain – her gaze fixed on me. A small pool of blood had started to form on the floor next to her, and its potent smell all but tingled my senses.

I smiled again, and put a foot on either side of her helpless body before straddling her.

I sat on my heels and continued to watch her, but she made a weak attempt to move away from me, and that didn't bode well with me.

"Seriously?" I mused, and chuckled when she tried to get away again.

"For how diabolical I thought you were, you're being one hell of a stupid cunt right now," I told her.

She made a sound – somewhere between a sob and a scream – making me roll my eyes.

"Didn't think I had it in me, did you?" I said, and then looked at the bloody nail file in my grasp. "Well, you should have thought about the consequences of your blatant cruelty before treating me like complete trash." I twisted the filer this way and that, and when a few thick drops of red dripped down to my fingers, I brought my hand over to my lips and licked my palm.

The smell, paired with the iron-and-salt taste of warm blood, hit me all at once, resulting in heat to rise in my neck and chest.

Mom made another sound – this one resembling something close to a gag.

I grinned at her as I rose on my knees. "I've gone rogue, Mommy," I said to her, then leaned over her in order to bring my face close to hers. "Wanna beat the defiance out of me this time as well? Or would you like to have me raped by random men again, just to fulfill some sick fetish of yours?"

Her lips trembled as she stared up at me, and a few tears slipped down her temples.

I have to admit: I was surprised to see them. In all my sixteen years of existence, I'd never seen the woman cry. Not once. So, to watch her in the state she was in, was a new experience. One I wish I could capture, but alas, I couldn't.

"You know, I would *love* to drag this one-on-one thing we've got going," I told her, "but I'm absolutely *done* watching you breathe. Because every breath you're taking right now is grating on my nerves." I canted my head and winked at her. "Time's up, Mommy. May you rest in fucking *hell*." I pulled my hand back, and then brought it forward, stabbing the nail file into her throat.

Her body arched against mine, and her mouth fell open as she choked on a scream.

I twisted the filer into her throat, appreciating the way her skin broke under my command; how her eyes started to turn glassy.

She thrashed under me, so I stabbed her in the same spot again, and again, and again. Each time I did it, the wound in her throat widened. Tiny lumps of her flesh stuck to my blood-drenched hand, but I kept on stabbing. I was in a daze of sorts – one I didn't wish to come out of.

I don't know how long I'd been doing it for, but when the sound of sirens hit my ears, I let go of a breath and finally sat back on my heels again.

I stared at Mom's expressionless face, at her parted lips. At the ghastly opening on her throat, and at the beautiful mess that I'd made.

Mission accomplished.

I was dimly aware that cops were outside the house – most definitely as a result of Marco having called them and told them what I'd done – but I honestly couldn't give a shit about any of it. I was so at peace with the view before me, with the realization that she was gone, that I couldn't help but smile again.

She was really fucking gone.

Gone.

I started laughing, then – *truly* laughing. I tipped my head back and let my joy be known to the walls around me; to anything and anyone who would witness and listen.

And to think that I'd spent *years* cowering before her, when I could have simply ended her like I had in that moment.

Man, I was so fucking crazed with happiness. It was a feeling so addicting that I wanted it to take over each and every one of my senses.

Footsteps sounded from behind me, putting an end to my brief moment of elation. They were more in number at first, but soon reduced to a single pair.

Momentary silence took over, probably to get a quick study on my behavior, but then those footsteps resumed their journey.

The hair on the back of my neck stood as I felt a brief presence behind me. It shifted before I could get a glimpse of it, though, resulting in goosebumps to prick my skin.

I felt a movement on my peripheral. It was quickly followed by a tall figure taking up most of the space to my left, making me smirk a little.

His arms were stretched in front of him, with his gun drawn in my direction – ready to blow my brain off if I so much as *tried* to be smug.

"*Jesus Christ*," he muttered under his breath, having finally witnessed my handiwork.

I tilted my head again and gave Mom a quick glance.

"Beautiful, isn't she?" I said. "I like her like this – so at peace and…quiet." I swallowed and let go of a chuckle. "I especially like the fact that I won't have to hear her voice anymore. Or do what she wants me to. It's absolutely *liberating*."

Sheriff Christopher Solo whispered a curse and angled his gun closer to me. "Drop your weapon and step away from the body," he ordered.

I leaned in and moved some of the bloodied hair away from Mom's face. "You think she can hear me right now, Sheriff Solo?"

"Dorran…" There was a firmness in his voice – one that made my spine stiffen a little.

I clicked my tongue and straightened. "Of course she can't," I stated, then grinned. "It's because she's fucking *dead*." I started laughing, and it was the kind that didn't stop, just kept on going.

"Drop your weapon, Dorran," Sheriff Solo commanded again. "Fucking *drop it* and step away from the body."

I whipped my head in his direction – my laughter cut short for the second time that night – and gritted my teeth. "Or what?" I challenged. It's the first I'd noticed the flashing red-and-blue lights outside, and how they reflected against the glass window behind the sheriff.

"Or I'll be forced to put a bullet in you," he spat at me. With his customary uniform and badge, and the noticeable presence he commanded, Sheriff Solo should be someone I should fear. But there was something in his clear blue eyes that made me stop and look at him.

Empathy.

There was an understanding in his gaze, although he'd just threatened to shoot me. Not pity or disgust or confusion, or any of the other emotions a normal person would have upon having witnessed a son straddling his dead mother's body – *knowing* he'd been the one who'd killed her. Out of the dozens of things he could have expressed while pointing his gun at me, he chose to display empathy.

Towards *me*.

Towards my appearance, my condition. And that was something that instantly gravitated me to him. Because for the first time in my life, someone had openly reacted that way towards me.

He'd been the one who'd delivered the news of Dad's death to Mom and I two years ago. At the time, I hadn't thought much of the condolences and assurances he'd given us. I'd always thought to myself: *He's just doing his damn job. It's in his nature to be monotonous in situations like this.*

But maybe it wasn't just part of his job; maybe he really *did* sympathize with us. Not that Mom cared one bit. She didn't so much as shed a single tear that day, or at the funeral. Or during the weeks that followed.

Not until I had her at my mercy a few minutes ago.

Bravado born out of cruelty can only go so far, after all.

I sniffed and let the nail file slip from my fingers, resulting in it to make a wet *cling* like sound when it hit the floor. Pushing Mom's right arm aside, I managed to shift sideways. I yanked at the hemline of the dress I was wearing, then stumbled a little before finally getting to my feet.

"Turn around," the sheriff said.

I brought my hands in front of me and wiggled my bloody fingers. "You really wanna cuff me like this?" I told him. "I'm sure you're good at what you do, given your rank, but even your law-abiding ass wouldn't want blood on your person."

He scoffed. An unreadable expression passed over his features, but just as quickly as it'd been there, it was gone before I could put a name to it.

He jerked his head toward the sink in the kitchen. "Be quick about it."

I walked over and twisted the faucet's knob, then placed my hands under the thick stream of water. Deep red droplets tainted the otherwise grey sink, and again, the smell of blood hit my nose, making me lick my lips.

I pumped some dish-wash liquid into my palms and began rubbing it between my fingers. "Mind if I change?" I asked. "I'll make a better killer with some decent clothes on."

"Don't test me, kid."

I chuckled. "Have it your way." I turned the knob and stepped away from the sink, then walked over to Sheriff Solo before putting my hands behind my back.

"You wanna tell me what happened here?" he asked.

"If I do, will it change what's about to happen to me?" I countered.

"Absolutely. If you haven't done th–"

I snorted, cutting him off.

"Dude, if you think I didn't do this," I nodded towards Mom's cold, wretched body, "then you seriously need to fucking *retire*."

The sheriff placed the cuffs around my wrists. "If you're trying to save some–"

"It had to be done," I cut him off again, then stared at the pool of blood on the floor. "I *had* to do it; I had no other choice. I was sick of it – so damn tired of the pain, the bruises, the insults. The…the rapes." I swallowed, and blinked when my eyes stung. "I couldn't take it anymore. It had to go – *all* of it did. But it wouldn't while *she* was alive." I laughed a little. "And so, I changed that."

I heard Sheriff Solo let go of a shaky breath behind me. "Well then," he said, and tightened the cuffs around my wrists.

I closed my eyes when the suffocating steel bit into my skin, and smiled when the sheriff started reading me my rights.

You have the right to remain silent…

You hear that, Mom? I thought to myself. *Silence. Peace.*

Retribution.

18. Past

Year 2008

My bare feet pressed against the cold floor as I stepped inside the sheriff's office. The air around me had a slight chill to it, and the office smelled like a combination of body odor and cleaning supplies.

Insistent chatter, along with the occasional static of radios going off every few seconds, filled the clustered room, and as Sheriff Solo led me further into the large area – with a hand wrapped around my left arm – I noticed the quizzical glances the deputies gave me. I realized that despite having seen a lot of weird shit in their line of work, they mustn't have witnessed a teenage boy dressed like a girl as a prisoner. I could only imagine the scenarios and assumptions they must have created in those bland little heads of theirs when I passed them by. Their curious eyes travelled over me – amusement and confusion clear on their faces – which only made me chuckle.

I winked at a couple of deputies in the back, who scowled at me and got back to whatever it is they were doing before they decided to ogle me like I was a piece of evidence or something.

Assholes.

But I guess not everyone had the ability of showcasing empathy. Most people only see a person's exterior and form a complete biography about them in their minds, but they fail to understand where that person is coming from.

As Sherlock Holmes, penned by Arthur Conan Doyle, had said: *You see, but you do not observe.*

That's exactly what most people do. They see you, they judge you, and they form an opinion about you without you even having opened your mouth to explain yourself.

Such is life, I guess.

Sheriff Solo led me away from prying eyes, and towards a slightly darker and chillier part of the office. This room had cinderblock walls, a white tiled floor, and twice as many cameras as the ones in the main office.

There were two very large, very glaringly bleak-looking cells in there, and my skin pricked with goosebumps at the idea of having to be *inside* one of them.

A table with a computer and some other shit was set up in one corner, with a disgruntled looking deputy sitting behind it. It was clear by the curl of his top lip and his bunched-together brows that he wanted to be anywhere *but* in that confined space, and honestly, I could relate, because *my God*, the stink in that room was appalling, at best. It was making me nauseous; making my damn nose burn. I was seconds away from heaving on the floor, and that says a *lot*, because I'm the kinda fucker who gets hard over the smell of *blood.*

Sheriff Solo stopped in front of the cell that was on the left side of the room, then let go of my arm and began unlocking it.

"We've got a full house tonight, kid, so you'll have to adjust," he said, then jerked his head toward the other cell, which was full of people I'd rather not share a close vicinity with.

Because of the damn smell, of course.

When I didn't respond to him, the sheriff rolled his eyes, took the handcuffs off my wrists, and all but shoved me inside the surprisingly empty cell.

I turned, just as he shut the door and locked it with a resounding *clank.*

I wrapped my fingers around the bars and shifted on my feet. "So…this is goodbye, then," I told him.

He let go of a tired breath and shook his head at me. "You're trouble, you know that?"

I grinned. "Of course."

He clicked his tongue, then swiftly glanced sideways before leaning close to the cell. "Gimme a few hours," he whispered, and his expression softened as he smiled faintly. "I'll be back for the two of you."

I stared at him in confusion. "Wh–" I clamped my mouth shut when he gave me a quick nod and walked away from me before I could ask him what he meant.

Alright, then.

Sighing, I stepped away from the bars, and was about to sit down when a voice stopped me in my tracks.

"I wouldn't do that if I were you."

I turned around so fast that I stumbled a little. My heart was in my fucking throat as I looked at the figure sitting opposite me – with the back of his head resting against the wall behind him, his knees folded and his forearms perched atop them, and a bemused smile playing across his young face.

No wonder Sheriff Solo had said he'd be back for the *two* of us.

"I may or may not have taken a piss on the floor over there just to annoy the in-charge outside," the guy said to me.

I swallowed and straightened, then walked further into the cell. "You fucking scared me, man," I told him.

He chuckled and raised his hands. "Sorry." He then gestured at the empty space next to him. "Come, join me."

"How chivalrous," I quipped, then settled down next to him.

"I am, after all, a complete gentleman," he said, and grinned when I looked at him.

Up close, I could easily see the bags under his brown eyes, the streaks of dirt on his jaw and neck; the holes and tears on his purple Henley and faded jeans. His hair was buzzed close to his scalp, and while that made him appear disheveled, his tone and posture were anything but.

"A gentleman who takes a leak on the floor just to rile a cop?" I asked.

"Obviously." He gave me a once over, so I brought my knees up and wrapped my arms around them.

"Don't fucking ogle," I muttered, then looked around the cell.

The walls and floor were nothing but hard concrete. There was a metal pissing pot in one corner, a bunk bed in the other, and a sorry excuse of an air vent on the top left side of the cell.

"I'm not *ogling*," the guy responded. "I'm…"

"Curious? Perplexed?" I provided, then looked at him again. "Amused?"

He searched my face for a moment, then shifted so that he could face me. "Why would I be amused?"

I shrugged. "I must look funny to you. A guy in a woman's dress – arrested for Christ knows what."

"I'm here too, y'know," he countered.

"But you aren't–"

"What, wearing a damn dress?" he said, cutting me off. "Doesn't fucking matter, man. I'm not judging, so relax."

I swallowed. "Sorry. I'm just…overwhelmed, I guess."

"You look like you've been through a lot, so feeling what you are right now is valid as fuck," he said, and my throat tightened at his words.

"That obvious, huh?" I snarked.

"You wouldn't be here otherwise."

I chuckled. "Touché."

"I'm Jayce," he said, then offered me a hand.

I shook it, and grinned before saying, "Dorran."

"How old are you?" he asked.

"Sixteen. You?"

"Nineteen," he said. "So, Dorran," he then added, "what the fuck did you do to get arrested? Because last I checked, having a bad sense of fashion isn't reason enough to be behind bars."

I couldn't help it; I laughed. "You're a smooth motherfucker, aren't ya?"

"Helps me get a dick every once in a while."

"You into guys?"

"Sure am," he said with a grin.

"No wonder you were ogling me," I teased, then raised a brow.

"Dude, trust me, if I wanted inside you, you'd already be on all fours, screaming my name."

His words made me inhale sharply, and a chill crawled up my spine as memories of the last two years started resurfacing again.

Hands holding me down.

Hands pulling at my clothes.

Hands pressing my face against the wall.

The whispered insults. The cruel fucking. The punches that would send me reeling.

Mom's lifeless eyes staring into nothing. Her blood on my hands, on my tongue. Her body pinned under mine. Her–

"Dorran?" Jayce's voice sounded concerned. "Hey, buddy; what's wrong?" He placed a hand on my shoulder and shook me slightly, making me jolt.

"Whoa." His eyes widened as he stared at me. "You okay, man?"

I pushed my hair back and took a few slow breaths in an attempt to knock aside the vivid images in my head. "Yes," I answered a bit hoarsely. "Yes, I'm…I'm fine, thanks."

"Was it something I said?" he asked.

I swallowed again and gave him a nod. "Yeah, actually." I then told him everything that'd happened to me ever since my dad's passing – including that night's events – and with every incident I relayed to him, Jayce's demeanor crumpled further and further.

"Sooo," he started once I'd finished, and lifted a shoulder. "You're here because you well-deservedly killed a cold-hearted bitch who traumatized you for *two fucking years*?" I expected him to be shocked or disgusted over the fact that I'd killed my mother, but instead, he was angry on my account, as if what I'd done made complete sense.

It did to *me*, of course, but I was glad I wasn't the only one in thinking so.

"Yup." I leaned back against the wall and stretched my legs out in front of me. "But I only gave the sheriff a brief overview of things, and didn't go into any sort of detail like I did with you."

"Well, you should have told him everything," Jayce said.

"Did you tell him your story?"

"I did."

"And did it make a difference?"

He shrugged. "Not exactly, but he at least *knows* the truth."

I gesture at my outfit. "I'm pretty sure he got a proper picture of what was happening in my house before he arrived," I stated. "That, and I don't think I'd have done a very convincing job of retelling everything like I did to you." I was quickly feeling at ease around Jayce, and that was both grounding and scary, because I'd never exactly had anyone in my corner until him.

He mirrored my position and stretched his legs out next to mine. "The truth doesn't have to be convincing, Dorran," he said. "The truth is the truth. It just *is*; it doesn't have to be bounded by anything."

He was right, of course.

"And you think Sheriff Solo is the kinda guy who'd see my truth for what it is?" I questioned.

"He *is* a human being, isn't he?"

I smiled and glanced sideways at Jayce, who did the same to me.

"Touché," I said for the second time that night, making him chuckle.

A comfortable silence filled the air after that, but to me, it was loud – *too* damn loud. I needed to keep my thoughts occupied until I felt sleepy or something, otherwise I'd be pulled back into the depthless pool that was my past.

I cleared my throat and nudged Jayce's bare feet with mine. "So, why are *you* here?" I asked him.

He turned his head towards me and gave me a tired smile. "Killed my elder brother." His tone was so casual that it made me wanna laugh.

"When?" I asked.

"Yesterday."

"You seem relaxed about it," I remarked.

"He deserved it," Jayce said. "I delivered justice where it was due."

"Care to elaborate?"

He scratched his jaw and rubbed a hand over the side of his neck, as if bracing himself for what he was about to say.

"Jeremiah was the golden kid of the family," Jayce began. "The eldest, the smartest. My family is dirt-poor, but he never let that affect the way he carried himself: with style and an air of humble superiority. He always knew what to say or what to do, and Jenny and I looked up to him as if he were God or something." He let go of a humorless laugh. "I'll cut to the chase," he then said, and cleared his throat. "He got into drugs last year, and, as usual, it started messing with his head. He got fired from his job at the insurance company he worked at, and because he was home all the time, he started being salty about it. Jen and I had school, and she worked part time at the diner next to our house, and that didn't sit well with Jeremiah.

He began lashing out at us, and even our parents. Then, as a revenge of sorts, he got Jen hooked on the same drugs he was on. He tried forcing me to do them too, but I knew better than that. Jen, on the other hand, didn't. She loved him; admired him. And, because he meant so much to her, she didn't hesitate in indulging his demand." Jayce closed his eyes and clenched his jaw, and his expression was so full of pain that it made my chest feel heavy.

"I found out too late," he all but whispered the words, then opened his eyes and looked at me. "I found out too fucking late that she was addicted. At first, she missed school and work every two weeks or so, and seemed completely alright when I asked her if everything was okay. But then she started skipping classes and shifts every other day, and that worried me enough to confront her about it. It was a fruitless effort, really, because it was like my words simply weren't getting through to her. She'd turned into Jeremiah, and he thought it was okay for her to do what he was making her do. Our parents thought both him and Jen were lost causes, and refused to help me in getting them into rehab. *It will bring shame to the family name and leave us disgraced in the eyes of peers and elders alike*, they said to me, and simply gave up on two of their own children." Jayce ran a hand over his jaw and blinked at me. "Jen was fifteen, Dorran," he told me. "Fucking *fifteen*!"

The hair on the back of my neck stood at the pain in his voice. "Was?" I dreaded asking that, especially because Jayce looked about ready to fall apart before me.

"She OD'd last week," he stated, then gritted his teeth. "Fucking Jeremiah didn't even attend the funeral. He was at home – high as a damn skyscraper." He sniffed, and his eyes gleamed in a way that made goosebumps prick my skin. "I left the chapel early and drove home. I was mad, upset, and so fucking broken. Jen was gone, and Jeremiah didn't even care enough to be there when our parents and I buried her." He shook his head as if he still couldn't believe his brother had done that.

"I found him on the living room couch, half asleep and barely coherent." Jayce paused and ran a hand under his nose. "It was so *easy*, Dorran," he told me, then laughed. "I didn't even hesitate; I just did it. I grabbed the landline's receiver, wrapped its cord around his neck, and pulled. He barely fought me, and it was over so quickly that I couldn't even believe it at first."

"How did you get arrested?"

"My dad saw me doing it," Jayce said. "Called the cops and had me taken away. Apparently, he'd seen me rush out of the chapel in a fit of anger, and had decided to follow me in case I did something stupid."

"Jesus," I breathed. "But he knew Jenny had OD'd because of Jeremiah, and he still called the cops on you?"

Jayce shrugged. "I had killed my own flesh and blood."

"Is that the reason he gave you for having you arrested?"

"Uh huh."

"And what Jeremiah did to Jenny – wasn't *that* killing your own flesh and blood?"

"According to Daddy Dearest, that wasn't intentional. He said that Jenny had brought her death upon herself by choosing to take drugs."

I scowled. "Oh, for fuck's sake."

"Yeah." Jayce scoffed. "And Mom was here yesterday. Gave the other prisoners quite a show, too. Called me an abomination; said she hoped I rot in this cell for the rest of my days."

"All because you ended a worthless life."

"Exactly," Jayce conceded. "Sucks when your own family fucks you over, huh?"

I scoffed. "Don't I know it."

Again, a blanket of comfortable silence fell over us, but this time, I let it wrap itself around me. I guess I found a shred of solace in the fact that I wasn't alone; that I actually had someone I could talk to – albeit temporarily – about the things I felt, and the things I'd done. Honestly, it was more than I could have asked for. Kind of like an oasis in a desert, but better.

"Hey." Jayce touched his shoulder to mine. "You wanna get some sleep?"

"Yes please."

He gestured a hand toward the bunk bed. "Pick one."

"Well, I ain't climbing in this dress," I said to him.

"Of course. I'll just have to be a proper gentleman and let you take the bottom bed, then."

I snorted and got to my feet. "Go fuck yourself, man."

He laughed. "Aye-aye, brother."

19. Past

Year 2008

Someone placed a firm hand on my arm and shook me gently.

"Dorran? Dorran, wake up."

I tried to blink, but my eyelids felt weighed down.

"Dude, seriously; wake *up*." More shaking.

I tried to move away from it, but ended up groaning at the stiffness in my neck and shoulders.

"Dorran, I swear to God, if you don–"

"Fine, fine." I finally managed to open my eyes, and found Jayce looking down at me.

"What the fuck is wrong with you?" I asked as I sat up. It was so dark that I could barely see him, with only a faint streak of moonlight streaming into the cell. It illuminated the dust particles surrounding us, and not the actual room.

It was also disgustingly hot, which was making me break into a sweat.

Jayce jerked his head to the side, and when I followed his direction, I found Sheriff Solo sitting in a chair a few feet away from us.

"Sheriff," I greeted clinically, then sat up in bed and moved sideways to make space for Jayce to join me. "Buried my mom's body yet?" I asked.

The sheriff arched a brow at me. "Sure did."

"Was an autopsy performed?"

He shook his head. "No."

Interesting.

"Where was she buried?"

"Next to your father."

"And I assume she got a proper burial?"

He pursed his lips as he studied me. "Only the basic formalities were undertaken, I'll tell you that."

That was still more than what she deserved, which was absolutely *nothing*.

"Right." I sniffed and pushed my messy hair away from my face. "So, to what do we owe the pleasure, then?"

The sheriff again lifted a brow, and glanced between Jayce and I. "So, it's '*we*' now, is it?"

"Let's just cut to the chase, shall we?" Jayce stated, and I realized that his posture was rigid.

Sheriff Solo chuckled. "Well, if we're being blunt," he said to us, "then let me be open and tell you that I have a proposition for the two of you."

I looked at Jayce, who in turn looked at me.

"A proposition?" he asked carefully.

"One that comes with your immediate release from this prison," Sheriff Solo added.

I scoffed. "Go fuck with someone else, Sheriff, because I sure as hell am not in the mood."

"I'm not here at 4 in the morning to crack a *joke*, Dorran. I meant what I said, so you can either choose to listen, or I can leave right now and save my time and energy."

"We'll hear what you have to say," Jayce piped in, then sent a quick glance my way.

I wanted to glare at him, but realized he was right in wanting to know what the sheriff had in mind. The two of us didn't exactly have much to lose anyway.

"Dorran?" came the sheriff's voice.

I blinked and cleared my throat. "Yeah, let's hear it." I gave him a nod.

"Perfect." He leaned back in his chair and crossed one ankle over the other. "So, how does killing for cash sound to the two of you?" he asked casually, like he hadn't just thrown a fucking grenade in my direction.

"I'm sorry, *what*?" Jayce said, appearing thoroughly bewildered.

"Told you he was fucking with us," I muttered.

"I'm really not," the sheriff countered. "You're good at what you do, and that's exactly what I need: the best there is."

"I didn't realize I was auditioning to be your puppet when I killed my mother," I told him.

"You know that's not what I meant."

"Didn't you?" added Jayce. "Because it kinda sounds like you did."

"We didn't kill for passion, Sheriff," I said, then clenched my jaw. "We killed because it was *necessary*."

Jayce looked at me, and gave me a slight smile to let me know that he agreed with what I'd said.

"And still, the thrill of it made you feel indestructible; made every single bone in your body thrum in delight," the sheriff stated.

"Fuck yeah, it did," I admitted. "But that doesn't mean every kill's gonna have the same effect."

"Why not?"

"Because we wouldn't be executing those for *ourselves*," Jayce provided.

"Unfortunately, not everything in this world is about *you*." Sheriff Solo exhaled audibly and ran a hand over his slicked-back hair. "Have you thought about how many people there might be in Riverside that don't have the opportunity, strength, or means of discretion to do what the two of you have done?" he asked. "People of power; people who simply want justice. Victims of violence, theft, abduction, trafficking." His eyes bore into mine. "Rape."

My entire body went cold at that. My throat closed up; my palms turned clammy.

"But why should we kill for others?" Jayce inquired. "It's not like we owe them anything."

"True, but it's the right thing to do, don't you think? And, you'll only kill those who deserve to be killed."

I let go of a crude laugh. "We're not vigilantes, Sheriff."

"Of course not, but there's a motherfucking load of money involved in this – enough to keep you and your future secured. If the idea of being righteous isn't your forte, then maybe being rich is."

"For how long are we to do this?" I questioned.

"Until you don't wanna do it anymore. You say the word, and you're out. I won't ask questions or force you to stay if you don't wish to."

"And what about the safety of our person?" Jayce asked.

Sheriff Solo leaned in and placed his elbows on his thighs before giving us a smirk. "You'll be untouchable. *Invincible*."

"Why us, though?" I had to know. "There's literally a prison full of potential candidates just outside, and yet, you chose to pitch your proposal to me and Jayce."

"Let's just say I have a soft spot for assholes who talk back," he answered.

I snorted, whereas Jayce chuckled.

"So…" The sheriff's eyes gleamed against the dwindling nightlight as he straightened. "Are you guys in?"

"Do we have time to think about it?" Jayce asked.

"Given how the two of you are to meet the magistrate in a few hours, I'd say no."

"And if we decline your offer?" I added. "What then?"

Sheriff Solo lifted a shoulder. "You'll be tried for murder, of course, and will have to serve time. 20 years, if not more."

Again, Jayce looked at me, and I looked at him. And, even though we'd barely known each other for a few hours, I knew exactly what he was thinking, and exactly what his answer to the sheriff's proposition was going to be.

20.
CIGNETTE

"So, you and Jayce said yes to him," I state.

"Yup," Dorran says, then gives me a roguish smile. "Best decision of my life."

I chuckle, then fix one of his vest's straps into place. "I still can't believe Chris is your boss. He's always been so…I don't know, *mundane,* I guess. At least that's how he appears whenever I see him during events and such."

He laughs. "Solo is an ethical motherfucker in his own right. All of us are."

"So..." I shrug. "You like it, then – killing people?"

The corners of Dorran's mouth twitch as he looks at me in silent amusement. "It's far more than that, Little Swan," he tells me. "It's an extension of me, I suppose, so it feels innately stimulating." He pushes some of the fallen strands of my hair behind my ear. "I gotta admit, though: I was overwhelmed at first. I thought I'd dipped my toes into something that was too incomprehensible for my mind to grasp, but it quickly became second-nature. The excitement was – *is* – constant, and with every corrupt asshole I killed, I became addicted to it – to the process and its outcome. After a while, I couldn't even bring myself to *think* about walking away from it. And then, of course, Varsha and Alex came along, and the five of us turned into a fucked-up little…"

“Family,” I complete for him, and my throat tightens at the way the word tastes in my mouth.

“Yeah,” Dorran agrees, and something passes over his features as he searches my face.

“You’re lucky to have them in your life,” I tell him honestly.

He slowly wraps his arms around my waist and pulls me closer to him. “I’m feeling pretty fucking lucky being here with you right now,” he says, then tugs my bottom lip between his teeth.

“The infamous Dorran Ledger being romantic? Riverside will *fall*,” I muse.

He grins. “A small price to pay for the spark that just lit up those beautifully haunting eyes of yours.”

A flush rakes up my chest at his words. I lean in and press my lips to his, ignoring the pain that ignites in my cheeks.

Dorran parts his lips and kisses me back, then tilts his head and places feather-light pecks on the side of my neck. When he moves back, he stares at my throat with an unreadable expression, and I know he’s looking at the finger imprints on my skin.

“Hey.” I cup his jaw and lift his face so that our eyes meet. “It’ll be okay,” I tell him.

His nostrils flare. “I’m going to end her,” he vows with conviction. “I’m going to fucking make her pay for what she’s been doing to you for all these years.”

Please, I wanna beg him. *Please*, *do it*. But something tells me that if I do that, he’ll rush up to Mom’s room in a heartbeat and live up to his word without hesitation. And I can’t have that, especially because I know it won’t end well for either of us.

I push aside the thoughts in my head and smile up at him. “You remember what you promised me during our video call the other day?”

His brows crease for a moment, but then rise just as fast when he recalls our previous conversation.

"The thought of your lips tainted with my blood – it makes me so fucking wild, Dorran."

"Then ask me for it the next time you and I see each other, and I swear I'll give it to you."

"Only if I get a taste of you in return."

He shakes his head. "Not tonight."

"But you said I could ask you for it the next time I saw you," I argue. "You're here now, so why not?"

Dorran's stare turns hard. "I said: *not tonight*."

I glare at him. "*Why?*"

"Because you're hurt, damn you!"

"And?" I scoff. "Trust me, out of all the scars I have on my body right now, the one you give me will actually be a welcoming one."

He frowns. "Cignette…"

I lean in and brush my lips over his. "I need this," I whisper. "*Please*, Dorran."

Distract me, I wanna tell him. *Take my mind off things before you see my bruises again and decide to do something impulsive.*

I don't say any of that out loud, even though I want to. I just hope he sees my desperation, and gives into it without reluctance.

He lets go of a breath, then places a quick yet rough kiss on my lips. "Fuck you for saying please," he mutters, making me chuckle.

Thank God.

He shifts a little and retrieves his switchblade from the back pocket of his jeans. The moment he flicks it open, my breathing turns erratic.

The worn handle appears matte under the moonlight, but the black blade shines beautifully when Dorran twists the weapon in his hand. I notice his initials, *D.L.*, carved in silver on the switchblade's handle, along with a very intricate set of designs around it, that look like a den of snakes at a certain angle.

I can't believe I hadn't paid attention to any of these details until now.

"Wow," the word escapes me in a rush.

Dorran smirks as he once again twists the switchblade in his hand. "Solo gave it to me a month after Jayce and I started working for him," he says. "Now I can't even imagine going a day without this little fucker, let alone perform a kill with anything other than this blade."

"It's absolutely gorgeous," I tell him. "And it complements you really well."

"Thanks." He grabs my right hand and presses a few kisses on my palm. "You sure you wanna do this?" he then asks.

I nod, and again, my breathing picks up.

Dorran flattens my hand, gives me a brief look, and touches his blade to the tip of my index finger. He then presses its sharp edge onto my skin, breaking it, and drags it down a little before pulling it back.

I flinch, and when blood starts seeping out of the small gash Dorran has given me, I look up at him.

"Do it, Little Swan," he all but commands.

I shake as a sudden thrill courses through my body, and when Dorran gives me another roguish smile, I bring my hand forward and touch my bleeding finger to his mouth.

His eyelids flutter, and he groans when I drag my finger over his lower lip first, then slowly trace his top lip before retracting my hand.

With his chest heaving, and his midnight gaze fixed on me, Dorran starts licking his lips, and I watch – completely transfixed – as his tongue taints red with my blood.

If getting high on someone is a thing, then I'll gladly admit that I'm hooked on every single thing this man does. He awakens something untamed in me; he makes me wanna throw morals out of the fucking window so that I can indulge in what my mind and body actually need.

"You taste so fucking good, Cignette," Dorran says, then swallows and licks his lips again. "Like strength and glory – you taste *divine*."

His words of admiration are a song that travel over my harmonized skin, turning me on to the brink of madness.

"Kiss me," I tell him.

Dorran grins. "Patience, Little Swan." He flips his switchblade and offers it to me – handle-first. "It's your turn."

I take the blade from him, then run my eyes over him. I rise on my knees, ignoring the pain that shoots through my ribs at the movement, and Dorran stretches his legs out so that I can straddle him easily. His cock presses against the inside of my thigh, turning me on further.

"Can't pick a spot?" he muses.

"Something like that." I smile at him, and what he does next – it's one of the most erotic things he's done since I've known him.

Dorran tilts his head to the side, giving me full access to his neck.

His muscles flex and shift, and I swallow, restraining the urge to put my lips on him.

"You trust me enough to put yourself in such a vulnerable position?" I ask him.

He straightens his neck and looks up at me. "You could cut me open right now, Cignette, and I'd still trust you – have faith in you to put me back together."

I cup his face with my free hand. "Why?"

Dorran holds me around the waist and shrugs. "Because I'm a sucker for you," he says easily. "And trust me, it's a little scary for me to admit that, but I've chosen to accept the idea of *this*," he gestures between us, "instead of being afraid of it. We'll just have to figure shit out as we go, and I think I'm okay with that."

I laugh and shake my head. "And to think we've barely known each other for a week."

"Sometimes the best things in life take the least amount of time to get hooked onto."

"Mm…" I drag the tip of his blade below his right collarbone. "I've yet to determine that on my behalf." I push the blade into his skin, but he just chuckles.

"Press harder, Cignette," he tells me. "I'm way tougher than this."

I oblige, and when he moans at the pressure, I pull the blade back and drop it to the side.

A thick bead of his blood shines through the small cut, and I don't know why, but I'm spellbound by it.

"I…I did that," I voice. "I actually did that."

Dorran's shoulders shake in silent laughter, and when I swat him on the arm, he only laughs harder.

"Sorry," he says, "but that was simply too precious."

I roll my eyes. "Shut up; let me revel in it."

"Why don't you do that by getting a taste?" he sasses. "Unless you've changed your mind, of course."

I click my tongue. "Careful, Ledger. Your desperate side is showing."

He winks at me. "Fuck you, Adler."

I grin and place a kiss on the corner of his mouth, then drag my lips lower. I let them trail over his skin, and smile when I feel him get harder against my thigh.

I widen my legs so that I can settle down further, and then, I finally lean in and lick the blood off of Dorran's collarbone.

My senses immediately overwhelm by the heady taste that surrounds my mouth, and I suppress a moan.

"Fuck," he whispers, and his head falls forward. "Do that again."

I drag my tongue over the cut, then suck on it, earning a grunt of approval from Dorran.

I move back and slide my fingers into his soft curls before giving them a tug. "God, you're *stunning*," I tell him, admiring the faint flush on his cheeks, his flared pupils, and his inviting lips.

He grins lazily. "Fucking kiss me, Cignette," he says, and so, I do; I kiss him with every ounce of strength in me.

I bite, tug, and suck, and Dorran perfectly mirrors each and every one of my actions.

I touch my tongue to the roof of his mouth, and our teeth clash when he presses forward and takes my bottom lip between both of his.

My grip on his hair loosens as I rock my hips against his, and the harsh denim of his jeans brushes against the flimsy fabric of my underwear, making me ache for more.

Dorran grabs my waist and breaks the kiss. "Careful," he tells me. "Limit your movements. Let me help you." He thrusts his hips upward, and his hard-on rubs against my clit.

I arch my back and cry out, then whimper when Dorran sets a thorough pace of rocking his cock against my soaked underwear.

I press down on him and move against him slowly, then cup the sides of his neck and bring our faces closer – so much so that every time he pushes his hips forward and I push mine downwards, we share the same breath.

"That's right, Little Swan," he whispers against me. "Use me for your pleasure. Take what you want – how much you want. Ride it all out and stain that underwear for me like a good little girl."

My nipples harden as my orgasm builds. His words spur me on, creating a heat in my belly.

"I can smell you, Cignette," Dorran says, then licks my lower lip. "My God, I can *feel* your sweet pussy weeping for release. You want that, don't you? You wanna come for me?"

"Yes," I hiss. "Fuck yes."

"Then do it," he commands, and claims my lips in a dizzying kiss. "Come all over my jeans. Fucking mark me with your arousal."

My clit throbs, seconds before my orgasm hits. I tip my head back and moan Dorran's name, riding my release as he continues his movements against me.

"Look at you," he all but rasps. "Look at you lighting up the fucking night with your beauty, Little Swan." He grabs my ass and rubs his hardness over my sensitive pussy. "You're so damn perfect."

My heart thrashes against my chest as I catch my breath. Swallowing once, I look down at Dorran, and when our eyes meet, we laugh and share a lazy kiss.

"That was…" I close my eyes and sigh softly against his mouth. "Thank you, Dorran."

He chuckles. "Thank *you*," he says. "Witnessing you let loose like this is fulfilling as fuck."

"Hmm." I smile and kiss him again, then open my eyes and scan his face. "But the next time you make me come, I want there to be no barriers between us." I bring a hand over his still-hard cock, and give it a squeeze. "Is that understood, Ledger?"

He groans and pushes his hips further against my grip. "I don't take orders from you," he tells me, and his eyes gleam as he gives me a smirk.

"I know you don't," I say. "But then again, no one is capable of making your dick as hard as I do, so you've got no choice but to listen to me."

He flashes a manic smile at me. "You're a fucking menace, Cignette Adler," he spits the words at me.

I squeeze him tighter and grin down at him. “Tell me something I don’t know, sweetheart.”

21.
DORRAN

To say that this woman has me by the balls – both literally and figuratively – would be an understatement. She brings out a side of me that I didn't even think existed. She challenges my instincts and distracts my focus whenever I'm with her, and for someone like me, that's a dangerous situation to be in. But in all honesty, I can't bring myself to give a fuck.

After I'd helped her clean up around five hours ago, we lied in her bed and shared a few random memories from our past with each other. It's kinda riveting to know that Cignette has had a childhood just as broken as mine. Our problems may have varied in their nature and circumstances, but they are still similar in ways only her and I can understand. And that, right there, is the beauty of our instant attraction.

The cracks in our interiors that only the two of us can see.

I yawn behind a hand and look down at Cignette, who is sound asleep and snoring softly against my ear. Careful not to wake her, I place a soft kiss on her forehead, and inhale the sweet smell of her skin.

Oranges. Always oranges.

She had initially had an issue lying down because of her bruises, but had ended up managing by pressing herself against the side of my body. She'd said that the pressure created by leaning onto me was helping her relax without feeling any pain, and because I was all for making sure she didn't feel discomforted, I was glad I could help her in any way possible.

She'd fallen asleep while listening to me talk, and that'd been around four hours ago. It's almost 6a.m. now, and she's still in a slumber, with my right arm under and around her, her head on my shoulder, and her right leg draped over mine. I've dozed off a few times, but haven't been able to sleep properly. Despite everything we shared in the last few hours, my focus keeps going back to what Miranda did to her. And for what? A dress that doesn't even exist yet? Un-fucking-believable.

I may have told Cignette that I won't do anything against it, but I sure as fuck am not going to stay true to my word. I'm itching to give Miranda a taste of what happens when someone messes with those I care for, but I won't be able to do shit if I don't get my ass out of Cignette's bed soon.

I shift sideways, and grimace when she groans in protest. There's no way I'll be able to free myself without disturbing her, so I decide to wake her instead of accidentally scaring her out of her sleep.

I push her hair away from her face, and stifle the urge to grit my teeth when I see the scar on her cheek.

Yet another reason for me to leave now so that I can actually do something about it.

"Cignette?" I brush the pad of my thumb over her chin and shake her gently. "Cignette, hey."

Her eyelids flutter, and a second later, she sluggishly opens her eyes.

"Sorry to have to wake you," I tell her. "It's almost 6, and the sun's about to rise. I'll have to leave now while I've still got some darkness to cover me."

She frowns. "Okay," she says groggily, then makes to rise, but I stop her.

"Don't." I shake my head once. "Go back to sleep, and text me later. Don't open the door for anyone but your bodyguard, and if there's anything you need, or if you feel even remotely unsafe or scared, call me right away."

She nods.

"Words, Little Swan – give them to me."

She swallows. "I'll call you if I feel like something's off. I promise."

"Good." I give her a quick once over, then press a kiss on her lips. "You good, right?"

She smiles. "I'm fine." She scans my face and runs the back of her fingers over my jaw. "Message me when you reach home?"

I chuckle. "I will."

She smiles again. "Okay."

God, I don't wanna leave her, but fuck, I *have* to.

And so, before I end up changing my mind, I pull my arm from under her and get to my feet. Grabbing my phone and opening my chat with Jayce, I shoot him a quick text.

Me: *Meet me at the gym in three hours. Text the others. Keep Solo out of this.*

His reply, surprisingly, is quick.

Jay: *It's adorable that you have to ask me to keep Solo in the dark.*

Me: *Don't test me.*

Jay: *You know I've got you, so relax.*

Me: *Thanks, man.*

Jay: *Don't mention it.*

"Dorran?"

I look at Cignette, and find her holding my switchblade out to me.

"You forgot this," she says.

"I wonder who's to blame for that," I muse as I take it from her.

She rolls her eyes. "Go away. I'm too sleepy right now to have a back-and-forth with you."

I grin and start back-walking towards her balcony. "Get your rest, then." I wink at her, pocket my phone and switchblade, then turn around and escape into the rising morning.

22.
DORRAN

"You do know that Miranda is Chase fucking Adler's sister, right?" Jayce asks.

I take a drag of my cigarette, then blow the steam out deliberately as I look around the dark, quiet alley.

"Yup," I answer.

"And I hope you realize that both Chase *and* Miranda are our clients," he added. "And that if Miranda is harmed, she won't waste a second in reaching out to her brother – who, in turn, will reach out to Solo. Who, let me remind you, is someone you wanted to *keep out of this situation*."

I give Jayce a bored look. "I'm not going to do anything to her," I tell him. "*Yet*."

"Ledge," he says in warning, and his eyes harden as he glares disapprovingly at me.

A few cars pass by the alley, and their headlights temporarily illuminate the otherwise dull night.

"Have faith in Dorran, babe," Alex assures him. "He's never steered us wrong so far. Plus, we're only here to do what we discussed earlier at the gym."

And that is to give Miranda a clear warning, that's all.

"I still think we should reconsider," adds Varsha from next to me. "Chase has kept us safe and away from prison for all these years. We're kinda in his debt. Breaching personal grounds and going for his family could put us in a seriously dicey position." She looks at me. "Is Cignette really worth risking our necks for?"

"You know I wouldn't have asked any of you to be here if she wasn't," I tell her honestly. "And besides, we've more than paid the debt we owe him by killing whoever he's wanted us to kill. It's not like we're pressed on his goodwill or somethin'."

"But that's the thing, Ledge – our rapport with him and Miranda is an ongoing thing," says Jayce. "It's not a one and done; it's still going to exist after tonight." He pauses and glances unsurely at me. "At least that's what I'm hoping will be the case."

I grit my teeth as I throw my cigarette on the ground, stomp on it, and turn to him. "The fact that you're not even *trying* to put an ounce of your trust in me right now, is baffling to me. Because you of all people know that I wouldn't be so stupid as to indirectly put Cignette in danger by causing too big of a problem with her mother."

He scoffs and raises his arms by his sides. "So it all just boils down to *her*, then, and not us or, I don't know, our *safety*."

"Of course it does," I tell him. "I wouldn't let anything happen to the three of you."

"And what about *you*?" asks Varsha, then folds her arms across her chest.

I shrug. "I know y'all love me too much to let anything happen to me, so I'm not worried about myself," I muse.

"I'm going to shove you in that dumpster over there and let you choke on trash-fumes just for being a disgustingly cocky bastard," Alex says with a scowl.

Jayce chuckles, and Varsha simply rolls her eyes, although I do notice a smile at the edge of her mouth.

When we'd met at the gym earlier today, I'd told the three of them about what Miranda had done to Cignette, and why. And then, I'd also told them what I planned on doing tonight, and they'd agreed to back me up – of course they had – albeit being a little hesitant about it.

The thrum of an engine takes over the silence, and the alley floods with golden light as a car starts turning into it.

Me and the crew immediately take cover behind the massive brick wall that's a bit further on the inside, and when I chance a glance at the alley, I see Miranda getting out of her silver Lexus with an air of arrogance that falls short only to the one her brother exudes.

Alex had learnt from one of the guards stationed at Miranda's estate – who, in turn, had learnt from Steven, Miranda's bodyguard – that she was going to have dinner at *Mario's Place* tonight. All by herself, might I add.

I'd kept tabs on Cignette via text messages throughout the day. No one but *Mave* had been with her for most of it, and when he'd left for the day, she'd called and asked me to come over.

It'd taken every bit of my restraint to stop myself from saying yes, because really, all I wanted to do was be close to her. But I couldn't, not tonight.

I'd told Cignette that I had to stay at *Finesse* and work on a few cars, and despite her having caught my lie – because let's face it, it wasn't exactly a good excuse to begin with – she'd refrained from calling me out on it, and had instead promised to keep her bedroom door locked and turn in early for the night.

Even though Miranda is here – right in front of me – I'd rather Cignette not take her chances and let her guard down. I've already gotten a glimpse of the things her mother is capable of, and with me indisposed tonight, I'll have to worry about Cignette's safety a little less, at least, knowing that she is secure in her room.

"She's on the move," Alex whispers, pulling me out of my thoughts.

I look ahead, and sure enough, Miranda says something to Steven – most probably asks him to wait in the car for her – before heading inside *Mario's Place* through its backdoor. It's something her and quite a few elites do when they wanna avoid media and spectator eyes alike, so that they can relax and have an undisturbed meal.

Like fuck I'll let that happen.

The backdoor closes, and silence resumes its symphony.

I purposefully press one of my boots against the ground and give my feet a couple of twists, resulting in gravel to crunch under it.

Steven, who is about to make his way back to Miranda's car, stops at the sound and brings a hand close to the gun attached to the holster on his hip.

I smirk, and slither out of the shadows before coming face-to-face with the guy.

I don't know him that well. We've met in passing during my meetings with the Adler siblings, but other than that, I don't know shit about him.

Not that I care, really. If something doesn't interest me, I usually don't go 'round sniffing in its direction.

"Dorran?" he asks. He's surprised to see me, and rightfully so, but doesn't take his hand off his gun.

Smart.

"Hey, man," I say, like I'm here to take a drag with him or something. From my peripheral, I notice Jayce sneaking out from behind the wall and making his way to the other side of the alley.

Steven appears thoroughly confused as he continues to look at me. "Hey…?"

I chuckle and take a few steps toward him. "You know what happens to those who see things for what they are, and yet, decide to unsee them and go about their business like nothing even happened?"

His brows crease as he stares at me.

Cignette had told me how, despite seeing what Miranda had done to her, this bastard had refused to show even a speck of sympathy towards her. He'd bowed his head and ignored Cignette; left her alone. And, because I can't get to Miranda – for now, at least – Steven will have to suffice.

He's suspicious of me now. "What are you doing here, Dorran?" he asks, and I notice that his complexion has paled a little, and beads of perspiration are marring his forehead and temples.

"It's too cold tonight for you to be sweating so much, man," I tell him, then grin. "It feels as though you've seen the Reaper or something."

He's full-on shaking now, and it only serves my rising excitement.

"Look, I don't know what you're up to, but if–"

"You turned your back on her," I say through gritted teeth, then get close to him. "*You fucking left her alone.*"

"What?" he shakes his head. "Who are you talking about?"

I gotta admit: watching a grown-ass dude, especially someone as tall and built as him, quivering the way he is right now, is amusing. Steven and I may share the same height, but he easily has a few extra pounds on me.

"Cignette," I tell him, and his eyes widen. "You saw what her mother did to her, didn't you? And you still did *nothing* for her."

He gives me an incredulous look. "Why would I?" He scoffs. "Just to put myself at a possible risk of losing my life?" He has the audacity to laugh. "Fuck *no*. I barely know the chick. What if she deserved the beating she received? Have you even thought of that?"

I'm so fucking enraged by his words that I legit see red. I grab his collar and align his face with mine. "Trust me, asshole, she *didn't*." I shake him once, and he sucks in a trembling breath. "But what's about to happen to *you* will be very well deserved, I'll tell you that." I look beyond his shoulder and nod, then shove him back before stepping away from him.

Steven makes to turn, but before he can so much as shift, silver flashes against the dark, and Jayce deftly wraps his curb chain – his weapon of choice – around Steven's neck before pulling at the chain's ends to choke the stupid fucker.

The chain is thick enough that it covers most of Steven's throat, and cuts off his access to any kind of movement. When he tries to claw at it, Jayce simply tightens his grip, and Steven's eyes bulge almost comically, while his face reddens.

He opens his mouth to draw a breath, but it's futile. He then tries to shoulder Jayce in order to break his hold, but that effort is just as fruitless.

Once he's got you where he wants you, no one, and I mean *no one*, can escape Jayce. And I'm not just saying that from a bias point of view; I'm saying it because it's a damn *fact*.

"It's hard, isn't it?" I tell Steven, who is still clawing at his neck and throat. "Scares you on the inside – knowing any given moment could be your last."

He brings a leg up in order to kick me, but I laugh and easily sidestep it.

Varsha and Alex join us, and the latter grins at his husband before settling on the car's hood.

I look at Jayce and point a thumb over my shoulder. "Bring him here," I say to him, then walk over to the empty space next to the dumpsters.

Jayce unfurls his chain from around Steven's neck and shoves him in my direction. The asshole gasps for air as he stumbles to stay afoot, and when he's close enough to me, I grab the back of his neck, bend his upper body forward, and knee him in the nose.

"Fuck," he hisses, and before he can rise again, I punch him in the gut, resulting in him to cough and double over.

He struggles to take a proper breath as he falls on all fours, then spits on the ground before rasping, "You're a cunt, Dorran."

"What the fuck did you just call him?" Varsha asks, and pulls her .38 Ruger S&W out of her denim jacket.

"Varsha." I put a hand up to stop her.

She glares at Steven with murder in her eyes, but steps back regardless.

I crouch so that I'm eyelevel to the asshole. "You know," I start, then tilt my head a little, "I was gonna let you go right now – I really was. But then you had to go and insult me like that, and now I've lost the very last shred of kindness I had for you in the deepest recess of my heart."

Steven makes a sound in the back of his throat. "Fuck you," he says. "Miranda will have your ass for this."

"It's cute that you think she cares," I muse, then get to my feet. "But you'll learn too late that people like her only care for themselves." I kick him in the ribs, and watch as he yelps and falls on the ground with an unflattering *oomph.*

"Gimme the car keys," I order.

"What?" he whispers, then wipes at his bloody nose. "You're crazy."

I sigh. "Don't make me repeat myself, Steven," I say. "It seriously takes away the fun."

He stares at me with so much anger on his face that it makes me chuckle.

"Keys, Steven – give them to me."

He flinches as he shifts to grab them from his pant pocket, then hands them to me with a tick in his jaw.

"Wasn't so hard, was it?" I say, then turn around and throw the keys at Alex, who catches them midair. "Turn on the headlights for me, will you?" I tell him. "The main event needs some kind of…*pizzazz*, methinks."

My crew laughs, and Alex hops off the car's hood to go turn on the headlights.

A few seconds later, the dark alley brightens to gold.

Looking down at Steven's struggling form, I put a leg on either side of his waist and touch my knees to the ground as I straddle him.

"What are you doing, you *freak*?" he asks, and tries to move away from me.

I click my tongue and punch him in the jaw, making him grunt. "Don't do things that are useless against your fate, man," I state. "It makes you look far more stupid than you've already proven yourself to be."

"You–"

I punch him again, putting a stop to whatever it is he's about to say. Then, I sit back on my heels and contemplate my next move.

"Hammer or blade?" I think to myself, then lazily roll my head to the side and look at my crew. "Thoughts?"

Steven jerks under me. "You're mad!" he shrieks. "You psycho. Let me go!"

I roll my eyes and punch him for the third time, then look at my crew again. "Thoughts, guys; come on. I ain't got all night."

"Hammer," Alex says with a grin, mainly because that's his weapon.

"I concur," adds Jayce.

"Seconded," Varsha agrees.

"Perfect." I grin and look at Steven. "You see that? We've got a weapon picked out for your demise, bud."

"Dorran…" Steven starts crying in between bouts of tremors. "We can come to an agreement, please. I'll…I'll leave Riverside. Yes! I'll fucking leave this godforsaken place. I'll go as far away from here as I can. And I…I won't say anything about what happened tonight to *anyone*. I promise. Just let me go, man. *Please*. I–" He stops talking, and ends up gurgling blood when I slit his throat with my switchblade. He was so busy groveling that he didn't even notice me sliding my blade out of my pocket. Stupid fuck.

Steven cups his throat and starts thrashing wildly, to which Alex sighs and shakes his head.

"I wanted to see you hammer his head in," he tells me, then purses his lips as he glances at Steven. "Too bad he wasn't cooperative."

I chuckle, and reach out a hand towards him. "Give it to me," I tell him.

Alex's gaze darkens as he eagerly puts his staking hammer in my waiting palm.

It's a beautifully deadly thing, with a sturdy wooden handle, and a metal-made head that consists of two ends – one that is clawed, and the other that's blunt.

I throw the hammer in the air, and catch it as it falls, then look at Steven, who's barely got any life left in him.

With the clawed end of Alex's hammer facing forward, I rise on my knees, pull my arm back, and then bring it down right in the center of Steven's forehead.

A loud, wet crunch of bone and skin breaking under the hammer's sharpness, hits my ears, and Steven immediately stops moving.

"Okay, that's super hot," Alex comments, making me laugh.

I pull my arm back a second time, then hit the same spot on Steven's head again, resulting in blood and chunks of brain to splatter on my forearm, neck, and face.

"God, that's disgusting," Varsha mutters, and turns her back to me. "Dorran, that's enough."

"It's not like you've never seen me covered in a person's remains before, sis," I tell her, then spit out a questionable piece of skin before standing and handing Alex his hammer. "Besides, didn't you say yes to me using the hammer around five minutes ago? Don't fucking contradict yourself like that."

She doesn't answer me, and instead, chooses to flick a middle finger at me.

I smirk. "Real mature, V," I tell her, then step away from Steven's body and turn around, only to find Jayce looking coolly at me.

"You happy?" he asks.

"*Very*," I answer with a grin.

He rolls his eyes. "I texted Eddie and asked him to send a cleanup team. He said they'll be here in 20. Let's head inside so that I can help *you* clean up all the mess you've got clinging on yourself."

"Always the nurturer," I muse.

He scowls. "Shut it, asshat."

I raise my hands and admit defeat, because testing Jayce's temper right now is not something I want to do, especially after the thrill of a successful kill.

Me and the crew make our way to the backdoor in order to sneak into the restaurant's bathroom, but I pause when I suddenly remember something.

"Guys."

They stop and turn to look at me.

I wink at them. "Before we go, I've got just one little thing that I need to do."

23.
DORRAN

M*ario's Place* is lit up like a chandelier house. As the crew and I step out of the bathroom and into the main dining area, I'm met with a crowd of servers bustling around, trays full of food in hand, their expressions sullen, and their footsteps hurried.

The warm lights in the restaurant complement the wooden interior, and the classic Italian music playing in the background really helps set the mood. But the air in here screams money in the most straightforward way possible – which, I guess, is exactly what the owner had in mind for this place while creating it.

As the four of us walk between the tables, I catch the eyes of a few elites who've hired me in the past. Their gazes meet mine, but they immediately look away and squirm in their seats as if maintaining eye-contact with me will make me wanna spill all of their sadistic little secrets out loud for those who'll listen.

It's baffling how they think they matter to me, when all I care about when I take up a kill is the act itself, and the fuck load of cash that comes along with it. I couldn't give a rat's ass about these uptight motherfuckers, and unless they've messed with me or the people I'm close to, I prefer to stay as far away from them as I possibly can.

Speaking of keeping a distance…

I wish I could distance myself from the nauseating smell of flowers that's wafting off of me right now. Out of the various types of soaps available in the market to choose from, the people in charge of toiletries at *Mario's Place* picked the one that smells like a fucking funeral bouquet.

And they use the words "lavishly elegant" to describe their services.

Lavish, my ass.

"Four o'clock," Jayce whispers in my ear.

I blink and look to my right, and find a waiter serving Miranda her meal.

Tenderloin Steak and a glass of sparkling red wine.

Some of the diners give me and the crew judgmental once-overs, clearly thrown off by our choice of clothing. I mean, with Jayce in a flannel, Alex in a letterman hoodie, Varsha in her signature denim, and me wearing a slim-fit vest, we belong in McDonald's or a burger joint, not in a sophisticated restaurant.

But then again, if we start giving a fuck about what these people think, then the world will come to an end. And so, I ignore their visual inspections and lead the crew over to Miranda's table. The waiter has left, and she's about to commence her meal in expected bliss, but stops short when she sees me.

"Miss Adler," I address her with a casual smile. "Fancy meeting you here."

Jayce, Alex, and Varsha occupy the table opposite Miranda's, while I slide into the chair that's directly in front of her.

She lifts her chin and assesses me, then slowly raises a well-trimmed brow at me. "What do you want, Ledger?" she questions, and her eyes crease near the corners when she narrows them. "If it's not something that requires my immediate attention, then I'll ask that you wait outside while I finish up here."

Arrogant bitch.

Her jewelry glints against the surrounding lights, and as she waits for me to speak, I notice that there's a stiffness in her posture, like she's on edge and eager to know why I've disturbed her.

I'm rattling her right now, but she's too stubborn to let it show.

I lean back in my chair and stretch my legs out against the table.

"Believe me, Miranda, it *is* urgent," I tell her.

She notices how I address her, and she doesn't like it.

"Did my brother send you?" she asks. "You should have gotten in touch with my bodyguard first, and *then* made yourself so…frank in my presence."

"Hmm." I cant my head a little. "My bad."

She's physically bothered by me, and I know that it's absolutely *killing* her to see me so calm.

I glance at Jayce. He taps a finger on his watch, silently asking me to hurry. He knows that if Miranda decides to call security, or worse – her brother, then me and the crew will get into a tight position. I have to be brief, and I have to make sure she understands what I have to say to her.

Miranda places her forearms on the table and gives me an annoyed look. "I'm running out of patience, Ledger," she tells me. "If it's money you want, you'll have to go to Chase, because I'm not at the–"

"Cignette," I voice the name with enough conviction that she stops talking and stares at me with a horrified expression on her face.

"My daughter sent you?" she inquires, and there's a tremor in her voice that's just so satisfying to listen to.

"Look, I can pay you ten times more than what she has," Miranda says with an urgency. "You don't have to go through with this, Ledger; you owe me and my brother your continued freedom, your–"

"Hold up," I stop her. Then, because I *really* can't keep it in, I start laughing. "You think Cignette hired me to kill you? Is that why you think I'm here right now?" I laugh some more, and my crew joins in on it.

And here I thought that the woman who literally created an entire fashion empire from the ground up would at least have a fragment of commonsense. But nope, these elites continue to disappoint me. I guess I should just stop expecting much of anything from them.

If Miranda thinks her daughter can contract her murder, then she probably knows she went too far with Cignette this time. She realizes she overdid it, and that fact is settled somewhere inside her.

She looks utterly ghastly and dumbfounded as she glances between me and the others. "Then why are you…" She swallows. "If not to…W–"

I bang a fist against the table so loudly, that it not only clatters the items on it and makes Miranda jump in her seat, but also terrifies the nearby patrons and servers.

"I'm here, you senseless *bitch*," I say between gritted teeth, earning a glare from her, "to *warn* you – to make sure you hear me nice and proper when I tell you to stay the *fuck* away from Cignette." I lean in. "Your daughter is under my protection now, and if I find out that you've dared to touch her again, or *hurt* her like you did yesterday, then things won't end well for you. That's a promise."

"*How dare you?*" she hisses, having finally regained herself from the initial shock. "How dare you threaten me, or even think that it's appropriate for you to interfere in my personal matters?"

"Abusing your daughter isn't a personal matter, Miranda; it's a fucking *crime*."

"You are in no position to–"

"Just because your brother has kept my crew and I's personal information out of the criminal database, doesn't mean you get to treat us like we're beneath you." I arch a brow at her. "Because trust me, we're *not*. We've more than shown our gratitude to you and Chase by eliminating your rivals and competitors at your request, so the least you can do is treat us," I jerk my head towards Jayce and the others, "with some *respect*."

Miranda's chest rises and falls at an erratic rhythm as she continues to glare at me. "Stop it," she spits the words, then glances around in panic. "Just fucking *stop*."

"Don't want the people to find out the kind of person you really are, do you?" I taunt. "Then do as you're told, or I'll make every single moment of your life a fresh kind of hell you'll want nothing more than to escape from."

She seethes at me and curls her shaky hands into fists. "What did she have to do to persuade you into doing this?" she asks. "Did she spread her legs for you, or suck your cock in some shit-stained alley?"

I clench my jaw and stifle the urge to drive my switchblade into her eye. "You'd really like to know, wouldn't you?" I manage to keep my voice stable, because fuck if I'll give her the pleasure of knowing that she's hit a nerve.

Alex looks my way, so I nod subtly to let him know that I'm good.

"To bring a man such as yourself to the other side of the spectrum must have taken quite a lot," Miranda pushes, and a sinister smirk takes over her face. She isn't giving up, which is good. I would have been so disappointed if she hadn't even tried. It means that I get to play one last hand before I can finally claim my victory.

"Cignette sure has what it takes to keep a man rooted in place," I say, then grin darkly. "She's the adrenaline that's coursing through my veins. The very reason I'm here right now." I click my tongue. "Not that you'd know anything about that. Because if you did, then you wouldn't have to rely on a different man every other week for your desires and thirst for companionship, and instead, would still have your daughter's father in your life."

She sucks in a breath at my words, and looks at me like I've just slapped her or something.

"Fu–"

“Uh-uh-uh.” I shake my head at her. “Cursing out loud in public? Miss Adler, what would the people say?”

“And what would Christopher say when I tell him that his minions are here to harass me?” she counters.

I place an elbow on the back of my chair and gesture at her purse on the table. “Go ahead; do it,” I say to her. “Call Solo right now and tell him everything.” He’ll probably have my balls for what I’ve done tonight, but he’ll back me up anyway, I’m sure of that.

Miranda hesitates, and her temporary bravado dwindles.

I smile triumphantly and get to my feet, and my crew follows suit. Looking down at Cignette’s mother, I decide to repeat myself in case she hasn’t fully grasped onto the meaning behind my being here.

“Stay away from Cignette,” I advise. “Do not even *think* about touching her again. And, if you try to outsmart me, or tell anyone about our meeting and conversation, then you’ll find yourself dolled up in a coffin – six fucking feet under, and very, *very* dead. I hope I’m clearly understood.” I remember the thing I’ve been carrying in my pocket since I left the alley, and decide to pull it out before throwing it on the table – right in front of Miranda.

She half-screams, half-cries, then covers her nose and mouth with her hands as she stares at Steven’s tongue staining the otherwise white tablecloth red.

“Also, your bodyguard spoke too much,” I say. “So, make sure the next one you pick doesn’t have the same habit. It’s not very flattering or tolerable, especially during work hours.”

Leaving her twice as horrified as a few minutes ago, I turn around and walk away, with my crew right behind me.

Mission accomplished.

24.
CIGNETTE

The iridescent dress glimmers against the fading afternoon light as I pull it over my body. The beautiful charmeuse glides over my skin, and as I move in front of the mirror, I notice how snugly it wraps itself around every inch of me that it touches. Its hem brushes against my toes, and opens into an upside-down V-cut that ends at the middle of my right thigh.

Pink, lavender, green, blue, silver, golden – the dress changes its color with each twist.

I turn sideways, and smile when I notice the low-cut back – exactly how I wanted it. My tattoo is on full display, with the swan appearing prettier than it is because of the subtle glint in my dress.

I push my shoulder forward and arch my back as I continue to inspect myself in the mirror, and the feathers inked on my skin shift with my movements.

Julian had driven over to the estate earlier today to safely deliver the dress to me. Mave had been the one to bring it up to my room, and when I'd opened the garment bag, I'd had to hold my breath upon seeing just how stunning the dress looked.

I turn again, and then stare at my reflection in the mirror.

I haven't done much of anything to hide the scar on my right cheek. To be honest, I don't exactly *want* to hide it. It's just another remnant of the battle I won against my mom's cruelty, so I'd much rather flaunt it than conceal it under layers of makeup.

The elites at the gala will notice it for sure, but no one will dare to inquire after it.

It's been four days since Mom's episode. The redness on the other side of my face has all but vanished, and the finger imprints on my neck, too, have faded. The bruises on my stomach and ribs, though, have darkened. They hurt, sure, but not as much as they initially did, so at least there's that.

I let go of a breath as I grab a comb and a few pins, then quickly tie my hair into an effortless French Twist. I spritz some perfume on my neck and wrists, and am about to step away from the mirror when there's a knock on my bedroom door.

"It's open."

A couple of seconds pass, then Mave pokes his head in and searches my room until his eyes meet mine.

"Hey," he says around a smile, and walks over to me.

"How do I look?" I ask as I smooth my hands over the front of my dress.

He stops in front of me and slides his hands into the pockets of his pants.

He's dressed in a white suit, with a black accent tie, black lapels, and silver cufflinks. His hair is coiffed, his facial hair is trimmed, and the familiar smell of his spice-and-mint cologne puts me at ease – ease in the fact that he's going to be by my side tonight.

"Absolutely radiant," he tells me, then scans my face. "You sure you wanna go, though?"

"Julian worked so hard on this dress. It'd be a shame not to show it off."

Mave shakes his head. "You know that's not enough, Nettie."

"I know," I say. "But I really *do* wanna go, Mave. It's been a while since I've seen Uncle Chase, so I'd like to change that. Also…" I quirk a brow. "There's gonna be free champagne. I don't even remember the last time I got drunk off my ass, and because I've got *you* to look after me tonight, I plan on downing as much booze as I can." What I don't say out loud, or show, is my unwillingness in wanting to come face-to-face with my mother. I haven't seen her or heard from her since the morning she attacked me, and as much as I wish I could keep things that way, I know it'll be impossible to avoid her tonight.

Mave seems unconvinced of my claims, but chuckles anyway. "Sure, but just know that if you throw up on yourself, I'm not going to clean you up. Been there, done that. You're not a cooperative drunk, and you sing – awfully too, might I add – while you're inebriated, so there's always a chance that I might lose my eardrums. Little good that'll do for my professional career."

My lips twitch as I look up at him. "You're so full of shit."

"I'll record you the next time you do it. *Tonight*, perhaps."

"As if I'll give you the satisfaction, you asshole," I tell him, making him chuckle again.

"Ready to head out, then?" he asks.

I nod. "Yeah." I quickly touch up my gloss, grab my white clutch from the dressing table, put on my silver spool-heel tie ups, and glance at my reflection in the mirror one more time.

I am an anomaly. A deviation from sanity.

A beautiful disaster.

And I've got this. I *know* I've fucking got this.

25.
DORRAN

I drop the towel from around my waist and grab my deodorant. Swiping it on my underarms a couple of times, I place it back on the dresser, then walk over to my closet before putting my clothes on.

I'm ecstatic about tonight, but I can't help but be anxious as well, because Cignette will be at the gala, and so will Miranda. If the latter pulls any kind of a stunt, I'll be too distracted to focus on the kills, and if the kills take all my attention, then I won't be able to keep an eye on Cignette.

My crew has agreed to watch her tonight, and despite knowing that it's unfair of me to ask them to do that, I'm not going to stop them. Four pairs of eyes are better than one, after all.

When I'd texted Cignette earlier today, she'd sent me a photo of her dress, and had told me that even though she was confident she could attend the gala and keep her wits about her, she was not ready to act social and jovial with Miranda. At one point, she'd even said she wished I could be there with her, and if I wasn't so duty-bound, I would have told her that I will, indeed, be there with her.

The thing is: I'm not sure how, and for how *long*, I'll be able to go undetected by her. Because something tells me that she'll find me out, and she'll do it before I've had the chance to finish the job I've been assigned to do.

I shut my closet door and make my way over to the mirror. Tucking in my sky-blue shirt, I zip my pants and put my belt on. I'm not one for ties, so I keep the first few buttons of my shirt undone.

I hear the ping of a new text as I'm pulling my navy-blue suit jacket over my shoulders. It's Jayce.

My phone's on the dresser, so I unlock it and tap on the message.

Jay: *We're here. You ready?*

I ruffle my still-damp hair, fix my collar, button-up my sleeve cuffs, and spray some cologne on my neck. I then grab my phone and switchblade, shoot a quick response to Jayce, then pocket both the items before heading out of my loft.

Me: *omw.*

I am a poison. A contradiction to stability.

A formidable calamity.

And I'll gladly destroy those who try to get in my way.

26.
CIGNETTE

The air conditioners in here aren't doing their damn job. Or maybe it's the crazy amount of body heat emanating off of the elites in this room that's making me feel as though I'm in a sauna. One would think that this place would have the best of everything, given how it's an Adler-family property, but alas, that is not the case.

I've lost count of the number of times I've pressed a hand over my face and neck to wipe the perspiration off my skin, and even though I've tried to fend it off, I simply can't seem to get rid of the obnoxious smell of mixed-up colognes around me. It's a very questionable blend, too – like jasmine and musk and aqua, all combined together.

"Need that drink yet?" Mave asks against my ear. "You look about ready to scream your lungs out. Some alcohol will help in putting your nerves at ease."

I turn my head and glare up at him. "I'm two seconds away from pushing you towards the champagne tower," I say, then give him a saccharine smile. "So if that's what you want, then go ahead and provoke me more. If not, then shut the fuck up and help me get out of here so that I can get some fresh air."

I've been standing in a corner and entertaining baseless conversations with bored elites for the last two hours. Some of them not-so-subtly tried asking me about the scar on my cheek, but their questions weren't anything

I couldn't easily evade. I obviously couldn't tell them the truth – because imagine the *scandal* that it would bring upon my *illustrious* family – so I could either lie, or not say anything at all and move on.

I chose the latter.

Uncle Chase is running late, and until he gets here, the winter-wear reveal cannot actually happen – which means I'll have to continue to spend agonizing seconds stuck in a room full of pretentious asswipes who think they're better than everyone in attendance here tonight.

In all honesty, though, if it wasn't so hot and congested in here, I would have actually looked around and admired the stunning décor without the fear of accidentally meeting someone's eye and then having to engage in a one-on-one with them. Because really, the ballroom is gorgeous, but feels like a fucking poultry farm with the colorfully annoying people occupying it.

The room's ceiling is dark, with a series of lights – glass tubes, more like – designed in the form of tidal waves spanning the entirety of its length. It's a work of art, for sure, and illuminates the place with a subtle, sensual glow.

The floor and walls are black-and-gold marble, and there's a massive screen and stage on the far end of the ballroom. A high-concept bar and champagne tower are set up on the right, and there's a lovely, flower-studded balcony on the left, with three donation boxes next to it. *The Chase Adler Foundation* is written on all of them, but I know for damn sure that every single dollar in those boxes is going to end up in Mom's pocket.

Speaking of my mom…

She's been ignoring me constantly since I arrived at *Imperia*. I've mostly seen her floating around the room like a middle-aged bee in her atrocious, floor-length and full-sleeved golden cocktail dress – mingling with the guests – but other than that, she's made herself scarce in my presence. Our gazes *did* lock a couple of times, but she averted hers so fast that it left both Mave and I confused and unsettled.

Mom also has a new bodyguard now, which is strange, because Steven has been with her for over a decade. Mave has no idea why Mom replaced Steven, or where he is, but the new bodyguard, Riley, is a fresh recruit with barely any field experience. I'm pretty sure she picked him for his boyish looks, green eyes, and short blond hair. Typical of her to go for the good-looking one.

"Forget fresh air," Mave whispers, and his voice all but jolts me out of my thoughts. "You've got incoming."

I look ahead, and curse inwardly when I see Waleed Najimi, flanked by three guards, making his way over to where I am.

He's wearing a beige-and-blue Armani three-piece, and appears just as put together as he did the last time I'd seen him.

"Cignette, my dear!" he sings, and comes to a stop in front of me. "I hope you are having a lovely time tonight." He then looks me over, and gasps before saying, "What do I see, now! *Ya 'Iilahi*, a beauty such as yourself with no glass in her hands! You must not be fully sober whilst dealing with a crowd such as this one. Did you not know that, *Eazizi*?" He makes a face and gestures around us, and I laugh earnestly.

"I've vowed to stay away from alcohol tonight," I tell him.

"Pssh." He waves a hand in the air. "Whatever for?"

I point a thumb over my shoulder at Mave. "This guy says I'm a very loose drunk, so I'm trying to avoid giving him the pleasure of witnessing me in that position."

Waleed laughs, and his eyes suddenly land on my scarred cheek. He must not have noticed it before, but he now stares at it with a flash of anger on his face, which surprises me.

"*Eazizi*…" He meets my eyes. "Who has done this to you? You must tell me at once." He reaches a hand out to touch my cheek, but Mave shifts from behind me and cups Waleed's wrist so fast, that I have to suck in a breath and blink at the swiftness of it.

"*Sir*," he says to Waleed, then drops his hand down. "I would like to respectfully ask that you maintain your distance." He moves closer to me.

Waleed arches a brow and steps back. "I meant no harm," he tells us. "I was simply inquiring. I wish to punish the person responsible for marring such a wonderful beauty."

"I assure you, sir, the matter has been dealt with," Mave states, and his voice sounds clipped. Almost like he doesn't appreciate Waleed complimenting me.

"Good." Waleed nods, then glances between Mave and I. "Good."

"May I be so bold as to step in?" comes a commanding, silk-smooth voice.

I turn, and grin up at the Administrator of Riverside County.

The guests around us have either quieted down or moved out of the way, and so has Mave.

"Uncle Chase!" I wrap my arms around his neck, and he holds me in close for a tender hug.

His team of bodyguards steps out of our way and gives us some space.

"Sweet pea." Uncle Chase moves back and looks down at me, and his smile fluctuates when he, too, notices my scar.

He frowns and cups my cheek, but of course, doesn't say anything. "You look radiant," he tells me, then places a kiss on my forehead. "Remind me to thank Julian on the amazing job he's done with your dress." His dark eyes shine with genuine admiration.

Uncle Chase is wearing a crimson tux and a black bowtie. His grey hair is parted sideways, which is how he's *always* worn it. He looks truly sophisticated and regal – fit for the position he holds in Riverside.

"Julian accepts your thanks, sir!" chimes Julian himself, having popped out of nowhere.

Uncle Chase chuckles. "Enjoying yourself tonight, son?" he asks him.

"Sure am. Thank you for the invite, sir."

"It's not *me* who you should thank," Uncle Chase says, then gestures at Waleed. "It's our generous host and sponsor."

Waleed looks flustered. "Always the charmer, aren't you, Mr. Adler?"

"Only where it matters."

The two of them share a laugh, and then Uncle Chase looks around at the gathered group. "You," he points a finger at Mave, then does the same for his and Waleed's guards. "All of you – go relax a little; have fun. This is a secure event with trusted people as guests, so you don't have to look so attentive and official."

Mave and the others share a look.

"But sir–"

"*That's an order*, Maverick," Uncle Chase cuts him off, then jerks his head towards the bar. "Grab a drink or two, come on. Live a little, for Christ's sake."

Mave clears his throat, and I turn a little so that I can smirk at him. "Maybe it's *me* who's going to have to endure your vile singing tonight, after all," I say softly. "Want me to record you while you give me a show, *Maverick*?"

He puts his tongue to his cheek and narrows his eyes at me. "With all due respect, Nettie, *fuck you*."

I chuckle, and get out of the way when a couple of guards come barreling over and wrap their arms around him. They start leading him to the bar, with the others right behind them, and as he gets dragged away, Mave looks back and mouths, "*Stay close*."

I smile and give him a nod, then turn to Uncle Chase. "I forgot to ask y–"

"Mr. Adler," one of the event organizers cuts me off.

Uncle Chase gives me a sympathetic smile. "I'm sorry, sweet pea," he tells me, then faces the organizer with an arched brow.

"Miss Adler needs you on stage for the reveal, sir."

Uncle Chase nods. "Let her know that I'll be there in a minute." He looks at me. "You were saying?"

I swipe at my upper lip and neck, then fan myself with my clutch. "Can you get the air conditioners in here to work somehow, please?" I say.

He laughs. "I may run this county, Cignette, but even *I* can't make these damn electronics work when they're most needed to work."

"*Language*, Uncle," I remark around a smile. "We don't want to give you a bad rep in the presence of your adoring fans."

He chuckles. "Most certainly can't have that." He then sighs and gives me another kiss on the forehead. "I have to go," he says with reluctance. "But let's spend an evening together – just the two of us. With coffee and our favorite macaroons, of course. How's that sound?"

I chuckle. "Absolutely perfect," I say. "I look forward to it."

Uncle Chase grins, then faces Waleed, who is busy talking to Julian. "Waleed?"

He immediately stops and gives us his complete attention.

"Should we join Miranda on stage?" Uncle Chase asks.

Waleed claps his hands together. "But of course! Lead the way, Mr. Adler."

Uncle Chase gives me a wink, then leads Waleed into the crowd.

"Good *Lord*, that Waleed guy talks *a lot*," Julian says, then comes to stand next to me.

I laugh. "He's eccentric for sure."

"Try *moot*."

I laugh again. "Well…that, too."

"You doing okay?" Julian asks.

"Yeah," I look at him. "You?"

He shrugs. "Same old." He takes a drink from the glass of bourbon he's holding. "I haven't seen you at *Lure* in a few days," he says. "And now I see *this*," he gestures toward my cheek, "on your face. You really sure you're okay, Cigs? In case you didn't know, I'm well-trained in taekwondo, and can take a fucker out with a neat roundhouse kick or two if you need me to."

I chuckle and give his arm a grateful squeeze, overwhelmed by the kindness in his eyes.

"Thanks, Julian," I say with a smile. "Seriously, it means a lot. But I'm good, I promise."

He smiles back. "I'll take your word for it."

A loud screech of a microphone silences the entire room. Julian and I look ahead, and I watch as my mom, uncle, and Waleed take the stage. The massive screen behind them lights up, and every eye in the ballroom is focused on the three of them.

I feel my phone vibrate in my clutch. I pull it out, just as Uncle Chase starts speaking to the gathered crowd, thanking them for attending the gala and being generous with their donations. I'm pretty sure he knows Mom isn't going to give a dime from tonight's collection to the women and children in our foundation, but again, he's going to ignore her shortcomings by brushing them under the rug.

I sigh and look down at my phone. Gavin has texted me, which immediately makes me scowl.

Gavin: *Baby, you've been avoiding me for days now. Did you find a better cock for that eager pussy of yours, or are you just playing hard to get?*

Wow…

I can't believe I fucked this dense asshole. *Multiple* times.

But then again, I was only looking for pleasure, and not substance, and he's *very* good at providing the former, so I didn't really care at the time.

Not until recently.

But given how Gavin cheated on Varsha with Nicole, and on Nicole with *me*, no one should expect any kind of substance from a guy like him anyway.

I glance sideways, and notice that Julian is busy listening to Mom, who has now taken the mic from Uncle Chase, and is rambling about the hard work she put into creating this new winter-wear collection.

What a joke.

I glance at the balcony, and find that it's occupied by a few elites who are smoking and vaping whilst chatting among each other. They have no interest in Mom's announcement, and I can't say I blame them.

I once again look at my phone, and type out my response to Gavin.

Me: *The former. And, if you like your cock attached to your body, you'll refrain from being so fucking candid with me next time.*

He begins typing seconds after reading my text.

Gavin: *Dorran will chew you up and spit you out. You're better off with me.*

Again: WOW.

Me: *Does being a pretentious cunt come naturally, or have you advanced in it somewhere?*

Gavin: *We're so good together, Cigs. Think about it. We're perfect for each other.*

Oh, he did *not* just say that.

Me: *We fucked, Gavin. A few times. That's it; that's all it was.*

Gavin: *For you, maybe, but not for me. Maybe it was at first, but my feelings have changed.*

I suddenly feel hotter than I did minutes ago. I start sweating in earnest, and the air around me feels too thick to breathe in.

Me: *This is not what we agreed on, Gav.*

I've never expected anything more than sex from guys, and Gavin isn't an exception.

Gavin: *So? Don't you want something more?*

With him? Absolutely not. Especially because he's got a girlfriend. And also because he hasn't got a single loyal bone in his body.

Me: *Where's this coming from, Gav? And what about Nicole? You can't keep doing this to the women in your life.*

Gavin: *Being away from you for a week has made me realize things. I don't want Nicole anymore. I want you.*

I close my eyes briefly, take a couple of deep breaths, and face Julian.

"Will you excuse me for a moment?" I tell him. "I need some fresh air." More like a ton of it.

Julian seems confused. "Now?" he glances at the stage, where Mom is displaying the new winter-wear on the screen. "During the reveal?"

Fuck.

"Yeah, I just…" I pretend to act tired. "The crowd is making me claustrophobic."

He furrows his brows in concern. "I can come with you," he suggests. "Maybe get you some water as well."

I shake my head. "That's not necessary, but thanks, Julian."

He nods. "Of course."

I give him a quick hug and practically run out of the ballroom.

I all but sprint through the empty hallway, and the cool air from the cassette air conditioners brings a much-needed chill to my sweaty body.

Fuck this night. Fuck that ballroom. Fuck those elites. *Fuck everyone*.

I'm so close to bending over and screaming until I can't feel my throat.

Mave was right in his assumption about my mood earlier. I just wish I had a drink in my hand right now. It'd make things endurable to some extent, at least.

I continue to breeze through the massive hallway, but come to a stop when I find a gorgeous, gold-threaded divan placed against the marble wall just ahead of me.

"Thank fuck," I whisper, and all but slump on it, only now realizing how much my legs and hips hurt from standing for hours without a break.

I look at my screen again, and, because I have no other choice but to set things straight, I continue my chat with Gavin.

Me: *Look, Gav, I'm really sorry. I can't do this; this isn't what I want.*

Gavin: *From me, or you don't want it in general?*

I grit my teeth at his audacity.

Me: *Unfortunately for you, that's none of your concern.*

Gavin: *I can't believe you're ditching me for a motherfucking KILLER, Cigs. A murderer. You and I both know that one of these days, Dorran is going to end up in jail, or worse. You really wanna waste your time on someone that can't even promise you forever?*

Me: *Who says that's what I want?*

Gavin: *It's what you deserve.*

I have to scoff at his text.

Me: *I'm done having this conversation with you, Gav. Again: I'm sorry. Whatever we had was fun, but it's over now.*

I wait for a few minutes for him to reply, but when he doesn't, I throw my phone into my clutch and let go of a slow breath.

I know I can be inconsiderate, but I kinda hope I didn't hurt Gavin's feelings. Even though he's kind of an ass.

Sharp footsteps sound from below me, followed by a set of voices. I can't make out what they're saying, but there's something about one of those voices that causes goosebumps to prick my skin.

I get to my feet so fast that I feel momentarily dizzy, but manage to grab the black railing in front of me before I can stumble.

My heart races, and I feel restless as I look around the foyer beneath me.

Nothing.

I almost convince myself of being wrong, when suddenly, I see a flash of blue, followed by a very similar head of jet-black curls.

Every bit of rationality leaves my body when I see Dorran, flanked by his crew, walking hurriedly towards the bathroom on the ground floor – his shoulders stiff, and his gaze darting around every other second.

And here I thought this night couldn't test me any more than it already has, but nope, I was wrong.

Fuck my life.

27.
DORRAN

I sneer and kick Andres in the ribs. "Die." Another kick. "You stupid." And another kick. "*Motherfucker*."

Beside me, Alex sighs. "He *is* dead, you weirdo."

"Not enough," I hiss, and stare at a very-unalive Andres at my feet.

His gangly frame is twisted in a very awkward position from my brief assault on him, and his face is starting to turn grey – almost ashen.

Our initial kill-order and plan had changed when, upon entering *Imperia*, Solo had called and informed me that he'd seen Andres entering the restrooms on the ground floor. When my crew and I found him in there, the asshole peed his pants, then tried locking himself in one of the stalls. And, when I didn't let him do that, he called me a "*stupid bitch*" and threatened to end me.

Big mistake.

I was going to make him bleed, but Jayce beat me to it and choked the fucker until he was dead.

"You should have let me cut him open," I tell Jayce, who is fixing the lapels of his grey suit jacket in one of the restroom's mirrors, but stops and narrows his eyes at me.

"And turn this room into a butcher shop?" he states. "No, thanks."

I ground my teeth. "It's what he deserved," I argue.

"For calling you a bitch?"

"Among other things."

Jayce sighs. "Look…" He faces me fully. "Chase was generous enough to grant us and Solo an open ground for our kills tonight, and Waleed's influence can only keep things under wraps to a certain extent. I understand that bringing these bastards pain is fun, and I fucking *love* watching you deliver justice, but if we can avoid that for once – especially tonight, when we still have 2 more kills to perform – then we should definitely give it a shot, don't you think?"

I scowl and cross my arms across my chest. "*Nope*," I say.

Jayce's mouth quirks up as he fights a smile. "Asshole."

"Fuck you."

"No, thank you."

I roll my eyes, and Alex chuckles at Jayce and I. "*Real Housewives* could *never*." He then walks over to Jayce, rises to kiss him on the lips, and places an elbow on his shoulder before looking at me.

"Jayce is right, though," he tells me. "Let's just be quick and neat, and leave before some random elite sees us and creates a situation of panic in the building. Because escaping *that* would be a mess, but leaving with our hands clean and the job done – it doesn't sound so bad, now does it?"

I glance at the cyan suit he's wearing. "You just don't want any blood on this…" I vaguely gesture at him. "Do you?"

He arches a brow. "So what if I don't? It's a Tom Ford original, okay? Cost me a shit ton."

"Focus, boys," Varsha says as she walks over to us. The knee-length red dress she's wearing complements her golden skin perfectly, and her short hair is parted sideways, which makes her appear classically elegant.

She casually places a heeled foot on top of Andres's stomach and waves a phone in front of her. "I've just texted Tomas from Andres's cell, asking him to meet here."

"Did he reply?" I ask.

Varsha nods, then glances at the phone before reading, "*Be there in 30. Should I bring Rizwana?*"

"I'm pretty sure he thinks Andres wants to discuss their latest shipment of girls that Waleed has already interjected," Alex provides.

"Highly likely, but it seems that he's unaware of the shipment's outcome, or of the fact that the girls are in the process of being sent back to their respective homes," Jayce answers, then looks at me. "How do we respond to Tomas's text, though?"

I work my jaw as I think things through.

"We can't stay in the same room for too long," I start by saying. "There's a strong chance someone might come in here and find us out. Because Varsha has already asked Tomas to meet "Andres" here, let's just deal with him ASAP, then move around a bit before we finish off Rizwana." I jerk my head towards the phone in Varsha's hand. "Tell him not to bring Rizwana. Tell him it's something only the two of them need to discuss."

She nods and begins typing.

"What about the body?" questions Jayce.

I pull my phone out and shoot Eddie a quick message. He's on the guest list, thankfully, so the crew and I have one less thing to worry about.

Me: *Send cleanup at the ground floor restroom.*

Eddie: *Any blood?*

The universe is out to get me, it seems.

Me: *No. Just the body.*

Eddie: *Team'll be there in 10. Northwest kitchen entry open?*

Me: *Yup. Solo made sure of it.*

Eddie: *Perfect.*

I slide my phone back into my pocket. "Cleanup will be here in a bit," I tell my crew. "One of us should stay back in case there's an unexpected hiccup. The rest of us can scatter, then meet back here once the cleanup is done with."

"I'll stay," Varsha offers. "It'll be fun to watch the team work their magic."

"You sure?" I ask.

She nods. "Absolutely."

I give her arm a squeeze, then lead Jayce and Alex out of the restroom.

"Text if you need help," I tell Jayce, then look at Alex. "Don't distract him too much."

The latter rolls his eyes. "As if."

The three of us nod at each other, and I watch as Alex all but drags Jayce towards the empty dining room.

I chuckle and turn around, and am about to take a step forward, but stop when I see a flash of silver before me.

I look up, and see a familiar head of pink hair. Her back is to me, and it seems as though she's searching for something. Even in the slightly dim hallway, her well-fitted dress glimmers against her enticing body, resulting in my cock to twitch.

"Where the fuck are you?" she mutters, and continues to look around.

I smirk, intrigued by her evident frustration, and start erasing the distance between us by making my way over to her.

28.
CIGNETTE

My heels press into the plush grey carpet as I take a left and enter another part of the hallway – this one a little more subdued than the previous.

Uncle Chase had told me recently that all this empty space was soon going to turn into a set of dining rooms to match the one that's already on this floor, but until that happens, I'm going to have to endure the dizziness that comes with going around in circles in this godforsaken place.

I rub a hand over my arm at the chill around me. It feels so different to everything else in *Imperia* – like this part of the hallway is an entirely separate entity of sorts.

I let go of a breath, and am about to take a step forward, but stumble a little when a calloused hand wraps around my wrist and turns me around with sudden force.

I gasp, and my clutch falls to the floor with a dense *thump*. I find myself pushed against the ice-cold, wallpapered wall, with my arms risen above my head, and twinkling, all-encompassing eyes looking down at me.

"*Little Swan*," he all but sings those words – recites them with agonizing desire. "You're so goddamn *beautiful*."

His compliment makes me blush, but I can't focus on anything but *him*, because *my God*, he looks even more breathtaking in a suit than he does in his usual vest and jeans. The angle of his sharp jaw is accentuated under the lights in here, and the smirk he has on those full lips of his – it's making me hot with need.

His smooth chest heaves, and his smirk broadens when he sees me checking him out.

"Like what you see, I presume?" he says. "I have to say, though: I'm impressed you found me so early. I mean, I knew you were going to eventually, but this level of swiftness is worth admiring."

"What the fuck are you doing here?" It's plausible how I still hold a shred of commonsense in me to ask him about his presence here tonight, and not completely give into him. I deserve a fucking medal.

Dorran brings a knee forward and parts my legs, then steps closer to me still, lets go of my hands, and cages me in with his arms. "I'm here on contract," he says matter-of-factly, but there's absolutely *nothing* casual about it because…

"You're here – on my *uncle's* property – *to kill someone*?" I question. My voice may have sounded a bit squeaky, but it goes without saying how understandable that is.

Dorran gives me a slightly unhinged smile. "Scared, are you, Little Swan?" He leans in, and our noses touch. "I love it – the smell of fear on you. It's considered a hot commodity in my line of work, and to have you wearing it like this…" He hikes his knee up and brushes it against my underwear. "It's so fucking titillating."

"Just because you've got a suit on, doesn't mean you have to be formal with your words," I tell him.

He chuckles. "And here I thought I could woo you with my extensive vocabulary."

I let go of a breath and swallow. "Dorran…" I place my hands on his chest. "Just…" I sigh. "Who are you here to kill?"

"Not your mother or uncle, that's for sure," he muses.

I grit my teeth and fist his shirt. "Don't fucking mess with me." I shove him a little. "Tell me."

"Rizwana Hafeez, Tomas Aetos, and Andres Salazar," he says. "We've already dealt with Andres, though, so we've only got the other two left."

Up until this moment, I'd only *imagined* Dorran doing his job, but now – in this very moment – shit's gotten way too real, and although I'm worried about his safety, I can't help but be fascinated by what he does. He's in work mode, and I'm so intrigued by the mere idea of him being here to end *actual lives* tonight, that it should be questionable. But it isn't.

Jesus, take the wheel.

"Do you know them?" Dorran asks.

I blink at him. "Huh?"

He purses his lips as if he's trying to stifle a smile. "The kills – do you know them, Cignette?"

I furrow my brows. "Umm, not exactly. I've had very brief introductory chats with them, but no, I don't know much about them. They are, however, far more loaded than some of the other elites here."

Dorran scoffs. "Makes sense. These assholes traffic women to wealthy clients all over the world. They fucking *swim* in money." He rubs a hand over his jaw. "They were ready to ship another group of women outside US borders, but it's a good thing Waleed and his team cracked the location's coordinates before it–"

"Hold on," I cut him off, and my eyes widen in surprise. "What the hell does *Waleed* have to do with any of this?"

"He's our client," Dorran tells me. "He's the one who contracted the kills."

I open my mouth, but nothing comes out.

It's a lot of information to take in. Those elites trafficking women, and Waleed wanting them dead for the same.

I may not be a saint of a human being, but I don't think I've ever wanted to fill my pockets by ruining other people's lives.

Stripping women of their power and independence – just to toy with them and treat them like *objects* – is the ultimate, self-made ticket to the deepest chambers of hell. And I'm so glad Dorran and his crew are here tonight for Andres, Tomas, and Rizwana's deliverance.

"You seem surprised," Dorran notices.

"I'm…" I shake my head. "It's just so…"

"Unbelievable?"

"Intense," I say. "And Waleed is actually a good guy in this situation? But he's…he's banging my *mom*."

"I know."

"You *do*?"

Dorran laughs. "I'm pretty sure all of Riverside does, Cignette."

I snort. "Touché." I then remember my conversation with Waleed from tonight.

"We spoke earlier – him and I," I inform Dorran. "And, I don't know, he seemed concerned after seeing the scar on my face. Like, *really* troubled."

Dorran stiffens, and his demeanor shifts. "Did he touch you?" he asks with molten anger in his voice.

"No." I roll my eyes. "But he wanted to. Mave stopped him, though."

"I would have done far more than that," he grits out.

I chuckle. "I know." I bite my bottom lip as I hook a finger into the waistband of his pants, then pull him closer. "Tell me you've taken precautions and have been careful in coming here tonight," I whisper against his lips, even though his intoxicating warmth is making it hard for me to think straight.

He runs a finger over the left spaghetti strap of my dress and pushes it down my shoulder, his anger now forgotten. He then moves the fabric away from my left breast, and pinches my nipple to the point of pain, making me cry out.

"Would it make you feel better if I say yes?" he whispers back, but with a slight smirk.

"Yes." I close my eyes and breathe in every one of his exhales. "Fucking tell me."

He bends and takes my nipple into his mouth, sucks on it, then roughly tugs it with his teeth before bringing his face over mine again.

"Solo's taken care of it," he says, then pushes his hard length against my stomach. "Fuck, Little Swan; you're driving me *insane*."

I smile and open my eyes. "And we haven't even done anything yet," I say.

"Oh, but I'm about to, because fuck if I'll let you walk away without making that pretty pussy of yours come under my command." With a grin, he gets on his knees before me, spreads my legs wider, and hoists my right leg over his shoulder. "No barriers, remember?" he recalls my demand from our previous encounter.

"No barriers," I concede. I'm out of breath as I watch him lift my dress up through its v-cut, and when he groans after seeing the silver satin of my underwear, I move my hips forward – silently asking him to get me out of my fucking misery.

I don't care if someone walks in on us right now. I'm way past the point of return with this man. I'm drugged on him; exalted by the very essence of him.

"Hold this for me," Dorran orders, referring to the lifted opening in my dress.

I do as I'm told, then suck in a breath when he haphazardly pushes my underwear to the side, parts my pussy lips, and leans in to kiss my clit.

"*Dorran…*" I moan, and use my free hand to run my fingers through his curls.

He grabs my ass and pulls my hips forward, then takes my clit into his mouth before pressing his teeth onto it.

I arch my back at the delicious pressure, and at the dull, throbbing pain in my ribs from my still-healing bruises, then tighten my hold on his hair when he alternates between licking and sucking my mound.

"Keep those eyes on me, Little Swan," he says, meeting my gaze. "I want you to watch me as I fuck you with my tongue." His warm breaths brush against my aching pussy, making my legs tremble a little.

Dorran runs his nose over my bud, drags his tongue over my slit, then circles it on my entrance before pushing it in.

"Fuck!" I cry out. "Harder, Dorran." I keep my eyes on him, and watch as his head bobs back and forth with each unrelenting thrust of his tongue.

The sound of wet skin against my arousal fills the silence around us, and it's so fucking filthy, yet so fucking hot, that I grin down at Dorran.

He returns it, then curls his tongue inside me, making me rise on my tiptoes as a wave of heated pleasure rolls through me.

I grip his hair tighter, then rock my hips in time with his tongue.

Dorran groans. "That's right, sweetheart," he says. "Ride my face. Just like that. Use me without restraint."

I move faster, and he pulls his tongue out of me before bringing his mouth back to my clit again. He sucks on it, tugs at it, then repeats, making me lose sense of everything around me.

"Pinch your nipple," he orders against my skin. "Tell me how hard it is; tell me it fucking *hurts* because of how good I'm making you feel right now." He squeezes my ass, then brings a hand forward before slipping two fingers inside me.

"Oh God," I rasp, and my eyelids flutter as my release builds under his touch. I cup my exposed left breast, then roll my nipple between my thumb and forefinger, only to hiss when a painful buzz zaps through it. "So good."

My hand slips away from his hair, and I press my palm on the wall next to my waist.

"Mmm." Dorran smirks up at me as he finger-fucks me faster, and presses the pad of his thumb over my clit. I can see my cum glistening on his lips and chin, and that drives me mad in a way I can't explain.

He glances between my legs, and his gaze darkens to the point where it looks black when he whispers, "You're dripping down my fucking fingers, Cignette. Christ, look at that compliant pussy stretching for me." He increases his pace.

"Dorran…"

"You close?" he asks, his voice like dark velvet.

"Yes," I breathe, and my body jerks against the wall. "Dorran, please."

His gaze seers into mine. "Clench around my fingers," he commands.

I do, and he in turn increases his speed.

A sharp moan rings out of me at the burning sensation that courses through my pussy, and Dorran chuckles. "You're so pretty like this, Little Swan – taking every bit of the pleasure I'm giving you." He curls his fingers inside me and continues fucking me with them. "Come undone for me. Show me how you let go."

And that does it for me. I press the back of my head against the wall, arch further against it, and tremble as my orgasm takes over. My clit throbs, and heat pulses through my center. My ears buzz, and my vision turns spotty. I close my eyes and scream Dorran's name – completely blatant as I express how he makes me feel, and what he does to me.

He pulls his fingers out of me, grabs my hips, and brings his mouth back on my pussy. He all but laps on my sensitive core, and eats me out with crazed resolution.

His tongue flicks my slit, and every other second, he makes a husk-like noise in the back of his throat that's so fucking hot.

He pulls at my still-sensitive clit, grazes his teeth over it once, then moves back, takes my leg off his shoulder, and gets to his feet.

"Fucking come here," I grit out, and fist the lapels of his suit jacket before pulling him to me and crashing our mouths together.

Dorran laughs against my lips, then opens them for me and kisses me back in a frenzy. The salt-like taste of my cum, mixed with Dorran's hot breaths, drives me wild. I fist his hair and push his face closer to mine as I take his tongue between my lips and start sucking it.

Dorran grunts, then pulls back and grabs my jaw in a firm grip. "Open your mouth," he orders.

I scan his face. His pupils are flared, and the sharp angles of his cheekbones are flushed a lovely shade of red.

I press my knee against his rock-hard cock, then slowly part my lips for him.

Dorran pushes his length against me and leans in before spitting in my mouth. He then stretches my neck and cups the side of it, places a thumb directly over my throat, and smirks down at me. "Swallow it."

I do – hard enough that I feel the press of his thumb in the process.

He spits into my mouth again, then slides his tongue over mine as he kisses me.

I moan and fist his hair tighter, and when he slides his tongue out, saliva and cum strings between our mouths before dropping onto my chin.

"I wanna taste you," I tell him honestly. "God, I want you in my mouth, Dorran."

He groans and licks my chin, and I feel him getting harder against me. "That so?" He wraps his fingers around my throat and squeezes. "Does this trigger you?" he asks, and I know it's because of the imprints my mom had left on me.

I shake my head, because really, I hadn't even thought about it until he'd pointed it out just now. But then again, I lose the ability to care about everything else when him and I are together, so it's only natural to forget.

"It doesn't, no," I answer.

"You sure?" he confirms.

I nod. "Yes."

He smirks. "Good, because I absolutely *love* how your pulse beats against the callouses on my fingers." He squeezes my throat further, making me gasp.

"Kiss me while you choke me," I croak out. "I want you to feel how my breaths stutter for you."

Dorran's chest heaves as he stares at me. "Jesus Christ, woman; you're going to be the end of me." He presses his lips to mine, and maintains a firm hold on my throat as he opens me for him and kisses me feverishly.

I bring a hand over his belt buckle and start to undo it, and run my other hand up and down his straining cock.

"You're so fucking hard for me, Ledger," I whisper against his lips. "Tell me, do you want your dick in my mouth?"

"You fucking know I do," he hisses. "Pull me out, Little Swan. Look at what you do to me."

I bite my bottom lip and start stroking him from over his pants. "Do you wanna come down my throat?" I ask him. "Or do you want it dripping down my face?"

"Cig–"

"I think I'd rather you cream my already wet cunt with your release," I say, and squeeze his base, making him arch into me. "Have it flowing down my ass and thighs."

Dorran grits his teeth and starts fucking my hand. "I'm going to make yo–"

"Ledge?"

It takes Dorran only a brief moment to lift my dress over my exposed breast and swivel in the direction the voice had come from. It happens so fast, that I barely have time to brace myself against the metaphorical avalanche that has collapsed over me – instantly ridding me of my state of arousal.

I fix my dress's straps and turn, only to find Jayce glancing between Dorran and I with a scrutinizing expression on his face. Alex is next to him, and looks just as disheveled as I feel right now. When our eyes meet, he gives me a knowing smirk, and I can't help but wink at him in return.

"What is it?" Dorran asks Jayce, who looks uncertainly in my direction.

"She knows," Dorran tells him, and Jayce whirls on him in surprise.

"*What the fuck?*" he hisses. "You can't just give out the kill names, Dorran! The hell is *wrong* with you?"

Dorran grits his teeth and takes a step toward him. "Let's not do this again, shall we? You know she's an exception."

Something in my chest tugs at his words, and when I glance at him, he subtly brushes a hand against mine.

"And if she rats us out?" Jayce questions. "Will she *still* be an exception?"

"Rat you out to *who*?" I find myself asking.

The boys look at me, and I scoff. "You think I give a shit about these people?" I say. "For everything they've been doing to those women, these elites deserve more than death. If anything, I'd like to help if I can."

"What can you possibly assist us with?"

"Babe." Alex glares at Jayce in warning.

"Guys."

We divert our attention towards the voice, and find Varsha making her way to us.

"Tomas is here," she informs, then gives me a curt nod. "Cignette."

I give her a smile. "Hey."

"What's the status on him?" Dorran asks.

"He's called Andres's cell a couple of times, and appears a bit agitated," Varsha says. "If we don't move quickly, he might leave."

Dorran nods, then bends to grab my clutch from the floor before handing it to me.

"You good to go back to the ballroom?" he asks me.

I take my clutch from him, then bite the inside of my cheek. "I kinda don't want to," I tell him, then suggest something that shocks not only him and the crew, but also myself.

"Can I…join you guys?"

Maybe it's the lack of alcohol in my veins, or the high from the orgasm I just had. Or maybe it's the cold around me that's making me this bold. Either way, one thing's for sure: I've lost my shit. Completely.

"*Abso-fucking-lutely not*," Jayce says, at the same time Dorran chimes, "Fuck yeah."

"Sweet baby Jesus," Alex mutters, then runs a hand over his messy hair.

Varsha simply looks amused as she glances at everyone.

Dorran sighs and looks at me. "Stay here if you don't wanna go back," he tells me, then tilts his head to the side. "Alex and Varsha can keep you company while I'm gone. That sound okay?"

I fix the collars of his jacket and shirt, then give him a reluctant nod.

Maybe he's right; maybe I should stay back. But wouldn't it be great to witness what he does?

"You'll stay *right here*, Cignette," Dorran presses. "Understood?"

I click my tongue. "Loud and clear, sir."

He fights a smile as he assesses me, so I rise on my tiptoes and press a kiss on his lips.

"Stay safe, okay?" I whisper.

He grins. "Never. But I'll try for you."

"I'm serious, Dorran." I kiss him again. "Please."

His expression softens. "Okay." He steps away from me and joins Jayce, and I watch as the two of them turn around the corner before heading into a different part of the hallway.

"Alright, then." Alex slumps onto the floor and presses his back to the wall. He then looks up at me and offers me a hand. "Sit with me, Cigs," he says. "I can call you that, right? Or does *Little Swan* apply to all of us?"

I laugh, and Varsha chuckles. As I lift my dress and settle down next to Alex, she does the same against the wall opposite me.

"I'm pretty sure Ledge will have your ass if you call Cignette 'Little Swan' in his presence," she states.

Alex hums. "Then I'll definitely do that," he sasses. "He's irresistible when he's angry." He gives me a wink. "You should see him when he's in the zone. He could give Leatherface a run for his money."

I tip my head back and laugh again, but this time, it's louder, lighter. And for the first time in my life, I feel like I truly *belong* somewhere. It's something I don't wanna let go, not when I've only just found it.

29.
CIGNETTE

"I was their client," Alex says. "I'd hired Ledge to kill my uncle."

My eyes widen. "I'm sorry, *what*?"

Varsha chuckles. "It's true; he was."

"I'm going to need more than just *that*, guys," I say.

We're sitting on the hallway floor, waiting for Jayce and Dorran to return. And so, to spend the time I have on my hands, I decided to ask Alex and Varsha if they'd be comfortable in telling me how they met Dorran, and how they came to be a part of his crew.

"My parents separated when I was six," Alex starts. "My dad changed states, remarried, and didn't want anything to do with Mom and I. Soon after, the two of us started living with her elder brother, Declan, and things were back to normal. I mean, as normal as can be for a middleclass bunch like us." He lets go of a breath and picks at a lint on his pant. "Declan owned a diner, and Mom and I helped him with it as much as we could. I had to drop out of school because we were always low on cash, so most of my time was spent in the diner's kitchen – cooking.

When I turned 17, Mom was diagnosed with AML – acute myelogenous leukemia. Doctors said it's treatable, but again, we didn't have the money for it. I…" He swallows, and his eyes glaze over a little. "I had to watch her die," he whispers. "She wasn't the strongest person I've known, but she still stood strong against everything that came her way. Until she *couldn't*." He laughs and shakes his head. "But life isn't fair, especially to people like her." He sniffs a little. "So anyway." He waves a hand in front of his face. "A couple of years after Mom passed, I came out to my uncle; told him I'm gay. And, well, let's just say he didn't take it well. He beat me up so bad, I could barely see straight for days. He took me to church, tried to "change" me by showing me "the Lord's way", but I kept telling him that who I was, was never going to change." He's staring straight ahead – at nothing – as if he's lost in a memory from his past.

I place a hand over his and give it a squeeze. "That's awful, Alex. I'm so sorry you went through that."

"Thanks, Cigs. I appreciate it."

A person's sexuality – whatever it may be – is their identity, sure, but it's also their own damn preference and business. *No one* is allowed to judge another for who they love or feel attracted to. Having a sense of independence in one's desires is so important, and so fucking beautiful. It shouldn't be taken away from anyone.

I rub the pad of my thumb over Alex's palm. "Is that why you had him killed?" I ask him.

He clicks his tongue. "No. It was because he tried to lock me inside his diner's walk-in freezer," he says.

"*What?*"

He gives me a rueful smile. "Yeah. I'm pretty sure he thought he could get away with it – call it an accident, maybe – and wash his hands of a *sinner* like me. But unfortunately for him, I managed to escape." He turns his hand and twines his fingers with mine. "I ran to the sheriff's office, told Solo everything, and he offered to assign Jay, Varsha, and Ledge to kill Declan. I immediately said yes, but I also had to keep my mouth shut about everything if I didn't wanna end up underground." He chuckles. "The four of them came over to my house a few days later like they were there to have a fucking friendly dinner or something – all casual and shit – and when Jay saw me, I think it triggered something in him, because he was on Declan in seconds. He finished him off before the rest of us could say anything, and Declan was a skinny motherfucker, so he didn't stand a chance against my guy." He laughs again. "Ledge asked if I wanted to get a farewell retribution, to which I said *hell yeah*, and put all my strength in smashing Declan's head in with the first thing I could find: a metal vase." He grins. "That feeling of his skull cracking open for me was just…" He shudders a little. "*So hot*. I still remember how Jay had looked at me in that moment – like he was transfixed by me. It's something I'll never forget, and it's also one of the reasons I asked Solo if I could join the crew."

I chuckle. "You and Jayce are adorable together."

Alex gags, and Varsha makes a sound between a cough and a snort.

"What?" I ask, glancing between them.

"If you call us adorable in front of Jayce, he'll probably choke you for it," Alex tells me.

"And then have the street dogs feast on your bones," adds Varsha.

I raise a brow. "Seriously?"

"Yup," Alex says. "My husband doesn't do *adorable*."

I shake my head. "When did you two get married anyway?"

"Last year," Alex provides, then grins again. "And in the same church Declan used to take me to, to *cleanse me of the evil inside me*."

I laugh. "Savage."

He joins me. "I know; I had so much fun. And then Ledge killed the pastor because he kept telling Jay and I how we'd sinned in the eyes of God, and my wedding day got *so* much better."

I don't know why, but I can't help but laugh at that. He's so fucking ecstatic as he says all that, that I can't control myself.

Varsha laughs along with me, making me feel validated.

"I'm serious!" he says. "I mean, have you seen the guy ending a life? He's magnificent while he works." He fans himself.

I swat him on the arm. "If you got married to Jayce last year, when did you join the crew?" I ask.

"Three years ago – right before Solo retired."

I turn to Varsha. "And you?"

"Five years ago," she tells me. "Dorran and Jayce found me naked and starving in an alley after my parents threw me out of the house upon having found me fucking a guy in my bedroom."

I open my mouth, but nothing comes out, because *what the fuck?*

Varsha chuckles. "Confusing, I know. The thing is: I'm an Indian, so my family was very conservative when it came to a lot of things. No smoking or drinking, no sex before marriage, etcetera. My dad, especially, was too overbearing. When they found a guy balls-deep inside me, they lost their shit. They tied me up, hit me, and shaved my head, then kicked me out of the house. For days, I lived off of scrapes I found in dumpsters, and I had to stay in the shadows as I had no clothes on me. I think it was a week after living hidden in the alley that Jayce and Dorran found me. They took me in and treated me like family, and if it wasn't for them and Solo, I'd have rotted in a darkened corner, and no one would have even cared."

My chest tightens at her words; at the haunting expression on her face.

I make my way over to her, and Alex does the same.

"I don't think saying I'm sorry is enough for what you've faced," I tell her. "But still, I'm so very sorry, Varsha."

Her expression clears as she smiles at me, then nudges my shoulder with hers. "Thanks. You've been through a lot of shit yourself, so I'm sorry, too, Cignette."

"Me too," Alex adds. "I apologize for not having said it sooner, but I mean it."

A lump forms in my throat, but I swallow it down and give them a grateful nod. "Thanks, guys."

"V, you *have* to tell Cigs how Ledge killed your parents," Alex urges, then sighs. "I wish I'd known you guys then. It would have been so cool to watch their demise."

Again, the three of us laugh at Alex's eccentricity.

"Well, Dorran cut my parents into pieces – while they were *alive*," Varsha provides. "He asked me to watch as he took turns dismembering them, and even though it was a lot for me to witness, I enjoyed every single one of their screams."

"You had every right to," Alex tells her. "It's a good thing we've got Cignette's uncle at our backs, or else we wouldn't have the kind of liberty we do right now."

My breath catches in my lungs as I stare at Alex, and a chill runs through my entire body as I'm completely taken over by shock.

"What did you just say?" I all but whisper the question.

Alex blinks at me. "Huh?"

I'm breathing a little heavily now as the impact of his words finally takes over.

"Cignette?" Varsha looks at me in concern, then places a hand on my shoulder. "Didn't Dorran tell you that Chase and Miranda are our top-tier clients?"

I thought I'd heard it all, but I apparently haven't.

"My mom's involved too?" I sound and feel so dumb right now.

"I wouldn't say they're *involved*," Alex says. "We kill whoever they want us to kill, and in turn, Chase keeps our information out of the law's hands. And, if there's any evidence against us, he extracts and destroys it. It's sort of a barter system, nothing more."

My head feels heavy; my body feels hot. There's a pressure on my chest that makes me wanna heave, but I need to know more, so I press on.

"Did Dorran know about me before last week?" I question.

"The whole of Riverside knows you, Cignette," Varsha states. "But if you're asking for specifics, then no, none of us knew anything about you but your name and relationship to the Adler siblings."

"Is that what you call Uncle Chase and Mom, then?"

"Among other things," Alex chimes, and I can't help but smile a little.

"So, my uncle has contracted kills to you?"

"Your mother as well, yes," he says.

"She's basically a demon, so I'm not surprised, but my *uncle*..."

"He's just as ruthless towards his rivals," Varsha provides. "We've ended quite a few lives for him."

I shake my head in disbelief.

I know Uncle Chase is driven – towards his job, his responsibilities to the county, and towards Mom and I – but I've just now grasped the full extent of his power, and how it works in his advantage when he needs it.

"When did this start?" I ask. "I mean, when did my uncle and mom get involved with you guys?"

Alex huffs a little. "Again: I wouldn't use the word *involved* to–"

"You know what I mean," I say, cutting him off.

"It started when Dorran and Jayce got out of prison," Varsha informs me. "Chase helped in making sure there were no records under their names, and ever since then, he's sort of always kept us out of legal trouble or binds."

I run my fingers through my hair, messing up my hairdo a bit. "And I'm assuming he knows you're here tonight?"

"Yup," says Alex. "Even the security here is aware of our presence. Just not the elites, of course."

"Does our regular security know about you?" I ask.

"Yeah," Varsha tells me, then gives me a faint smile. "And yes, Maverick knows about us too."

I don't know why, but I'm not as shocked to learn that, and it's because I know Mave's #1 priority is to keep me safe. He'd *never* tell me about Dorran and the crew, especially because he knows firsthand how dangerous they are.

Same goes for my uncle, I'm presuming. He wouldn't want me knowing Dorran or getting associated with him in any manner – for the exact same reason as Mave's.

Little good that did, though.

It now makes sense why Dorran chooses to sneak into the estate to see me, but still, there's something I don't understand…

"Why did Dorran keep something like this from me?" I say, then shake my head again. "I mean, I–"

"I kept *what* from you?" comes Dorran's voice, seconds before he reaches us. He's got a piece of paper towel in his hand, and he's absentmindedly cleaning tiny drops of blood from his now stained shirt, but stops when he's in front of us, and raises his brows at me.

"I thought Jayce had advised you against drawing blood tonight," Alex remarks.

"Tomas was getting a bit…fidgety. He deserved that quick stab in the throat, I promise."

Alex chuckles. "*Right*."

Dorran flips him off, then turns his attention to me again. "What did I not tell you, Cignette?"

Jayce walks in and stands next to Dorran, and looks exasperated as he glances around at the four of us.

"What the hell are y'all talking about?" he asks.

"About Dorran hiding the fact that my uncle and mom are your clients," I provide, then bunch the hem of my dress, get to my feet, and face the man in question. "Were you even going to tell me?"

He shoots daggers at Alex and Varsha, then brings his intense gaze to me. "Honestly? I don't know. I *seriously* don't know. Maybe, maybe not. I'm content with how things are, and I didn't wanna fuck anything up."

"Telling me the truth wouldn't have changed things between us," I say truthfully.

Dorran sighs. "I'm sorry," he tells me, and his crew whip their heads at him like he's said something forbidden.

"What?" He glares at them. "I'm capable of accepting when I messed up, okay?"

Jayce makes a grunt-like noise, whereas Alex remains surprised. Varsha, on the other hand, has her signature all-assessing look on her face.

I cross my arms over my chest. "It's not gonna work if you keep things from me," I address Dorran. "I need to know shit so that I'm well-prepared for certain situations."

He nods. "I agree."

"So?"

His brows furrow. "So what?"

Sweet Jesus, gimme patience.

"Are you hiding anything else from me?" I grit out.

He thinks on my question, then clears his throat and slides his hands into his pant pockets.

"Well, Solo doesn't know about us," he confesses. "I've been meaning to tell him, but I don't know how. So, if you see him tonight, just act indifferent. Or better yet, ignore him until I've told him everything."

"And when will that be?"

"Not tonight, I hope," Jayce cuts in. "I wouldn't want the old bastard getting a coronary in a room full of unsympathetic elites. It wouldn't be pretty, even by his standards." He chuckles, and the rest of us join in.

"So…" I let go of a breath and try to sort the facts in my head. "Solo doesn't know about us, and neither do Mave, my uncle, and my mom. Right?"

"Correction: Miranda knows," Jayce says. "Dorran made sure of it, by not only murdering Steven and cutting off his tongue, but also threatening your mom with it, and letting her know that you're under his protection. You should have been there. It was a whole thing."

"Jayce," Dorran warns, his voice clipped and laced with anger.

Fuck me ten ways to Christmas.

"Why *the fuck* would you do that?" I ask. "If Mom tells Uncle Chase about this, the–"

"She won't," Alex states, then gets to his feet and stretches his arms above his head. "If she knows what's good for her, she won't. Besides, Chase thinks Miranda fired Steven for misconduct. He doesn't know about Steven's murder. Not that he'd care if he did."

No wonder she's been ignoring me tonight. Giving her a verbal warning is one thing, but killing her bodyguard and in turn taking away her assurance of being protected? Yeah, that's some next-level shit.

"I screwed up, didn't I?" Dorran asks me, and there's this vulnerability on his face that's so beautiful in its rarity, that I have to blink just to make sure it's actually there.

It is.

"I'm not an ungrateful bitch," I say, then walk over to him before fixing some of the curls on his forehead. "You killed a damn human being for me – just in warning. And, as crazy as it sounds, I appreciate it. It may make me seem fucked up or weird, but I don't care. I like this; I like *us*. I don't know what this is, but it's good, and it's something I want more of."

Dorran smiles. "Don't go soft on me now, Little Swan. You know I'll kill anyone who tries to wrong you or hurt you, and when I do, I'll take all the fucking pleasure in it."

It's a little questionable, but that promise of his turns me the hell on.

Dorran smirks, knowing he's got me, and damn if I'll deny it.

There's a ping of a new message, and a second later, Jayce pulls his phone out. He reads whatever is written in the text, then scowls and looks at Dorran.

"It's Solo. He says it's tough to separate Rizwana from the crowd. She's a social fucking bee, but she's trying extra hard tonight. You think she sensed something?"

"Perhaps," Dorran says, then works his jaw. "We need to isolate her in order to finish her, and she's making it impossible for us to do that. She either knows we're here, or she's trying to win the elites over in order to secure a position in next year's elections. This gala is the perfect opportunity for her to make some fans, after all."

"Maybe I can help," I provide, and the four of them look at me.

"I can pull Rizwana out of the ballroom," I add.

"How?" Jayce asks.

Well, fuck if I know.

"Umm, I'll find a way," I tell him. "Just…give me a chance; I'll come up with something."

"We don't have time for trials, Cigs," Varsha says as she finally gets to her feet. "We have to leave before a former client finds us out and informs the others. Can you imagine the chaos that'll create?"

"Do you have another idea?" I counter.

"We don't," Dorran answers, then gives me a nod. "Do what you gotta do, and when you have her alone, text me the location, and we'll be there."

To my surprise, Jayce gives me a nod as well.

My phone buzzes in my clutch. I pull it out and glance at the screen, then look at Dorran after reading the name flashing on it.

"It's Mave," I say, before receiving the call. "Hey."

Booming music hits my ears, followed by Mave's voice. "Where the hell are you, Nettie?"

"With a couple of *Lure's* sponsors," I lie immediately.

Dorran grins at me, making me roll my eyes.

"What floor are you on?" Mave asks, and I catch a slight slurring in his words, which means he's had a few drinks for sure. "I've been looking for you in the ballroom."

Fuck.

"I'll be there soon, okay?" I tell him. "Please don't stop having fun on my account. I'm fine, Mave."

"Nettie." There's a couple of voices in the background, but I can't understand what they're saying. "Nettie, hold on."

"Yeah, okay."

Dorran rolls his arm in a "*wrap it up*" gesture, to which I nod.

"Hey, okay; sorry about that," Mave says. "You still there, Nettie?"

"Yes, I'm here."

"Uh, yeah, alright. So, where are you? Because I need to come and get you right now."

"You don't–"

"Dorran Ledger and his crew are in the building tonight, Cignette," he says firmly now, like he's suddenly sober. "I need you close so that I can keep an eye on you."

My heart thuds in my chest, and I glance at Dorran and the others.

"Who are you talking about, Mave?" I ask, then quickly pull my phone away from my ear and put it on speaker.

"The Bloody Prince," Mave's voice filters through the phone. "He's here tonight, and so is his crew. I need to know where you are so that I can come get you."

Dorran arches a brow, and a look of amusement takes over his features.

"How do you know they're here?" I ask, even though I already know my uncle has informed every security personnel about the crew's presence.

There's a pause on the other side, and the speaker's audio cracks against the loud music.

"One of the hotel's external guards saw him and let me know about it," Mave answers. "Just…just tell me where you are, Nettie. I'm–"

"I'll be there in a few, I promise," I tell him, then disconnect the call and throw my phone back into my clutch.

I grab a lapel of Dorran's jacket and pull him in for a kiss. "I should go before Mave starts looking for me," I say against his lips. "But I'll text you as soon as I've got Rizwana."

He smirks and kisses me back – hard enough that it makes me a little dizzy. "Show me what you've got, Little Swan."

30.
CIGNETTE

The ballroom is just as suffocating as it was over two hours ago. If anything, the crowd in here has somehow multiplied, making things way more congested than before.

It doesn't help that I had to spend all of 35 minutes listening to a 60-year-old Michelin-star chef talk about how he marinates his chicken, all the while giving me looks that clearly suggested what it is exactly that he wanted to *marinate*.

Disgusting fool.

Mave has been calling me nonstop, but I've had to ignore him. And, whenever I see him glancing around the ballroom from his place at the bar, I blend in with any available group of chatting elites that's close to me.

I have to continue avoiding him, because if he finds me, he won't let me out of his sight, and that'll fuck everything up for Dorran. I can't have that.

I wipe the sweat off my neck and chest as I search the thick crowd for Rizwana, and as I do, Mave swivels in his seat – drink in hand – and starts looking around again.

"Fuck," I mutter, then turn so that I can find a spot to cover myself, but stop when I see Mom and Waleed in conversation with a few elites.

Fucking great. Just what I needed.

I clear my throat and beeline over to them – anything to prevent from getting spotted by Mave.

"Mom!" I all but chirp, startling her.

She whips her head at me with rage on her face, but when I give her a knowing smirk, all color vanishes from her face, and she neutralizes her expression before giving me a wobbly smile.

"Daughter," she addresses me with an icy tone.

I lean in and press a soft kiss on her cheek, then take advantage of our close proximity to whisper in her ear, "Relax, Mommy. Fear isn't exactly a good look on you. Think of the spectators and media in the room. What will they say if they see you like this?" I move back and give her a plastic smile, then quickly greet the elites in front of me before glancing at Waleed.

"I hope my mom's keeping you busy tonight," I tell him.

He winks at me. "In more ways than one."

I laugh, but internally, I go, *ewww*.

I know he's a good guy, but like…still, *ewww*.

"The new winter collection looks absolutely amazing," one of the elites praises.

"Indeed," I say, even though I have no fucking idea what it looks like.

I take half a step back and chance a glance at Mave, and find that he's turned his back to me and is now doing something on his phone.

A couple of seconds later, *my* phone vibrates in my clutch, and I know it's him.

"Excuse me," I say to Waleed and the elites, ignoring Mom's pointed stare, then make my way toward the empty spot just outside the ballroom's balcony.

I pull my phone out and look at the screen, and sure enough, I have a new text from Mave.

I click on it.

Mave: *Do you seriously want me to stumble around this building in search of you? Where the hell are you, Nettie?*

I sigh and glance at him again.

His shoulders are hunched, and the other bodyguards around him are forcing their conversation on him, but I can feel his disinterest and worry even through the distance between us.

I swallow and start typing a response.

Me: *Switch to water, Mave.*

He replies instantly.

Mave: *I will – when you join me at the bar.*

I frown a little.

Me: *I need some time. I'm trying to woo a potential sponsor, but they're playing hard to get.*

A lie, of course.

Mave: *Why? Why the fuck are you helping Miranda by doing good on her brand?*

Me: *I may loathe my mother, but I still care about Lure, Mave.*

It's funny, though, right? I despise the woman who created this empire, but I don't hate the empire itself.

Mave: *Alright. I'll give you an hour, and then I'll come looking for you. I'll crawl if I have to, but I'll get to you.*

I shake my head.

Me: *You're a dramatic drunk, Maverick. I'll be there within an hour.*

Mave: *Fine.*

Me: *Fine.*

A ridiculously boisterous laughter meets my ears, and I immediately snap my head up.

Rizwana.

I may not know much about her, but I do know that laugh. She's known for it, after all.

I scan the room, and spot her near the stage. She's chatting animatedly with an elite I don't recognize, and merely a few feet from her, Christopher Solo is busy conversing with the sheriff and his son. I know he's keeping an eye on Rizwana and looking for an opening to talk to her, but if he waits too long, there's a chance she might slip, and I most certainly won't let that happen.

I brace myself, let go of a breath, and make my way to her.

"And to think, I was going to hire them for my nephew's–"

"Rizwana," I greet her with a clinical smile, then look apologetically at the man she's talking to. "I'm sorry, but can I borrow Miss Hafeez for a moment?"

He nods and excuses himself, leaving me and Rizwana alone.

From what I can remember about her, she's in her late forties, unmarried, and deals with the import and export of exotic spices. One would think a business such as this wouldn't be much profitable, and they'd be right. It's what she does outside of her business that makes her ridiculously rich.

"Miss Adler," she says, then gives me a quick once over, her gaze pausing briefly on my scar before continuing downward. "You look absolutely radiant."

I look at her dark hair tied high above her head, her bold makeup, her black-and-red embroidered kaftan dress, and the gold jewelry she's adorning, then incline my head a little.

"Thank you. And you look positively breathtaking, yourself. I'm in awe of your outfit and aesthetics."

She's a little surprised by my compliment. "I appreciate you noticing that."

"Of course," I say. "Your designer did a lovely job in terms of showcasing authenticity."

Again, she's taken aback by my words, but I mean every single one of them.

She may be a bitch, but I can at least praise the person who designed her dress. But when I think of where most of her wealth comes from, and how she pays for the privileges she has, it makes me sick to my stomach.

And brings me back to the reason I'm even talking to her to begin with.

"You've actually caught me at the wrong time, Miss Adler," Rizwana tells me.

"Hm." I arch a brow. "How so?"

"I was actually about to head out to get some fresh air. I need a break from all of this." She gestures around us. "I think you understand."

She thinks I'm here to breach her pre-election promotion session, which is laughable, because I give zero fucks about any of that.

I glance around, but don't see her bodyguards nearby. A small miracle, really.

"Well, that's a coincidence, then, because I was just about to head out myself," I say, then give her another clinical smile. "Join me, Miss Hafeez; I insist. I would love to know more about your fashion preferences and designer's details."

She opens her mouth, then thinks better of it and shuts it. She knows she can't deny an Adler at an Adler gathering. It makes for a bad rep.

"I would love to," she voices instead, then motions behind me. "Please, lead the way."

"Excellent!" I turn, letting go of a relieved breath, then shoot Dorran a quick text as I start making my way to the ballroom's exit.

31.
DORRAN

"How long has she been gone?" Varsha asks.

"Almost 45 minutes," Jayce answers, then stretches out in the chair next to mine before looking at me. "Should we check in?"

I take a long drag of my cigarette, then shake my head and lean back in my seat. "Give her time; she's got this. Besides, Solo still hasn't been able to get ahold of Rizwana, so let's wait it out a little."

We're sitting around a corner table in the darkened dining room on the ground floor, waiting for Cignette. I know she's taking long, but I also trust her enough to know that she'll get the job done. From what I've seen, she isn't one to give up easily.

I take another drag, then close my eyes and let it out slowly. The smell of tobacco and smoke hits me, and I sigh a little.

"Are you trying to trigger the fire alarm?" Jayce questions, irritation clear in his voice.

I pop open an eye and glance at him. "It's not on my list of agendas for tonight, no."

Alex and Varsha, who are sitting opposite us, laugh in unison, but stop when Jayce glares at them.

"Quit being so restless, man," I say to him, then offer my cigarette to him. "Try not to let your nerves get to you."

"We're running out of time."

"What time?" I ask, then turn sideways to look at him proper. "I don't see the need to rush things."

"If someone were to come in here–"

"It'll be their funeral," Alex says. "Like Dorran said, babe: relax; try to lighten your head a little."

Jayce sighs and takes a pull from the cigarette, and I watch as his shoulders slump when he exhales the smoke.

"Feel better?" I ask.

"Fuck yeah," he mutters, making me chuckle.

My phone buzzes with a new text.

I swipe it off the table, glance at the screen, and say, "It's Cignette." I then open the message, and grin after reading it.

Cignette: *I've got her. 1st floor dining room.*

Me: *omw.*

"She did it," I tell my crew, then get to my feet and button up my suit jacket. "Buckle up, guys; it's time to kill a bitch."

32.
CIGNETTE

"I'm very lucky to have hired him before someone else snagged him," Rizwana is saying, but just like the last few minutes, I zone her out and stay alert as I lead her towards the dining room.

Now that I have her, things are starting to feel realer. I'm literally leading this woman to her death, but still, I don't feel an ounce of sympathy towards her, or hesitation in doing what I'm about to do.

"Very lucky, indeed," I state absentmindedly, then take a sharp left from the 1st floor railing.

My heart is thudding so fast that I can feel it at the base of my throat, and my hands feel slightly clammy, making it hard for me to keep a consistent grip on my clutch.

"Where are we going?" Rizwana asks, and I think I hear suspicion in her voice. "There's a perfectly open spot for air just behind us."

I let go of a calming breath through pursed lips, then put a bright smile on my face before turning around to face her.

"*That?*" I gesture towards the divan I'd sat on earlier. "Well, it's too public for me. I'd rather no one disturb us while we talk."

Her eyes narrow as she assesses me, then something in her demeanor changes, and she gives me a smirk. "I'm fine with the idea of having some privacy, if that's what you're looking for."

Oh, dear Lord. She thinks I'm into her. Well, if it works in my favor, why the fuck not?

"*Now* you get it." I wink at her, then jerk my head towards the hallway. "Follow me," I say, then practically rush in the dining room's direction. Once inside, I don't stop until I've crossed half the room, and when I turn this time, I find Rizwana glancing around the quiet, dark expanse with an impressive look on her face.

"I like it," she praises, then eyes something over my shoulder. "And it's got a view."

I follow her direction, and find a beautiful archway on the furthest wall, that not only showcases the violet sky and shimmering stars, but also *Imperia's* illuminating entrance.

Hands cup my waist, and I feel the heat of Rizwana's breath against my ear, which makes me stiffen.

"You're a pretty little thing, aren't you?" she says a bit hoarsely. "Wanting to sneak into an empty room with me like this." Her hands travel up and cup my breasts. "You want me to touch your pussy, princess? You want my fingers inside you, fucking you till you're coming all over them?"

I close my eyes and will myself not to shiver. I wanna jerk away from her, but in doing so, I might provoke her to leave.

All I have to do is wait; bide my time. Dorran will be here soon, and then, all of this will be over.

Rizwana parts the opening of my dress and brings her fingers dangerously close to my underwear, and I swallow the dryness in my throat in order to avoid coughing.

"If I slip a hand inside you right now, will I find you wet for me?" she whispers. "Will you beg me to put my mouth on that cunt of yours?"

My body fails me and starts trembling a little, but I stay rooted and wait.

Patience – I have to have patience.

"Look at that. You're turned on, aren't you?" Rizwana misreads my body language, and it only spurs her on. She starts pushing her hand in through the waistband of my underwear, but a sharp *bang* of a door slamming shut makes her stop abruptly.

"I wouldn't do that if I were you," comes a voice that immediately slithers itself over me; wraps itself around me. "You're touching a woman who's *mine*."

Rizwana pulls back, and I promptly step away from her before pivoting on my feet.

Dorran is standing a short distance from us, with his hands in his pant pockets, and his crew by his side. He gives Rizwana a look that's laced in flesh-tearing ice, and I can't help but admire him for the way he looks right now.

Dorran is night personified – a blanket of darkness that overpowers everything in its path.

"Ledger," Rizwana all but spits his name. "Fancy meeting you here." She appears both shocked and terrified, but it's impossible to say which of the two emotions takes precedence over the other.

Dorran tilts his head and gives her a smirk. "Hey, Riz; sup?"

She scoffs. "Didn't know you'd recruited a posh bitch in your group of fuck-ups." She glances sideways at me to emphasize her point.

Dorran starts reducing the space between us by taking slow, deliberate steps in our direction. "I'll repeat myself to you, but just this once: I'd be *careful* if I were you, Rizwana. Using slurs on Cignette isn't exactly going to work in your favor." He stops directly in front of her, then looks at me and lifts a brow in silent question.

I nod, letting him know I'm okay.

"As if I have a chance," Rizwana says.

Dorran grins at her. "You're right, you don't."

She steps back and starts running towards the dining room's entrance, but as soon as she reaches it, Varsha tackles her and drops her to the ground.

Alex hops onto a nearby table, and starts swinging his legs as he watches Varsha punch Rizwana in the face.

Dorran sighs and rolls his eyes, then lifts my chin. "You look a bit shaken, Little Swan."

I swallow and shake my head. "I'm alright."

He runs the back of his fingers over my jaw, then leans in to press a long kiss on my lips. "I'm glad," he whispers, then moves behind me before wrapping his arms around me. "You wanna watch as Jayce ends her?" he asks, then gestures ahead. "Or do you wanna get outta here?"

I swallow again and look at Rizwana. Jayce has a thick chain wrapped around her throat, and she's struggling fruitlessly against it. Something about the strain on her face, and her mere helplessness, intrigues me, and I want to see where it all leads.

"I'll stay," I tell Dorran.

He chuckles. "Good girl," he says. "Jayce?"

He looks up at us. "Yeah?"

"Bring her closer," Dorran orders.

Rizwana continues to struggle as Jayce drags her over to us with a hand on his chain, and the other in Rizwana's hair.

Dorran places his chin on my shoulder, then parts my dress enough for my underwear to show.

I suck in a breath. "Dorran…" I whisper. "What are you–"

"You trust me?" he asks.

"Of course, but–"

"Good." He cups my pussy, making me arch against him.

Alex and Jayce seem unfazed by what's happening, but Varsha's face flushes pink. She averts her gaze, but I notice a slight smirk on her face regardless.

"Dorran, your crew is watching," I rasp, then bite my bottom lip when he presses the heel of his palm to my clit.

"You're still so wet from the orgasm I gave you earlier," he says. "Or…is it Rizwana's touch that's done this to you?"

"Fuck you for assuming that," I sneer. "I–"

He laughs – a beautiful action that sets me on fire. "So quick to defend yourself, sweetheart." He starts rubbing my center. "Your clit is so fucking hard right now," he states. "Does it hurt when I do…this?" He circles my bud, and I let go of a sharp cry.

"Mm…" He hums. "You seeing this, Riz?" he addresses Rizwana. "This is what you wanted, didn't you? This is what you hoped you could have." He strokes me with fervor, and my stomach knots as my orgasm builds.

Rizwana claws at Jayce's chain, her face now red. "You two deserve each other," she croaks. "Messed up little sluts, both of you."

Dorran laughs again, but this time, there's no warmth in it. His movements between my legs stop as well. "Too bad you can't ship us off somewhere to be whores, though," he says. "We're already too screwed up for your standards."

Her eyes widen, and what happens next is a blur, because I can barely keep up with the chaos that ensues before me.

Rizwana digs her long nails into Jayce's wrists, who groans and steps away from her, his chain falling to the floor with a heavy *clink*. She then pulls out an unusually-thick, strange-looking hair-stick from her bun, and makes to stab Jayce with it, but Dorran slides away from me and rushes in front of Jayce with such speed, that I realize a little late that it's *him* who has taken the brunt of Rizwana's attack.

"Dorran!" I scream, just as Rizwana pulls her hair-stick out from his left side and stumbles to her feet.

"You bitch!" Alex rushes at Rizwana and kicks her in the gut, twists the arm in which she's holding the supposed weapon, and pulls it out of her grasp.

I run towards Dorran, and catch him before he can trip, ignoring the pain that shoots through my ribs as his weight presses against me.

He's breathing a little unevenly, and his shirt is stained red with how much he's bleeding.

He groans and presses a hand on the wound, then leans on me for more support.

Jayce and Varsha are at his side, and the shock on their faces matches the one I'm experiencing right now.

Chairs screech as Rizwana tries to get out of Alex's hold, but he knees her in the face, making her fall to a crawl.

He heaves a breath and spits at her. "You shouldn't have done that," he tells her. "*You shouldn't have fucking done that.*" He bunches her hair and tilts her head all the way back, raises the hand in which he's holding the hair-stick, and brings it down, stabbing her in her left eye.

She screams, and it's a cry filled with so much pain and terror that one would want to look away or flinch against it. But I don't. I watch it; watch *her*. I watch as she's given what she deserves.

Alex stabs the same eye again, and again, and again, and a sick, wet, crunch-like sound fills the air, making me feel nauseous.

But I don't look away, though. It's like I *can't*.

Rizwana's body slumps on itself, but continues to jerk violently each time Alex stabs her eye.

She's dead – just like that.

So fragile is a human life. So easily breakable. Erasable.

Alex roars and moves onto her next eye, leaving the previous one a pulpy, bloody mess. He's in a different kind of zone now, unaware of everything else but his task. He keeps on stabbing – his hand coated in blood and skin.

"Stop," Dorran pants, and tries to stand up straighter, but ends up losing his balance and falling back against my arms.

"Stop," he says again – to Alex, who doesn't seem to have heard him. "*Fucking stop!*"

Alex finally, thankfully, listens, and lets go of Rizwana. As her lifeless body all but drops to the floor, he throws the hair-stick on her corpse and steps away from her.

Dorran groans again. He's sweating a little, and his complexion has paled. "Text Eddie for cleanup," he tells Jayce.

"I've done that already," Varsha says. "And I've sent Solo an SOS, letting him know you've been injured."

Dorran nods, then straightens again. "We need to…get out of here," he grits out. "All that noise could have attracted unnecessary attention."

My eyes sting as I notice the exertion on his face. I glance at his hand on the wound – now covered in his blood – then look at Jayce. "Hold him."

He immediately switches positions with me, and as I step away from them, I hear Jayce say, "I'm sorry, Ledge; I fucked up," to Dorran, who grunts and replies, "Just don't let me bleed out, and we can call it even."

I walk over to the nearest table, grab its white tablecloth, and place my clutch on one of the chairs. Dorran and his crew watch me as I tear the tablecloth into two long pieces, fold those pieces into thick rectangular blocks, then walk back to them.

"Take your hand away from the wound," I tell Dorran, then glance at Alex. "Grab another tablecloth and tear it in half for me."

He nods and gets to work.

I look at Dorran's left side, and, because his hand isn't covering it, I can see the wound quite clearly. The outer shell is swollen, and the hole is as wide as a bullet wound would be, but in his case, there's no actual bullet to stop him from bleeding out.

I swallow and press the cloth pieces over the wound, and Dorran cries out – a sound that's so sudden it makes me jolt.

"I'm sorry," I say, then glance at him. "I'm so sorry."

"This won't be enough, Cignette," he tells me.

"I know. But it'll be enough to get you out of this place without losing too much blood."

His eyelids droop a little as he scans my face. "Thank you," he whispers.

I cup his jaw and kiss him once. "Don't. I just want you to be okay."

"I will be."

I move back. "That better be a promise."

He chuckles – *tries* to, more like – but ends up hissing in pain.

"You're so damn corny, Little Swan," he muses.

"Fuck you," I counter, then roll my eyes.

"Here." Alex comes to stand next to me, and offers the requested tablecloth pieces.

"Wrap one of these around Dorran's waist," I tell him.

Varsha lifts Dorran's jacket from behind, and Alex starts wrapping the cloth around his waist. Jayce steps closer and support's more of Dorran's weight on himself. With the folded pieces still covering his wound, I pull my hand away, just as Alex secures Dorran's left side with our makeshift bandage. I take the other piece from him and wrap it over the first one, tightening it overall.

Dorran grunts again, but says nothing.

I tie the ends of both the pieces into a knot, then sigh and take a step back. "This'll do for now." I then look up at Dorran, and when he gives me a lazy smile, I swipe the sweat off his brows, fix his disarrayed hair, button-up his suit jacket, and return his smile with one of my own.

"Let's get you outta here," I tell him, then grab my clutch and brace myself as I start making my way towards the door.

33.
DORRAN

It's uncomfortable as fuck here, and the pain in my side isn't helping one bit.

The five of us were almost at *Imperia's* exit, but an elite interrupted our path by approaching Cignette and deciding to engage in small-talk with her. It's a relief that my crew and I were a few steps behind her, and were able to take cover behind the foyer's stairs before we could be spotted. Still, I'd have much rather gotten out of here than hide and spend another moment inside this fucking hotel.

Rizwana's attack had been an unwelcoming surprise. Me of all people knows how deadly some of the mundane things we use in our day-to-day lives, can be. I killed my mother with a goddamn nail file, for fuck's sake, so for Rizwana to use a hair accessory – most definitely custom-made for her protection – is kinda plausible.

Unexpected, too, but I guess that was one of the intentions with which it was made.

I glance at Cignette again, and scowl at the sleazebag who just won't let her go. She's trying to wrap up their conversation by physically stepping away from him, but he keeps shifting closer to her. If I wasn't feeling like I could drop and fall asleep at any moment, I'd have cut the fucker open. But alas, he gets to live.

I give Alex, who is standing next to me, a once over. "I thought you didn't want any blood on your Tom Ford," I tell him, then jerk my head at his chest, where Rizwana's blood is splattered over his shirt, and the lapels of his jacket. "This looks an awful lot like the opposite."

He rolls his eyes. "First of all, shut the fuck up, and secondly, no one hurts either of you assholes and gets to live, so *yeah*. Tom Ford be damned; that bitch deserved what I served."

I smirk and ruffle his hair. "That is true." I then click my tongue and gesture vaguely at Cignette. "Text her and ask her to change the exit route," I say. "Ask her to move towards the kitchen."

He nods. "You got it." He pulls his phone out and does as I've asked.

I shift under Jayce's hold and try not to curse as a throbbing pain ignites my left side.

Fuck Rizwana and her dead ass.

Cignette's phone pings with a text, and I watch as she pulls it out, reads the message, and then looks up at her admirer with an apologetic smile. She tells him she has to go, and he nods and gives her a lust-filled grin before finally getting out of her personal space. She touches his arm and says goodbye, and I grit my teeth when the asshole takes that as an opportunity to check her out.

Cignette pivots on her feet and beelines for the kitchen, relief clear on her face.

I step out of Jayce's hold. "I'll manage on my own until we're outside," I tell him. "Don't want the waiting staff to get suspicious."

His jaw ticks – a clear sign that he wants to protest. He doesn't, though, and instead just nods.

I start making my way towards the kitchen, and with each press of my left shoe on the carpeted floor, pain shoots through my side. It's hard not to let it affect my gait, but I'm trying. I know I'm limping a little, but we're very close to getting out of here, so I can't fucking slow down now.

We reach Cignette, who is standing outside the kitchen. She gives me an uncertain look when she sees me walking on my own, but I give her a nod and gesture behind her. She sighs and turns, then pushes open the kitchen's revolving door before leading me and the crew inside.

Every single staff member stops what they're doing when they see her, and a chorus of "*Good evening, Miss Adler*" and "*Can I get you something, ma'am?*" fills the room as Cignette clears a path for us.

None of the staff even remotely notices me or the crew; they're all too busy swooning over Cignette. And, as we reach the kitchen's exit, I notice that a few of them sigh in evident longing when Cignette passes them by. If this moment could be played in slow-motion, it'd make for a hilarious SNL act, and if I wasn't so damn amused by these fuckers, I'd have pulled their sockets out of their heads and shoved them into their drooling mouths.

I'm full of threats tonight when it comes to my Little Swan, aren't I?

Cignette hurries out into 17th Ave, then turns right.

The crew and I follow her, and now that I'm walking on rock-hard ground, the pain in my side has only multiplied. But thankfully, Jayce wraps an arm around my waist and guides my steps forward.

"You don't have to do this, you know," I tell him.

"I'd rather you not fall on your ass and make a fool out of yourself," he jokes, but I can see the guilt on his face for how things turned out during the kill.

"Beating yourself up about what happened won't change shit, Jay."

He meets my eyes. "It won't, but it'll help me hate myself for what I let happen, at least."

"Don't do that to yourself," Varsha says. "It was an accident; it wasn't your fault."

"It was *stupid* – that's what it was," he spits out.

"And it's in the fucking *past*," Alex adds. "We dealt with it, and it's over. No reason to let it overcome the present."

Jayce doesn't respond to that, but he does relax his posture a little.

The last thing I want him to feel is guilt. We weren't aware that Rizwana was armed, nor had we hoped that she'd fight back. It's things like this that make our job unpredictable, and even though I prefer to avoid collateral damage, in this case, I'm glad it was me and not Jayce or the others.

We enter the parking lot, and Cignette suddenly stops short when she sees Solo ahead of us. He's leaning against his SUV, and when he glances up and sees her, his expression morphs from one of worry to one of complete stupefaction.

He instantly glares at me, knowing without words that Cignette's presence here is on my account, but I shake my head at him.

He opens his mouth to say something, but I raise a brow and shake my head again.

He clenches his jaw, and his nostrils flare as he continues to glare at me, but he thankfully says nothing.

I nod at Jayce, and he lets me go. Grunting a little, I make my way to Cignette, and place a hand on her lower back. "Hey."

She looks up at me. "He wants to kill me, doesn't he?"

I grin. "If he does, then I'd love to see him try."

Solo scoffs, making me grin wider.

"Did you drive here?" I ask Cignette.

"No. Uncle Chase had one of our Limos pick me and Mave up."

I nod. "I can drop you home," I tell her, to which she immediately shakes her head.

"I'm coming with you."

"But your bodyguard–"

"Won't be a problem," she says. "I'll talk to him."

As if on cue, her phone rings, and when she pulls it out of her purse and looks at it, I know it's Maverick before she can even confirm it.

"It's him," she says, then excuses herself and walks towards the other side of the lot to receive the call.

I reach my Harley – that's parked next to Solo's SUV – and take a sharp breath in before quickly straddling it. It's only when I settle onto it that the ache from my wound registers again, but I try not to let it get to me and pull my keys out of my pocket.

"You sure you good to drive?" Solo asks. "Varsha or Alex can bring it over instead if you're not comfortable."

"I'm fine," I tell him, then push my hair back and stretch my neck side to side.

A bout of silence follows, and I watch as Jayce, Alex, and Varsha get into the former's jeep, while Cignette continues to speak on the phone. Her voice has elevated a little, and even though I can't make out what she's saying, it's obvious that her and Maverick are having an argument.

"You know you've messed up, right?" Solo says after a while.

I smirk at him. "I knew I'd fucked up, and was utterly fucked, when I first got a taste of her."

Solo's jaw tightens at my words, and he purses his lips a little. "She's an Adler, Dor. A fucking *Adler*." He sighs and places his hands on his hips. "It could have been anyone – *anyone* but her."

"But it *is* her," I tell him, and make sure I'm looking him in the eyes while I do it. "It's *her*, Solo, and nothing you say to me is going to change that."

He searches my face, then snorts and shakes his head. "You're fucked," he muses, then chuckles. "Goddamn you, Dor. You've dug a hole for yourself, and now the rest of us will fall right into it with you and your little Barbie."

I scowl. "Why do you guys keep calling her that?"

He seems confused by my question. "Keep calling her *what*?" he asks.

"A *Barbie*," I sneer.

"Because she fucking looks like one," Solo states. "Pink hair and shit – I don't know."

I roll my eyes. "How insightful."

"You fucking asked."

"My bad."

He pauses and looks at me. "I'm serious, though; you're putting the entire crew in danger."

"They know what they're getting into," I say. "Besides, you know I wouldn't have risked things if she didn't mean shit."

He crosses his arms across his chest. "And why, exactly, *is* she the shit?" he asks.

"Because she's a reflection of who I used to be," I answer easily. "And I may sound crazy, but I find myself being...I dunno, gravitated towards her every time we're together. Like calls to like, and all that."

Solo sighs again. "I get–"

"Dorran?"

Cignette walks over to me, and even though she seems troubled, she gives me a barely-there smile. "I'm sorry for interrupting," she says to Solo, then looks at me again. "I'm ready to leave when you are."

I push a few errand strands of her hair behind her ear. "He's pissed at you, isn't he?" I ask, but only because I don't like the idea of her being upset.

She lifts a shoulder. "I wasn't exactly receptive to his concerns, so he's got every right to be mad."

"What reason did you give him anyway?" I question. "I can't imagine he let you go that easily."

She swallows. "I told him I was going home with a potential sponsor."

"The supposed sponsor's home, you mean?"

She nods. "Yeah."

"Did he ask for a name?"

Cignette bites the inside of her cheek and shifts on her feet. "I made one up." When I lift a brow in silent demand, she exhales in exasperation and says, "Ivan Caruso."

I smirk. "*Yikes*."

She rolls her eyes. "Shut your face; it's the only one that came to mind at the time, okay?"

"And what a name it is," I say. "Full-on mafia vibes."

She makes a small sound in the back of her throat, and Solo coughs in the background.

"Be grateful, you stunted dick," she tells me. "I'm doing this for *you*."

"I know." I run my eyes over her tensed shoulders, and the sweat on her forehead. "I'm sorry. I didn't mean to contradict your intentions."

"Don't." She clicks her tongue and licks her lips. "I just…I didn't mean to snap. I'm fucking sorry."

"Hey." I lift her chin. "You can change your mind," I tell her honestly. "I can still drop you to the estate."

She shakes her head, and her posture slackens. "I'm coming with you," she repeats herself from before. "I just…I need to know you'll be okay."

"He's too stubborn to die on us, don't worry," Solo adds, and earns a glare from Cignette in return.

"I'm going to pretend you didn't just say that, Chris," she says to him. "For your own safety."

Solo blinks at her – a little dumbfounded by her threat.

I chuckle, then put the key into my Harley's ignition before twisting the throttle. "Hop on, Little Swan," I tell Cignette, "before Maverick tracks your phone and fucks shit up for us."

She lifts her dress and straddles the Harley. "Well, he can fucking *try*, that stubborn asshole."

I chuckle again. My *God*, she's on fire tonight. And it's hot. All kinds of hot.

"Atta girl," I praise, then turn the Harley around with a resounding screech before speeding it out of *Imperia's* parking lot.

34.
DORRAN

"The stitches should dissolve within two weeks," Dr. Myers says. "Make sure to change the bandage after every shower, and keep the stitches as dry as possible. We wouldn't want them getting infected, or worse." He pushes the waistband of my navy-blue sweats down a little so that it doesn't press against the bandage, then clicks open his pen and starts writing something on a prescription paper. "You can take Ibuprofen for the pain, but – and that's a *huge* but – if the pain is too much to handle, here's something stronger." He hands me the prescription, which I pass on to Solo, who is sitting in a chair next to my bed, with Jayce on his right.

Dr. Myers is a general practitioner at the Riverside County Hospital, and the only one me, Solo, and the crew call upon for medical assistance when we need it. He's been a trusted ally of ours for years now, and his penchant for loyalty is nothing short of admirable.

He closes his bag and gets to his feet, and when Solo offers him a thick wad of cash, he accepts it eagerly. He then gives the three of us a quick nod, pockets the money, and deftly takes his leave.

"You feeling any pain right now?" Solo asks.

I'm lying in my bed, so I shift a little and turn my head so that I can look at him. The moon casts a faint shadow on the back of his head through the massive floor-to-ceiling windows behind him, and I can see the outside world on complete display for me – noiseless and paused for the night.

My loft is a simple yet thematic blend of comfort; completely wood-made and warm. My sanctuary of sorts. There's a living room, fireplace, and a kitchen, along with a small set of stairs that lead up to my bedroom – which is just as minimalistic. It's got floor-to-ceiling glass windows on the right – my favorite – a king size bed, an attached bathroom, and a fireplace with a TV right above it.

Like I said: simple yet comfortable.

"Nah, I'm good," I tell Solo.

My wound feels kinda numb right now, thanks to the gel Dr. Myers injected into it before stitching it close. I also feel a little queasy, but he says it's an aftermath of the shock I must have experienced after being stabbed.

When I drove Cignette to *Finesse* an hour ago, I was pretty close to passing out. Again: the shock of what happened was settling in, and it was paralyzing my nerves; making me feel light-headed.

It's funny, though, because when it *did* happen, I didn't think too much of it; just about getting out of *Imperia* before me and the crew were spotted. But I guess my brain triggered my body to act in a certain way, and now that everything is over and done with, shit is finally starting to affect me.

Dr. Myers was waiting for me and the crew by the time we reached *Finesse*, and the minutes that followed after Solo and Jayce carried me up to my loft, went by in a blur.

I stare at the wooden ceiling – an exact replica of the walls and flooring in my loft – and sigh.

To say that I'm lucky to have Solo and my crew in my life would be an understatement. There's not much to be grateful for in my line of work, so the fact that I have an entire group of people by my side – one I consider *family* – is something I'll never take for granted.

"You sure you don't want an Ibuprofen or somethin'?" Jayce inquires.

I face him and shake my head. "All good here, don't worry." The air conditioner above my bed makes a muffled buzzing sound, and a wave of ice-cold air hits my naked chest and upper body, resulting in a sharp sting of pain to shoot through my fresh stitches.

"Can you turn this off, please?" I tell Jayce, and gesture at the AC. "Fucker's making my side hurt."

He does as I've asked, and when he settles back down next to Solo, the latter leans forward in his chair and gives me his full attention.

"You feel coherent enough to talk?" he asks me.

"For fuck's sake, Solo, not *now*," Jayce interjects. "You can do this later; let him rest tonight."

Solo glares at him. "He was stabbed tonight, Jayce," he hisses. "Fucking *stabbed*. Never, in the sixteen years of us working together, has something like this occurred. So no, I *can't* do this later, because I need to know what the hell happened with Rizwana – right fucking *now*."

"I–" I start, but Jayce cuts me in.

"It was my fault."

"Jayce," I say in warning. "*Don't*."

Solo glances between us, then focuses on Jayce. "Elaborate."

Jayce tells him everything – from Cignette's involvement to Alex killing Rizwana after she attacked me, and by the time he's done, Solo's expression holds something I can't exactly put a name to.

"You involved Cignette into this…" he *states* rather than *asks*, and his voice is so icy that it puts even my air conditioner to shame.

"She wanted to help," Jayce provides, at the same time I say, "You were taking way too long in getting Rizwana alone, and Cignette merely wanted to speed things up for us."

Solo takes turns to properly shoot daggers at both Jayce and I, then runs a hand over his mouth before letting go of a frustrated breath.

"I want to strangle the two of you right now," he begins, then shakes his head. "I wanna fucking blow your heads off."

"Uh, I think I'll pass on that offer, thanks," I say, then yawn behind a hand. "I've spent way too much money on this loft, so I'd very much prefer not to stain it with blood and…brain particles." My eyes droop for a moment, but I snap them open just as quickly.

Fuck, I'm tired.

Solo gives me a razor-sharp glare. "Don't fuck with me right now."

Jayce clears his throat, and when I glance at him, he shoots me a quick '*What the fuck?*' look.

I sigh and click my tongue. "Look, Cignette was merely *assisting*," I tell Solo. "And she did a damn good job of it."

"So, what, she's part of the crew now?" he hisses. "You want me to throw her a welcoming party or some shit?"

My nostrils flare, and I grit my teeth. "I didn't mean th–"

"Of course you didn't," he spits at me. "Because you haven't been thinking with your head since you got involved with her. A fucking *Adler*, for Christ's sake." He rubs his jaw like it has personally offended him, then shakes his head again. "Fucking her is one thing, but bringing her into this – into our *work* – that's too much, Dor. She's a liability, at best, not to mention, our benefactor's *family*."

"I thought we'd already established her importance, but if you want me to, I can readily jog your memory for you," I tell him darkly. "Besides, we don't owe our choices to Chase; we haven't been living off his goodwill. For everything he does for us, we pay him back with the blood of his enemies. Him and us – we're on equal footing."

"Don't sass with me," he sneers. "You and I both know how merciless Chase is. We've killed people for all but *nothing*, just because he *wanted* us to kill them. Once you get on his bad side, you don't fucking survive."

"I think you're underestimating our strength as a unit, Solo," Jayce says. "I think we can take on the odds – whatever they might be."

"And you think it's always about strength and numbers with that guy?" Solo counters.

I narrow my eyes and assess him. His white shirt is stained with sweat, his hair is slightly messy, and his posture is somewhat stiff.

"You're scared, aren't you?" I deduce.

He laughs and leans back in his chair. "I'd be stupid not to be."

"Why?" I ask plainly, because I've never considered equating the term fear with Solo. Ever.

"Because I don't want to be put into a situation where I'm forced to do something I'd never want to do," he admits, and his eyes darken. "I'll die before I'm pushed to that limit, but I'd much rather things don't come to that." He'll die before he lets Chase order him to kill me for what I've dared to do, is what he means.

"If it *does* come to that, you won't have to be the one to end things," I tell him. "You have my word, Solo."

"Ledge, come on." Jayce looks at me with an agonizing expression on his face. "Don't fucking say that, man."

"Don't gimme the martyr speech, kid," Solo says to me – his gaze pinned on mine. "For as long as I live, no one gets to touch any of you idiots. You're family, and I protect those I care for."

"God, you're a sappy motherfucker, aren't ya?" I muse, then pause, swallow, and incline my head at him. "But I appreciate it, though – everything you've done and continue to do. You know that, right?" My eyes droop again, and this time, it takes a bit more effort to pop them back open.

Solo chuckles. "You've already sworn to put me in the grave by being a reckless asshole, so I'm just validating the inevitable by offering myself up as sacrifice. In advance."

Jayce chuckles. "I think I signed up for it before you did," he tells Solo. "So get in line, man; I get the first place here."

I laugh, but it morphs into a yawn. "Fuck the both of you," I mutter, then yawn again. "Righteous little shits."

There's a knock on the door, followed by it opening partway into the threshold.

Cignette enters the room, and her gaze zeros in on me.

I run my eyes over her – over her soft pink hair that's tied up in an untidy fashion, her face devoid of the makeup she had on earlier; the white Geralt of Rivia hoodie she's wearing, and her exposed thighs and legs. The need to pull her close and watch her gasp is strong, but so is the invisible force that's keeping my ass rooted to my bed.

I meet Cignette's stare and wink at her, and she smirks in response, making me grin.

"I think Jayce and I'll take our leave," Solo starts, and both him and Jayce get to their feet. "You two look about ready to fuck each other, and I definitely don't wanna be here when that happens. Christ knows how much bleach I'll need to wash *that* vision out."

The rest of us laugh, and I flip Solo off as him and Jayce walk out of the loft.

The soft *click* of the door shutting behind them fills the air, and Cignette lets go of a tired breath before climbing into my bed. She props an elbow on the pillow next to mine, then lies down beside me – our feet bumping against each other's.

She slides the fingers of one of her hands into my hair and starts massaging my scalp, while the fingers of her other hand daintily brush the white bandage that's stuck to my left side. A haunted kind of look crosses her beautiful features, and her eyes darken further – as if she's lost in thought.

"Hey," I tell her, then cup her jaw to bring her close to me. "Hi."

She blinks at me. "You have abs," she says, pulling herself out of that momentary lapse.

A surprised laugh leaves me at her words. I pull my hand away from her jaw and place it under my head. "I thought it was a given that I'd have them."

She meets my gaze again, and when I grin at her a second time, her eyes clear over. "Why is it a given?" she asks, then runs the pads of her fingers over every muscled indent of my abs.

"I mean… I'm hot, for one. And I own a Harley. And a garage. And let's not forget that I'm a killer, which also makes me the most dangerous guy in all of Riverside. And I've got the personality of a–"

"Dick-deprived salamander."

I choke on a laugh as I stare up at her, and she looks back at me with a plain expression on her face.

"Excuse me?"

"I said what I said," she says matter-of-factly. "You were turning into a narcissistic version of Shakespeare; I had to put a stop to it."

I chuckle. "Touché."

She rolls her eyes, then frowns as she scans my face. "You look so tired," she observes.

"I mean, I *did* get stabbed tonight," I counter. "Also, you look so fucking sexy in that hoodie."

She exhales in annoyance. "You're such a…*guy*."

"I know." I yawn, and it's so intense that it makes my vision a bit spotty.

"You need to rest, Dorran," she says, then massages my scalp again. "Get some sleep."

I hum. "Yeah…" The word comes out slurry, and it's followed by yet another yawn.

"You need any meds?" she asks.

I shake my head.

She cups my jaw and presses a kiss on my lips.

I groan, and my cock shifts behind my sweats when I get a taste of her.

I hold her jaw in place and part her lips, then suck on her tongue before merging our mouths in a way that makes it impossible for either of us to breathe. But I don't stop; I continue to kiss her. Because *fuck*, who needs air when I've got her gasping against me like this.

"Dor…" she whispers my name, then punctuates it with a soft kiss before moving back just slightly. "You need to sleep." She nudges my nose with hers, then runs her knuckles over my cheek.

"Will you be here when I wake up?" I ask, and realize that it makes me appear vulnerable. It's not like I care, though, simply because I've been nothing but transparent with Cignette since we started this – whatever this is between us.

She can take my memories, my weaknesses, and my strengths. And, because I'm only human – however ruthless I can be during the times that call for it – I like to believe that I still have a lot of flaws. Cignette can take them all, and I can carry hers, because we're sides of the same coin; a combination of divergence and similarity, molded into sculptures of flesh and bone and blood.

Her face softens as she smiles at me. "Of course," she answers easily. "I wouldn't trade this position for anything." She kisses me again.

I close my eyes and smile against her mouth.

Whoever says morally grey guys don't appreciate tranquility and wholesome moments in their lives, is full of shit. Because I'm as grey as grey goes, and I've still got a boner as hard as a fucking brick from the brief cheese-talk Cignette and I just had.

It's all about enjoying the moment and calming your inner demons – albeit temporarily – and mine drift away without hesitation when Cignette takes over my mind. Deep shit, right?

Yeah, I think so too.

35.
CIGNETTE

He's so beautiful while he sleeps – like a prince of darkness contained by slumber.

It's almost 4 in the morning, and even though I've tried, I haven't been able to get a shuteye. The moment when Rizwana stabbed Dorran keeps playing in my head, and despite being brief, it still makes me shiver.

To me, Dorran is invincible, but what happened at the gala proves otherwise. I'm terrified of it, and *scared* of feeling terrified.

If all of this had happened a week ago, I wouldn't even have known about it, much less cared for it. But now – after everything I've seen and everything Dorran and I have shared – it seems as though we were predestined to coexist; to entangle and become irreplaceable facets in each other's lives.

My phone vibrates in my hoodie pocket. I slowly, tentatively, pull my hand away from Dorran's hair and sit up on his bed, then slide my phone out and open the text that's flashing on my screen.

Alex was generous enough to lend me his spare – and *absolutely priceless*, according to him – hoodie when I'd freshened up in *Finesse's* bathroom earlier. He'd also ordered McDonald's for him, Varsha, and I while we'd waited for Dr. Myers to finish treating Dorran. The mood around us may have been heavy, but the three of us had still managed to enjoy our meal and talk about random shit to help us pass the time.

The glass windows in Dorran's bedroom showcase the sky and the empty street below us, and it's such a peaceful view that it takes great effort for me to pull my eyes away from it.

I sigh and bring my attention to the message Mave has just sent me.

Mave: *You okay? I'm sorry I yelled at you earlier.*

I let go of a breath and press my fingers to my forehead. Fuck, I can feel a headache coming in.

Me: *It's okay. And I'm sorry I lost my temper with you. That was totally uncalled for.*

Him and I had had an argument on the phone when he'd called me while I was in the parking lot with Dorran and the crew. I have to say: I behaved insensitively, and didn't value his concerns at the time because my focus was entirely on Dorran.

His reply is almost instant.

Mave: *You don't have to apologize.*

Mave: *Why are you up, though? Are you still with that Ivan guy?*

A pang of guilt tightens my chest.

I've lied to him in the past about my whereabouts and such, but it never feels good, or gets easy. But it does suck when he takes his job too seriously and tries to suffocate me with the rules, given how well he knows me.

Me: *Yeah. We had a few drinks, and he let me stay over in his guest room.*

I'm gonna go to hell for lying to him.

Mave: *I can pick you up if you'd like.*

Me: *It's okay. He said he wanted to discuss investing into Lure during breakfast, so I think I'll stay.*

Mave: *I still don't get why you're so adamant.*

Me: *I told you: I care about the brand.*

He takes a couple of minutes to reply this time.

Mave: *Fine, but if you need me to pick you up before I start my shift, let me know.*

Me: *You can come in late if you wanna. I'll be here a while.*

Mave: *You're seriously pushing it, Nettie.*

I sigh and type back a response.

Me: *I'll be at the estate by 10. 11 at the most.*

Mave: *9, and that's it.*

Me: *This isn't up for negotiation.*

Mave: *Like hell it's not.*

Me: *Don't make me use the boss card.*

Mave: *I'd love to see you try.*

Now *he* is the one who's pushing it.

Me: *Well, you asked. You'll start your shift at 10a.m. today, and that's an order, Maverick Constance.*

I'm pretty sure he's fuming right now, but it's not the first time, and it most definitely won't be the last.

I pinch the bridge of my nose when my head starts throbbing.

Me: *I think I'm going to head to bed. All that alcohol is getting to me.*

I haven't had a drop of it tonight, but he doesn't need to know that.

Mave: *Please don't tell me you sang in front of that guy. Because if you did, then you should kiss all your hard work and schmoozing goodbye before it's too late.*

I chuckle, but stop when Dorran groans and shifts in his sleep.

Me: *Screw you.*

Me: *But no, I haven't sung. YET.*

Mave: *Lord have mercy on the poor chap.*

I roll my eyes.

Me: *I'm done with you. Bye. Good night. And fuck you.*

Mave: *Night, Nettie.*

I place my phone on the nightstand, then lie down next to Dorran again.

He shifts, then moans as if he's in pain.

I notice beads of sweat on his temples and neck, so I get out of bed and turn on the air conditioner.

I've just placed the remote back on the mantel and sat down on the bed again, when Dorran's eyelids flutter open, and his gaze lands on mine.

"Hey," he croaks. "What're you doing?"

I lie next to him and smile at him. "You're sweating a little, so I was just switching on the AC."

"Okay," he whispers, then closes his eyes.

"Are you in pain?" I ask softly.

He shakes his head faintly, and I exhale in exasperation. He's stubborn, and until he *says* he needs them, I can't force him to take any painkillers. All I can do is ask, and hope that he decides to say yes.

"Okay." I adjust my head on the pillow, and stifle a groan when it throbs twice as strongly as it did a minute ago.

"You're staying, aren't you?" Dorran mumbles, and it's a little incoherent, but still understandable.

I inch closer to him and kiss the sharp angle of his cheekbone. "Don't worry, I'm not going anywhere," I whisper, and can't help but think how unfair it is that I only get to spend borrowed time with him.

If he were any other guy, things wouldn't have been so complicated. But he's the most feared man in Riverside; my uncle's personal executioner. And despite all of that, I still want him. Most of all, I wanna be with him without having to rely on lies, or be haunted by restraints and fear.

And I know I've lost my shit when I say this, but I think it's time that I loop Mave into all of this so that I don't have to continue fabricating people and instances to him anymore, or sacrifice my needs when it comes to Dorran and I.

Fuck, this is going to turn into an absolute shit-show, isn't it?

36.
DORRAN

My eyelids feel leaden, but I still manage to blink my eyes open. There's a flare of sunlight reflecting through the massive glass windows – my daily wake-up call of sorts. I start shifting towards it, all the while groaning at my stiff lower back.

The bathroom door opens, and the smell of my shampoo wafts through the chilly room. I try to turn over, but end up cursing out loud when a pull-like ache cuts through my left side.

"Dorran?" Cignette comes running to me – her hair wet from the shower she's just taken. "What's wrong?" she asks. She's wearing one of my old sweatshirts, and the long, blue sleeves are all but hanging off her fingers.

I use my hands to push myself up, then rest my back against the headboard before facing her. "Can you get me some Ibuprofen? Bathroom, third drawer."

"Of course."

I close my eyes as I wait for her to return. Distinctly, I hear the opening of a drawer, the sound of items being shifted around, followed by the clink of tablets in a bottle, and approaching footsteps.

I open my eyes, just as Cignette walks out of the bathroom, grabs the half-full glass from the nightstand, and hands both the medicine and the water to me before sitting down next to me.

"Thanks," I say after having taken the pills, then place the empty glass back on the nightstand.

Her brows are furrowed as she looks at me. "Does it hurt too much?"

"I'll be fine," I tell her. "I've had nastier wounds than this."

"But Alex said you've never been wounded during a kill – ever."

I sigh. "I haven't, but you forget that my mother was a monster. I've experienced my fair share of bruises during my teens."

Her frown deepens, so I tug at one of her floppy sleeves and urge her closer. "C'mere."

She climbs onto the bed, then straddles my thighs. When I smile up at her, she bends and presses her lips to mine – hot and demanding.

I slip my hands under the sweatshirt and grab her waist, only to realize she isn't wearing any underwear.

"Little Swan…" I breathe against her, and when our eyes meet, hers glaze over.

"Pull your hair up," I tell her.

She straightens, and uses the band around her wrist to secure her hair above her head. She's looking at me with an intensity that's so fucking foreign to me, yet so fucking hypnotic, that I momentarily lose my train of thought.

Cignette is a sight to behold. With the morning light casting bright haloes around her, she's a living portrait of suave beauty.

I yank at the hem of the sweatshirt. "Take this off," I command, and clear my throat at the subtle husk in my voice.

She shifts and does as I've asked, and her pussy presses against my growing erection behind the thin fabric of my tracks, making me groan.

She throws the sweatshirt on the floor, and my chest heaves as I take in her naked body with unabashed desire.

Her skin appears illuminated under the sunlight, and somewhat hides the healing bruises on her ribs. I trace my eyes over the high peaks of her breasts; her dark nipples that are pebbled and begging for attention. Her slender waist is a delight, and her pink pussy is a damn beckon to my growing hunger.

"This, too," I say, and gesture at my sweatpants.

Cignette grins and slides down my legs, then grabs the waistband of my tracks and pulls. I lift a little, and she drags it all the way down before letting it fall to the floor.

She looks at my cock, then, and sucks in a breath when she sees the slightly curved barbell pierced across my crown. The large beads on either side of my dick's head are coated in precum, and as Cignette licks her lips before meeting my eyes, I grin and make a come-hither gesture.

She gets on all fours and crawls the small distance to me, and when she's close, I fist her hair and pull her head back before spreading my legs wider.

"Your mouth – open it for me," I order.

She does.

I use my other hand to roughly cup her jaw, then lean in before tugging her bottom lip between my teeth. "So fucking compliant today, Little Swan," I remark, then spit into her mouth. "Don't swallow."

She grabs the wrist of my hand that's on her jaw, then digs her nails into my skin.

I grin again. "Pull your tongue out."

She makes a sound of protest, but when I raise a brow at her, she does what I've told her to. Her tongue is filled with my saliva, which makes my cock harden further.

I bend and spit into her mouth again, then yank at her hair a second time. "Now, be a good girl and suck my cock," I tell her.

She shudders a little, and moans sharply when I all but shove her face towards my groin.

Cignette drops my saliva onto my cock, then mixes it with the precum before rubbing it over the entire length of me. She takes one of the beads between her teeth and tugs, making my hips buck on their own accord as pleasure zaps through my balls.

"Take me in your mouth, Cignette. *Now*," I say to her, feeling a hot flush creep up my chest and shoulders.

She squeezes my base with unforgiving pressure, then parts her lips before sucking on my crown. She moans, and the sound vibrates against my skin.

I push her head lower, forcing her to take more of me. "Suck harder." Her mouth feels warm and firm, and my spine stiffens with how fucking *good* she feels around me.

She relaxes her jaw and continues to suck, and a few strands of her hair fall out of my grasp, brushing against the insides of my thighs.

I press her face even closer, and she gags. But I don't stop; I keep my hold steady.

Cignette claws at my abs, tries to move back, but it's futile.

"Choke on it," I grit out, then look at the mess she's made on my dick with her drool and tears.

She once again digs her nails into my skin – this time on my pelvis – then takes me to the very back of her throat.

I tip my head back and cry out, because *fuck me*, I feel myself draw up close to my release by that single move alone.

I pull her head back, and she gasps audibly. Letting go of her hair, I let her breathe for a couple of seconds, then wrap my fingers around her throat and bring her mouth to mine.

I kiss her – hard enough that it makes my vision hazy. I kiss her, because she's so damn delicious and I can't help but force her lips apart and thrust my tongue into her eager mouth.

And I kiss her, because I'm a madman; because I'm helpless to her taste, to her smell.

She breaks the kiss, and I grab her left thigh before bringing her over to straddle me again.

I let go of her throat and wrap my fingers around my erection, then start rubbing my crown over her wet cunt.

Cignette bites her lower lip and smirks at me – her dark gaze far more depthless than it usually is.

I smirk back at her, and can't help but admire her disheveled state. Her hair's a mess; her cheeks are tinted red. Her lips are a little swollen, and her eyes still hold tears from the brief face-fucking.

"You're a *vision*," I tell her honestly. "A beautiful illusion come to life."

Her eyelashes touch the tops of her cheeks as she blinks, and her face flushes to a deeper shade of red at my compliment.

"You just *have* to say shit like that to completely contradict your nature, don't you?" she says.

My smirk broadens at her words. "And what exactly is my *nature*?"

She aligns her face with mine. "An unyielding one," she whispers.

I bite her lower lip and bring my cock over her entrance. "Is that supposed to be a compliment?"

She leans in further. "It can be whatever the hell you want it to be." She hisses as she takes me in, then stops halfway before rising a little.

"Make it fit, Little Swan," I tell her. "Because you don't want me to be the one to do it for you, trust me."

She grits her teeth and slides her pussy over my crown, then pushes herself down in a single thrust.

"*Fuck!*" she all but screams, just as I grunt and remove my hold on my dick.

Cignette shudders, then rises again, right before slamming down all the way.

"God, *yes*," I groan. "You take me so fucking well, sweetheart." I grab her ass and spread her cheeks, just as she starts a slow up-and-down rhythm, clenching her walls around me in a way that makes my spine tingle.

"Ride me," I order, then spank her once. "And don't stop until you're done using me."

Her breasts move in time with her hips as she fucks my cock, and every time she takes me in from tip to base, the insides of her thighs slap against mine.

My body contracts in response to her movements, and causes bouts of pain to cut through my left side, but I ignore them.

Our breathing is erratic – a desynced harmony that reverberates through the room.

Cignette rides me faster, and I feel her clench around me. My balls tighten in response – because the constraint around my dick feels so damn *nice* – and my stomach knots as my orgasm builds.

"God, that piercing hits *so* good," she rasps, and starts moving her hips in deep, slow circles. She then wraps her fingers around my throat – surprising me – and puts enough pressure that it stops my proper breathing pattern.

I draw even closer to my release. "Tighter," I tell her. "Squeeze tighter."

She grins and presses her fingers further into my skin, then rocks against me harder. She's so fucking wet that I can feel her dripping down to my sack, and it only serves to make me wild for her.

I'm way past the point of sanity right now, and I can see nothing but my need to let go.

I cup her breasts and pinch her nipples, making her tremble as pain mixes in with her growing pleasure.

She lets go of my throat and fists my hair with both hands, then crashes her mouth down to mine before forcing my lips open for hers.

I groan as I kiss her back, then bring a hand down between us to slap her clit with my fingers.

"Fuck you," she hisses, and tugs painfully at my hair, making me laugh a little. She's riding me with unrelenting speed, and we're sweating, despite the room being cold.

"That's what you get for being a good little slut for my cock," I tell her, then start rubbing her clit because I'm seconds away from my release.

She shudders again, then clenches around me a second time, right before tipping her head back and screaming my name.

My shoulders stiffen; my hips draw up. And just like that, I join her, shooting my load into her cunt.

Somewhere between coming, we start kissing again, and every little whimper Cignette lets out, I swallow it eagerly, because I fucking relish the idea of *me* being the one to have coaxed them out of her.

"Fuck," I breathe, and touch my forehead to hers. She's panting, and her damp body all but molds into mine when I let go of her ass and wrap my arms around her waist.

"Fuck is right," she answers, making me chuckle.

We're silent for a while, with only the sounds of our steadying breaths, and the chirping of birds outside keeping us company.

This shit is too mundane for me – staying entangled after sex, I mean. I've never done this before; never even had the *urge* to. But with Cignette, it's like these things happen naturally. On instinct. I always wanna be close to her, and where this revelation would have pushed me far, far away from her a few days ago, right now – in this moment, after everything I've seen and heard – it feels…I don't know, *okay*. Perfect even, if I dare to be more specific.

My cock's still buried inside her, so when she shifts and starts to absentmindedly run her fingernails over my chest, I feel myself harden again. But it's when I look at the expression on her face that I realize she's deep in thought. Lost in her own mind.

I lift her chin, then search her eyes. "Hey," I say softly. "What's up?"

She sighs and takes my hand away from her face, then places it between her breasts. Again: it's something I'd never let a woman do, but it's Cignette, so it's *okay*.

"I…" She swallows. "I have a crazy thought."

I nod. "Tell me."

She licks her lips and works her jaw. "I think we should tell Mave about us. About everything." She grimaces a little after saying that, as if she's unsure of how I'll react to it.

Honestly, I'm not fazed by it. I don't care who knows and who doesn't. I know what the truth is, and I'm willing to fight anyone who isn't onboard with the idea of Cignette and I. Plain and simple.

"Okay," I tell her. "Let's do it."

Her eyes widen. "Seriously? You won't tell me how ridiculous of a suggestion that is?"

"Why would I do that?"

She clicks her tongue and gets off my lap to sit next to me, and I immediately miss her warmth. I also notice how she keeps her thighs closed in order to avoid soiling my mattress with our combined releases.

It's cute.

"Because Mave can very well tell Uncle Chase about us, and shit could – no, wait, *will* – get out of hand. And I'm pretty sure I don't have to tell you how my uncle'll react to everything."

"But Maverick won't tell anyone anything," I say simply.

Cignette raises a brow. “You seem confident about it.”

I lean back against my headboard and smirk at her. “Sweetheart, that man is in *love* with you, and the last thing he’ll wanna do is put you in any kind of danger, let alone jeopardize your standing in front of your uncle. So, if you wanna tell him about us, then go ahead; I’m okay with it.”

She sucks in a breath. “He’s not–”

“What?” I challenge, then grin.

She glares at me. “He’s *not* in love with me,” she says tersely.

“Right, and I’ve got dicks for arms,” I muse, earning a solid punch in one of said arms from Cignette.

She looks contemplative as she stares at the floor for a few long seconds, then brings her gaze to mine again.

“What about the others?” she asks.

“What of them?”

She pushes her tangled hair behind her ears. “What if they aren’t okay with Mave knowing?”

“How is any of it their problem?” I start, then shake my head. “Cignette, this is about you and me, not *them*. Maverick already knows about all of us; he just doesn’t know about *this*.” I gesture between us. “And, if we want him to know, then it doesn’t matter what Solo or my crew think. It’s *our* goddamn business.”

She again falls into a lapse of silence.

I give her time to either talk herself in, or out of the decision, because I’m fine with either.

“Okay,” she says finally, then exhales heavily. “I’ll call Mave and ask him to come to *Finesse*. That alright with you?”

“Absolutely.”

She purses her lips. “I can’t guarantee he won’t burn the place down the second he gets here, though.”

I laugh, then scratch the area around the stick-on bandage. “Let him try, Little Swan,” I say with a grin. “Let him fucking try.”

37.
CIGNETTE

"*Are you out of your goddamn mind?*" Mave yells, and tires screech against the asphalt when he stops his Range Rover at *Finesse's* entrance before making his way to me.

"What the fuck are you doing here?" he questions with pure rage in his eyes, then gives me a once-over. "And what the *hell* are you wearing?"

When I'd called him fifteen minutes ago and asked him to meet me here, I hadn't waited to hear his response. And yeah, I was expecting him to be mad, but this – this is an entirely different shade of anger that I'm not sure I want right now.

I glance at the sweatshirt hanging off my frame, and Dorran's too-big black boots covering my feet, then look up at Mave.

"What's wrong with what I'm wearing?"

He pinches the bridge of his nose and takes a deep breath.

He's in jeans and a red flannel, which means he drove here from his place. At least he didn't defy my order of staying in and reporting late.

"You." He points a finger at me, then at his car behind him. "Get in there – *right fucking now*."

"Can you just calm down for a moment?" I say, then push my hair away from my face when a gust of ice-cold wind blows it over wildly.

"*Cignette*." There's a warning in his voice, one that brings goosebumps to my skin. Also, he used my name instead of calling me Nettie, which means he's seriously pissed.

"I'm *fine*, if that's what you're worried about," I tell him.

"What I'm worried about right now is getting you out of here before you attract unwanted attention, and I want you to fucking get in my car so that I can take you the hell away from this place." He's seething, and it's absolutely *not* working in my favor.

"Look…" I bring my hands in front of me. "I want you to trust me, and I want you to follow me. There's something I wanna tell you, but I can't do it here."

He narrows his eyes at me. "No."

"Mave, come on–"

"I said: *no*," he grits.

I clench my jaw. "Then you can go back the way you came, because I'm not coming with you."

He scoffs and takes half a step back, then an entire one forward. "You don't get to fight me over this," he tells me. "Do you even know where you *are*?"

"Outside Dorran Ledger's garage and loft," I say easily, earning a look of complete surprise from Mave. "I know exactly where I am."

"You–"

"Are you coming with me, or not? Because I'll only ask once."

"What the fuck have you done, Nettie?" he questions, then swallows before running a hand over his jaw. "Fine," he relents. "I'll give you twenty minutes, and then we're getting outta here."

I sigh. "Thanks." I grab his hand and start leading him to the back of the garage, where there's an emergency door meant only for Dorran and his crew. And me, too, I suppose, given that Dorran gave me the code to unlock it.

I feel rustling behind me, and turn to find Mave pulling his gun out of the back pocket of his jeans.

"Fucking *seriously*?" I hiss.

"I'm coming with you, aren't I? You don't get to comment on me taking necessary precautions."

"For fuck's sake," I mutter, then focus on the door again.

"How do you know the code for this?" Mave inquires when I punch the 7-digit code in, then push the door open.

I don't answer him, and once we're inside *Finesse*, I shut the door behind us before leading him up the stairs that are behind the main counter.

"Nettie, stop." He tugs at my hand. "Where are we going?"

I look over my shoulder. "Just trust me, please," I say.

He sighs in evident annoyance, but nods and follows me.

We reach the top of the stairs, and I pause to collect myself before sliding open the door to Dorran's loft.

Here we go.

Biting silence fills the air when Mave and I enter the living room, and, as soon as he sees Solo, Dorran, and the crew occupying the massive couch before us, he lets go of my hand and whirls me around to face him.

"What the fuck is this?" he spits, then briefly looks over my shoulder. "Nettie, what the fuck is going on?"

"Do try not to be so dramatic, Maverick," comes Dorran's silk-smooth voice. "Cignette, come here." He's wearing a green vest and grey sweatpants, and as casual as he *looks* right now, his tone is giving off completely different vibes.

Mave's eyes widen in shock. "Nettie–"

"Just listen to what I have to say," I plead. "*Please*, Mave."

"We are *leaving*." He makes to grab my hand, but I move back.

"No." I raise my arms to my sides in defeat. "Just…just relax and listen to what I have to say, okay?" He tries to protest, but I cut him off by saying, "That's an *order*."

His nostrils flare as he scowls at me. "This is borderline *madness*, Nettie."

"And I thought you'd be willing to cross the damn threshold with me."

He scans my face – reluctance and confusion still strong on his.

He's quiet for a while, but then swallows and jerks his head forward. "Be quick about it," he finally says.

I nod. "Let's settle down." I walk over to Dorran, who's sprawled on the couch, and grins when I sit next to him.

Mave hesitates. He's trying to balance his emotions right now, and it's pretty clear from his fluctuating expressions that he doesn't trust a single person in this room. Myself included.

"Oh, come on, you goddamn idiot," Solo says to him, then shifts before patting the empty space next to him. "Sit your ass down so that we can get this over with."

Mave cautiously joins Solo – gun still in his hand – then glares at me.

Dorran straightens a little and places his arms on the back of his couch, then widens his legs, which results in our knees to touch.

Mave notices, of course, and bristles visibly.

I lean forward and place my elbows on my thighs. "You'll listen to me," I tell Mave, "and you won't interrupt me until I'm done. Deal?"

He scowls, but nods stiffly.

I take a deep breath in, let it out slowly, then tell Mave everything – from meeting Dorran at *Finesse* for the very first time to get my car fixed, to the events that took place after, including what happened last night, and the names of everyone who currently know about him and I.

When I'm done, I blink at my bodyguard, but his features give away nothing. It's like he's made of stone or something; he's barely moving.

"Mave…" I voice, trying to test the waters.

He blinks back at me, but stays silent, and it fucking gnaws at me.

"Say *something*," I urge.

At my request, the expression on his face morphs to one of pure rage again.

Fuck me.

"Oh, so you're expecting me to *say something* after you've gone and literally *fucked everything up*?!" He practically yells the last three words, making me cringe.

"That's what I've been sayin'," Solo mumbles from next to him, earning a kick in the shin from Varsha, who is sitting to his left.

Dorran shifts and leans forward, bringing his body closer to mine. "Watch your tone, Maverick," he warns in that signature spine-chilling voice of his.

"Or what, fuck-face?" Mave challenges.

Within seconds, the crew is on their feet. "The fuck did you call him?" Jayce says, and starts to walk towards Mave, but Dorran rises and pushes him back.

"Don't." He shakes his head to emphasize his point, to which Jayce's jaw hardens, but he does step back.

Solo is keeping Alex and Varsha in line, who look about ready to tackle Mave to the floor.

Mave stands – seemingly shocked by what he sees – and I follow suit.

"You've doomed me to hell by telling me everything," he addresses me, then puts his gun away. "You could have just kept me in the fucking dark."

My throat tightens as I watch the struggle on his face. "I didn't wanna keep lying to you. I didn't want to have to come up with names and scenarios just to put you at ease about my safety," I say. "Because, Mave, I know you care, and I'd feel so fucking *guilty* if I'd have to put up a façade every time I needed to get away from the estate. It wouldn't have been fair – to either of us."

"What's not fair, Nettie, is you making me choose, because that's *exactly* what I'll have to do." He scoffs and runs a hand over his hair. "I've been working for Chase since I was your age. Hell, *younger* than you, probably. And I've *always* been loyal to him; always followed his orders. I just…" He closes his eyes and exhales heavily. "You're making me *choose*," he says again – quietly – then looks at me. "And Christ damn me, but I'm going to have to pick you. I'll always fucking pick *you* over Chase."

My heart beats in my throat as I stare at Mave. Because right there, in his clear grey eyes, I see the one thing I was scared I'd find; the one thing Dorran had so confidently assumed would be there.

Love.

I see *love* in Mave's eyes. For...for *me*.

I wanna say that I know how this emotion feels, but that'd be a complete lie. Experiencing it and having it directed towards me are two very different things, and despite being uneducated in the former, I can sense it being projected at me through Mave, and that's something I don't need experience for. That's something I simply *know*.

"So, what, you called me a fuck-face just for the sake of it, then?" Dorran says, and his voice pulls me out of my thoughts.

Mave clicks his tongue. "To be honest, I've wanted to call you that for a long time now."

Jayce folds his arms across his chest, whereas Alex and Varsha scowl. Solo, on the other hand, coughs behind a fist, making me shoot daggers at him.

Dorran chuckles. "Man, I kinda wanna stab you right now," he tells Mave, who smirks.

"Go ahead and give it a shot…*fuck-face*."

I groan. "For the love of *God*," I mutter.

"So you're part of the team now?" Alex asks Mave. "Do we hug or high-five or somethin'?"

"I wouldn't go *that* far," Mave responds. "I'm only risking my neck for Nettie. The rest of you are a…" He purses his lips as he looks for a term.

"Necessary bargain?" I provide.

He shrugs. "Yeah, that."

"Jeez, don't treat us with so much respect, man," Jayce voices. "Gives me acidity just watching you *try*."

"I, for one, am glad there's someone in this band of misfits who sees sense in the fucked-upness of this entire situation – like myself," adds Solo, earning simultaneous glares from me and the crew.

Mave stifles a smile, and I relax, knowing I won't have to pretend or lie to him anymore; knowing he's here, and always will be. And, as selfish as it is, I'm glad about it, and him.

When he meets my eyes, I smile and mouth, "*Thank you*," to him.

He shakes his head. "*You're a menace*," he mouths back, making me chuckle.

Dorran nudges my shoulder with his. "Hey," he says to me, then grins down at me.

I grin in return. "Hey."

He bends to place a kiss on my lips. "You feel good, now that he knows everything?" he asks, nodding in Mave's direction. "Or do you regret it?"

"It's perfect," I say. "I'm relieved, if that makes sense."

"It does."

"Thank you," I tell Dorran. "For being patient and calm. I know it's tough to trust people, especially someone who works for my uncle, but I'm happy you decided to take a chance today. It means a lot to me."

"Come now, don't go soft on me. He can still mess shit up, and when he does, I'll be there, waiting to put an end to him."

I raise a brow. "*If* he messes up – which he *won't*."

"Don't be so damn sure about it. He's only human."

"And you–"

Someone clears their throat, making me look ahead.

It's Mave, and the expression I notice on his face is one that's very easy to decipher.

Envy.

I don't know what to do with it, or how to counter it with something that might make it better.

When he sees me watching him, he quickly neutralizes his features, then looks at Dorran.

"I hope you know being with her has naturally put a target on your ass," he says. "You can't rest easy or get cocky; can't even minutely trust Miranda to keep her mouth shut. She's a fucking ticking bomb, that bitch, and Chase is just as vicious."

Dorran puts an elbow on my shoulder and winks at Mave. "Oh, I *know*. This is, after all, just the beginning, and I'm *so* ready to see what's in store for me next." He smirks down at me. "For *us*, I mean," he adds, then presses his lips to mine again.

The hard part is over – or at least I think it is. I could be wrong, though, but I won't know what challenges await me until I actually step into the next phase. And even though it's terrifying, I'm ready to see what the future holds for Dorran and I.

Part Two

THE *Reckoning*

38.
DORRAN

3 months later

I duck in order to avoid getting punched by Jayce, slide under his arm, then turn around, just as he does, too, and jab him in the stomach.

His upper-body bends forward at the impact, and he hisses out a curse.

I tighten the tape around my palm and fingers as I wait for him to recover. “It’s been *months*, Jayce,” I tell him, then shake my head. “You’ve gotta stop going easy on me. I know for a fact you could have stopped that blow. Come on, man; just fuckin’ let it *go*.”

We’re both panting from being at it for over an hour now, and the sweat coating my body is just as inconvenient as Jayce’s stubbornness towards…well, letting it go.

He straightens, and the flickering overhead lights in the underground gym throw a brief spotlight on his hardened features.

“I dunno what you’re talking about,” he says a little hoarsely, then clears his throat before resuming his fight stance.

I mirror him, then go in for another punch.

He swerves just in time, then reels an arm back, but I block him when he’s close enough, and hit him with an uppercut – right in the chin.

He barely manages to keep his balance, and spits blood on the concrete floor before wiping his mouth with the back of his taped hand.

"*This* is what I'm talking about," I say, then push my damp curls away from my forehead. "Every day we do this, you give me stupid fucking openings to hit you; to fucking *hurt* you. You really thought I wasn't noticing any of that?"

He ignores me and moves forward, but I step away, making him meet my eyes.

"Jayce, come *on*."

"What the hell do you want me to say?" he sneers.

"That you're done blaming yourself for what happened 3 months ago," I sneer back, then get in his space.

He huffs out a chuckle. "You know I can't do that."

"Why not?"

"Because it's a crucial enough mistake that I *need* to remind myself of it in order to not repeat it."

"Bullshit," I spit out. "And for the last time: it was an *accident*. Nothing more, nothing less. So you better get your shit together, Jayce, because if you don't, then so help me God, I'll shove common-fucking-sense down your throat if that's what it'll take for you to wake the hell up."

We stare each other down, and through the array of emotions I see in his eyes, the one that shines quite clearly is acceptance. It's something similar to what I'd seen all those years ago in the prison cell, when he'd told me why he'd been arrested, and how *right* it'd felt to have killed his brother.

He's accepted his fault with what happened with Rizwana, but what he's also put into his head is the wrongful idea that he somehow *deserves* to be forever punished for his little slip-up. And that's not good. Far from it, actually.

"Do you want me to punch you in the dick, or have you understood everything I've just told you?" I say.

"It's not a button I can switch off on a whim, Ledge," he states.

"Well, then tell me what'll help. I wanna be able to do *something* about it."

"You've already taken the brunt of my stupidity," he tells me with furrowed brows. "And, it'll be a while before I stop accusing myself for letting that happen, but I'll do it; I'll forget."

"Only because I'm forcing you to?" I ask.

He shakes his head. "You're not forcing me; you just care in your own way. Besides, if you and Alex and Varsha don't push me to move on, then who will? I just have to come to terms with…I don't know, the thoughts in my head. And when I do, I'll be less of a douche to you and the others."

I smirk. "You know we love you for your douchery. You wouldn't be as exciting otherwise."

"First of all, douchery is not a word. Second of all, stop looking so fucking smug, or else I won't hesitate in wiping the floor with your pretentious little ass. And you know just as well as I do that you do *not* want that."

My smirk widens at his words. "Do your worst, brother. I can take ya, you know that." I pull my damp vest off my body and throw it behind me.

Jayce chuckles and does the same with his t-shirt, then quickly goes in for a strike.

I evade it with ease, then jab him in the gut. He groans but recovers quickly, then socks me in my now-healed left side, making me laugh.

We parry each jab with counter-punches of our own – completely out of breath but still pumped by adrenaline. The thrill is too high, and so is the need to be the one to land the final blow.

Duck, rise, block, hit, and repeat. It's like a dance of sorts – one we've been mastering for over a decade now.

I press my feet on the ground, then use my bodyweight to push myself up into a jump. My fist is ready to hit home, but at the last minute, Jayce moves to the opposite side, rendering me off balance, then slides behind me before grabbing me into a sleeper hold. His arms are locked around my neck, and he pushes my head forward against his vise grip, leaving me with no other choice but to tap his bicep in submission.

I let him move away from me, let him put his guard down, and then, when I'm sure he isn't expecting it, I turn around and spear him with all the strength I've got left.

My right shoulder throbs at the force, and Jayce and I all but crash against the floor in an unceremonious heap.

"*Motherfucker*," he hisses as he clutches his middle whilst lying on the concrete. A few seconds of silence follow, and then, he starts laughing out loud. "Fuck, man," he says, then laughs again. "You really got me."

I laugh along with him, then lie down next to him. "You okay?" I ask.

"I think I broke a rib or two."

"Too bad. I was aiming for all of 'em."

He chuckles. "And you?"

"Probably sprained my shoulder."

"Good."

I laugh again and turn my head in order to look at him. He does the same.

"You excited for your date tonight?" he questions with a gleam in his eyes.

A grin creeps its way up to my lips. "Yeah." My voice sounds a little foreign to me, given how there's a jovial tone to it. But I embrace it, because it feels good to be enthusiastic about something like this.

I've planned a date for Cignette and I tonight, and I've decided to cook something for us instead of ordering in or going to a restaurant. Mad, isn't it?

Alex is the cook of our family, and as someone who's been living off of his beautifully put-together meals for over three years now, I can safely say that me making something edible might quickly turn into a delicious hazard for Cigs and I. But I'm going to try, because:

A) Alex will be there to make sure I don't end up burning the house down.

B) How hard can working in the kitchen actually be, right? I'm already an expert at slicing meat, so this should be a piece of cake.

Or not.

I honestly don't know.

I shift and get to my feet, cursing at the sharp pain in my shoulder.

"Where're you going?" Jayce asks from the floor.

I rotate my right arm to release some pressure, then look down at him. "The grocery store."

He visibly chokes on his words. "Wh-*what*?"

"I'm going to the grocery store, you asshole."

He clutches his stomach and starts cackling – *really* cackling. "*Dude…*"

I roll my eyes and walk away from him – towards the gym's locker room. "I hope the ceiling falls on you and ends up breaking all your damn ribs to dust," I mutter.

"I heard you!" he hollers, making me chuckle and shake my head.

39.
CIGNETTE

My mauve skater dress is doing absolutely *nothing* to aid me against the brisk wind, but the view around me is worth enduring tonight's weather. It's almost 9p.m., and the hustle in this part of Riverside is finally slowing down. Less honking, less chatter. More peace.

The moon is a lovely crescent, with stars scattered around it like pins on an endless map that is the sky.

I turn and look at the pale fairy lights strung above me, looped through the four poles surrounding the small rooftop. They're twined among each other into intricate and unique patterns, and brighten the space with a soft yet clear ambience.

I shift my attention from my surroundings to Dorran, who's sitting opposite me. He looks *beautiful* – yes, beautiful – in a lavender dress shirt and black pants. And, as dramatic as it may sound, I quite literally lose my ability to breathe every time his curls blow over his forehead against the force of the wind, and his eyes shine against the nightlight.

"This is amazing," I say to him, then nod at the table between us. "And so is this."

Dorran Ledger *cooked* for me. I mean, does it *get* any more perfect than that?

When he'd picked me up a mile away from the estate an hour ago, he hadn't said much about where we were going. Mave had wanted to come along, of course, but it wasn't gonna happen, and I'd made sure he understood that quite clearly. He's still not used to, or okay with, the idea of Dorran and I being together, but it is what it is, and there's nothing he can do or say that'll change things.

The last three months have mostly been a breeze for us. With Mave on my side, I've been able to spend time with Dorran, and successfully give hours at the *Lure* HQ, managing my social media team.

Speaking of Dorran…

He didn't tell me where he'd planned our date to be, not until we reached the apartment building his crew lives in. One elevator ride up to the rooftop, and here we are.

"Are you sure?" he asks now, and his throat bobs as he swallows. "We can order takeout, or I can ask Alex to make someth–"

"Stop." I place my hands over his and run the pads of my thumbs over his knuckles.

"This is lovely, Dorran. I *promise*."

There's roasted chicken, mashed potatoes and peas, along with red wine and a tray of very delicate-looking chiffon cake slices, topped with orange meringue, all plated elegantly on a round table.

Like I said: *lovely*.

Dorran sighs. "Well, if you're sure." He gestures at the food. "Let's get to it."

We quickly serve ourselves, and as I take my very first bite of the chicken, I can't help but moan at the taste. The spices put my senses on alert, and the chicken itself all but melts on my tongue.

Dorran chuckles, then takes a drink from his wineglass. "I don't think I've ever moaned while eating roasted chicken," he says, then puts a forkful of it into his mouth, and his eyes widen almost comically as he chews on it. "Fuck, I've outdone myself," he mumbles.

I grin. "Exactly."

He gives me a pensive smile. "This is the only thing my mom would make on the days she'd decide to cook for the two of us," he tells me, then spreads some mashed potatoes over the chicken in his plate. "And hers was…I don't know how to put it into words." He laughs to himself. "It'd feel rubbery, smell like smoke and dull chilies, and the taste…" He shakes his head and meets my eyes. "It didn't even feel like actual food, Cignette. Most of the time, I was glad when she refused to cook for me, because then I could buy those frozen, ready-to-eat packets that tasted a hundred times better than what she made. And I know I shouldn't say this because food is a blessing – whatever it may be – but I just…sometimes I couldn't stomach even *looking* at it. I remember washing it down with soda most of the time, and on the days when I wasn't brave enough to eat it, I'd trash the whole thing and stay hungry instead."

I place a hand over his wrist. "I'm so sorry, Dorran."

He shakes his head again. "Nah, it's good. It's just that whenever I make this – because it's the only thing I can cook without burning anything – I can't help but think of the past; of the slowly ticking moments in the kitchen where I was forced to spend time with my mother who simply didn't…care. Because that's all she had to do, Cigs: fucking *care*, show some shred of humanity towards me." His gaze turns distant for a moment, but when I move my hand from his wrist and twine our fingers together, he looks down at them with an expression on his face that's so purely guileless, yet so profound.

Dorran is a man shaped by his past. Who he is today is a sculpture that took years to mold and perfect – years of pain, anger, betrayal, and suffering, all put together to form the layers that constitute a human that's so fucking special. To me, and to the people who care about him.

"I know exactly what you mean," I tell him, and when he brings his eyes to mine again, I smile at him.

"Ever since my mom started involving me into the society – forcing me to socialize and suck up to the people who barely gave a shit about me – I've hated it. And I'm not saying I'm unique in my distaste towards it, or I'm not like the other girls. But fuck, the kind of lifestyle she is obsessed with, is not the kinda lifestyle I want. It's as simple as that."

"You should have the right to choose," Dorran says.

"Precisely. But she didn't think I needed to have a voice, and so, I started doing what I thought was right: living my damn life the way I wanted to. Mom didn't like that, of course, and you've seen firsthand how she retaliates when she thinks I've wronged her."

Dorran's jaw tightens, and he squeezes my fingers in silent comfort. "Fucking leave that stupid estate and that life, then."

I chuckle ruefully. "I can't."

"Why not?"

"Because, aside from my mom and uncle completely losing their shit over me for disregarding the luxury, fame, and respect that comes with the Adler name, if I *do* decide to leave, then I won't have a claim at *Lure* anymore, and I seriously can't have that."

Dorran's brows crease. "You care about the brand, then," he states.

I nod. "I think it's the only thing my mom's done that I don't hate. *Lure* is a palace of possibilities, but because Mom's in charge, it feels like a prison of sorts. Both to me and the hundreds of employees that work for us."

"And if Miranda is gone…"

"I get to take over, yes."

Dorran smirks and leans back in his chair. "Well, that can be easily done."

I laugh. "At the risk of my uncle finding out and killing you for it? No, thank you."

"But just imagine you getting to be at the head of the table," he says, and his eyes gleam in genuine excitement. "The queen, commanding her little shit-faced acolytes to do her bidding."

I laugh harder. "Hey, now. Those acolytes are hard-working people who are sincerely interested in making *Lure* as unique and popular as possible. But alas, none of their ideas are as great as Mom's vision, which is absolutely one-dimensioned and trashy, at best."

Now it's Dorran's turn to laugh. "Well, my offer stands indefinitely, so you can cash it in whenever."

I chuckle. "I appreciate it."

We get back to our food, and as Dorran and I fall into a debate about which vintage car is the classiest, I realize that I've never spoken as much in my life as I do when I'm with him. Not at work, not during events, and most certainly not with Mave. And, it's not a comparison, just an observation – one that makes me feel things I've never even dared to think about.

40.

CIGNETTE

"I love how quiet everything is right now," Dorran whispers against my temple, then tightens his arms around my waist.

"Me too." I shiver against the wind, but smile when he runs a hand up and down my arm, and his callouses kiss my bare skin, leaving goosebumps in their wake.

We're standing behind the rooftop's stone railing, watching the night darken before us. The fleeting hustle from earlier has lulled completely, with only the sounds of June Bugs and owls echoing against the peaceful silence.

I spoon some chiffon cake and meringue from the plate that's on the railing, then turn around to look up at Dorran. "Open up."

He takes a huge sip of his wine, then grins and parts his lips.

"Suck on the spoon," I say once he's taken the cake into his mouth.

He arches a brow, but obeys my little command.

I hold in a breath as his cheeks hollow; as his tongue darts out and licks the back of the frail object in my grasp.

My God, I'm going to lose it. He's barely done anything, and I'm already so fucking wet for him.

I pull the spoon out of his mouth, and watch – transfixed – when the strong column of his throat moves as he swallows the cake.

"You know why I asked Alex to use orange meringue with our dessert?" he questions, then smirks before stepping closer to me.

I set the spoon back onto the plate, then return his smirk with one of my own. "Tell me why."

Dorran leans in and touches his nose to mine, resulting in our breaths to merge. "Because you always smell like them – like fucking *oranges*." He presses his lips to mine, and distinctly, I hear his wineglass crash against the floor, which makes me chuckle.

He grabs my neck and starts fucking my mouth with his – tongue and teeth and bruising nips that ignite me like a damn inferno – and when his cock pushes against my stomach, I bite his bottom lip and cup him from over his pants.

He breaks the kiss and lets out an unrestrained moan, and it's so fucking hot that I wanna hear more of it.

I drag my long nails over his growing erection, and Dorran's gaze turns molten. "I like having you at my mercy," I tell him. "I fucking *relish* it."

He cocks his head to the side. "That so?"

"Mm-hmm." I run the back of my fingers over his cheekbone, and then, with my eyes on him, I go down on my knees before him. The harsh ground bites into my knees, but I don't care, because damn it, Dorran looks *stunning* like this – all worked up and flushed. The fairy lights cast an outline around his form, and his face is mildly shadowed by them.

He's a God – picture-perfectly sinful – but it's me who's going to make him sing my name like a damn prayer tonight.

"Unbutton your shirt," I tell him. "But don't untuck it."

He chuckles and starts moving his fingers over the buttons of his shirt, revealing his smooth, muscled skin for my viewing.

I rise on my knees and place open-mouthed kisses on his abs, and when he thrusts his hips forward in response, I laugh and unbuckle his belt, then unzip his pants before shoving both it and his boxers down enough to expose his jutting cock for me.

My pussy aches at the sight of him, so I press my thighs together in a vain attempt to dull my need of wanting him inside me.

I grab his base and lick the precum off the slit on his crown, then take one of the metal beads of his piercing between my teeth and tug on it roughly.

Dorran lets go of a broken grunt, and bunches my hair in a vise grip while heaving out rapid breaths.

I grin up at him, then touch my nose to the patch of dark hair on his pelvis before inhaling, and my clit throbs as his scent overtakes my senses. I slip my other hand under my dress, move aside my underwear, and push two fingers inside my wet pussy.

"Fuck," I whisper, then lick the thick vein on the underside of Dorran's cock.

"*Cignette…*" he groans, and tightens his hold on my hair, silently commanding me to speed things up.

I move my fingers in and out of me at a steady pace, then swallow as much of Dorran into my mouth as I can, all the while stroking him with fervor.

"Take me deeper," he rasps. "I know you fucking can." He's out of breath, flushed from face to chest, and makes for an impossibly euphoric sight.

I hum against him and loosen my jaw, then take him in all the way, gagging when his piercing hits the back of my throat. A few tears roll down my cheeks, briefly making my vision hazy.

Dorran groans again, and it's enough encouragement for me to start working faster. I bob my head back and forth as I continue to suck him, and with each slide of my lips along his pulsing cock, he moans, taking every bit of the pleasure I'm giving him.

"Fuck yeah, Little Swan," he says around a smile. "You feel so good fucking my cock with that hot mouth of yours."

I quicken my movements. His body has gone rigid above me, and I know he's drawing closer to his release.

I continue to finger-fuck myself as my other hand slips over Dorran's length with ease, and when I pull my mouth away from his cock to wrap my lips around his balls, his hips jerk forward.

I run my tongue over his sack, then suck on it – gently yet firmly – at which Dorran growls.

He widens his stance and looks down at me. "Just like that – taste every inch of me, Cignette, and don't you dare stop; I'm fucking close." His eyes are hooded, and his lips are parted.

I pop his balls out of my mouth, then start stroking him harder, all the while circling my clit with my thumb. I'm close, too, and it's so hard to hold myself back when all I want to do is come.

"I wanna taste you so fucking bad, Dorran," I tell him. "Hot and thick – just for me." I stick my tongue out and slap his cock over it a couple of times, and when I feel him throbbing against my palm, I moan his name and take him into my mouth again.

That does it for him. He tips his head back and roars, pulling at my hair as he basks in his orgasm, and spurts of his cum fill my mouth. I retch a little at the overwhelming sensation of being full, and swallow every drop of Dorran's heady release. My own orgasm follows, rendering me weak as I come all over my fingers. I whimper as I continue to rub my pussy. My ears are buzzing, and a flush creeps up my body as I come down from the high.

I pull Dorran's cock from my mouth, and he all but falls on his knees in front of me. He's panting, and so am I, and when our gazes meet, we grin at each other. He grabs the hand I'd used to fuck myself, then sucks on my wet fingers, maintaining eye contact with me.

“You loved touching yourself with my cock in your mouth, didn’t you, Cignette?” he asks, then starts working himself, hissing while he does it. “You liked it when I came down your eager little throat, hoping it was your cunt, hoping I’d have–”

Dorran’s words are cut short when the rooftop’s door slams open, and familiar voices fill the space.

I look over his shoulder, and see his crew making their way in, only to stop short when they see us.

Alex’s face contorts to one of pure shock. “*Nope*,” he says, then shakes his head vigorously. “I did *not* just see that. I repeat: I did *NOT* just see that.”

Jayce mumbles something and glances away, whereas Varsha raises her arms in annoyance and walks back into the building.

Dorran clicks his tongue. “You *actually* can’t see shit, Alex. I’ve got my back to you; stop overreacting.”

“I CAN SEE YOUR ASS CRACK!” he yells. “Your. Fucking. ASS CRACK!”

I purse my lips in an attempt to stifle my amusement, but fail and end up laughing instead.

“I thought you liked my ass,” Dorran quips, then fixes his boxers and pants before getting to his feet. He zips the latter, leaving his belt undone and his shirt unbuttoned, then offers me a hand.

I wince as I get to my feet, and he smirks when he sees my sore knees.

“Yes, but when have I ever mentioned being fond of the crack?” Alex says. “*Never!*”

Dorran and I face him. He’s standing with his arms folded across his chest, with Jayce by his side, who looks like he wants to crawl into himself.

“What are you guys doing here anyway?” I ask.

“We thought you two must’ve finished dinner by now, so we wanted to come get the dishes and stuff,” Jayce answers.

“Well, we are done, now that you fools have interrupted us,” Dorran states, then sighs and waves a hand in the table’s direction. “Cigs and I’ll bring everything down to your apartment.”

I nod, and Alex glances between Dorran and I with a smirk on his face.

“Since when do the two of you carry *dishes*?” he teases.

“Fucking zip it,” Dorran mutters, then walks over to the table and starts piling the plates together.

I join him, and ignore the looks of complete hilarity on Jayce and Alex’s faces. But when I chance a fleeting glance at the latter, he winks at me, making me chuckle to myself.

41.
DORRAN

I crouch to make sure the oil has drained completely into the oil pan I'd placed under the grey Honda HR-V I've been working on for the last couple of hours. Seeing that it has, I set the pan aside and lie on my orange Creeper, then roll under the car. Locating the space where the oil filter should be, I grab a new one from next to me and start screwing it on slowly, making sure not to put too much pressure. I then slide out from under the car, pop open its hood, and uncap the oil-fill port before pouring fresh oil into the reservoir. Once I'm done, I cap off the port and close the hood, and have only just picked up a cloth to wipe my hands, when my phone pings back-to-back with 2 new messages.

I throw the cloth on my toolbox, then pull my phone out from my jeans pocket before reading the texts.

Solo: *sent a photo.*

Solo: *Colton Davis. 21. Raped our client's 13-year-old sister. The fucker's gonna be at Aurea Vista tonight at 10. I've informed Eddie.*

I grind my teeth as I scan Colton's photo. It's a selfie, and the asshole is grinning in it. Brown hair, green eyes – he's a living, breathing cliché. Not for long, though.

Me: *And our client?*

I look at my crew as I wait for Solo to respond. Varsha is tallying up our monthly finances on the garage's laptop behind the main counter, whereas Alex is working on a customer's Kawasaki, and Jayce is changing the tires on a blue Corvette.

I grab a metal chair from next to my work station, then settle down in front of the Honda, just as a new text from Solo comes in.

Solo: *Bryce Landers. Him and Colton are seniors at the same college. Mostly acquaintances before the incident, which took place during a party at Bryce's house last week. His dad's paying for the kill, and has asked for proof as well.*

I smirk as I type my response.

Me: *Perfect. I'll tell the crew.*

Solo: *Text me if there's a hiccup. I'll be waiting for your call.*

Me: *Got it.*

I close the chat page and open the one that's directly below his.

Me: *Wanna help me with a kill tonight? Aurea Vista, 10p.m.*

I look up from my phone. "We've got a kill tonight, guys," I address my crew, and when their heads turn to me, I lean back in my chair and relay to them the details Solo gave me. Once I'm done, I clear my throat and add, "I've asked Cignette to join us."

"Oh, dear Lord," Alex mumbles, and Varsha exhales heavily before shaking her head a little. Jayce, on the other hand, narrows his eyes at me in a way that's both scrutinizing and threatening.

I click my tongue. "She'll be fine," I say.

"Oh, I know," Jayce counters. "It's *you* I'm worried about."

"What's that supposed to mean?"

"You lose focus when she's around you, Ledge," Alex states with a faint smile. "And don't get me wrong, we adore Cigs–"

"–Adore is a very strong word," Jayce cuts in, but Alex glares at him and continues.

"Like I was *saying*…" He gives his husband a look full of warning. "We adore Cigs, but when she's around you during a kill, shit goes awry."

I raise my hands in defeat. "That was *once*. And we've already established that it was an *accident*."

"Could happen again," says Varsha. "Besides, this is our first kill after Rizwana. I think we'll do better if we stick to the usual routine."

I clench my jaw, but what I instead wanna do is huff in displeasure. I don't, though, because the last thing I wanna come across to my crew as, is immature. They're only being cautious, despite also being unreasonable. But I'm a stubborn asshole, and I'm not gonna back down easily. Well, unless Cignette doesn't wanna join us tonight, that is.

I scratch the side of my neck as I glance around at my crew. "Look, let's wait and s–" I stop when my phone rings with an incoming video call from Cignette. I answer it, and grin when her face fills my phone's screen.

She's wearing a black silk blouse, and her long hair is braided over one of her shoulders. There's a faint tint on her cheeks that's fucking adorable, and her lips are painted red.

"My *God*, you're beautiful, Little Swan," I say by way of greeting, and hear Alex sigh in the background.

"I'm a mess," she states, just as someone next to her asks, "Is that what he calls you – *Little Swan*? What the fuck kind of term *is* that?"

"Good to see you're still as dense as yesterday, Maverick," I snark.

He bends so he can look at me through the screen. "Hey, fuck-face," he all but chirps, to which Jayce coughs, and Alex and Varsha full-on laugh.

"Y'all suck," I tell my crew, then focus on the call again. "Kindly take your face off the screen, Maverick. It's shriveling up my perfectly functional cock."

Cignette elbows him and shifts her phone away from him, and now that I see it, she seems tired. Mostly annoyed, but tired too.

"You okay?" I ask her.

She exhales with her entire body. "Maybe? I don't know. My team and I just had a meeting, and I'm on my way to another one with the marketing team. It's a shithole of a day here, but I'll be fine." She pushes some of her errand hair away from her face. "So, who are we killing tonight?"

"Jesus, Nettie; talk a little louder, why don't you," Maverick mutters.

She rolls her eyes. "We're in an *elevator*, for fuck's sake."

I wanna laugh, but it's something she just said that has completely taken me off guard.

Cignette used the word "we", and I don't know why, but it fucking hit me in all the places such a small word *shouldn't*. And I'm so damn flabbergasted by it that it takes me a moment to realize that she's calling my name.

I blink and swallow, then shake my head. "Yeah?"

She narrows her eyes at me, and I hear the *ding* of the elevator as it stops on her floor.

"Shit, hold on." I watch as she steps into a posh-looking hallway, and nods at someone I can't see. She pauses for a beat, then clicks her tongue and looks at me again.

"Yeah, okay. So, *Aurea Vista*, right – the nightclub at University Ave?" she says.

"Yup. At 10 tonight."

"Perfect." She then glances around the hallway. "Tell me about the kill."

Aaaaand I'm hard, just like that. She's so invested in this, that I can't help but feel twice as thrilled about killing the bastard. And my dick really appreciates her intrigue, so that's a bonus.

I quickly fill her in on the details, then minimize our call so that I can text Colton's photo to her.

"Got it," she tells me. "Piece of shit," she then mumbles.

I chuckle. "Not your type?"

She puts her tongue to her cheek. "Fuck you, Ledger."

I wink at her. "Wear something easily accessible tonight."

"For Colton, or for you?" she sasses with a smirk.

A flash of anger cuts through me at her words, and I grit my teeth before glaring at her. "Say that again, Little Swan, and see what happens."

Her smirk vanishes, and she audibly sucks in a breath while her gaze darkens.

Maverick once again shoves his face in front of the screen. "Was that a threat, Ledger?" He looks pissed, but it's laughable compared to how I feel right now.

"Move. Your face. *Away*," I grit out.

He scoffs and opens his mouth to say something, but the phone is shifted away from him, and Cignette comes into view again.

"I was joking," she tells me, then rolls her eyes. "You're going to kill the guy anyway, so I deserve to at least crack a joke on his behalf, don't I?"

I tilt my head to the side. "On his behalf? Since when have you turned into a martyr for the unlawful?"

"*Since when have you turned into a martyr for the unlawful?*" she says in a mimicky voice, making the crew laugh.

"You go, Cigs!" Alex hollers. "Stay classy, you *queen*."

She chuckles. "Aww, thank you, Alex." She raises a brow at me. "See? That's called appreciation."

"I'll show you appreciation tonight," I tell her.

She purses her lips. "Promises, promises," she sings before smirking at me again. "I'll see you later, then, princeling," she says, and disconnects the call, leaving me aching for more of her.

Fuck my life.

"She's good, huh?" Varsha muses, having noticed my state.

"The best," I tell her with a shake of my head, then rise before getting back to work.

42.

CIGNETTE

"I'm coming with you tonight, since you've decided to become so stupidly *unhinged*," Mave says as soon as I put my phone back into my purse.

"Correction: you're going to drop me off at the nightclub, and then you're going to go home."

He reduces the space between us and glowers down at me. "I will do no such thing."

I cross my arms across my chest. "Oh, but you *will*."

He scowls. "If you simply needed a chaperone to go meet your psycho boyfriend whenever he calls on you, then why the hell did you even involve me into all of this? If you didn't actually need me, why didn't you keep me out of this bullshit?"

"I think I've already told you why, Mave." I uncross my arms, then grab one of his hands and give it a squeeze. "Lying to you *sucked*, and I wanted to put a stop to it. Also, keeping things from you just felt…*wrong*."

He studies me for a bit. "I get that, Nettie, and I respect that. But it's my job to protect you. Hell, it's more than that for me. I don't like it when you're alone with Dorran and his friends; I'll feel at ease if I'm close by and can keep an eye on you."

I swallow when I see the raw emotions in his eyes. He genuinely cares about me, but I've yet to convince him that so does Dorran.

I squeeze his hand again, then let it go before smiling at him. "I'll be fine with Dorran," I say, and avoid flinching when his expression hardens. "And, if something goes wrong, I'll call you."

"You wouldn't have to if I'm already at the club with you," he counters.

"Please?"

He doesn't say anything.

"What girl meets her boyfriend with her bodyguard by her side?"

Dorran and I haven't exactly established titles for each other, let alone our relationship. But I do like the sound of being his girlfriend, and even though it's a new experience for me, I have to say: I'm not mad about it.

"The girl whose boyfriend is a contract killer, and has all but invited her to join him while he conducts a goddamn *murder*," Mave states the obvious.

I exhale. "Can I fire you for one night?" I ask.

He chuckles. "As if. You can't get rid of me that easily."

I pout, which is quite unlike me, and then I frown, because I can't think of anything else to say to him.

"Let's just get through this meeting," I say, and make to turn around, but Mave grabs my wrist and stops me.

"Fine, you win," he relents. "But only if you promise to call me if something goes wrong."

I grin at him, then rise on my tiptoes to give him a quick kiss on his cheek. "I promise."

He smiles and shakes his head, then nods in the conference room's direction. "Let's get to that meeting, then. You've got a murder to witness later on, after all."

I scoff and roll my eyes. "And you call *me* a menace," I say, then swivel on my feet, fix my beige pencil skirt, and start walking down the hall. With Mave right behind me, of course.

43.
CIGNETTE

I enter the chilly room to a chorus of '*Good Afternoon, Miss Adler*', and look at the people gathered around the massive glass table in the conference room. Each an expert at marketing and finance, these people know exactly what they're doing, and how to bring *Lure* back on top, because by the looks of it, the brand is seriously suffering. Despite the investors, sponsors, and donations.

My team and I discussed potential promotional methods earlier today, but until and unless we have a full grasp on the amount of damage *Lure* has recently seen, we can't move forward with our plans. That, and I need proper financial guidance from the marketing team to better understand what I'm dealing with.

Sunlight reflects against the wide floor-to-ceiling glass windows around the room, showcasing iridescent prisms throughout the space.

As I take a seat at the head of the table and set my purse on it, Raj and the rest of my social media team nod at me from where they're gathered to my left.

I nod back at them, and when Mave steps away from me, I quickly look up at him and whisper, "Sit next to me."

He gives me an incredulous look. "*What?*" he mouths.

I glance at the chair to my right, then at him. He seems hesitant, but swallows and does as I've asked.

I sigh, because it's good to have him here, then clear my throat and face the crowd. "Whenever you guys are ready," I address the marketing team.

A few of them look at Mave with skeptical and unsure gazes, but I pay them no heed. Mave does, though, so I place a hand over his knee from under the table, and when he looks at me, I give him a smile, which makes him relax a little.

"Our sales have gone down by a minimum of 17% since last year," a member of the marketing team announces, and when I look ahead, I notice that he's opened a file in front of him and is gesturing at a PowerPoint presentation on the screen behind him.

"Minimum?" I say.

"Just the online sales," he clarifies. "Offline sales have been next to non-existent, especially since the summer of 2022."

"The reason?"

"A massive increase in our prices," another member – Erin, I believe – says. "*Lure* has been focused on limited edition and seasonal wears for the last few months, and we've noticed that it's since then our margins have dropped significantly."

The conference room's door opens, and every single person at the table gets to their feet. Mave included, although he does so reluctantly. I remain seated, and try not to cringe when the smell of *J'adore*, by *Dior*, fills the air, making the hair on the back of my neck stand, and goosebumps to prick my skin. Her heels click against the Oakwood floor, and a second later, she enters my peripheral, which leaves me with no other option but to face her.

Her white blazer dress washes out her complexion, making her look distasteful, and her fully-done makeup only adds to her lack of sense in decorum.

"*Mom*," I make myself say.

Her vacant eyes narrow. "Cignette."

Everyone settles back into their chairs, but not Mave. He subtly tilts his head, letting me know he's going to be by the door, standing guard with Riley, then offers his seat to my mother before walking away.

I clench my hands into fists, but say nothing, and when Mom occupies Mave's chair, she sends a fiery look my way, clearly rattled that I've seated myself in her rightful place. If she's expecting me to move, then she's going to be disappointed. I'm very comfortable where I am, and I don't plan on getting up any time soon.

She notices that, of course, and shifts her attention from me to her employees, who quickly catch her up on what has been said in the meeting so far.

"But our price range has always been well-received," she argues. "And, with the introduction of limited-edition clothing, we are establishing the fact that our brand is to be held under the same light as those that cater to luxury wear."

"If that was your goal, Mom, then you should have expanded *Lure* to cities like LA, NYC, or even somewhere in Europe," I counter. "But all our offline stores are limited to Riverside, and whatever online sales we were making, dropped significantly when COVID and lockdown hit. Avenues and lifestyles have changed now; people are prioritizing money over luxury. If *Lure* wants to survive, it'll either have to reduce its product prices and focus more on everyday clothing, or expand to cities, or countries, where it would gain some rightful traction."

Mom looks beyond livid, but she's hiding it well. "I wouldn't be so dramatic with my approaches, Cignette," she bites out. "I'm sure there's something that can be done to save face and go about in the same direction as we are right now."

Waleed "broke up" with her a week after the charity gala 3 months ago. Not only that, but he also stepped down as *Lure's* sponsor, and headed back to Abu Dhabi to resume his family business. Kinda sucks because his money was good for *Lure*, but on the other hand, I don't pity Mom at all.

"I'm afraid Miss Adler is right, ma'am," Erin says. "For *Lure* to survive, we must at least consider one of the two suggested options."

"Which are?" Mother Dearest asks dumbly.

Erin and the others look mildly irritated, and I have to purse my lips to stop the smile from taking over my face.

"Uh, about the extension of *Lure* in other cities, or the reduction of prices, ma'am," says another member of the marketing team.

"Or we can have a clearance sale," Raj suggests. "For now, I mean."

"*A clearance sale?*" Mom places a hand over her chest as if that's the most appalling thing she's ever heard.

"Those *are* pretty popular," Lexie, my team member, says. "And, from what I've seen on our website, we've got quite a lot of apparels from the last three years that could sell out rapidly if they're available at half their original prices."

Misty, *Lure's* customer service in charge, puts forward a file in Mom's direction. "Around 70% of the recent customer complaints I've received, have been about the price increase and stock limitations. A clearance sale could be an immediate relief mechanism while the other teams work on additional options."

Please don't ask what the additional options are, I pray.

Mom grabs the file and takes a good amount of time going through the customer emails and DMs, then clears her throat and looks up at Erin. "Would introducing more…casualwear be a solution?"

"That alone? I doubt it, ma'am."

Mom places her forearms on the table and steeples her fingers together. "Minus 25% on all current prices – including the cost of limited-edition clothing. Should that be enough?"

Erin glances at her team members, then gives Mom a hesitant nod. "Temporarily, yes."

"What is that supposed to mean?" Mom asks in a raised voice. "I created *Lure* for success, not for charity. And you all have been hired to help me achieve that. What you're asking of me is preposterous, but I'm still willing to try because I cannot think of anything else that might aid us right now, and you're still not fully sure if that's enough?"

"In a long run, most definitely not," I say, and when Mom whips her head at me, I lean forward and arch a brow at her. "What you're doing right now with your launch decisions makes *Lure* seem like a brand fit for costume parties. We've got fur, leather, glitter, gossamer, skimpy, bold, and extravagant, but our catalog lacks the induction of plus size apparels, diversity options, along with casual and comfortable clothing. Maybe if you spend more time in understanding customer needs, and less on forcing our designers to make clothes that are red-carpet worthy, and not couch-appropriate, we'll be able to save *Lure* from drowning after all." I get to my feet and grab my purse. "Now, if you'll please excuse me, I have another engagement I need to get to. I've put forth my suggestions regarding this issue here today, but if there are other ideas discussed in my absence, I'd appreciate it if I'm made aware of them." And with that, I turn around and start walking towards the exit.

Mave opens the door for me, and once we've left the room and crossed at least half the hallway, he starts laughing, making me stop and do the same.

"Oh my God, did you see her *face*?" I lean against the wall and continue to laugh.

He joins me. "Atta girl; I'm so proud of you."

I smile at him. "Thanks. It was…liberating."

"I bet. Riley wasn't amused, though. He looked quite offended on Miranda's behalf."

I wave a hand dismissively. "They deserve each other."

"Quite." He nudges his left shoe against my pumps. "You said you have another engagement. Am I missing something?"

I wink at him. "I have a very private, one-on-one appointment with my bed in about…" I check my watch. "20 minutes – if we can successfully evade Downtown traffic."

He pulls his car keys out of his pant pocket. "Leave that up to me," he says with a grin, then leads me towards the elevator.

44.

CIGNETTE

I close my eyes and move my body to the pounding drumbeats booming throughout the club. The local rock band playing live here tonight is really good, and the vocalist's voice, paired with the lyrics of the songs he's performing, are helping me let loose after the stress of seeing my mom earlier. The nap I'd taken hadn't done shit for me, but this music – it's fucking working.

The thump of feet jumping around me joins the electric tunes of the guitar being played, and the smell of deodorant, mixed with body odor, fills the packed space. It's not exactly my ideal place to indulge in, but tonight, I need it – need the sweat that's coating my skin, the dizziness that comes with dancing without reserve. I feel alive; almost weightless against the overpowering music.

My feet are aching already, but it's only because of the nude stilettos I've got on, that work so damn perfectly with my red, thigh-length cocktail dress and beige clutch that I just couldn't resist the urge of putting them on.

I step away from the group of people around me and look at the bar area to my left. There, with a drink in hand and two of his friends beside him, is Colton. I'd caught his eye the second I'd entered *Aurea Vista* a few minutes ago, and despite him having checked me out more than once in that short period of time, he hasn't acted on it, or even approached me yet.

I suck in a surprised breath when a pair of demanding hands cup my waist, seconds before I'm pushed further into the thick crowd. My back presses against a hard chest, and then, I feel the warmth of his breath on my neck.

"My, my, Little Swan; what's gotten into you tonight?" he all but purrs. "Dancing with strangers like this, giving them a show of what's *mine*." He drags the tip of his nose over the shell of my ear. "Inadmissible, don't you think?" His hands move higher, and he flicks the top of my dress down to cup my breasts, making me gasp.

"Dorran, there are *people* arou–"

"You didn't think much about that when you were shaking your pretty little ass in their midst," he says. His tone sounds casual rather than accusatory, which sets me at ease.

I glance around, and realize that no one is actually noticing us. They're too busy dancing or making out or singing along with the band.

"Is this your way of staking your claim – by grabbing my tits in a full-house club?"

He chuckles. "Oh, sweetheart, I don't *have* to stake my claim on you anymore. You belong to me, plain and fucking simple." He pushes me back against him further, then kneads my breasts between his fingers.

I swallow and relax into him, and when he starts kissing my neck and shoulder, I exhale shakily and say, "Colton is here."

He stops what he's doing. "I know."

"He's checked me out a few times but hasn't made a move yet."

He hums. "Has he, now?" He discreetly fixes my dress, and when I turn around to look at him, I have to hold in a breath as I give him a once over.

Dorran's wearing a white vest, a black leather jacket, and his signature faded jeans and dark boots. His hair is a ruffled mess of curls, and the angles of his face are edged out against the bold lights in the club.

"Wow," I whisper, then clear my throat and repeat myself. "*Wow*."

He laughs. “So easily pleased.”

“Only because it’s *you*, dumbass.”

He laughs again. “*And* refined.”

I roll my eyes and look away from him, only to find Colton excusing his friends’ company to head to the bathroom.

“Dor–”

“Follow him,” Dorran orders. “Distract him. I’ll get the crew and join you in a minute.”

I nod, and make to leave, but he grabs me by the wrist and pulls me to him again. “Also, you look unholy as fuck in this red dress, Cignette.” He gives me a chaste kiss. “Just thought I’d tell you that.”

I smile and kiss him back, then step away from him. “I can’t wait for you to take it off me later,” I tell him.

He grins. “I’ll make a show of it for you,” he muses.

I chuckle and shake my head, then turn around and push through the crowd in order to make it to the bathroom.

45.
CIGNETTE

Two guys are busy making out with each other outside the bathroom. When they see me, they simply wink my way, then get back to practically mauling each other off.

Well, then.

I push open the ivory door next to them and step in, but stop when I see Colton. He's washing his hands in the sink, and a couple of girls are fixing their makeup next to him.

He glances up, and our eyes meet through the mirror in front of him. He smiles at me, then turns around and faces me.

The girls, engrossed in a conversation among themselves, walk by me without even looking at Colton and I, and when the door closes behind them, he shoves his hands into his jeans pockets and gives me another smile.

"You're Cignette Adler, right?" he asks, then scratches the back of his neck as a sheepish look takes over his features. "I saw you earlier but didn't know how to walk up to you. I mean, you're *you*, and I just…" He chuckles, and it's so innocent that it's a little hard to believe that he's someone who raped a minor only a week ago.

"I'm making an ass out of myself, aren't I?" he says, and I realize I've yet to speak.

I run my fingers through my hair and purposefully mess them up in a way that makes Colton swallow. He drags his eyes over the length of my body, then shifts on his feet, clearly affected by what he sees.

"I am," I finally say, then bring one of my legs in front of the other. "And, you're not making an ass of yourself. It's totally normal to be…*nervous*." I lick my red lips, and his gaze zeroes in on them.

"You wanna go over to my place?" he questions boldly, a little out of breath – his shy-guy act totally forgotten. "I'd love to show you a good time, baby."

Baby.

He's not even looking at my face; he's too busy ogling everything below my chin. And that, right there, showcases his true personality to me.

"Is that what you promised Bryce's sister before forcing yourself on her?" I say.

His head whips up, and he finally meets my stare. I smile at him, and his complexion pales. He all but staggers on his feet in a haste to create more distance between us, and his brows furrow as he now looks at me with a completely different sort of expression.

Fear.

"Wh-wh-what are you talking ab–"

The bathroom door opens, followed by four pairs of footsteps walking in. There's a click of the lock being secured, and then, a familiar arm wraps around my waist.

"Now, now, sweetheart; you've terrified the poor bastard," Dorran says to me, and when I look up at him, he chuckles, making me do the same.

"There were a couple of guys outside when I came in," I tell him.

"There was no one there when we got here."

I sigh. "Good."

He smirks. "Relax, will you?"

"I'm trying," I tell him. "I'm more worried about us being found out than I am of watching the asshole die."

Dorran chuckles again. "Everything's okay. Don't psych yourself up; enjoy the thrill of the moment."

"The *thrill*?"

He grins. "It's *intoxicating*," he provides. "It's buzzing through me right now, and I *love* it." His eyes gleam, and he looks so dangerous that someone with a sane mentality would want to run away from him. But I – I can't stop thinking about kissing him until I can't breathe.

"Pity you have to die," Alex says to Colton, and his words pull me out of my thoughts. "You're…I don't know, *cute*, I guess."

Colton moves further away from the 5 of us. "Who are you?" he asks as he frantically glances between us. "Let me fucking go, okay?"

Jayce sighs. "Could you be any more of a cliché?"

Varsha folds her arms across her chest. "Cooperate with us and we'll make it quick, because you and I both know you're not leaving this bathroom alive. So, don't waste our time, alright?"

Colton stumbles, then falls. "Please…" he begs, and when none of us say anything, he fucking bursts into tears. "Please let me go. *Please*."

Dorran leaves my side and crouches next to him, then roughly grabs the collar of his grey t-shirt before hauling him forward.

"Is that how Harper pleaded with you when you *raped* her?" he sneers at him, making him shake his head. "She must have, but you filthy piece of shit – you didn't fucking stop, did you? Not until you got what you needed." He gropes Colton's crotch, making him scream. His face is strained and sweaty, which shows how painful Dorran's grip is.

"Please…" Colton whispers. "I'll do anything…I'll give you anything you want. Just…just please…"

Dorran clicks his tongue, clearly annoyed, and moves his hand away from between Colton's legs. I watch with bated breath as he slithers the same hand under his leather jacket, then slides his switchblade out from the back pocket of his jeans.

Jayce sees it too, and kneels in front of Colton before holding down his legs, while Alex and Varsha move behind him. I step closer, but stay on the sideline.

Colton is flat-out horrified now, and starts screaming and thrashing. He tries to push Dorran off him, but Jayce punches him in the jaw. "Fucking stay still, dimwit."

Dorran clicks open his switchblade, and when Colton sees the weapon, he screams even more.

"Someone help me!" he shrieks. "FUCKING HELP ME!"

Chills run over my entire body when I hear the desperation in his voice, see the fear on his face, and the helplessness in his eyes.

"Fucking shut up," Dorran hisses. "And try not to flail too much. It's a new jacket, and my Little Swan seems to like it a lot. So let's not stain it with your blood, shall we?" He bunches the top of Colton's hair and pushes his head back, then brings his switchblade forward and slices Colton's throat open in a single sweep.

His eyes widen as sprays of blood flow out of the cut, and he starts gurgling on some of it as well. His body convulses and jolts for a few seconds, and then, it stops. *He* stops.

Jayce and the others get to their feet, but Dorran remains crouched next to Colton's body. He twists his switchblade this way and that, then brings it to his mouth before licking the thick line of blood off the sharp edge of his blade.

There's something about that little act that makes fire burn under my skin. Maybe it's the way the blood taints his tongue red, or maybe it's the way his lashes touch his cheeks when his eyelids flutter before he swallows. I don't know what it is, but it's almost hypnotizing, and all kinds of arousing.

He's so addictive to watch – a symphony of madness and deviance. A variation from normalcy, and a good-looking one at that.

My beautiful freak.

"How's it taste?" Jayce asks Dorran.

He grins. "Like dead frat boy."

The crew laughs, and I can't help but join them.

Dorran stands and walks over to the sink, then runs his switchblade under the water. While he does that, he also fixes his jacket and hair, which were already immaculate to begin with.

Varsha takes a picture of Colton's corpse, then types something on her phone before looking at Dorran. "Proof sent."

He nods, then glances at Jayce. "Text Eddie."

"Did that already," Varsha says.

"Perfect." Dorran pockets his blade and makes his way over to me.

"Need a gum?" I ask.

His lips twitch as he tilts his head at me. "And here I was, about to ask if I could kiss you."

"In your dreams, Ledger."

He laughs. "Fine, I'll take the gum, then."

I open my clutch and hand him a couple of mint strips, and right before he takes them from me, Dorran quickly leans in and gives me a brief kiss on my lips.

I gasp and try to push him, but he steps back and pops the gum into his mouth before giving me a rogue smirk.

I must admit, though: the smell of blood on his mouth, and his breath, turned me on, but I'll be damned if I tell him that.

"Let's get outta here, guys," Alex says, then gestures at Colton. "That dead face of his is starting to get real unattractive, and I'm *so* not digging the vibes."

"Yeah, let's," Dorran concurs, then takes off his leather jacket before moving behind me. "Raise your arms a little," he tells me.

I shift my clutch from one hand to the other as he slides the sleeves of the jacket in through them. He then pulls it up and over my shoulders, and I wrap it snugly around my front. When he circles back to me, I raise my brows at him in silent question.

"It's cold outside," he says easily, then clears his throat. "And I wanted to see you wearing my jacket." He looks me over with a burning gaze. "It looks better on you than it did on me," he remarks, then winks at me before leading the crew and I out of the bathroom.

We pass through the crowd – now thicker than it was before – and exit the club. Once outside, we take a left and enter an alleyway parking area. There are buildings on either side of the expanse, with rusted bicycles chained to poles that are decorated with half-torn flyers and random phone numbers. The air in here is stale, and smells of smoke, piss, and something pungent I can't exactly put my finger on.

Our footsteps echo against the quiet, and gravel crunches under our feet, amplifying the eerie silence around us a little too much.

A cat mewls somewhere, startling me. I swallow and stay close to Dorran as he leads the crew further into the alleyway, and release a relieved breath when I spot Jayce's Jeep and Dorran's Harley parked next to a graffiti wall on the far right.

"Dorran Ledger?" comes a voice from behind us, making us stop. We turn, and find 7 men standing before us, barricading the alley's entrance. In our case, our *only* exit.

Dorran steps forward, then places a hand on my hip and pushes me behind him. "Who're you?" he assesses the men with calm calculation.

Jayce and Alex flank his left and right respectively, and Varsha comes to stand beside the former.

"Stay away from Cignette Adler," one of the men says.

Dorran lets go of a surprised chuckle. "What the fuck kind of joke is this?"

"It's a *warning*," another guy states. "One we suggest you don't take lightly."

Dorran shakes his head. "You punks seriously think you can threaten *me*?" he sneers, and I notice his posture stiffening against his evidently building anger.

I suck in a breath and look over his shoulder. The crew seem just as confused by the strangers as I do, and rightfully so.

"You think my mom sent them?" I ask Dorran, then glance at the men again. "They don't exactly seem like the kind of people she'd have any sort of association with, though."

"After my threat to her, I don't think Miranda has it in her to play tricks on me," Dorran responds. "She knows I don't take kindly to bullshit."

The men fidget and look among each other – agitated.

Dorran sighs and spits the gum he was chewing, on the ground. "Are you morons going to do something, or should we leave?"

I make a sound in the back of my throat, while the crew simply laugh.

Goddamn psychos, all of them.

At Dorran's question, the gang of 7 pull out a series of weapons from under the hoodies they've got on – knifes, sharp-edged knuckle rings, metal rods, and even a couple of guns.

My chest tightens in fear, and I quite literally can't feel my legs.

"*Now* we're talkin'," Dorran says, excitement clear in his voice.

"It doesn't have to come to this," the guy in the middle – probably their leader or some shit – says. "Leave Cignette Adler here, and you can go without getting hurt."

"Really?" There's so much amusement in Dorran's tone that it makes me smile a little.

"And what exactly will you do with her if I leave her here?"

"Deliver her to our client, of course."

"And I'm assuming you won't tell me who this client of yours is?" Dorran asks.

The guy in the middle scoffs. "Do I look stupid to you?"

Dorran clicks his tongue. "Positively, yes." He quickly pulls his switchblade out of his pocket, and the blade all but glints against the hovering moonlight. "And you're about to find out just how much of a dumb fuck you are for even *suggesting* I leave Cignette with you."

The men step forward, and I brace myself for what's about to happen.

46.

DORRAN

The sound of muted gunshots hits my ears, just as I drive my switchblade into one of the thugs' eyes. I kick his screaming ass off, and he lands on the ground with a sick crunch, writhing in pain. Wiping his blood off my jaw with the back of my hand, I pocket my switchblade and turn around before raising my arms at Varsha, who has got her brand new 9mm – suppressor in place – angled at the men Alex and Jayce are dealing with.

"Why the fuck would you do that?" I ask her, then groan when my right boot presses against the blown-out brain of one of the guys she's shot. His head is cracked open, and he's bleeding a goddamn river. It's flowing down the cracks in the ground in an almost mesmerizing stream, and it takes great effort for me to look away from his vacant eyes, but I manage to do it anyway.

"What, making quick work of these assholes before the cops come on their usual nighttime rounds and end up finding us here?" Varsha retorts.

She's right. If the deputies or the sheriff witness us in this situation, Chase *and* Solo will have a hard time getting us out of this mess. And, if they *do* decide to persuade the law in our favor, it'll put them both in dangerous and compromising positions – something neither of them can afford.

"Well, when you put it like *that*…" I glance sideways, and find Jayce all but breaking a guy's neck with how hard he's choking him with his curb chain. And, let me add by saying how much he seems to be enjoying himself whilst watching the life dim from said guy's eyes.

Someone screams, and I whip my head to where Cignette is. She's holding onto a pole for dear life, trying to avoid getting blood on her heels, all the while watching Alex smash a thug's skull with his hammer with stark fascination on her face.

"Why are you screaming?" he asks her, then brings his hammer down on his victim again. The poor fool's face splits open in two while his body continues to jerk, and I can see the very muscles of his cheek from how beautifully Alex has broken him.

"You almost got chunks of brain on my dress," Cignette argues. "And this is a pretty special one, too. It's one of Julian's originals!"

Alex huffs and steps away from the battered dead body. "Wait, who's Julian?"

She rolls her eyes. "Forget I said anything."

"Ledge, behind you!" Jayce calls out.

I pivot on my feet and grab the wrist of the guy who was about to – or had planned to, at least – stab me in the back. He's the one who'd warned me to stay away from Cignette, and to leave her here for his client.

Perfect.

His knife falls to the ground as I twist his arm behind his back. "Seriously?" I spit the question at him, then kick him in the shin to get him to fall on his knees, but he ends up elbowing me in the ribs, taking me off my game. I let go of his wrist as the wind is knocked out of me, and when my crew starts making their way to me, I raise a hand to stop them.

The guy turns to face me and goes in for a punch, but I duck in time, then clock him in the groin.

He howls and bends over in pain. "Fuck you," he grunts.

I grin, then fist the collar of his hoodie, because there's nothing else on him for me to hold onto; the fucker's bald as an ass.

"Unfortunately for you, I'm not into street filth." I knee him in the face, making him stumble away from me.

He recovers quickly, though – his nose now bloody – then brings a left fist forward, and as soon as I move to block it, he uses his other fist to punch me in the jaw.

Razor-sharp pain shoots through the lower half of my face, and my ear, and I shake my head to get rid of the wave of dizziness that clouds my vision.

"*Nice*," I say, and when Baldie tries to come at me again, I slip to the side, then jab him in the ribs.

He doubles over at the impact, and I use that as an opening to punch him in the face, then deliver an uppercut to his throat.

He gasps and clutches his chest, then coughs and falls to his knees. I'm about to retrieve my switchblade so that I can put an end to him, but Jayce's words stop me from doing that.

"Ledge, wait. He's the only one left."

I give him a quick look, then sniff and settle down on a clean spot next to one of the dead bodies so that I can catch my breath. Straightening my legs out, I press my palms behind me on the ground, then lean my weight against them.

Jayce comes to stand behind Baldie, and I cock my head to the side as I study the latter. He looks young – maybe in his late twenties – and has aged scars peppering his face and neck. The circles around his eyes are prominent, and his drooped lids indicate that he probably uses, or drinks often.

"What's your name?" I ask.

He glances around frantically, but when I lift a brow at him, he exhales in defeat, and his shoulders slump in on themselves.

“Graham,” he answers forcefully.

“Graham…” I stretch my neck to relieve some of the tension there. “For all that verbal foreplay we had, you and your buddies turned out to be complete disappointments.”

“The men you killed tonight were a thousand times better than you and your friends,” he rasps.

I grit my teeth. “Is that why they decided to take money from someone to come fight me, then – to prove their fucking *superiority*?”

He snorts. “We needed that money, however small the amount. It was better than what we made at the boxing arena.”

Made. He’s already talking about himself in the past tense.

“You wanna tell me who hired you to do this?” I ask.

He swallows and meets my eyes. “Will it make a difference if I do?”

I work my jaw and shake my head. Letting him live will be too big of a liability, and it’ll be foolish of me to even consider it.

He laughs humorlessly. “Well, fuck it. If I’m gonna die for something that wasn’t even my business to begin with, then so should he.”

“*Who?*” I push.

Graham sniffs and lets go of a cough. “Gavin,” he says.

Surprised, I look at Cignette and my crew, only to find them wearing a similar expression on their faces.

“Gavin, as in the tattoo shop owner?” I question.

Graham nods. “Yeah. My friends and I always got our inks done from him. He priced us reasonably, and was fun to be around. We weren’t exactly friends, but we did hang out a few times in the last couple of years.” He shifts on his knees. “When we met last month, he told us about Cignette, and how she broke up with him to be with you. That’s when he suggested we threaten you to stay away from her, and that he’d pay us if we said yes. A couple of the guys weren’t onboard with the idea, but I *forced* them into it, and they…” He looks around at the decimated bodies of his friends with pain and regret on his face. “In a way, I killed them too, didn’t I? I should have just said no to Gavin, should have…”

I zone him out, because what he’s saying doesn’t matter now, and it most definitely doesn’t mean shit to me.

I glance at Varsha and give her a subtle nod. She returns it, then points her gun at Graham. The sound of a muted gunshot cuts through his rambling, followed by a bullet piercing one side of his head, and exiting through the other.

Cignette gasps and places a hand over her mouth at the suddenness of it, and her eyes widen a little as she stares at the exit wound on his temple.

His body falls over with a loud *thump*, and Jayce steps back before raising his arms and looking down at his white t-shirt, which is now splattered with blood.

“Jesus *fucking* Christ.” He glares at Varsha. “A warning next time, maybe?”

She shrugs and puts her gun away. “You knew it was coming; you shouldn’t have stood so close to him.”

He rolls his eyes at her, but says nothing.

“Relax, babe,” Alex chimes, then circles a hand over the stains. “That’s…a good look on you. Totally complements your complexion.”

Jayce scowls at him, then turns around and heads for his Jeep.

Alex clicks his tongue and stomps after him, and with a shake of her head, Varsha follows behind them, leaving Cignette and I alone.

I get to my feet and dust my hands off as I examine the dead bodies around me. “Fuckers didn’t even care to call cleanup,” I mumble, then shoot a quick text to Eddie, asking him for immediate assistance. Once I’ve done that, I look up as I’m pocketing my phone, and find Cignette – with a hand covering her nose – sidestepping brain matter and gore. She manages to make her way over to me without vomiting, or worse, tripping over the sticky trails of blood.

"Oh God," she whispers, but the words come out muffled. "I can't breathe; this place *stinks*. It's like a goddamn meat market in here."

I chuckle, then grab her by the waist when she stumbles.

I jerk my head at the chaos beneath us. "They make a pretty portrait, though, don't you think?" I tell her, just to get a reaction out of her.

She moves her hand away from her face to glower at me. "Take me home before I paint you right next to them."

I choke on a laugh as I look her over. "Who are you, and what have you done to my Cignette?"

"She tripped and fell face-first into a boulder of depravity." She pats my cheek. "Now, get me out of here before I scratch your face off your chiseled body."

My God, why the fuck did that comment turn me on so much?

Maybe because I'm a degenerate, but eh, that's already an established fact, isn't it?

I bend and lift Cignette in my arms, earning a surprised intake of breath from her, then start walking us to my Harley.

"Sooooo, are we keeping this to ourselves, or are we telling Mave and Solo about the turn of events?" she asks, then wraps an arm around my neck.

"Maybe once I've gotten some sleep. I don't think I have to energy to deal with either of those idiots right now," I say.

She nods, because she looks just as tired as I feel.

"Who knew Gavin had it in him, huh?" I wonder out loud.

Cignette sighs. "I told him I didn't want anything to do with him. I guess he didn't like that."

I grunt. "He for *sure* didn't like that. Asshole fucked up a perfectly good kill-night for me and the crew."

Her lips twitch as she studies me.

"What?" I ask.

She lifts a shoulder. "There's this ease with which you talk about murder and death. It's hot. I never thought I'd like that, let alone *think* about liking something of that nature, but here I am; I'm addicted to it, and you."

I smirk. "Although I appreciate the fuck out of what you just said, I have to ask: aren't you even *remotely* concerned about Gavin?"

Her eyes shine as she grins at me, then leans in and kisses me, making me groan.

"Why would I be, when I know you're going to take care of it the way you always take care of things," she says against my lips, then fists the hair at the nape of my neck and kisses me again.

I stop when we reach my Harley, then open my mouth and slide my tongue against Cignette's. My boner brushes against her ass, making her moan against me.

She has indirectly asked me to do something that I'd already planned on doing even before Graham revealed his client's name. Gavin signed his sentence the moment he decided to get in my way, and because I'm the type of guy who doesn't appreciate annoying child-play, I won't make things easy for him.

A loud honk makes Cignette and I break the kiss. I glance at Jayce in the driver's side of his Jeep, then shoot a quick scowl at him.

"We've gotta go," he says coolly.

"I *know*, asshat," I tell him, then place Cignette down on her feet before straddling my Harley. Once she's done the same, I speed us out of the alleyway and into the vibrant streets, with the lamp posts illuminating us in half-cast shadows as we breeze past the unaware citizens of Riverside.

47.
DORRAN

I push open *Radical Ink's* glass doors, and the moment I step into the shop, the smell of burning incense sticks hits my nose, making me scowl. The waiting area is empty, save for Nicole, who is sitting behind the front desk and talking to someone on the phone. She stops when she sees the crew and I, then gulps and shakily puts the receiver down on the table before getting to her feet.

"Dorran, hi…" Her eyes ping-pong between the 4 of us. "Umm, come here to get matching tattoos?"

"It's too early in the morning for you to get on my nerves, Nicole," I tell her, then walk over to the desk. I place my forearms on it and lean over, and Nicole's chin starts trembling in time with the rest of her body.

"Where's Gavin?" I ask her.

She's panting a little, perhaps from having held her breath. "He's not in yet," she says.

I chuckle, and she looks on the verge of bawling. "Wrong answer," I tell her. "Try again."

"Dorran, please…"

"*Tell me*, Nicole, and I'll let you go. I promise."

She blinks at me, and a few tears slide down her face, smearing her eyeliner as they go. "I–I swear he's not–"

I slap the front of the table so hard, it makes her yelp, and for the table itself to rattle, resulting in the contents it held to crash against the tiled floor.

"Don't fuck with me," I sneer at her. "Tell me where Gavin is – right fucking *now*."

She shakes her head, and that does it; that breaks my resolve of keeping my shit together.

I fist her hair and slam the side of her face against the embossed wall behind her, and when she screams, I press harder. "Now, have you decided to stop bullshitting me, or should I keep going?"

The door to one of the private rooms slams open, and a second later, Gavin walks out. His hair's tied above his head, and he's wearing a black apron over his blue jeans and t-shirt. He's also got rubber gloves on, which means he was probably getting ready for a client, and that someone could walk into the shop at any time now.

"What the fuck is happening here, Nicole?" he asks, then comes to a stop when he sees the crew and I. "Dorran," he addresses me with an icy glare, then glances at the hold I have on Nicole's hair. "Let her go."

I grin and pull back my hand, then turn and fold my arms across my chest.

"Hey, Gav," I quip.

He snorts, seeming irritated. "I don't know why I'm surprised to see you here, but I kinda am."

I can't help but laugh at that comment. "Did you really think your little *chums* could scare me away?" I click my tongue. "They weren't even a proper *challenge*, man."

His face tightens, and his nostrils flare. "You killed innocent people last night, Dorran. Doesn't that fucking bother you at *all*?"

"Wouldn't be the first time I've done it," I say in honest indifference, then take a step forward, bringing myself a bit closer to Gavin. "Besides, they wanted my Cignette – to *deliver* her to you. I couldn't possibly let that happen, could I?"

"You don't deserve her," he hisses at me.

"And I'm presuming *you* do?"

His chest rises and falls unsteadily as he stares at me. "She means a lot to me. I wanted to change for her; be someone she needs. But then *you* came along."

"Are you saying you know exactly what Cignette needs, Gavin?" I chuckle. "Seriously, dude, have you figured her out so easily – just by fucking her a few times?" The last 6 words taste acidic in my mouth, but they are, unfortunately, also true.

"Well, she doesn't need a goddamn murderer in her life, that's for sure."

"Gavin…" comes Nicole's weak voice, and it's clear that she's shocked by what he's saying. I'm not, though, because I know how men like him are: unreliable, untrustworthy.

Fucking absolute pieces of shit.

The shop's doors open, making me look over my shoulder. Two girls – laughing among themselves whilst holding hands – start walking in, but one look at me, and they stop.

"*Leave*," I tell them, and that simple word triggers their senses, because they practically rush away from the shop and into the street opposite ours.

With a roll of my eyes, I face Gavin again. "So, where were we?"

He looks unsettled by the absence of seriousness in my tone. "You're only playing with her, aren't you?" he says to me. "You think you're so cool – toying with her like she's a fucking puppet or something. You don't care about her. Hell, you don't care about anything but *yourself*."

"You assume too much," I tell him. "What I feel for her, you never fucking can. And you know why?" I tilt my head a little. "Because what Cignette and I have is bound by blood – of our pasts, of our hardships, and of our will for survival. We're both volatile in our own ways, but we stabilize each other when we're together. And that, Gavin, is something you never can, or will, have."

I realize after saying all that, that my throat has closed up. My chest is warm, and my head's a bit heavy. Maybe it's the weight of the things I've just confessed, or maybe it's the truth in them that's making it hard for me to breathe, but either way, I love it; I love how I feel right now.

"Fuck you, Dorran," Gavin spits out, because he can't counter what I've said with anything remotely as meaningful.

"Watch it, Gavin," Jayce warns.

"It's fine, Jay," I say.

His jaw bunches up, but he gives me a subtle nod regardless.

"You must think you're above us all, don't you?" Gavin remarks, then laughs. "You go around threatening and killing people; you've got your ass secured by elites, and loaded with money. You've fucking got it all, but that doesn't, not even for a second, change who and what you are, Dorran Ledger."

"Gavin, shut the fuck up," Nicole says.

I glare at her, to which she squirms and shrinks into herself, then look at Gavin again. "And what exactly *am* I?" I ask him.

"A monster," he sneers at me.

I laugh, then rub the space under my chin. "That's it? That's the best you got? A monster? Gav, tell me something I don't fucking know, man." I arch a brow. "Don't you people call me the Bloody Prince or some shit like that? Doesn't being *that* come with an obvious stamp of also being a…*monster*?" I laugh again, then shake my head.

His hands clench into fists as he seethes. "But that's what you are, Dorran; what you'll always be – a sadistic, uncaring *monster*. I know you don't care about it, but you should. And damn Cignette for choosing you over me, damn all those who think you're someone to be feared. Because

I'm not fucking scared of you; I pity you. I pity the life you lead, and the things you do in order to convince yourself that you're superior to everything and everyone. I pity the morals you stand for, and the–" He stops, and his eyes widen in complete shock. A second later, he looks down, and when I do the same, I notice blood spreading steadily across his chest. From a bullet wound on his left pec.

Nicole screams, and the shots keep coming. Two more on his chest, followed by one on his right shoulder, one on his stomach, and another that pierces right through the center of his forehead. And, it's only when Gavin drops dead on the floor, do I blink myself out of my trance and turn to Varsha, who looks like she's in an entirely different zone.

She's about to pull the trigger again, but I wrap my fingers around the gun and stand in front of her.

"Varsha, *stop*," I say, and when she doesn't even look at me, I pull the gun away from her and hand it to Jayce. "*Varsha*."

She meets my stare, and what I see in hers makes my stomach knot.

Hurt.

She wasn't over Gavin having cheated on her, so she took it upon herself to give herself what she needed: a final salutation to the relationship they once had.

"He won't get away with everything he just said to you, Ledge," she tells me. "He's going to have to pay."

"He's *dead*, Varsha," I say, then frown. "He's fucking gone."

She continues to look at me, all the while breathing heavily, and then, her eyes glaze over. Her tears slip through before she can stop them, and my heart fucking aches at seeing her like this. She hasn't shed a single tear since her breakup with Gavin – not until now, when she's finally ended things for good. The way *she* wanted them to end.

“Oh, Varsha.” My voice is constricted as I pull her to me and wrap my arms around her. “I’m so sorry, sis,” I whisper, then press a kiss on her forehead.

She fists my vest and holds onto me, and a moment later, Jayce and Alex join us. The latter runs a hand up and down Varsha’s back, while Jayce looks completely crestfallen.

A crunch-like sound gets my attention, making me look in its direction. Nicole – who was trying to get away while me and the crew were distracted – stops short, having accidentally stepped on one of the fallen items from earlier. She looks at us like a deer caught in headlights, and starts opening her mouth to say something, but I stop her.

“Going somewhere, Nicole?”

She’s flat-out shivering now, and I know it’s not because of the weather.

“I won’t tell anyone what happened here,” she provides. “I promise I won’t tell a soul. I’ll leave, and I swear you’ll never see me again.”

I disentangle myself from Varsha and walk over to her. “That’s the plan, isn’t it?” I say, then give her a wink.

A monster. That’s what you are…

Gavin’s words buzz in my ears, making me grin. I sniff and run a hand over my face, then focus on Nicole, who looks like she might faint if I so much as move a finger.

I sigh, give her a quick glance, then reach a hand out to Jayce. He offers Varsha’s gun to me, and when Nicole sees me holding it, she tries to make a run for it, but I grab her by the neck and push her back.

“No! Dorran, please… *Please!*” she begs as she struggles against me. “I won’t tell anyone. *Please*.”

I press the gun’s muzzle between her brows. “Look, I’m making it quick and easy for you, so just shut that bitch mouth of yours up and accept your fate. You’ve seen and heard more than you should’ve, which was supposed to be absolutely *nothing*. You're not walking out of here alive, Nicole."

She sobs and closes her eyes, seconds before I pull the trigger.

Her blood splashes across my face, and on instinct, I run my tongue over my bottom lip, tasting the familiar, iron-sweet flavor of it.

A monster.

A sadistic, uncaring monster.

Fuck yeah, I am.

Nicole's body loosens against my grip, so I let go of her neck, and watch as she falls in a heap at my feet. I then walk back to my crew and hand Varsha back her gun before saying, "Eddie will deal with this mess. Let's get the fuck outta here, come on."

She's so disoriented as she nods that it makes me burn with rage. If I could bring Gavin back to life and kill him myself, I would, because that asshole broke a piece of my sister today, and I know for a fact that it's one she'll never get back. It sucks, and I'm helpless against it, and that's the kind of situation I don't like falling into.

The urge to turn around and look at Gavin's dead ass one more time is strong, but I keep my eyes forward and follow the crew out of *Radical Ink*. It is, after all, the only logical thing for me to do.

48.
CIGNETTE

I'm flipping through yet another page of the latest *Vanity Fair* issue, when I see movement in my peripheral. I look up, just in time to see Dorran climbing up my balcony. His arms flex as he grabs the marble railing and lifts himself up and over it, and when I look at the time on my nightstand clock, I can't help but smile.

12:00a.m.

I'd texted and called him a couple of times during the day, but he hadn't responded to any of them. I'd had half a mind to visit *Finesse* in order to make sure he was okay, but I also didn't wanna be one of those people who crowd their partner's space at all times, so I hadn't acted on my instincts.

Dorran enters the room, and I turn to gaze up at him. My smile fades almost immediately when I see the expression on his face, and the way he seems weighed-down while standing before me.

I drop the magazine on my bed and rush to him. Up close, I can see the darkened stains of blood on his yellow vest, the circles around his eyes, the sweat and grease on his face, and the way his brows have knitted together, as if he's got something on his mind that's straining him on the outside.

"Dorran…" I cup his jaw. "Hey, what's wrong?" I wipe the grey smudges off his chin and nose, then frown when he doesn't answer me.

"You're scaring me," I confess, and run the back of my fingers over his cheek.

He leans into the touch, then lets go of a weak breath and closes his eyes. "I'm…tired, I guess."

I feel an ache in my gut as I watch him. I haven't seen him like this since I've known him, and whatever has caused this, has to be huge, or at least something that hit home for him somehow. I wanna know what it is, and I wanna fucking fix it for him.

"Dor–"

"I'm sorry I didn't answer your calls and texts yesterday," he says in a voice that's soft, yet broken. "Me and the boys were with Varsha for most of the day."

I blink, and my frown deepens. "What hap–" I lose my train of thought when Dorran opens his eyes and grabs my hand – the one I have on his cheek – and brings it to his lips before pressing a kiss on the inside of my wrist. Goosebumps prick my entire body, and when he touches his nose to the spot he just kissed, I feel a blanket of warmth wrap itself around me.

"Will you go for a ride with me?" he asks. "Right now."

I nod without hesitation. "Yes," I say. "Of course, yes."

He sighs as if he's relieved to hear my answer. "Okay."

I step closer to him, then rise on my tiptoes before giving him a kiss on his lips. The lingering smell of cigarettes on his breath is familiar, and also soothing in an innate sort of way.

"Okay," I tell him, then smile and give him another kiss.

49.
CIGNETTE

The wind whips by me as Dorran speeds his Harley through the dim streets of Riverside. The solid hum of the engine beneath me, paired with the distinct smell of smoke in the air, puts me at ease. I close my eyes and breathe it in, then place the side of my face on Dorran's back.

My white shorts and lavender hoodie are failing exceptionally against the cold, but I'm also enjoying the brittle weather tonight, so I can't exactly complain.

Dorran takes a left, and we enter yet another quiet neighborhood. I tighten my grip on his waist, then place a kiss on the back of his neck as I inhale his scent.

He hasn't spoken a word to me since he started driving us out of Upside, and even though I've wanted to, I haven't attempted at starting a conversation with him. I know I should, but I also want to give him time to clear his head, because I feel like he really needs it tonight.

We reach a pull-off, and Dorran turns his bike into it. The road is a bumpy high-rise here, so he slows down and drives at a neutral pace.

"Where are we?" I ask.

"You'll see," is all he says.

The ground transforms into a carpet of lush green grass the further we go, and when Dorran finally stops his Harley at a massive clearing, it takes me a moment to realize where we are.

I get off the bike and look around the hilltop we're on, and can't help but suck in a breath when I get an unrestricted view of the ocean in front of me. It's wide and calm, and the water all but glistens against the moonlight. Subtle waves crash and fall into each other, and with how coincided the sky and the ocean appear to be, I can see the stars reflecting in each ripple that passes and returns.

I turn around, and find Dorran sitting on the grass. His knees are folded and pressed to his chest, and his forearms are rested atop them as he stares at the ocean with a pensive look on his face.

I'm momentarily struck by how detached he seems; how he's hunched over a little, and how his brows touch every other second, indicating that he's thinking something.

I erase the short distance between us and sit next to him, then scoot closer to make sure we're touching. I'm about to place a hand on his arm and ask him what's got him this disheveled, but he beats me to it.

"Varsha shot Gavin yesterday. Multiple times." He then follows those words by telling me everything that happened at *Radical Ink*, and how he had to kill Nicole in order to avoid leaving any loose ends behind.

I open my mouth to say something – what, I don't exactly know. There's so much to unpack here that I have to sit quietly and process every bit of it before I decide to respond to any of it.

Firstly, what I personally feel after having just heard Dorran, is relief. Relief that Gavin's dead. As much as I didn't give a shit about him, he was starting to pose a threat, so he naturally had to go. And I know it's selfish of me to put my feelings first, but I'm not a goddamn saint, and I'm not ashamed to admit being happy about something, despite it being someone's death.

Secondly, Varsha shot Gavin, which I'm assuming is the reason behind Dorran's shift in mood. I know Gavin and Varsha had history, but from the extent of it I'm aware of, he cheated on her with Nicole. So, circling back to point one, I'm glad he's dead, and I'm glad Varsha was the one who put an end to him. But that also means killing him triggered her mentally, and in turn the entire crew.

"Tell me what you're thinking," I urge Dorran.

He looks at me, and there's literal pain in his eyes – one he chooses to let me see.

"Alex and I found Varsha crying in *Finesse's* bathroom a couple of hours after she killed Gavin," he says. "She's fine now, of course, but *fuck*, Cigs, I've…I haven't seen her like this since the day Jayce and I found her 5 years ago. And what happened with Gavin ended up breaking that cycle." He brings his knees down and crosses his legs before shifting to face me. "I'm fucking mad at that asshole, even though he's gone. I wanna kill him, have his blood on my hands, but he's already dead. Too easily forgiven and forgotten. And I can't help but think how unreasonable love is. Because that's what Varsha felt for him, didn't she? *Love*." He lets go of a crude laugh. "Such a small fucking word, and yet, it consumes a human being, makes them helpless to the point where they've got no other choice but to lose. Love is a weakness, a manifestation of all things wrong in this world."

I love you.

The three words echo in my mind so suddenly, that it makes my entire body go numb. My head buzzes with the realization, and a single tear falls down my cheek, but I quickly swipe it away before Dorran can notice.

I don't know when it happened, but it did. I think I've known it – subconsciously, perhaps, even before my brain fully registered it. It's sort of a blind revelation, but it's there; it *exists*. I love Dorran, and it's the goddamn truth.

"And yet…" he continues, then scoffs. "I love my crew, and Christ help me, I love Solo as well." He shakes his head after that last admission.

I manage to smile, but I can't help but flinch at the prickling pain in my chest. I know I shouldn't expect it, but it still hurts knowing I'm not one of the people he loves. But unfortunately for me, I'm far too into him to let the pain bother me.

I sniff and slide my hair behind my ears. "Varsha always seems so, I don't know…"

"Impassive?" Dorran provides.

"Levelheaded," I say. "She's always calm, always in control of things. She knows what needs to be done under every circumstance, and she does it without panicking or fumbling."

"She was none of those things earlier." Dorran pushes his curls away from his forehead, but they fall forward again. "I guess even the strongest of minds have their limit, huh?"

"Every human being does."

"True." He smiles ruefully. "But, being one of the shoulders for her to lean on today was draining. And trust me, I'm not complaining; I'm here for her whenever she needs me. But I gave her all I had, and now I feel kind of…empty. And let me tell you somethin': it's a scary fucking feeling, especially when I've got people relying on me. I can't zone out or lose focus; I simply can't switch off."

"But you *can*," I argue. "And you *should*, Dorran. I understand you've got a duty towards your family, but you've also got a necessary obligation to *yourself*. If the very foundation of an empire weakens, then it's only a matter of time before the rest of it comes tumbling down. And that's exactly what you are to your crew – the fucking kernel. Don't be afraid to step back when you need to, because every once in a while, you *do* need the space, even when you think you don't."

His throat bobs as he swallows. "It's not something I'm used to."

"Then don't make it a habit," I tell him. "Take a break only when you feel like you seriously can't handle shit."

He chuckles and shakes his head. "God, you're fucking perfect," he says, then grabs my chin and kisses me.

"I know," I whisper against him, then kiss him back.

Dorran wraps his lips around mine with such urgency, that it quite literally makes it hard for me to breathe. His tongue is sure as it slides against mine, causing a rush to flow through me.

His kisses are a lovely paradox of mild and commanding – a sweet, sweet torture that only makes me weaker for him. That burn my entire fucking world and blind it indefinitely.

I match his pace, and in turn, he kisses me like I'm made for it; for *him*.

He moves back and fists the hem of my hoodie, then pulls it over my head. Grinning when he sees my pebbled nipples, he then yanks at my shorts. "Up, come on."

I lift a little, and he pushes my shorts down my legs. A shiver runs through me as a strong breeze passes by me, and the dull ache in my clit heightens against it.

Dorran takes my shorts and drops both it and my hoodie on the grass, before getting to his feet. He then takes off his vest, and my breath stutters as I run my eyes over his broad shoulders and smooth chest; the prominent veins on his arms, and the impressive definition of his washboard abs. A thin trail of dark hair runs down his navel and behind the waistband of his jeans, making me swallow.

I catch his gaze, and find him looking smugly at me. "Take off your fucking jeans, Dorran," I tell him.

He smirks, and I get a sudden urge to touch myself when he unbuckles his belt and pulls his jeans and boxers down to his ankles before kicking them off.

He cants his head sideways and widens his legs. "Lie down, Cignette," he orders.

The crisp grass bites into my skin when I do as he's asked, earning a heated look from him.

"Spread those thighs for me and show me your pussy," he says next.

I do, and my hips arch on their own accord when a lick of air caresses my center.

Dorran spits on his palm, then fists his cock and starts working himself. "Touch yourself, Cignette."

I bring a hand to my pussy and start circling my clit with two fingers, while with the other I pinch one of my painfully hard nipples.

Dorran strokes himself faster, and this view of him right now – bathed in moonlight, stark naked and pleasuring himself to *me* – hurdles me over the edge. I writhe as I orgasm, making sure to keep my eyes on him until I'm done.

Dorran stops touching himself and kneels in front of me, then grins and places my legs over his shoulders before pulling me to him. "I want both your hands above your head," he commands.

I do as I'm told, and his eyes travel over every exposed inch of me. His precum coats his swollen crown and stains his piercing, and even though I wanna reach out and taste it, I don't.

"You're such a good girl, aren't you, Cignette?" he muses, then drags his tongue over his bottom lip. "Opening yourself up to me, surrendering to me like this…" He groans. "Makes me so fucking hard; so fucking hungry." He grabs his cock and positions the head against my sensitive entrance. "Did you like making yourself cum right now while watching me beat my dick to you?"

God, the words he uses – they make me mad with want.

"Yes," I answer easily.

He grins again. “Do you want me inside of you – fucking that greedy little cunt of yours and making you cum like a slut?”

“Fuck you. *Yes*,” I hiss, then raise my hips.

He chuckles and starts pushing himself in, and we moan together when his cock stretches my walls. The initial burn is strong, but it’s quickly taken over by Dorran’s deep thrusts as he starts sliding in and out of me.

I grab his bicep with one hand, and cup the side of his neck with the other. “Fuck,” I breathe when he fills me completely, hits me to the back with his entire length. “More, Dorran. I need more.”

He smirks and pushes my legs forward, in turn bending my body, then hovers over me. My knees touch my breasts, and when he shifts closer and starts pounding into me with short, rough thrusts, his balls hit my ass, and his thighs slap against mine.

“This what you want?” he asks, then fists my hair and brings our faces closer than they already are. “Fuck, you’re so tight, sweetheart. So fucking hot.” He ruts into me with abandon, and when his piercing hits me in just the right spot, I cry out and look down to see how he moves in and out of my pussy. His cock is coated in my cum, and there’s some of it on the patch of hair on his pelvis as well.

It’s such a raw feeling – knowing you’ve marked someone in a carnal sort of way. It’s something that exceeds everything else; every promise or declaration. And seeing my release on Dorran like this is the ultimate state of euphoria for me.

My breaths are broken hiccups in my throat as he continues to fuck me, and even though I feel a strain in my back and legs with how firmly he’s molded my body, I don’t mind it one bit. If anything, it turns me on even more, and brings me closer to my release.

Dorran grunts, and his eyelids flutter while his movements turn jerky. His fingers tighten in my hair, and his hot exhales fan my cheek. “I’m close,” he says, continuing his unrelenting pace.

I clench around him, and heat rushes through me. One final roll of his hips, and I'm hurtling over the edge. My back arches against the ground as my orgasm takes over, making me feel completely hazy.

"God*damn* it," he grits out, and crashes his lips to mine as his shoulders shake against the impact of his release. With his cock buried inside me to the base, Dorran's cum shoots into me in hot spurts.

I'm panting, and so is he after he breaks the kiss. Then, something crosses his flushed features, right before he pulls out of me and slides down my body.

"Push my cum out of you," he orders from between my thighs. His face is so close to my clit that every word he utters, vibrates against my bud.

I rise on my elbows and push, and get a feeling of dripping slickness on my slit, all the way down to my ass.

Dorran brings his mouth to my entrance and sucks, making me bunch a fistful of grass to avoid bucking against him. His head bobs as he alternates between licking and sucking, and once again, I'm entranced by him; by how eagerly he's eating his own cum out of my pussy.

"Dorran…" I whimper his name as I continue to watch him.

He moves back and crawls up to me, then grabs my chin and tugs my face to his. I part my lips for him, and he spits our mixed releases into my mouth. He then slides his tongue over mine, and when he pulls back, I see a thick string of cum on his.

"Swallow it," I command, then wrap the fingers of my left hand around his throat before squeezing it with enough pressure to make him grin at me.

I feel a shift on my palm, indicating that he's swallowed, and my vision blurs temporarily by how turned on I am by him.

I smirk and loosen my grip on his throat. "How's it taste?" I ask him, using the same question Jayce did the other night.

Dorran chuckles, then leans in. "Let me show you," he replies, then kisses me.

I wrap my legs around his waist and hold onto his neck as I kiss him back – all teeth and nips and moans – and he rises, settling me on his lap. His cock grinds against my aching cunt, and my eyes roll in ecstasy as I start gliding myself over his hardening length.

This is it for me – this man, this moment, and this feeling that I've got in the very pit of my stomach. It's ever-growing, all-consuming. And, as Dorran slides himself inside me again, I realize that it's also self-destructing.

I never said I liked it easy, did I?

50.

CIGNETTE

"Thanks so much for joining me, Cigs," Julian says. "I know this isn't an ideal hangout situation, but I'm glad you said yes nonetheless."

I smile. "Don't mention it. If anything, *I* should be the one thanking *you*. After that brainstorming session with my team this morning, I can barely see straight. I needed to get out of the HQ and look at something that isn't social media or *Lure* related. I swear, the words "discount" and "sale" are going to haunt my dreams for at least a month."

Julian chuckles. "I'm glad you find antique shopping relaxing."

"Honestly, though, it's a million times better, not to mention *interesting*, than staring at my computer until things start to obscure, and I just can't take it anymore."

When Julian had asked if I'd like to go to an antique store in Downtown with him during our lunch break, I'd said yes immediately. Because A) I've never been to one of those, and B) I *needed* to step away from work before I started pulling my own hair from my scalp.

I look at Mave from over my shoulder, who's walking merely a couple of steps behind me. Our eyes meet, and I flash my teeth at him in a too-wide smile. He returns it with a genuine smile of his own, but doesn't forget to shake his head at me because he knows I'm a complete pain in his ass.

Downtown is as busy as one would expect. With active shops on either side, the road in the middle is jammed with traffic. It'd rained an hour ago, so some people still have their raincoats on, while others carry their umbrellas in hand.

The three of us continue to walk on the busy pavement, and Julian has Maps opened up on his phone, and is guiding Mave and I to the store he'd found online.

"How much further?" I ask Julian, and sidestep a puddle to avoid staining my black pumps and crimson jumpsuit.

He frowns at his phone, then points ahead. "Should be here somewhere."

"What's the store called again?" Mave asks.

"*Aurora's Antiques*," Julian replies.

"Niiiiice," I can't help but muse.

He laughs. "Well, they claim to have the most unique artifacts and such, so I wanted to check them out." He then clicks his tongue. "Landon, my fiancé, has the weirdest of interests. Like, if you look at him in passing, he'll seem like a completely simple, sunshiny kinda guy. But when you see the things he likes to collect, you'll change your goddamn mind. I remember giving him one of those weird, rubber-made Frankenstein hands on his birthday the year we started dating, and he's still got it. He uses it as a paperweight in our condo office, and every time I see it just sitting there on the table, I swear it fucking moves an inch closer to the edge."

I chuckle. "Well, nothing wrong with that. I do love a combo of sweet and crazy myself." My cheeks heat immediately after I say that, and Julian, of course, notices.

"You little minx; you've been holding out on me!" He shoves my shoulder in a playful manner. "Tell me everything!"

I grin. "Not a chance, but I *will* say that he's sweet when he wants to be, and abso-fucking-lutely freaky when he's in the mood. He's just…I dunno, amazing."

Someone coughs behind me.

I turn and scowl at Mave, to which he slides his hands in his pant pockets and pretends to look up and around him.

"I'm guessing big guy here doesn't approve," Julian remarks.

I roll my eyes. "He doesn't approve of anything."

"Excuse *you*," Mave butts in.

"Careful where you're walking, Maverick," I taunt. "I don't want you falling on your ass and breaking your fragile hipbone or something."

Julian laughs, and Mave mumbles something I can't quite make out.

We walk past a few more stores, and then finally reach *Aurora's Antiques* at the very end of the street. It's a wood-finished store with a massive glass casing next to its entrance, which showcases a bunch of watches, globes, and vintage mirrors.

Julian pushes open the door and enters the shop, and I follow after him. An overwhelming smell of moth balls and polish permeates the stocked space, making me scrunch my nose against it.

The carpeted floor mutes our footsteps as we walk further into the store, and when I look around, all I see are chairs, more watches, globes, and mirrors, along with clay busts, miniature statues, rusted swords and armors, and Ouija boards.

"That deer head mounted on the wall is judging me," Mave says, startling me a little.

I blink and glance at the object he's talking about, only to suck in a breath at how real it looks. It's as if an actual deer shoved its head into the wall, and was paused by time to remain as is.

"It doesn't like your scent," Julian quips.

"Did you just quote Gruthum from *The Last Kingdom*?" Mave asks him.

I stop and face him. "Wait, you've seen that Viking show?" I question.

Mave opens his mouth to answer, but stops when a booming yet elegant voice rings through the store.

"Welcome to *Aurora's Antiques*. My name is Toyah; how may I assist you today?"

The three of us turn to the woman behind the glass display case. Her skin is a lush shade of brown, and she's wearing leather pants, along with a white silk blouse that's tucked inside said pants. Her dark hair is wrapped within a beautiful head wrap, while the gold bangles and rings she's wearing, clink against each other as she steeples her fingers and smiles at us.

Julian walks over to her, so naturally, Mave and I follow.

"Hey there. I'm looking for something small yet unique for my fiancé. It's his birthday this week," he says.

The woman nods, then gestures at the case in front of her. "You may have a look at these and see if anything piques your fancy." She has an English accent – Welsh, most probably.

Mave comes to stand next to me and leans against the case, while Julian and I look at the things on display inside it. Rings, bracelets, daggers, coins, and other trinkets I can't possibly identify. They look old and invaluable, but for all I know, they're made of brass and don't hold a single shred of connection to history. But eh, it's all about the appeal of these things anyway, and not their authenticity.

All of the items have been kept under a golden light, which makes them appear sparkly and enticing. Well, all except for one. It's black, square-shaped, with a skull, along with the words 'DEATH NOTE' embossed in gold on it. It's simple, yet it drew my attention the moment I laid eyes on it.

Just like Dorran had the day we met.

"What's this?" I ask Toyah, then tap my nail against the glass.

"A lighter." She opens the compartment and pulls the lighter out, then flicks its front panel to the side, bringing a lick of blue flame to life.

"It's beautiful," I say, then smile at her. "I'll take it."

"It'll be $150."

"*What?!*" Mave straightens, seeming thoroughly appalled. "It's a goddamn *lighter*, woman, not a handcrafted vase. You seriously think you can trick us int–"

"Mave." I place a hand on his forearm and shake it in warning. "Calm *down*, please."

He looks down at me. "I *am* calm, Nettie. You seriously think this trash costs $150? If you really need a lighter, you can find one for $3 at the fucking grocery store. And news flash: that lighter will do exactly what this one does."

Oh my God.

I glance at Toyah, but thankfully, she seems unfazed by Mave's outrage. It's probably because she deals with all kinds of customers on a daily basis, but still, that doesn't mean I'm not embarrassed by what he said.

I let go of his forearm as I glare at him, then face Toyah again. "I'll take it," I repeat myself, then pull my card out of my purse before handing it to her.

Mave looks displeased, but it isn't the first time I've gotten this reaction out of him, and it most definitely won't be the last.

Julian picks a charm bracelet for Landon, and as he asks Toyah about its origin, I quickly snap a photo of the lighter and send it to Dorran.

Me: *If you were an inanimate object…*

He takes a bit to reply, and by the time he does, Toyah has handed my card back to me, and Julian has paid for his bracelet.

Dorran: *That's actually pretty accurate. Biblical too, if you wanna look at it in that sense.*

Me: *I can't wait to watch you light your cigarette with this. It's going to do all sorts of things to my insides.*

Dorran: *You're so easy to please, Little Swan.*

Dorran: *Also, you didn't have to buy me anything.*

Me: *I've got two words for ya: shut up.*

Dorran: *I could skin you alive for saying that, you know.*

Me: *And yet you won't, princeling.*

Dorran: *You're way too confident for your own good. But fortunate for you, I'm going to enjoy fucking that assertiveness out of you later.*

"Cigs?"

Feeling flushed and a little out of breath after having read Dorran's text, I look up, and find Julian giving me a knowing smirk. "Let's go; we've gotta head back to the HQ."

I purse my lips. "Already?"

Mave opens the store's door for me and jerks his head to the side. "Get out of here before you make another impulsive purchase. Because I swear to God if you do, I'll lose every piece of my commonsense and do something I probably wouldn't want to."

My lips twitch as I fight back a smile. I then slide my phone and lighter into my purse, but not before responding to Dorran's last message.

Me: *I look forward to it.*

Me: *P.S. I gotta go, but I'll call you later.*

I turn around and give Toyah a wave, then walk out of *Aurora's Antiques*.

"Wanna grab a quick bite before we get back to work?" Julian asks once we've crossed the street and reached the other side.

"Yes, please," Mave and I say in unison, making him chuckle.

"I'm thinking extra cheese sandwiches, Greek salad, and some refreshing mojitos. My treat, of course."

I hum, then wrap an arm around his and follow him through the string of shops. "You're a heaven-sent, Julian. A true savior."

"I concur wholeheartedly," Mave says, making Julian and I laugh.

51.

CIGNETTE

I lip-sync to Miley's *Flowers* blasting through the speaker in my bedroom, and fluff my pillows before I can settle in for the night and give myself some much-needed self-care. I've got my face scrub, mask, and detoxing toner at the ready, and all I've gotta do now is find some snacks from the kitchen.

I make my way to the bedroom door, and have just opened it when my mom and her bodyguard come to a stop just outside my room. Her eyes are glazed over and red-rimmed, and her posture is loose. She's drunk.

The very first thought that enters my mind is: Mave isn't here, and it's after 12. I'm alone right now, with only the night-shift guards at the estate's entrance.

I swallow and tighten my grip on the door's handle. "Mom," I address her in a nonchalant tone.

"*Bitch.*" She takes a step in my direction, and on instinct, I move back. She laughs, then stumbles, but Riley catches her before she can fall.

"Take her up to her room," I tell him. "And make sure she doesn't choke on her vomit."

Mom scoffs. "You know what the people at the HQ have been calling me ever since that meeting?" she asks, then hiccups. "A *sellout.* A money-hungry hag. They laugh at me in my absence; they give me looks of mockery when I pass the hallways." She grabs the threshold and leans in.

"And it's all because of *you*," she sneers at me. "My employees think you're *Lure's* future, that you'll take the company to new fucking *heights*." She scoffs again. "So, I thought I should pay you a little visit tonight – to see the people's favorite in all her righteous glory."

Ice claws its way up my spine at her words, and a lump forms in my throat at her indirect threat. I can't get air in and out of my lungs, and my legs feel leaden.

Mom smirks, having sensed the shift in me. "What's wrong, *Miss Adler*? Feeling outnumbered, are you?"

My eyes sting with unshed tears, but I grit my teeth and manage to gather what little strength I have left. "You wouldn't dare," I tell her. "Not if you like your pathetic head on your shoulders."

Her lips spread in a grin. "I do like a good challenge." She hiccups again. "Especially if it'll end with you on the floor, screaming for help and crying for mercy."

I make myself move and push the door towards her. It connects with her head, making her shriek. I then turn around and climb onto the bed in search of my phone, but Riley beats me to it. He grabs it off the nightstand and throws it against the wall, then gets on my bed and fists my hair.

"I'm going to have too much fun dirtying you up, you sneaky little cunt," he hisses at me, then shoves me on the mattress.

I turn and try to move away from him, but he grabs one of my legs and yanks me to him.

"Let go of me!" I scream, and kick him in the jaw, which somehow ends up urging him on further.

"Defiant little bitch." He lifts my hoodie, exposing my breasts.

I make to push it back down, but he grips both my hands and slams them above my head.

He smirks and cups my right breast with his free hand, then kneads it painfully. "You've got the county's most dangerous man weak for you.

There really must be something in you for him to defy the people he should otherwise be grateful to." He drags his hand lower and grabs my center, making a sob hitch out of me.

My tears fall to my temples, and my vision blurs as I thrash helplessly against his hold. "Stop," I say, and can't help but cry when my plea makes him grin.

He unzips his pants and pulls his cock out, then starts stroking it while running his eyes over me.

This can't be happening…

Please, this can't be happening right now.

Mom enters the room, and when she sees Riley working himself to me, she bends over in laughter. "Serves you right," she says while laughing, then claps her hands like the mad-fucking-woman she is.

I thrash under Riley again, and try to kick him off me, but he doesn't budge. What he instead does is hook his fingers under the waistband of my shorts. He manages to pull them down, and when he glances between my thighs, he groans and strokes himself faster.

"If only your cunt had pink hair," he muses, then chuckles. "Would make you more special than you already are…*Princess*."

"Let me fucking *go*," I manage to say, then jerk under him.

He chuckles again, then positions himself at my entrance, making my heart all but stop.

No.

Please, no.

"You've got a pretty set of lips," he whispers, then hovers over me and lets go of my hands. "I'm gonna kiss them and see if they taste just as good as they look."

My heart is beating in my throat as my fear heightens. "Riley, no." I shove at his hips and shoulders, then slap him when he tries to kiss me.

"Fucking *stop*," I grit out, and claw at his cheeks when he forcibly brings his face closer to mine.

He grins through my assault, and when I press my nails further into his skin, breaking it, he pushes further. I turn my head to the side, and my eyes land on the lamp on my nightstand. My mom sees it too, and opens her mouth to warn Riley, but I'm faster. I grab the lamp by its golden, rod-like body and pull at its cord, then smash it against the side of Riley's head.

Shards of glass rain down on me, just as Riley howls in surprise and gets away from me. He curses when blood drips into one of his eyes from the gash on his forehead, then falls back onto the bed.

The song on my speaker changes to *Still Alive*, by Demi Lovato, just as I scramble to my knees, kicking away my shorts when they tangle between my ankles. I straddle Riley's waist, and as he looks up at me, his complexion pales when he sees the rod in my hand.

"Get off me," he rasps, then groans and grabs his bleeding head.

I'm breathing too fast, and I feel a strange sort of rush pumping through my veins. "Still wanna grab my tits, Riley?" I say, then run a hand under my nose to wipe away the snot. "Still wanna fuck me and taste my lips?"

"Get the fuck off him, Cignette," Mom warns, fully sober all of a sudden. She comes to a stand on the other side of the bed, and when I lock my gaze with hers, she gives me a look full of rage.

Riley starts sliding out from under me, and my attention snaps back to him. He's about to turn and make a run for it, but I raise my arm and stab the lamp's slightly bent rod right in the center of his chest. Blood splatters across my hair, face, and neck. His eyes bulge, and his mouth opens in a silent scream.

Mom gasps audibly and moves away from the bed.

I pull the rod out before bringing it down on the same spot a second time, a third, and then a fourth, and only stop when I'm sure Riley's dead, and the gaping hole in his chest is wide enough to showcase some of his insides.

I don't know where this strength came from, but I'm glad it did. Succumbing to fear and losing to it yet again would have been a massive mistake. It feels good to have taken matters into my own hands this time, even if it meant ending a life.

I spit at Riley's now-flaccid cock and get off the bed, putting distance between myself and his body. My hands are covered in his blood, and the white mattress underneath him is painted in it.

"What has he done to you?" comes Mom's voice. It's soft and unsure, as if she's scared of raising it in front of me. "What has he turned you into?"

I look at her, and notice that her face is completely ashen. She has pressed herself against the wall, and is clutching her pearl necklace for dear life whilst staring at me as if I'm a stranger.

Maybe I am.

Even *I* don't know who the fuck I am in this moment, so to expect her to be okay with this side of me would be a ridiculous notion.

"Leave my house," she says, then swallows. "*Fucking leave!*"

"He was going to *rape* me, Mom," I make myself say. "How…how can you be okay with that?"

She gives me a blank look, and the weight of everything that has happened in the last few minutes crashes into me all at once. It's like a headfirst collision of thoughts and mental pain and shock, and it's…it's a *lot*. It really fucking is a lot.

I make my way to the door, and Mom shrinks away from me. *Funny how the tables have turned*, I wanna tell her, but don't, and instead, walk out of my room. I cross the foyer and enter the garden, and only when I've covered half of it, do I let go of the pressure in my chest, and start crying. My voice rings out against the silence, and pairs with my sloppy footsteps as I pass by some of the figurines in the garden. The guards stop their chatter and give me horrified looks when I reach them. They're unsure of how to approach me, or even ask me anything, so they remain as they are, until one of them decides to unlock the gates for me.

"Thank you," I croak out, then head out into the streets, leaving the guards puzzled and tongue-tied behind me.

52.
DORRAN

"Liam Hemsworth can kiss my pale *ass*," Alex slurs a little, then pats his thigh. "Here, fucking *kiss it*."

I laugh, and so does Solo and the rest of the crew.

I glance at Varsha, and when she smiles at me, I reach out and squeeze her hand.

"Whoever made the decision of recasting Geralt is going to rot in hell," Alex continues, then frowns and takes a long pull of beer from the bottle in his hand. "Cursed hemorrhoid."

"Did you just call an actual human being a hemorrhoid?" I ask him.

"Fuck yeah, I did." He grins. "I'm very drunk, aren't I?"

"No shit, Sherlock," Jayce says from next to him, then kisses the top of Alex's head.

I widen my legs and lean back in my chair, then check my phone. I'd texted Cignette a while ago, asking her to come hang out with me and the others at *Finesse*, but she hasn't responded yet. I called her, but her phone's switched off. And her not getting back to me is grating at my nerves *and* making me uneasy. Wonderful combo, if I do say so myself.

Solo wanted to have a drink night with the crew and I, and had come to *Finesse* after closing time with way too many 6 packs. None of us could say no to that. And so, we're sitting outside the garage now, with a small bonfire in the center, listening to Alex whine about Henry Cavill being replaced by Liam Hemsworth as Geralt in *The Witcher*.

I throw the butt of my cigarette inside the empty beer bottle at my foot, then check my phone again, and when I see nothing, I grit my teeth and grab a chilled bottle from the cooler next to Jayce. I look up, and Solo, who is sitting opposite me, lifts a brow at me. I shake my head at him, and pop open the bottle's cap, then give into the beer's sweet taste by gulping it down in one go.

"Is it just me, or does Dorran have three heads?" Alex says, then bends and squints at me. "Nevermind, it's me."

Everyone laughs, and I can't help but join them.

"Dorran?" Varsha touches my arm, and when I look at her, the shock on her face is palpable as she points at something to my right.

I follow it, and my breaths stutter when I see her.

Solo, Alex, and Jayce turn when they see me, and the former curses when he, too, watches as Cignette, drenched in blood, makes her way to us.

Beer splashes on the ground when I throw the bottle that's in my hand, then rush towards her. She stops when I reach her, and looks up at me with wet eyes and trembling lips.

My heart is going mad in my chest, and it takes great effort to even breathe properly.

"What happened?" I ask her, and give her a once over. Her feet are bare and soiled, and she's holding something in one of her hands – a rod, I think. I take it from her and drop it to the side, then cup her face.

Solo and the others join us, but none of them utter a word.

"He tried to rape me," Cignette says softly, then starts crying. "And she…she just stood there and did nothing."

My blood is ice in my veins. "Who?" I swallow. My head feels heavy, and briefly, memories of my past resurface, reminding me of the teenage boy I once was.

"Riley…" she whispers, then tells me everything that happened in her bedroom, and how she left the estate and walked all the way over to *Finesse*.

To say that I'm angry would be laughable. I'm livid – both at myself and at that bitch, Miranda. I should have killed her the very first time instead of warning her to stay away from Cignette, but I softened; I let emotions cloud my judgment. And this – this very moment we're all witnessing – is the consequence of the mistake I made.

"Jesus Christ, what the fuck is *wrong* with Miranda?" Solo mutters. "Her own *daughter…*"

I blink when my eyes sting, then run my thumbs over Cignette's cheeks. "Are you hurt?" My voice cracks towards the end, so I clear my throat.

She steps closer to me, and her tears smear the blood on her face. "No."

I nod, and step away from her before looking at Varsha. "Take her to my loft." I then look at Jayce. "Carry her upstairs?"

"Of course." He pats my arm, then faces Cignette. "Is it okay if I…?" He gestures at her frame. "If I…"

"Yes," she says to him. "Yes, please. I don't think I can walk anymore."

I fist my hands as my rage multiplies. Fuck Miranda. Fuck the goddamn universe.

I wait until Jayce and Varsha have left with Cignette, then go to pull my phone out of my pocket, only to realize it isn't there.

"Here." Alex hands it to me, then places a hand on my shoulder. "It was lying next to the cooler."

"Thanks." I take it from him, and as I'm opening my list of contacts, I notice that my hand is shaking a little.

"Breathe, Dor," Solo says from next to me. "Fucking breathe."

I inhale and exhale unevenly, then nod to myself and put my phone to my ear.

"The hell you want, fuck-face?" Maverick grumbles, presumably half asleep.

"Not now, man."

He's silent for a beat, and I hear the click of a door opening. "What is it?"

"It's Cigs." I stretch my neck and brace myself to say the next words. "Riley tried to rape her, but–"

"*What the fuck?*" he yells.

"Listen to me," I hiss, and once I'm sure he's going to comply, I continue. "He tried, but *failed*. Cignette was able to escape, thankfully. She did, however, end up killing him, and when she left the estate, the night shift guards saw her. It's quite a bit of a mess, given that the body is still in her room and the guards are obvious witnesses of the state she was in. Think you can handle both situations on your own?"

"*Fuck*," he whispers. "Yeah, yeah, of course. The guards won't be a problem; they're acquaintances, and will keep their mouths shut if they know what's best for them. And yeah, I'll handle the body." He sighs, then curses again. "How's she? Is she okay?"

I sniff and run a hand over my jaw. "Mentally, I don't think so. Physically, yes, she's fine."

"Well, I'll fucking take it."

"Can you find where Miranda is?" I ask him.

A pause, and then, "Wait, she was there?"

"She stood by and let it happen."

"God, I'm going to cut that cunt to pieces," he sneers.

"Find out where she is, and we'll do it together," I promise him.

I'll damn everything to hell, and I'll make sure Miranda Adler doesn't see the morning sun, because that bitch just messed with the wrong guy – *again* – and this time, the only penalty for her actions, is *death*.

53.
DORRAN

I enter my loft's bathroom, and find Cignette standing in front of the wide mirror, staring at her reflection.

"I killed someone today," she says shakily, in between fresh tears. "Dorran, I *killed* someone…"

I walk over to her and take my place behind her, and when she looks at me through the mirror, I cup her shoulders and bend to press a kiss on the back of her head.

"You did it to protect yourself. You did it because you had no other choice, Cigs."

Her body succumbs to mine as she sighs. "But *he* did." She sniffs. "He could have chosen not to do the things he did, or say the things he said to me. He didn't, and so I…"

"You did what was *right*," I say, then turn her around so that I can look at her proper. "Men like Riley deserve death, and they deserve it from the hands of the people they have, or have *tried* to, assault. Our law is good and all, but it doesn't come with the guaranteed satisfaction of ending a life that did us wrong. And Cigs, what you did is justified; it was fucking self-defense."

She blinks at me as she cries, and fuck, I can't see her like this.

Twice now I've been robbed the chance of personally killing the men who hurt the women in my life. But nonetheless, I'm proud of Varsha and

Cignette for doing what needed to be done, even if it gnawed at their conscience.

"Will you let me clean you up?" I ask Cignette.

She nods faintly, then gives me a barely-there smile. I know it's not a lot, but it's *something*, at least.

I pull her hoodie over her head, and fix her hair when they stick up in odd places. "Go on; I'll join you in a bit."

She walks into the shower and turns on the faucet.

I straighten her hoodie, and am about to throw it into the washer, when I feel the weight of something in my hand. I dig into her pockets, and find the lighter she'd gotten me, in one of them. With a smile, I slide it into my jeans pocket and put the hoodie away. I then strip down to my boxers, set my clothes aside, and join Cignette in the shower.

Her eyes are closed; her hands are rested by her sides. Warm water, tainted by the blood on her body, cascades down the swan tattooed on her back, over the peaks of her breasts, and then gathers at our feet.

She makes a beautiful sight – a fallen angel washing away her sins, and her pain. She's the very definition of perfection – my unholy addiction.

She turns when she feels me behind her, then looks up at me with wet lashes and open eyes.

I join her under the spray of water and wrap my arms around her waist, and she, in turn, places a hand on my chest.

"Hey."

She smiles – genuinely this time. "Hey."

"Tell me what you're thinking."

She takes a moment to mull things over.

"I feel numb, I guess," she says after a short while, then swallows. "I'm more shocked by what I did than I am guilty. Is that…normal?"

"Yes," I answer honestly. "But the word normal has a different meaning for everyone, and the last thing I want you to do is compare your feelings to someone else's. Because Cigs, only *you* can put a label on what's going on with you right now, and whatever it is, it's *okay*."

She shakes her head. "I don't know, Dorran."

"But I do." I reach over and twist the knob that's on the wall behind her, shutting off the faucet. "Your courage, your determination towards life – these are layers of you; feathers that bleed out against the odds you've faced, and continue to face. You've been hurt, broken down to the point where you gave up on being strong for yourself, but you've got that part of you back now, and I want you to keep it. Because baby, fearlessness is a hot look on you, and fuck if I'm not weak in the knees for you."

She laughs, but she also cries at the same time. And then she just sobs.

"Cigs." I pull her to me.

"I want you," she whispers, then touches her wet fingers to my abs. There's an enticing tint on her cheeks, one that's putting my self-control to its limit.

I frown and shake my head. "Cignette, I can't. I–"

"I *need* you," she says, urgency clear in her voice. "Wash away his touch from my skin, his words from my mind. Because water won't be enough for either of those things, Dorran; it has to be *you*."

Fuck me, how am I supposed to say no to that?

I let go of a breath and press my forehead to hers. "Are you sure?"

"With you? Always."

I clench my jaw as a wave of emotions crashes against me at her confession. "Damn you for making me lose my resolve."

She pushes her fingers into my hair and touches her nose to mine. "Have me. Just…please, have me, Dorran."

Her plea does it for me; it cuts through the very last shred of my restraint. With my heart a rhythmic beat in my ears, I shift us so that her back is pressed against the steam-covered glass panel to my left, then move my hands away from her waist and bring them higher. I outline the swell of her breasts with my fingers, then go lower, until I've reached her thighs. I continue my ministrations and slide a hand over her pussy, making her gasp. I lean in and kiss her, swallowing the soft noises she's making in time with my fingers working her slit.

She whimpers against me, and when I break the kiss, she drops her head forward, resulting in her long hair to curtain the sides of her face. She's panting, and her breaths fan against my cheek. My cock strains against my wet boxers as I continue to drag my fingers up and down the length of her pussy, and when she groans, arching her back against the glass, I push two fingers inside her and press my thumb to her clit.

"Dorran…" she rasps. "It's not enough. Fuck, I need more."

I curl my fingers inside her, and she starts trembling. Her lips are parted and her eyes are hooded, which means she's close. She's so wet that I can hear the sound of my fingers moving in and out of her, and the way she's clenching around my digits is making my cock ache for release.

Cignette tugs at the waistband of my boxers. "Take this off and fuck me, Dorran," she urges.

I pull my fingers out of her and get rid of my soaked boxers, then grab her thighs and lift her up. She instantly wraps her legs around my waist, and once I've positioned my cock at her opening, I enter her slowly.

She encircles her arms around my neck and tips her head back, whispering my name when I pull out, and then push into her again.

I keep my movements slow yet consistent, and with each thrust inside her, I feel her clenching around me.

"God…" she moans, then fists my hair and pulls me to her. "You're perfect, Dorran. So good."

I grunt when my balls tighten at her praise, then widen my legs and rotate my hips in a way that allows me to fuck her deeper. She stretches so well for me, *feels* so good around me.

We're so close that we share the same breath. Her nipples brush against my pecs, and her eyes – hypnotic as always – hold mine as I continue to fuck her. Every time I thrust inside her wetness, she rocks against me, heightening our pleasures. I increase my pace, but just a little, only because I'm eager to feel her orgasm against my cock.

I love how we join; how every other feeling fails in comparison to her body on mine.

I groan and thrust forward, and her pussy squeezes around me – hard. Cignette presses her brows to mine and lets go of a sharp moan, seconds before her entire body shakes as she orgasms.

My release follows soon after. My spine stiffens, and my balls draw up as I spill inside her, with our lips merely an inch apart.

I stay with her like this for a while, basking in the overwhelming buzz I feel throughout me, then gently pull out of her before setting her on her feet. I clean the remaining blood off her hair and body, and once I'm sure there's none of it left on her, I lead us out of the shower.

We don't say anything, because really, no words could justify the calm between us. All I know is that it's there, and I know Cignette feels the same, because she's not as lost as she looked a few minutes ago.

I hand her a towel, and have just grabbed another one for myself, when my phone rings from the floor. Cignette leaves the bathroom and heads into my bedroom, and I pull my phone out from the pocket of my discarded jeans before receiving the call.

"Maverick."

"Body's been dealt with, and the guards have been spoken to," he informs.

"And Miranda?"

"She apparently has a very important last-minute meeting with a realtor in Paris."

What the fuck?

"*Paris?*"

Maverick sighs. "She's planning to open shop over there, it seems, and is in need of a property."

I arch a brow. "Tonight, of all nights?"

"Too convenient." He clears his throat. "How's Nettie doing?"

"She's fine. You heading to the airport right now? It'll take me at least 30 to get there."

"I've almost reached, actually," he says.

I grin. "Good; keep an eye on Miranda. I'm on my way."

"Gotcha." He ends the call.

I get dressed in the same clothes as before, and when I look up, I see that Cignette – still wearing the towel – is curled up on one side and is fast asleep on my bed.

I wish I could hold her, stay by her, but I've got work to do; a bitch to catch. And I won't rest easy until she's in my grasp.

I sigh and leave the bathroom. Staying as quiet as possible, I put a blanket over Cignette, making sure she's otherwise comfortable, then head downstairs.

Ready or not, here I come, Miranda fucking Adler.

54.
DORRAN

The airport's parking lot is thankfully secluded. It's lined with cars, sure, but there's not a single person in sight. Well, no one other than Miranda and her driver, who are currently still inside her silver Lexus. And from the looks of it, they seem agitated, but I can't be sure what exactly it is that they're doing.

"You see anyone?" Solo asks from next to me.

I shake my head, then look around. The airport is illuminated, given the hour, and there's distinct chatter of people, and sounds of various vehicles near the gates.

"There're CCTVs in the lot," I tell Solo. "But fortunately for us, there's none facing the direction Miranda is in right now."

He does a quick sweep as well. "Well, we're in luck."

I open the passenger side door of his SUV. "Let's be quick about it. It's a vulnerable spot as it is; we could have company at any moment."

"Agreed."

We get out of his car, and have merely taken a few steps towards the Lexus, when Maverick slips out of the shadows and joins us.

He greets us with a curt nod. "She just got here," he informs us. "She's got a 10a.m. flight, so I don't know why she's here more than 8 hours before boarding time."

“I’m sure she thought it’d be harder to find her here,” Solo provides. “She can easily gather an audience, or worse, get the attention of the airport security. She knows Dorran will come for her, so she’s chosen to stay here and bide her time.”

“And even if she went to her brother for aid, she knows I’ll find her and kill her anyway, so she’s decided to keep him out of this. She knows she’s messed up, and now she’s looking to run away.” I glance sideways at Maverick. “How do you know her flight timing anyway?”

He lifts a shoulder. “I’m the head of security. If my team hears tiny details about the Adlers, they let me know the same.”

“As long as it works in our favor, I’m okay with it,” Solo adds, and when I look at him, he hands me a pistol.

I take it from him, and make sure the suppressor is in place, then stretch the fingers of my free hand to rid some of the tension there.

I’m not one for guns, and using them always leaves me dissatisfied. But tonight’s situation calls for less blood and more action, and a pistol is perfect for that, I suppose.

I stop in front of the passenger side of Miranda’s Lexus. Her back is to me, and she’s typing something on her phone, so she doesn’t see me. Her driver, however, notices me almost instantly. His eyes widen, and he says something to Miranda, whose shoulders stiffen. She turns abruptly, and our eyes meet. I send a mock wave her way, and her lips press into a thin line.

She pushes the button to drop down her window’s glass, then swallows. “I’ll have you know that I’m untoucha–”

“Just get out of the goddamn car, you spineless cunt,” Maverick says, shocking her.

She gasps, then glowers at him. “How *dare* you talk to me–”

“You’re wasting our time, Miranda,” I cut in, then scratch my left temple with the suppressor’s tip. “You knew this’d happen; you know there’s no escape for you this time.”

She notices the pistol, and all color drains from her face, making her appear even more ghastly.

"You think I'm scared of you?" she braves saying, then glances between me, Solo, and Maverick. "You think I'll beg you to let me go?" She scoffs. "Fucking foolish."

I click my tongue. "I don't know what gave you the idea that I even *remotely* wanna hear your baseless nonsense, but either way, I couldn't care less. Just get out of the car and stop getting on my nerve."

She glares at me. "What's to stop me or my driver here from calling my brother and having you disposed for your blatant audacity?"

I tilt my head and look at the driver in question, and before Miranda can so much as blink, I point my gun forward and shoot the sorry fuck right in the center of his head.

So much for "less blood".

He falls backward at the impact, and his brain, along with his blood, splatters against the glass window behind him.

Miranda muffles her scream behind a hand, and her entire body shakes as she realizes that she's truly alone right now.

"*This*," I sneer at her, then grin and place a forearm on her car's hood before leaning in. "Now, unless you wanna test me further, I suggest you do as I've asked."

"Why not just shoot me as you did him?" she asks.

"And deny Cignette the golden opportunity of watching you grovel for your life? Not a chance."

She seethes in silence as she watches me. "You are nothing but an ungrateful dog," she hisses. "And I can't wait to have my brother drag you and your friends through the streets of Rive–" She stops when I sigh out loud.

"That sounds marvelous, really." I smirk. "But I want you to get out of the car now, Miranda. Because if you don't, then I'll have to pull you out of it. And make no mistake, I *will* do it, consequences be damned."

She opens her mouth to spew some random shit at me once again, but I press the gun to her lips, shutting her up.

"Out, *now*," I say. "Do it, because I won't fucking ask again."

She must see something on my face because she relents and does as I've asked. With her eyes blazing in anger – at me, obviously – she unlocks the door and gets out of her car.

"Was that so hard?" Solo says with a roll of his eyes.

She doesn't answer him, and when I push her forward, she stumbles, but rights herself and follows Solo to his SUV.

I turn to Maverick. "You joining us?"

He points a thumb at the Lexus. "Don't you think we should take care of this mess first?"

"I have a team that'll deal with it, no problem."

He nods. "Perfect. I'll follow you and Chris, then."

I nod back at him, then pull my phone out and send Eddie a picture of Miranda's car's number plate, along with instructions on what to do, and where to find the car. Once I've done that, I join Solo, and slide into the driver's side of his SUV. Shifting to look behind me, I find Miranda glaring murderously at me once again. This time, however, her hands are tied, and there's a piece of black duct tape covering her too-big mouth.

I glance at Solo. "How long have you been waiting to do this?"

He's sitting next to Miranda, and scowls when I smirk at him. "Go fuck yourself, Dor."

I chuckle and hand his pistol back to him. "Keep this close, in case she decides to go wild on you." I then look at Miranda. "Cliché formalities and all. They make for a good time, don't you think?"

Her nostrils flare, but because she can't speak, she decides to shoot daggers at me.

Not that I care.

I face forward, and before I drive us out of the parking lot, I send Varsha a quick text, asking her to bring Cignette and the rest of the crew to the underground gym.

55.
CIGNETTE

I follow Varsha further into the underground gym, wrapping my arms around myself when my nipples pebble against the chill. The overhead lights flicker on occasion – a usual trait here – and the smell of wet stone and sweat permeates the air. I've only been here a handful of times in the last few months, but this place has never ceased to make me shiver.

Varsha had woken me up earlier and told me that Dorran wanted us all at the gym. I'd still been half asleep when I'd grabbed a random sweatshirt and shorts from his closet and dressed myself, and had only gained a full sense of myself after Alex had shaken me awake multiple times during the ride here.

"Nettie."

I blink and look ahead, and find Mave standing next to a small dumbbell rack.

What is he doing here?

I smile, despite the confusion, then start making my way to him, but he rushes forward and wraps me in his arms, all but engulfing me in his warmth.

"I'm so sorry I wasn't there when it all happened," he says against my ear.

I hold onto him and close my eyes, sighing against his familiar presence. "You couldn't have known, Mave."

"But we know Miranda's impulses. We know she's a goddamn psychopath." He pulls back and looks down at me. "And I should have fucking been there – this time, of all."

I shake my head. "Maybe it was time for me to finally stand up for myself the way I should've since the very beginning."

He works his jaw as he studies me. "What you did was…huge. It'd be stupid to ask how you feel about it, but I really wanna know if you're okay."

I hug myself and shrug. "I guess I am. The event flashes in my mind in fragments; in bits and pieces. Maybe it's because I haven't let myself think about it fully. I'm scared that once, or *if*, I do, it'll take over me completely."

"I can understand that. It's not something you can just forget, or ignore indefinitely. But remember why you did what you did, Nettie, and know it's in the past now. And if you need to talk to someone about it when things get too hard to handle, there's always me, or we can get help–"

"I don't want that," I cut in, then swallow. "I… I can take it. I'll get over it."

Mave's brows knit together as he looks at me. "That's not how it works."

I shift on my feet and avert my gaze from his. "Dorran doesn't need therapy, and he's killed more people than you and I can count."

"You're not him," Mave argues. "And you never will be."

"But I'm getting there, aren't I?"

He places his hands on my shoulders and steps close to me. "Look at me."

I grit my teeth and keep staring at the dumbbell on the lowest shelf. The rubber around its middle has peeled off a little, and is hanging loose, ready to be pulled off. My fingers itch to do just that, but I also don't feel like moving my body.

"*Nettie*."

I reluctantly meet Mave's eyes. "What?"

He sighs. "You wanna tell me why you think you're like Dorran?"

I lift a shoulder. "He killed his mom for what she did to him all those years ago, and tonight, I got close to doing the same. I was consumed by something unnamable, and I wonder if I'd just *done it* instead of walking away…" I chuckle. "I think that's the thing I can't stop mulling over in my head the most."

Something like surprise takes over his features. "Done what?"

"Killed my mom, Mave," I say, then let go of a breath. "I don't think I've ever said it out loud, or even thought about it consciously, but the idea has always been there, isn't it? The desire, the *will*." I scoff and rub my hands over my face. "I want her dead, and I wanna do it with my own hands. I want her to beg me, to fall on her knees and just…*beg*."

Mave cups the side of my face and tilts it upward. "Then you'll be glad to know that your wish will be fulfilled tonight."

I frown. "I don't understand."

"Dorran called me earlier and told me what'd happened, then asked me to track Miranda. She was hiding at the airport's parking lot, waiting to leave for Paris for a *meeting*. We ended up finding her before she did, though, and fuck-face plans on killing her. It's why you're here; why we're all here."

I suck in a breath. "You have Mom?" A spark of something hot burns in my veins, and I suddenly don't feel so numb.

Mave nods, then gestures behind him at the open hallway. "He's in there with her. Go."

I swallow and step away from him. "You'll be here when I get back, right?" I ask.

Silver lines his expressive eyes. "Always, Nettie."

I squeeze one of his hands, then head towards the hallway. It's a wide piece of area behind a concrete wall, with nothing in or around it but a glass paneled door that leads to a dimly lit room, and an out-of-place leather couch Solo is sitting on, reading a Marvel comic.

"Ah, there you are," he says when he sees me, then drops the comic on the couch before getting to his feet. "He's in there," he tells me, jerking his head towards the door. "And now that you'll be joining him, I'll be outside. I've got stuff to prepare." He reaches me, touches one of my arms gently, then walks away.

Wow.

I make my way towards the door, and the closer I get to it, the more I can see what's beyond it through the glass panel on its top half. Saws, knifes, hammers, belts, cleavers, and some needle-like rods. Goosebumps mar my entire body upon seeing how well each and every one of these items is lined; how easily accessible they must be to the person who wants to use them.

I reach close enough to the door that I can twist its knob if I want to, and look inside, only to gasp and place a hand over my mouth when I see Dorran, all but bathed in blood, crouched before a body. He's got a kitchen axe in his right hand, and because his back is turned to me, I can't exactly see what it is that he's chopping off, off the corpse in front of him.

I'm beyond shaken, even though I know I shouldn't be. This is who he is, after all – dark, unforgivably unapologetic; insane in the face of ending lives. And God, I still love him, despite seeing him practically cut a human to pieces.

I look towards the other side of the room, and find Mom – her wrists and ankles tied, and her mouth taped shut – crying as she watches Dorran. Her face is streaked black from her mascara, and her hair is a dirty mess around her. Her grey pencil dress is smudged black, and so are her legs.

The sight she makes is beyond satisfying, and if I had my phone with me, I'd have taken a photo of her and nailed it to my bedroom wall.

She must've felt a presence or something, because she turns in my direction, and when our eyes meet, she starts fighting against her restraints. Every time she jerks to free herself, her back bangs against the steel cabinet behind her, making a loud thump-like sound.

Her actions make Dorran turn as well, and when he sees me, he grins and gets to his feet. Gone is the man who'd stood behind me and uttered words of encouragement in my ear only hours ago. Who'd fucked me in his shower and cleaned me up after. Because who I see before me is death itself – materialized; made human.

Dorran walks over to the door and stands in front of it, then places his left hand on the glass panel before looking down at me.

I align my hand against his, then scan his blood-splattered face. "What are you doing?"

He cants his head slightly and taps the tip of the kitchen axe to his earlobe. "I can't hear you." Whether he speaks those words or mouths them, I can't tell.

I gesture downwards, asking him to unlock the door. He nods, then steps back and pulls it open for me. Just as soon as he's done it, a too-strong wave of ice-cold air hits me, followed quickly by the overpowering smell of raw meat and blood.

"*Christ*," I whisper, then press the back of my hand over my nose. "Dorran, what the fuck?"

He chuckles. "Too much for ya?"

"You're cutting open a human being, damn you. And the air fucking *stinks*."

"Correction: I'm *dismembering* Toby over there, not cutting him open." He clicks his tongue, then waves towards *Toby*, whose bleeding arms are placed near his head instead of being where they actually should be.

"Besides, your mother needed a bit of entertainment before her reckoning, and that's exactly what I was providing. It is, after all, the least I can do for her."

I can't help but laugh. Like, a full-blown outburst. Anyone else would see me and think I've lost it, but Dorran just grins, making me laugh harder.

"You're unbelievable," I say with a shake of my head.

"And you're fucking priceless, Little Swan," he muses.

Six simple words, and yet, they warm me from the inside out. Only because *he's* the one who said them.

I take my hand away from my nose and try not to focus on the stench, then enter the room and stand directly in front of Dorran. He arches a brow at me, and I rise on my tiptoes to bring my face close to his.

"Say that again."

He smirks. "You're fucking *priceless*, my Little Swan."

I glance at his lips, and watch as they spread into a deviant smile. "Yours, huh?" I meet his gaze.

His pupils are flared, and the glint in them is unmistakable. "Did I stutter?"

I chuckle. "Kiss me, then," I say, and erase the space between us before fisting his soiled vest.

He lets go of a slight hiss, drops the kitchen axe, and pulls me to him. He then wraps the fingers of his right hand around my throat and squeezes, cutting off my air supply.

My lungs burn as I struggle to breathe, and when I let go of a strangled groan, Dorran laughs and presses his lips to mine.

My senses go haywire at the taste of blood, and for the man holding me at his mercy. I moan and kiss him harder, opening him up enough to suck on his tongue.

Dorran moans out loud, and it's a sound devoid of inhibition; it's husk and lust, molded together.

He loosens his grip on my throat, and I in turn bunch his hair in a fist.

"You've consumed me entirely, Cignette," he rasps against me. "And my God, I'm mad for you. Fucking ravenous." He all but crashes his mouth to mine, making me arch against him. I'm wet, I'm hot, and it's…too much.

"You're one to talk," I tell him, and when he chuckles, I press my teeth to his bottom lip, puncturing the soft skin there.

Dorran moans again – louder this time – then thrusts his hips forward, and his rock-hard cock pushes against my stomach.

I grin, then suck on his bottom lip, relishing the taste of his blood on my tongue. Getting high on the very essence that's a part of every inch of him. The thing that makes him who he is.

Dorran pulls back, then presses open-mouthed kisses to my jaw, my neck, and my collarbone. He licks a path from my throat, all the way up to my chin, then travels lower again. I close my eyes and massage his scalp as he bites and sucks on the skin behind my ear, and bring my other hand down between us to cup his growing boner.

He grunts and presses his nose to the side of my neck while he rocks his hips into my hand. His breathing is hard, heavy, and it only serves to make me wetter for him.

Something bangs against the steel cabinet – once, twice, and then a third time.

I blink myself out of the trance I'd fallen into, and let go of Dorran's hair. He scowls and turns around to face my mom, who is glaring at us from the floor.

"Too eager to die, are you, Miranda?" he taunts, then kicks at her tied-up feet, making her cry out. He then points at Toby's body, which is now turning blue in the face. "Wanna end up like him, then, or would you like the special treatment?"

Chills rake through me at the ice in his voice. It's leveled and calm – a deadly combination when it comes to him.

Mom thrashes against her binds, just like I'd thrashed under Riley, pleading with him to stop. Images from earlier assault my mind, but I swallow and push them away.

You're not the pain you've endured, I tell myself. *Chin up; stay strong*.

Dorran faces me, just as I steady my breathing and look at him.

"You alright?" he asks, then touches his knuckles to my cheek.

"I will be," I answer honestly, then give him a small smile.

He places a kiss between my brows, then presses his forehead to mine. "I'm here, okay? Always. Whatever you need."

Countless emotions tighten my chest. "I know," I whisper, then give him a brief kiss. "I know."

56.
CIGNETTE

"For the love of…" Dorran moves away from me and turns to look at Mom when she pushes the cabinet yet again.

I glare at her, but she keeps her gaze locked on him.

"Can't you see your daughter happy for one fucking minute?" he questions, then scoffs at what he's said. "Of *course* you can't. It's one of the reasons why you're gonna die tonight. Are you fucking excited about it? Because I sure as hell am."

I glance at Toby, and at the thick stream of blood that's surrounding him, and imagine my mom in his place. It wouldn't be wrong of me to say that I'm eagerly looking forward to watching her bleed out, but more than that, I'm excited to witness the process that will lead to it.

Mom falls sideways and starts shifting away from Dorran, and let's just say that it's…awkward.

He raises his hands in mock defeat, making my lips twitch. "You literally made all that noise to get my attention, and now you're moving away from me?" he says to her, and when she shakes her head and continues to slide away from him, he sighs and presses the heel of one of his boots to her bound ankles.

She cries, to which he rolls his eyes.

"I don't have time for this shit," he mutters. "Let's take you out of this room so that I can be done with you for good." He grabs her by the hair and starts dragging her towards the door, ignoring her broken sobs.

As he should.

"Dorran?"

He stops at my voice.

I walk over to him. "I can't hear her screams clearly enough," I say.

He blinks, then lets go of a surprised chuckle. "Do the honors, then," he states, and jerks his head at Mom.

I take a step back and look down at her, and when her teary eyes bore into mine, I give her a wink before pulling away the duct tape from her mouth with as much force as I can muster.

She yelps in pain, and it's a pleasing sound, albeit a short one.

Dorran grins at me, then resumes dragging her out into the hallway. She screams and curses all the way through, and it's ineffective enough that it doesn't even bother me.

Bitch. Cunt. Whore. Perfect nicknames for the Flawed Princess, I suppose.

We enter the main gym area, and I notice two metal chairs in the center of the room. They're placed in such a way that they're facing each other, and next to one of these chairs is a wooden table, upon which is a surgical tray. There're a couple of pliers in this tray, and I can only imagine how Dorran is going to use them on my mother. *If* he decides to use them at all, that is.

Mave and Solo are standing next to one of the walls in the room, half-shadowed by darkness, whereas Jayce and the rest of the crew have taken to the other corners of the room.

"Christ, fuck-face. What *happened* to you in there?" Mave says, giving Dorran repeated once-overs, clearly rattled by the amount of blood on him.

“He had fun, is what happened,” Solo provides, then chuckles when Dorran flips him off.

“If you plan on spending time with us, then you’ve got to get used to seeing Dorran like this,” Jayce says. “He’s our resident butcher, in case you didn’t know.”

“Yeah, and I’m itching to gut a pig next,” Dorran adds, giving Jayce a too-wide smile. “Wanna volunteer, my dear?”

Alex snorts, and Jayce grabs his crotch before mouthing, “*Fuck you*,” to Dorran.

Mave glances at them, then shakes his head and folds his arms across his chest. “Why the fuck did I even ask?” he mutters to himself, making us laugh.

Dorran shoves Mom in Varsha’s direction, then settles into the chair that’s got the wooden table beside it. “Get her ready,” he orders Varsha.

Alex joins her, holding onto Mom while Varsha unties her hands. He then pushes Mom down into the chair opposite Dorran’s, and Varsha secures her wrists to its armrests. Once they’re done, the two step back and join Jayce. Feeling out of place, I make my way to Mave and stand next to him.

“You okay?” he asks, then scans me from head-to-toe. “There’s blood on you.”

“Not mine.”

“I gathered as much.” A wistful sort of look takes over his face, but he brushes it away and nods ahead. “These people are crazier than I’d imagined,” he whispers. “But I have to say, though: Miranda has never looked as fucked up as she does right now.”

I chuckle. “True fashion icon, isn’t she?”

He makes a sound in the back of his throat, to which I laugh.

“Will the two of you stop giggling?” Solo hisses from next to Mave. The latter tries to protest, but Solo arches a brow, quieting him.

"Yo, Ledge; what's our plan here?" Varsha asks, and the three of us turn our attention forward again. "For shit to not go sideways, we'll have to make her death look like an accident."

"You dare speak about me as if I'm dead!" Mom sneers in a cracked voice. "You are nothing compared to me. *Nothing*."

"Oh, for fuck's sake," Mave mumbles, then marches towards Mom. He reaches her, and when she glowers at him, he rears his right arm back and punches her in the jaw.

Blood spews from her mouth at the impact, and a screech-like sound fills the air as her chair skids backward. For someone who has won-over wealthy investors with merely a shift of her brow, she isn't exactly doing well on her own right now.

"Step aside, Maverick," Dorran says in his signature, too-calm voice.

Mave grits his teeth, keeping his hand fisted. He stares Mom down with so much hatred that it makes my chest ache. He despises her for everything she's done to *me*; for how she's treated *me*.

"You don't deserve a daughter like Cignette," he says to her. "Hell, you don't deserve *anything*. The fame, the money, the forcibly-earned respect – you deserve none of it." He grunts and punches her again. And again. And each time he does it, he draws blood.

I feel the wetness of tears on my cheeks only when Solo places a hand on my shoulder, squeezing it.

"Keep it together, kid," he assures. "And don't even think of looking away. You'll watch what's being done to her, and you'll watch it until we're through with her."

I nod, warmed by his words, and the kindness in his eyes.

He gives me a small smile, then retreats his hand from my shoulder.

"*Maverick*." The warning in Dorran's voice is clear, and it's enough to change the atmosphere in the room.

Mave is in the middle of delivering yet another punch to Mom's already bruised and swollen face, but stops when he, too, senses the shift. He raises his hands by his sides, then spits at Mom's feet before making his way back to me.

"Feel good?" I ask, then glance at the redness around his knuckles. "Apart from those, I mean."

He sniffs and runs a hand over his mouth. "Plenty."

I notice a tick in his jaw as he stares ahead, and the stiffness in his posture. Deciding to let him be, I sigh and focus on Dorran.

He gets to his feet – his eyes on Mom – and starts pulling his chair closer to hers. The sound of metal grating against concrete echoes through the room, thickening the air with tension.

There's bloody saliva dripping down her chin, and she has all but folded in on herself. But when she sees how close Dorran's getting to her, she makes a weak sound of protest. He, of course, ignores it, and once he's satisfied with the new placement of his chair, he brings the table close as well.

Mom's eyes widen almost comically at the sight of the pliers. "Don't do this," she croaks out. "There's still time; don't do this, Dorran."

"And what, let you go? Forget about what you let happen tonight, and what you've been doing to Cignette for *years*?" he counters, then cocks his head to the side. "I don't think so."

Mom starts sobbing, then flinches when the action causes her pain.

"Hurts, doesn't it?" The question passes through my lips before I can even think about it.

Everyone in the room looks at me, Mom included.

"When you want to cry, but can't because you know it'll only hurt more if you do," I continue. "But those salty tears still fall through, making the bruises on your skin *burn*…" I swallow against the lump in my throat, and clench my jaw to stop my chin from trembling. "It fucking *hurts*, Mom, and it only grows. It breaks you from the inside; traps you in an endless loop of fear – both conscious and otherwise."

Dorran meets my eyes, and I see recognition there – towards my words, and the meaning they hold to the both of us.

"Cignette…" Mom's face crumples as she cries. "I'm so…sorry, my sweet. Please forgive me. Forgive me, and I promise to be a better mother to you. Get me out of here, and I swear to you that I'll change. I'll do everything you want me to, but just…please, just get me out of here."

"Are you seriously fucking negotiating with your daughter right now?" Jayce hisses, and makes to step forward, but Alex holds him back.

"I'm asking her for *forgiveness*," Mom argues.

"When you're so close to meeting your end? That's rich, Miranda," Alex counters. "Out of all the times you could have apologized, or even talked yourself out of assaulting Cigs, you choose *now* to atone for your wrongdoings."

"I don't need you, Mom," I say honestly. "Not after how much you've scarred me over the years just to make yourself feel better. You treated me like an enemy, and not like your own flesh and blood – which I fucking *am*. You've made me feel vulnerable and scared in my own skin, and now you want me to forgive you?" I laugh. "*No*. Just…no. You deserve everything that's happening to you right now, and you deserve it because you're a cruel, narcissistic human being, and you need to pay for all the damage you've done to me."

"I gave you money, a status in our society, a fucking house to live in!" she screams brokenly. "What else could you possibly want from me?"

"The fact that you even have to ask me that is proof enough that you shouldn't have been a mother to begin with," I tell her.

She pauses, as if my words have hit her all at once. But then her face contorts just as fast. "Fuck you, you ungrateful little *cunt*."

"Fucking end her before I do it myself, Ledge," Varsha says. "She's breathed long enough."

Dorran sniffs and looks at Mom again, then clocks her in the face, making her groan. "Haven't I told you before not to speak to Cignette with disrespect?" he says, then slaps her cheek. "Haven't I?" Another slap. "Fucking answer me!"

She trembles, then gives him a weak nod. "I'm sorry."

He laughs. "You're sorry…" He shakes his head a little, then slaps Mom again – harder this time. "Too. Fucking. *Late*." He grabs one of the pliers, then presses Mom's left hand flat against the chair's armrest.

She tries to push herself back, but it's of no use.

Dorran opens the plier, then closes it around one of her long nails. Giving her a wink, he pushes the plier back, paying no heed to her screams, and pulls the nail right off her finger.

"You know why I'm doing this?" he asks her, then plucks another one of her nails off, grinning when she begs him to stop. "Because you won't be needing your nails, not after people find you burnt to a fucking crisp in your own car."

She shakes her head, then screams when Dorran pulls off her ring finger nail.

"You were on your way to the airport – all by yourself – when your car caught fire," he continues. "Due to an electrical issue, of course. A few loose wires in the engine, along with some built-up hydrogen, and…*boom*. Goodbye, Miranda Adler."

Mom mumbles something, but it's not clear what she's saying. She's barely got any strength in her, let alone a voice.

Dorran throws the plier back into the tray, then leans back in his chair. "I'm bored," he says plainly, and takes a cigarette out of his jeans pocket. He puts it between his lips, then lights it up with a familiar lighter. The one I had planned on giving him, but hadn't had a chance to.

Death Note.

He takes a drag of his cigarette, and runs the pad of his thumb over the golden skull embossed on the lighter, all the while scanning Mom from top to bottom.

"You know, I thought I'd enjoy torturing you," he tells her. "But you're not fun enough. You beg for mercy one minute, then curse people in the next. Where the hell is your consistency?" He laughs to himself as he takes a second pull from his cigarette, then brings it in front of him. He twists it left and right as if assessing it, then presses its still-burning tip to the bleeding nailbed of one of Mom's fingers.

Her cry reverberates through the walls, making a chill crawl up my spine.

"*Jesus*," Mave mutters from next to me.

"Jayce," Dorran calls, then throws the cigarette on the floor and looks at me. "And you – come here."

I walk over to him, just as he straightens in his chair. When I've reached him, he gestures at his thighs. "Sit."

I do, and wrap an arm around his neck. He places one of his arms over my thighs, and rests the other one on my lower back.

"Remove the ties from around her wrists," he says to Jayce. "Let's give her a final fighting chance, even though she isn't merited to one."

"You are *sick*," Mom grits out, directing her words at Dorran as Jayce unties her.

"What I am, is *dangerous*," he tells her. "And the man who's about to put a full-stop to the never-ending chapter of your life." He nods at Jayce, who moves behind Mom, pulls his curb chain out of his jacket, and wraps it around her neck.

I hold my breath as I watch him, and my nails dig into my skin as my anticipation grows.

Mom's frail body jerks at the initial contact of Jayce's weapon, but when she realizes what's happening, she starts clawing at the chain. When that doesn't seem to work, she tries to break Jayce's grip by banging her fists against his hands. He in turn pulls at the chain, tightening it, and with a very subtle twist of his wrist, he ends up breaking Mom's neck.

Her body goes limp, and her hands fall on her lap. Her mouth opens in a silent scream, and her eyes roll upwards.

She's gone.

I let go of the breath I was holding, and let the rapid beating of my heart soothe me as I stare at my mom's dead body. Gone – she's fucking *gone*.

"Cigs."

I force myself to look away from the sight before me, and face Dorran.

He assesses me slowly, as if he wants to make sure I'm still with him.

"I'm fine," I say, then swallow. "I promise."

"You just lost the only parent you had, Cigs. And even though she was a monster, Miranda was still your mother."

"True, but would you blame me if I told you that all I feel right now, is relief?"

He smiles. "Of course not. I'd never blame you for feeling liberated."

My eyes turn misty at his choice of word. Wanting him closer, I slide my fingers into his hair and touch my forehead to his. "Thank you."

He tilts his head and presses a kiss on my lips. "I'll do it all over again, and then some, if it'll result in you not having to get hurt again."

I'm speechless, helpless against his devotion. And so, instead of answering him – because I don't think I can – I kiss him, relaying my gratitude the only way I'm able to right now.

My mom is dead, and that's going to change things. It may not seem like it right now, but I'm pretty sure the impact of her death will hit hard.

And when it does, it'll put me, and the people I've come to love, in serious danger.

57. CIGNETTE

Riley's hands, his breath – she can feel them on her body.

His words, his threats of dirtying her – they consume her mind, paralyzing her.

He's naked, hovering over her, but she can't move. She's frozen; drowned in shock.

There's laughter, and then there are screams. None are her own, she realizes.

Riley is closer – too close. He's smiling down at her, and it's making her insides burn. He bends to kiss her, but she shakes her head.

No…

Please, stop.

He gets closer still, but her body refuses to move. Her mind thrashes, but her lips can't form the words to put an end to this. He holds her down, and her fear multiplies. He leans in all the way, and finally, her mouth parts, and a scream rips its way out of her.

Stop! No, please…

Stop it…

Please, please, ple–

I gasp and jolt upright in bed, then look around frantically, only to realize I'm in Dorran's bedroom. He's sleeping next to me, and the early-morning sunlight peeking in through the floating curtains, outlines the ridges of his softened features.

I sigh in relief and close my eyes, then rub my hands over my face and tie my hair above my head.

I remember Dorran asking Mave to drive me to his loft while him and the others took care of Toby and my mom's bodies. And I remember all but falling onto the bed the moment I'd gotten here hours ago. What I don't remember is having a throbbing headache, which I'm assuming is the aftermath of my brief nightmare.

I hold my head in my hands and press my fingers into my scalp. As if I needed a goddamn migraine today.

"Cignette?" Dorran's voice is groggy, and when I turn towards him, he sits up and looks at me with sleepy eyes. "What's wrong?"

I fix his hair – still damp from the shower he must've taken – then shift close to him. "Nightmare," I say.

He frowns a little, then pulls me to him.

I wrap my arms around his waist and bury my face into the crook of his neck, relaxing into his warmth.

"Feel every bit of the fear and pain these nightmares bring," he whispers against my hair, then sets a soft kiss on my forehead. "Because the more you learn to embrace them, the less they'll haunt you – both in your sleep, and while you're awake. The tragedies you endure reflect themselves in your dreams. They test your internal strength; look for signs of weaknesses. If you let those demons take over you, you lose. If you learn to let them in, they'll surrender to you. And at the end of the day, that's all you need, isn't it? To win over the darkness inside you so that you don't lose your aim in life."

"But it's so hard to fight all these memories," I admit.

"It always is, Cigs, and I'd be stupid to say otherwise."

I pull back, then smile a little when he leans in to kiss me on the lips. I cup his jaw and kiss him back, then touch my nose to his, letting the calm of this moment steady me.

"Did you get everything sorted?" I ask after a while, then move back and look at him.

He nods. "We had her Lexus placed near a suburban neighborhood in Olivewood Ave. I made sure the car had loose wiring, but Eddie and his team did the rest. It's quite a full area, so I'm sure news has spread already. A few of his team members were supposed to be among the crowd of onlookers, so we can be assured that things won't stray off course."

I sigh, then bring my fingers to his bare chest. "You think my uncle will run an investigation?"

He lifts a shoulder. "I don't know. But for all our sakes, I hope he doesn't. We've been thorough with everything, but no crime is perfect. There is a chance we missed something, and if we have, then an investigation could reveal it."

I swallow, then nod. "If he does decide to go through with it, I'll try persuading him to take the other direction."

"That could make him suspicious of you," Dorran cautions.

"I'll be subtle," I say. "Besides, he is more likely to hea–" I stop when Dorran's phone rings.

He grabs it off the nightstand. "It's Solo," he tells me, then receives the call and puts it on speaker. "Yeah?"

"Chase is *devastated*," Solo starts. "He's called me for advice because he thinks Miranda's death might be a subterfuge and not an accident. He wants to run an inquiry, but his team of advisors think it's bad press, given how close the elections are. They want him to mourn for the media and the people, and gather as many sympathy votes as possible. Opening up an inquiry would give the opposition a chance to challenge his state of mind, or question his ability to handle matters of the county. Also, Chase doesn't trust the new sheriff and his son, and wants me in on the case. Well, *if* he decides on turning this incident into one, that is."

"But you're a citizen, Solo, not the law. Not anymore," Dorran remarks.

"I know, kid, and I plan on keeping things that way. I'm going to push his advisors to join me in influencing him to stick to their plan, because the last thing we need is an official investigation."

Dorran and I glance at each other, and I see how much he, too, wants Solo to succeed.

"Push him as much as you can, but if he doesn't budge, let me know, and I'll try talking to him," I say.

"You should be with him right now, Cignette. Perhaps your presence will make a difference," he suggests. "I'm curious why he hasn't reached out to you still."

And it hits me.

"Shit, I don't have my phone anymore. Uncle Chase must've tried calling me. *Fuck*, he must be worried."

"Relax, kid; I'm sure he thought you heard the news and are grieving or some shit. Don't panic, but do go see him ASAP. You being with him might make him see reason."

"Agreed," Dorran says.

"Alright, I've got to go meet him now, but I'll keep you in the loop. Alert the others, just in case."

"Will do," Dorran tells him. "And Solo?"

"Yeah?"

"Stay safe, alright?"

Solo chuckles. "You too. The *both* of you."

58.
CIGNETTE

There's not going to be an investigation.

Solo managed to convince my uncle to listen to his advisors, and my presence, as he'd predicted, helped Uncle Chase understand how an inquiry could affect both his, and my own, standing in the press. And if the press painted us in a bad light, then the people would lose their faith in the Adler family. And so, to keep our family's reputation intact, my uncle did what is in everyone's best interest: hold a funeral for Mom so that we can finally move on.

It's been almost three days since her death, and even now, as I'm standing next to Mave at the cemetery – surrounded by strangers – I feel absolutely *nothing*.

It's a sunny day today, so I don't have the guise of raindrops to act as my tears. I've tried keeping my eyes open without blinking in hopes of conjuring an illusion for the same, but that hasn't worked. And so, I'm keeping my head bowed, and using my hair as a cover to avoid catching any suspicion.

There's a dull murmur around me, which is irking me to the point where I find myself shifting on my feet and fidgeting with the napkin in my hand. I don't even know why more than half of these elites are here. I'm assuming it's just to brag about something extravagant they've done recently, or to have their faces captured by the media's cameras lurking nearby. I hear the click of shutters, and see brief flashes here and there, but I don't give them much attention. It's hard as it is to avoid the elites' eyes, but if a camera ended up catching my face sans tears or any sort of emotion, then there'll be a scandal too messy for even my uncle and his team to get rid of.

"It's reeking of perfume in here, and it's a goddamn open area," Mave mutters from next to me.

"Just put a hand over your nose and pretend to weep in agony," I say softly. "The people here will buy it, I'm sure."

"Have I told you recently that you're a fucking menace?"

My lips twitch, but I purse them in order to avoid grinning. "Not in the last few days, no."

"Well, I'll be sure to catch up, then."

A snort leaves me, but I quickly turn it into a cough. A few elites glance my way, but then look away when I avoid meeting their stares.

The murmur around me stops all of a sudden. I chance a peek ahead of me, and see a somber-looking Uncle Chase, joined by a few of his guards, carrying a casket on one of his shoulders. A casket that consists of nothing but charred bones of my mother. For everything that she was, and everything that she had, *this* is what's left of her; all that she has *become*.

Fucking crazy where her cruelty landed her, right?

59. DORRAN

I've been watching her for a while, and to say that she looks bored would be an understatement. I can tell by the agitation in her body language that she wants to run away from the crowd, but I guess that'll have to wait.

She's wearing a black dress, and it perfectly outlines each and every one of her curves with how snugly it hugs her willowy frame.

I lean against the massive olive tree I'm standing next to, and slide my hands into the pockets of my green hoodie. It's not the best outfit for camouflaging myself, but hey, at least I tried. There's sweat trickling down my temples from how hot it is today, and it is only amplified by the hood concealing my features.

The people gathered at the cemetery stop their chatter when Chase and some of his guards bring out the casket. They're burying Miranda's remains instead of simply cremating her. A public show of commiseration, no doubt.

The officiator is saying something as the burial liner lowers the casket into the ground, and the media representatives surrounding the cemetery go wild – flashing their cameras and capturing pictures of the moment, and of Chase as he all but breaks down in grief.

I roll my eyes and look at Cignette again, and what I see makes a grin spread across my face. She's smirking at the dug-up hole in which the casket has just been placed, and there's something about her expression that's so beautifully aberrant, that it makes a fire burn in the very center of my chest. I don't know what the hell it means, or why it's as strong as it is, but what I *do* know is that it's coming from so deep inside me, that it threatens to consume me entirely.

And if I'm being honest, I would let it scorch the fuck out of me if *this* is how it'll make me feel for the rest of my days.

The crowd starts to disperse, and I watch as Cignette heads towards the parking area with Maverick. The ceremony's over, it seems.

Turning away from the cemetery, I push back my hood, then ruffle my sweaty hair and start walking down the street to my Harley.

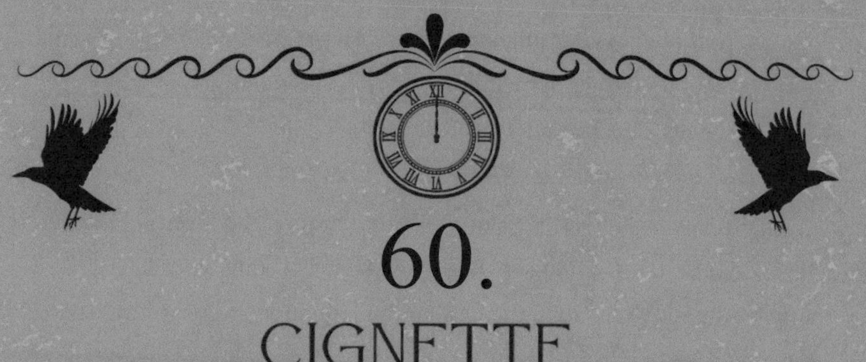

60.
CIGNETTE

"What?" I say in disbelief, staring at my uncle. He's sitting at the head of the conference room table in *Imperia*, surrounded by his team and a few investors. I'm standing next to him, with Mave behind me. I'm glad he's here with me, because there's a strong chance I might fall after having heard what Uncle Chase has just said to me.

I was in Mave's Range Rover, about to head back to the estate after the funeral ceremony, when I'd gotten a call from my uncle. He asked me to come to *Imperia* because he had something important to tell me, and even though I'd been *this* close to saying no to him, I'd agreed.

Now I wish I'd just said no.

"I don't want you to fight me on this, Cignette," he tells me with a frown. "Because my decision will not change."

"You're selling *Lure* to strangers, goddamn it! And you didn't even think of discussing it with me in private before holding a meeting about it."

Frustration flashes across his face. "This *meeting*, as you call it, is not about *Lure*; it's about my campaign. But because Mr. and Mrs. Goswami are here already, I thought I could finalize everything with them so that the paperwork process can begin. Besides, they aren't strangers to me. They're one of *Lure's* biggest investors, so it makes sense for them to buy the company, now that your mother is gone." His expression crumples at the last bit, but he manages to neutralize it without anyone noticing it.

My hands clench around the table's blunt edge. "*Lure* is mine by right. You can't take it from me like this."

"It was your mother's wish," he says, shocking me further. "She wanted *Lure* to be sold to someone who paid handsomely for it, and she wanted the sum to be used in our charities. But my sister wasn't the best when it came to handling wealth, so I've decided that the money Mr. And Mrs. Goswami have agreed to pay for *Lure*, will be transferred to your account." He shifts in his chair and moves closer to me. "You're an *Adler*, sweet pea. You've got money beyond comprehension. You don't need to run a company. Hell, you don't even have to *work*. Whatever I've done over the years, I've done for you. You've got everything you need; can't you see that?"

"Is this supposed to make me feel better?" I ask. "Or do you want me to build a temple in your name – with *Lure's* money, of course – and worship you like a damn God or some shit for the generosity you're showing me?"

"Cignette." His dark eyes narrow slightly, indicating that he's upset. "You will *behave*."

"Don't treat me like a child," I hiss.

"Then stop fucking acting like one!" He slaps the table in hopes of rattling me, but I don't even blink, which surprises him a little.

"I have a vision for *Lure*. I have things I want to do, to change in it. I wanna run the place; take it to new heights. Don't steal that opportunity from me," I say.

"You've never really shown any interest in the brand, so forgive me if I don't take your word for it," Uncle Chase counters. "I'd rather sell *Lure* and walk away from it with money, than watch it fall, and then beg people to invest in it. Because let's face it, the brand is struggling, and there's barely a chance it'll bounce back to how it used to be."

I don't know what to say to that. I'm hurt by his words, but he's right, isn't he? I've spent so long keeping my voice to myself in fear of enraging my mom, and in turn, him, that my intentions never really got a chance to be seen. I've spent *years* cowering and sticking to the sidelines, and it's only since Dorran came into my life that I've found the strength I didn't even know I had. And I know it sounds like I'm firing a gun from over his shoulder, but that's not the case. Dorran is the catalyst that broke my cycle of cowardice. He awakened in me what has been there from the very beginning: the power to fight for myself, and for what's mine. Seeing him, listening to him, and understanding the ways he works in, has inspired me to be stronger. There's nothing wrong with that, in my opinion, but I understand how some might think he influenced me the wrong way, or that I've become dependent on him in all the ways a woman shouldn't be on a man like him.

"Let me at least try to manage the HQ for a few months," I tell Uncle Chase. "One shot – that's all I'm asking for."

He shakes his head. "I don't have the time for it, nor the energy. *Lure* is a lost cause, and you'll do good by letting it go."

"You won't budge, regardless of what I say," I state the obvious, then step away from him. The people around the table pretend to focus on their laptops and files, but I know they've heard everything. "If you were going to be unreasonable from the start, why call me here? You should have done what you thought is right, because that's exactly what you've ended up doing anyway." I turn around, ignoring the eyes that track my every move, and walk out of the room.

I bypass some of the hotel staff on my way out, and stop only when I've reached Mave's car. I realize that my hands are fisted, and the anger I feel is making me dizzy.

I stop in front of the Range Rover and glare at one of its back tires. Digging my heels into the ground, I grit my teeth and ready myself to kick said tire, but before I can swing a foot to do just that, Mave grabs me by the waist and lifts me, then places me a safe distance from his car.

"No," he says when I sneer at him.

"How could he do this to me?"

"It's done, Nettie."

"I know, okay? But how could he fucking *do* this?" I raise my hands in exasperation and exhale heavily. "What the fuck was he thinking?"

"I'm sure he wasn't." He folds his arms in front of him. "All he cares about is winning the election so that his position is secured for a few more years. I wanna say that his grief is getting the best of him, but that'd be a lie. He's making sure the road ahead is clear for him, and that powerful people like the Goswamis are by his side when the need arises. He's sacrificing *Lure* in exchange for their continued support. I'd wager it's *them* who asked him for the company in the first place." He sighs and taps his shoe against my stiletto. "I wouldn't think much of it now, because there's literally nothing to be done. You can't win against him, simply because he's blinded by his goal."

"So what, I just spend all the money I'm going to get, and lie in bed all day reading magazines?"

Mave shrugs. "Better than attending 20 meetings a day where the same thing is repeated over and over again. Or deciding which shade of beige is better than the other. Or what thread needs to be used on what fabric. Frankly, I feel like everyone that works at *Lure* shits nylon and chiffon." He shudders, making me roll my eyes.

"But it's *fun*, though," I say.

"What, shitting nylon and chiffon?"

I shove him playfully. "Making fashion-related decisions, you asshole."

He puts his tongue to his cheek. "Still doesn't beat the alternative."

I sigh. "You think I should have fought harder?"

"It wouldn't have changed the outcome, so I'd say no."

I let go of a breath and try to calm myself the fuck down. Silence stretches between us as I let the weight of what's happened, sink in. It's true that *Lure* is lost now, and because my contribution to it has been next to non-existent, I can only argue so much. I can push, but I can't throw someone off their feet to get what I want. That's how my uncle does things, not me. And I know I'm once again giving up a fight, but this time, I really don't have a choice.

I pull my hair over a shoulder when a gust of warm wind blows it over my face, then look at Mave. "Want me to buy you the most expensive scotch available in Riverside, now that I'm going to be filthy fucking rich?"

He laughs, sensing my need to change the subject, then pulls open the passenger side door of his car for me. "Please, and thank you."

61.

DORRAN

She looks seraphic in her sleep. Her long, pink hair is fanned out over the pillow, and her body is listless against the mattress. Her shorts have bunched up a bit, and the white camisole she's wearing – it's barely concealing her pebbled nipples. Watching her so at ease makes me feel calm, but it also makes me hard as a fucking rock. Her safety relaxes me, and her body makes me mad with need.

I'm leaning against her balcony's archway, having just climbed up the railing. I'd thought sleeping in her bedroom after what happened with Riley would be difficult for her, but seeing her right now has cleared that doubt from my head. As long as she's comfortable at the estate, I don't mind visiting her like this. It's our little thing, after all – just hers and mine alone. And the smile that takes over her face when she sees me in her balcony? Yeah, that's something special; something I'll never get enough of.

She'd texted me a couple of hours ago and asked me to come over, but because I was at *Finesse*, busy servicing Solo's SUV, I'd seen her message a little late. I know I should leave, but I also can't stop looking at her.

She stretches her arms and shifts in her bed, then blinks her eyes open. Our gazes meet, and her lips slowly spread into a lazy, relaxed smile.

There we go.

"Were you watching me sleep?" she asks, then sits up in her bed. Bringing an arm forward, she wiggles her fingers, urging me to come closer.

I chuckle and start walking over to her. "It's your fault for looking so damn hot, even while asleep." I sit next to her when she shifts to make space for me.

"Is that why you're hard right now?" she questions around a smirk, then runs a hand over my growing cock.

I hiss at the pressure, then grab her wrist. "Do that, and I'll come in my fucking boxers."

"That's the goal, though."

I chuckle again. "So this is why you asked me to come over, then – so that you could make me jizz in my pants?"

She clicks her tongue. "Nope. I wanted you here because I needed to talk to someone about how my uncle stupidly, *impulsively*, decided to sell *Lure* to random investors instead of letting me run it."

I blink, not expecting her to say that. "Chase sold Miranda's brand?"

Cignette nods, then frowns. She then tells me about her conversation with Chase from earlier, and how he'd all but shunned her pleas of wanting to run the HQ herself.

"His lawyers contacted me a few hours ago, letting me know that the paperwork is being finalized. Mave thinks I shouldn't let it get to me because it's something that'll fatten my pockets, but how can I fucking *not*?"

"Of course he does."

"I don't know what to do, Dorran," she says, and her frown deepens.

I run the back of my fingers over her jaw. "Want me to be honest with you?"

She leans into my touch. "Always."

"You're rich, you're beautiful, and you've been through enough shit for multiple lifetimes. Take this time off to relax, enjoy the goddamn money, and find a purpose when you feel like you're ready to try something on your own." I soothe the lines between her brows with a thumb, then press a kiss there. "Besides, I'm always on the lookout for a chick who's willing to wash client cars wearing a bikini, and who can give me blowjobs in the backseat whenever I need them. So hit me up when the money runs out and you wanna make more of it."

Her mouth opens in surprise as she stares at me. Then, she grabs a pillow from behind her, and before I can stop her, she hits me with it – right in the face.

"You're such an ass!" She hits me again, making me laugh.

I duck and move away, then slide towards the other side of the bed. "I was only giving you some advice!"

She gets on her knees. "To wash cars wearing a *two piece*." She hits me in the back of my head. "Yeah, I heard."

I barely have time to avoid getting hit before she brings the pillow down on me once more. "You gotta admit: it sounds sexy," I say, then laugh again when she all but tackles me on the bed.

She's panting, and so am I. Her dark eyes glint against the silver moonlight as she throws the pillow to the side. Placing her hands on my chest, she straddles me, then presses her pussy against my boner as she settles on my hips.

"I meant the first part, though," I tell her, then hold onto her waist. "You've been through so much; you *need* some downtime to heal and reflect. Try not to think too much about Chase's decision, because there's unfortunately no way to change it. He's an adamant bastard, and as much as I'd like to ask you to fight him over this, I also know it'd be pointless if you did. And I'm not trying to discourage you; I'm only trying to save you the disappointment. That man is ruthless. It's the reason he's on top of the food chain right now."

Cignette fidgets with the fabric of my red vest, lost in thought. "I think you've said something like this to me before, but at the time, I didn't believe you." She sighs. "I always thought he was the reasonable one out of him and Mom, but I guess I was wrong."

"A person can only hide behind a mask for so long. Their true colors do eventually reveal themselves, and it happens when you're least expecting it. All you gotta do, Cigs, is pay attention," I say, then sit up. "I'm sorry this happened to you, but I know you'll get through this, too, just like you have with everything else. It'll pass, you'll see."

"I feel like I waited too long to raise my voice against things. That I've sort of made it a habit to rely on you for finding my strength and boldness. My weakness and fears made me appear careless to my uncle, and now I'm paying the price for it."

"Don't do that," I say, making sure she's looking me in the eye. "Don't fucking blame yourself or question your past behavior. Whatever you did, you did to survive, and that doesn't make you weak. It makes you strong – helpless against the cards life has dealt you, sure, but strong nonetheless."

She sucks in a breath, then lets it go slowly before swallowing. Cupping my jaw in a hand, she brings her face close to mine. "Thank you." She brushes her nose against mine, then kisses me.

My cock throbs as I get a taste of her, and when she closes her lips around mine, I groan. "I've got you, Little Swan. *Always*."

She kisses me again, and she does it with enough fervor that it drives me wild. Rocking her hips against me, she moves back a little, and when I moan, she smiles and presses her lips to the side of my neck. She pushes her teeth into my skin, making me impossibly hard, then runs her tongue over my collarbone.

I tip my head back, and her lips eagerly travel over the indents of my shoulder, then to the base of my throat. I slide my fingers into her hair and close my eyes, because fuck, this is making me all sorts of hot.

Cignette fists the hem of my vest, and is about to lift it, but I cover her hand with mine, stopping her.

She pulls back and looks at me, and I shake my head at her.

"Not here," I say, and when she lifts a brow at me, I grin. "Take me to your mother's bedroom."

62.
DORRAN

"What the fuck?" I say as I follow Cignette, and glance around at the blatant absurdity that is Miranda's bedroom. It looks like a Victorian era chamber or something, with white-and-gold furniture, a king size bed, and a vast balcony that's bracketed by long, beige curtains. There is a wide, mirrored screen directly opposite the bed, and each panel of this screen seems to be foldable, for it has a thick seam that separates one from the other. Talk about self-obsession.

The lights in the room are turned on, and it seems like no one has been in here for days. I mean, who would, right? It's not like the guards care about it, and Chase is too busy making stupid fucking decisions to visit his sister's room.

"Uh, Dorran?"

I turn, and Cignette points upward.

I look up, and my brows rise on their own accord when I see that almost the entire ceiling in the room is nothing but reflective glass.

"What the hell kind of sex dungeon bullshit is this?" I say.

"Don't ask me for details, because I've literally stepped into this room for the first time in *years*," Cignette says, then shudders a little as she glances around. "I think I was 7 when I was here last. I was looking to *borrow* a lipstick, but Mom thought I was intruding on her privacy. She kicked me out and asked me not to enter her room – ever. It's a small mercy I listened to her on *that*, at least."

I laugh. "I'm curious, though: why does a 7-year-old need a lipstick?"

She rolls her eyes. "I'd seen a picture of it in a magazine and wanted to try it out."

"Of course you did," I muse, earning a quick scowl from her.

"You think she has sex toys in here?" she asks.

"If she does, I don't wanna see them. Christ knows where she's used them, and on how many."

Cignette pretends to gag, making me laugh again.

I walk over to the dressing table in the room, then study the items strewn on it. They all look the same to me, so I pick up a long, purple tube, then twist it open before putting its wand under my nose. I regret doing that almost immediately, because a strong, ash-like smell hits my senses, making my eyes water. I cough and look to the side, then sniff and shake my head.

"For fuck's sake, Dorran, stop smelling the goddamn mascara." Cignette grabs the tube from me and throws it back on the table.

"It's *toxic*," I say, then wipe my nose and eyes. "What's it even used for?"

She blinks and stares at me. "It's used on the eyelashes," she provides plainly.

"Why?"

A small pause.

"Because it enhances them?"

"And what purpose does that serve?"

She purses her lips, and I know she's trying not to laugh at me.

"It doesn't," she says, then shrugs.

"Right." I nod. "Good to know."

She does laugh now, then walks over to me and cups the back of my neck with her hands. "You're cute." She kisses me. "*And* I want you to fuck me in front of those mirrors."

"Only if you promise not to call me cute again," I say, then pull her to me.

She grins. "Nope." She leans in and kisses me again. "*Cute* – that's what you are."

"Shut your face," I groan, and kiss her back. When she chuckles against me, I lift her up, wrapping her legs around my waist. I walk us to where the paneled mirrors are – our lips moving in abundance – then set her on her feet. We take our clothes off in a haste, and once we're naked, Cignette drags her eyes over me, then runs her fingers over my inner thigh.

"Touch yourself," she says to me. "And watch yourself while you do it." She moves to my side, and as I grab my cock and start stroking it, she bends and takes my right nipple into her mouth.

"Jesus," I hiss, and my hips piston forward. My dick pulses as I continue to fuck my fist, and my breaths turn heavy while I watch my reflection in the mirror. I'm flushed from the chest up, and my lips are slightly swollen from our kiss. I'm disheveled in the most vulnerable of ways, and I fucking love it.

Cignette snakes a hand downward and grabs my balls. She tugs at them, then bites my nipple, and my lids flutter before my eyes fall shut.

It feels so fucking *good*. The pain from her teeth on my skin, and the pleasure I'm giving myself, along with the one she's giving me by kneading my sack, are making me hot; making me wanna come all over the floor.

"Watch us, Dorran," she whispers, and I know she's close to losing it with how uneven her tone is.

I open my eyes and look down at her, just as she takes her hand off me. She halts my movement on my cock, then swipes the precum off my crown.

Bringing the finger between her lips, she sucks on it, and when she moans, I'm done for.

"Get on all fours, *now*," I command, and watch as her pupils dilate in response.

She steps away from me and turns, then gets into position. Shifting her hair over one shoulder, she aligns her body parallel to the mirrors.

I get behind her, then go down on my knees. I can see her tight ass hole, and wetness dripping down to her thighs from how wet she is for me.

I grab her cheeks and squeeze them, then spank them hard, making her jerk.

"Lift higher," I tell her, then slap them again.

She whimpers and raises her ass.

I look to my left – at the mirrors – and can see how beautifully her body has arched; how ready she is to take me. Her full tits hang against her frame, and goosebumps have marred her creamy skin.

I drag my fingers over her pussy, and she moans. I hold onto her waist and pull her back to me, and she, in turn, groans in frustration.

"Fuck me, damn you," she grits out. "Because my pussy sure as hell won't fuck itself."

I chuckle. "Yes, ma'am," I say, then slip my cock into her heat.

Cignette tips her head back and cries out as I fill her, then pushes back against me to take my entire length inside her.

"*Yes*," she moans, then rocks her ass again. "Fuck yes."

I move in and out of her at a steady rhythm, and watch as she coats my cock with her cum. The slick sounds of her walls swallowing me fill the room, and every time I thrust all the way in and my piercing hits that deep fucking spot of hers, her breath hiccups, and she tightens herself around me.

I grab her ass and spread her cheeks as I pound into her, and when I'm in her up to the base, I halt for a second and twist my hips, making her whimper.

She moves with me, fucking herself as I fuck her. She circles her pelvis, and I quicken my thrusts.

"Look at how well you take my cock," I hiss, then spank her. "Ah, *shit*; look at how your hungry little cunt squeezes it. My God, I love it when you use me for your pleasure, Little Swan." I glance at the mirror, just as she does, too, and the picture we make – it's beyond euphoric. I'm rutting into her wildly, and she's grinding against me just as fast. When I smirk at her reflection, she grins and licks her lower lip.

Fucking sexy as fuck.

I lean in and spit on her ass hole, then rub it in a circle with the pad of my thumb, lubricating her.

Cignette groans, and I once again look at her through the mirror.

"You okay with this?" I ask her.

She nods. "Use your fingers while your cock's still in me."

As if she could get any more perfect.

I can feel myself draw up as I continue to thrust into her pussy. I slowly push my index finger into her ass, and fuck me, she's so tight that I can't even imagine how good it'd feel to have my cock in there instead of a digit.

"Mm…" She rises on her hands and rocks against my ministrations. "Another finger," she pants, then grabs one of her tits and starts pinching her nipple.

My hips move hurriedly as my release nears, and when I push a second finger inside her ass, Cignette cries out, and her body surges forward.

"That's so good, Dorran," she moans. "Fuck me harder."

I do. Spitting over my fingers, I move them in and out of her ass, just as I pound into her pussy at an unrelenting pace.

She keeps whispering my name as she takes every inch of what I'm giving her, and soon, she clenches around me. Her back arches, and her body trembles as she orgasms against me.

I slow down and let her ride out her high; let her breaths even out as her body loosens under me.

I feel my spine stiffen as my cock continues to breach her walls, and when my balls tighten, I pull my cock, and my digits, out of Cignette, then fist myself. She watches my reflection with intrigue on her flushed face, and as I start running my palm up and down my length in quick, rough strokes, she brings her ass closer.

"Fuck," I whisper, then rise on my knees as my orgasm takes over my entire body. Thick, white spurts of my cum shoot out of my throbbing cock and fall on Cignette's lower back, and some of it drips onto her reddened ass cheeks. She keeps her eyes on me as I empty myself on her, and once I'm done, I let go of myself. I drag my fingers over her skin, spreading my cum further.

"Come here," I order.

She turns and reaches me, then levels herself to me.

I grab her by the throat, and catch her gasp against my palm. "You're such a good girl, aren't you, sweetheart?" I say, then grin when she makes a sound.

"Open up for me."

She parts her lips, and I slide my fingers into her mouth. Her cheeks hollow as she eagerly sucks my cum off them, and when I push them in deeper, she loosens her jaw and takes them to the very back of her throat.

"Fucking perfect." I pull my hand back, then bring her closer before crashing my mouth to hers.

She tastes and smells like me, and kisses me back like I'm her only source of sustenance.

I let go of her throat and pull her flush against me, then sit down on the floor. She straddles me and continues kissing me, bunching my hair up in a painful grip.

“God, I wish your dead mother is watching us right now from whatever pit of hell she’s in,” I say, then bite her bottom lip before sucking on it.

“Imagine her body turning in her fucking grave, restless at the sight of us soiling her *cashmere* carpet,” Cignette adds, then laughs.

I snort, then chuckle. “I’m sure we make a hot sight, though, so at least there’s that.”

She smiles down at me, and it’s the kind of thing that tugs at you; moves something inside you because it means more than you can put into words.

“The *best*,” she corrects me, then presses her lips to mine, engulfing me in her warmth.

63.
DORRAN

Let me set the scene for you before I tell you what's happening right now. Or better yet, what me, Solo, the crew, and Maverick are *enduring* in this moment. By the hands of my goddess of a girlfriend, of course.

The 7 of us are at Eddie's VIP club, *Indulgence*, and Cignette has downed one too many drinks, despite Maverick and I's attempts at stopping her. She wanted to treat us all with a night out in Downtown, but all she's been doing since we've gotten here, is drink.

And…now she's *singing*. Horrendously, too, if the buzzing in my ears is any indication.

"*And I keep dancing with my, eye-eye-eye-eyes, eye-eye-eye-eyes cloooooooosed.*"

I'm sitting on one of the velvet couches in one of the private rooms at *Indulgence*, with Cignette's head on my lap, and her mouth merely inches away from my innocent eardrums. My life's absolutely perfect, thank you so much for asking.

I guess her current state is also a byproduct of her losing *Lure* to Chase's stubbornness. She told me earlier that her account had been credited with a huge sum, and even though it's sort of a reassurance that Chase lived up to his promise of giving Cigs *Lure's* money, I understand how it must have hurt her. The finality of it all, I mean.

And let's not forget about everything that happened with Riley and Miranda a few days ago. That's a mental scar I know she'll always carry with herself, despite what she says. I can tell she's grieving in her own way, and I can understand that there's this inner turmoil that she's experiencing, but to say that I'm feeling it the way she must be feeling it, would be a lie. And it's because I'm not like her. A monster never mourns, so I'm pretty much an illiterate in this field. But I'm here for her, and if she needs anything, I'll do my best to give it to her.

"*Cause everywhere I look, I still see youuuuu,*" Cignette continues to sing, then laughs and hiccups. Her white cocktail dress has risen a little, exposing her thighs, and her heels are all but dangling off the couch's edge.

"Someone please stop this train wreck," Solo mumbles, then downs a shot.

"It won't stop until she falls asleep. Trust me, I've tried in the past," Maverick says.

"Let the poor woman enjoy her money, people," Alex adds. "Being rich means she can do whatever she wants."

"That shouldn't involve her making us deaf, babe," Jayce remarks.

"Whoever told her she can sing is the dumbest fuck in the world," Varsha remarks.

"I think she just assumes she's Solange when she's intoxicated," Maverick tells us, making us laugh.

"There is so much wrong with that sentence," Alex says, then shakes his head. "But I'll let it pass since we're all so drunk."

Varsha raises her glass, and the rest of us follow.

I lean back on the couch and take a drink of my bourbon, and almost spit it back out when Cignette sings another line from Ed Sheeran's latest single.

"God, I need to be more inebriated if I'm to continue to endure this shit," I mutter. I then snatch the shot glass Solo has just picked up, and chug it, letting the vodka burn my throat and chest.

Cignette shifts on my lap, then groans and sits up. With her hair knotted on the side of her head, and her eyelids drooped, she looks completely fucked up. And adorable.

She leans forward and makes to grab the half-empty bottle of scotch from the table, but I stop her.

"Nope." I pull her arm back and bring her close to me. "You've had enough for tonight."

She pouts as she blinks at me. God, even her eye makeup is smudged. How the hell did she manage to do *that*?

"One glass," she slurs, then runs her fingers over her throat. "My throat's…dry–*hiccup*–from the singing."

"Well, drinking more will make you sing more, and I can't let that happen."

She shoves at my chest, making my lips twitch. "Rude." She pokes my shoulder. "*Rude*."

I give her a quick kiss, and when that makes her smile, I do it again.

"I'm just saving all our hearings, especially mine. How else will I hear you moaning and screaming my name when I'm fucking you later tonight?"

She glances at my lips, and when I smirk, she brings her face close to mine. Her breath smells sweet, and I fucking lose myself in her when she glances up at me. A big mistake, because I realize too late that she's doing this as a distraction, and by the time I've blinked myself out of it, she's already moving forward and grabbing that bottle of scotch.

"Dorran, what the fuck?!" Maverick scolds.

Cignette puts the bottle to her lips and starts downing the remainder of the scotch that's in it. It takes my brain a second to signal my body to fucking move, and when it does, I pull the bottle from her and hand it over to Alex.

"*Rude*," she whispers, then hiccups.

I can't help but chuckle. "You fucking tricked me."

"You deserved it, *okay*?" She slumps against me. "I told you: my throat is *dry*."

"Let's keep it that way, then. Unless you want me to order you some water."

She scrunches up her nose, making me laugh.

The room's door opens, and the loud techno music playing outside, filters in. I look towards it, and find Eddie making his way to us, looking every bit like Alexander fucking Dreymon, but with dark eyes. It's uncanny, seriously.

He's in his early 40s, and everywhere he goes, he instantly holds people's attention. He's got that aura about him, I guess, what with owning a place like *Indulgence*, and doing the things he does behind the scenes. He's just as much a twisted motherfucker as the rest of us, but the way he carries himself – it masks who he really is, very well.

"Everything okay here?" he asks, then comes to a stop in front of the group.

"All good; thanks, man," Jayce says, tipping his glass forward.

Cignette turns and looks at Eddie, then makes a small sound in the back of her throat before getting to her feet. She fails, of course, and Eddie catches her before she can hit the floor, face-first.

Asshole.

"And who are *you*?" she says, then stumbles in her attempt at stepping back to give him a once over. "Whoops, excuse my…" She waves a hand in front of her face. "*Tardiness*."

When we got to *Indulgence*, Eddie was in his office, so him and Cignette didn't exactly have a chance to meet. I was hoping it'd stay that way, though, but I guess not.

Eddie smirks, then let's his gaze travel over the length of *my* Cignette's body.

Okay, that's *enough*.

I rise and wrap an arm around her waist, pulling her to me.

Eddie notices, of course, because I'm not being fucking subtle about it. He smirks, and I in turn scowl at him.

"Stay in your fucking lane, *Edgar*," I warn.

He chuckles, then raises his hands in surrender. "I was just lookin', man; I didn't intend to touch. Or *taste*." He winks at me.

"Oh, I'd love to see you try."

"Boys, boys, *boys*." Cignette clicks her tongue. "Stop fighting over lil ole *moi*. There's plenty of me to go around, alright?"

"I need to get you *home*," I counter.

"Psh." She turns around, stumbles again, then faces the others. "They're fighting over me," she tells them, pointing at herself, then giggles. Fucking *giggles*. "They're…fighting–*hiccup*–over meeeee."

"Good God, she's something else," Eddie says.

That comment makes me laugh. "Isn't she?"

He shakes his head. "I mean, you've risked your ass for her on more than one occasion, so she's most definitely gotta be."

"The things we do for the people we care for."

He looks at me as if he's studying me, then nods and gives me a smile. "You're lucky you have that – people that you're close to; a fond family of sorts." There's a suppressed sadness to him now, as if he envies me, but isn't malicious to act on it.

"You're part of it too," I say, simply because he's been there for me and my crew for years now, and it'd be unfair not to appreciate that.

He laughs. "Was that a lie to make me feel included?" He raises a brow. "That's not your style, Ledge; I thought you knew that."

I roll my eyes and give his arm a playful punch. "I meant what I said, so you best believe it, asshat."

He chuckles. "Thanks. I *think*."

I flip him off, to which he chuckles again.

"Dorran?" comes Cignette's voice.

I turn to her, and notice that her complexion has paled.

Fuck.

"I think…I think I'm gonna throw up," she says.

Maverick is on his feet in an instant, and so are Alex and Varsha. Jayce and Solo glance at each other, and then, with unison sighs, stand up as well.

"I wonder why that is," Solo comments, then averts his gaze when Maverick and I glare at him.

Jayce clears his throat, and I know he's doing so to stifle his laughter.

Dipshit.

Maverick makes his way to Cignette, and with a nod in my direction, he starts leading her to the bathroom on the other side of the room.

I sigh and look at Eddie. "I gotta go."

"Duty calls, I see."

I lift a shoulder, then bump my fist against his before following after Maverick and Cignette.

64.
CIGNETTE

17 days later

The floral and slightly fruity smell of amaryllises hits my nose as I enter my uncle's estate gardens. The entire area is vibrant, full of flowers and beautifully manicured grasses. It's well-kept and eye-appeasing – a complete opposite of the figurines on my estate grounds, which make absolutely no sense whatsoever. But the thing is: I don't care enough to get them removed, so I guess they'll be staying there until they fester and fall off.

Mave's held up at the estate's gate with a few of the guards manning it, so I've decided to move ahead since Uncle Chase had made an appointment for him and I to have macaroons and coffee in his lawn at about 10:30a.m. It's 11:12a.m. right now, so I'm already quite late.

When he'd asked me to come to his estate for coffee the other day, I'd had half a mind to refuse him, given his stupid fucking decision of selling *Lure*. I can be furious at him, despise him, but at the end of the day, he's family – the last of it, too – so I couldn't find it in me to deny his request.

I take a left and enter the lawn, and my hair, along with my lavender summer dress, flow sideways as a bout of air whips by me. The grass at my feet swishes as it shifts with the wind, and caresses my ankles as I walk further into the lawn. The sun is right above me, and even though I prefer the gloomier weather over this one, I'm absolutely loving the warmth on my skin today.

"There you are!" says Uncle Chase.

I put a hand over my eyes to shield them from the glaring sunrays, then look ahead. There's a set of white chairs and a table set up under the shade. Various biscuits and macaroons are plated on delicate crockeries, along with a pot of coffee that's placed right in the center of the table. Guards are surrounding the area, but they remain a respectful distance away from the setup.

I wave at my uncle, then make my way to him. "Your gardens are stunning," I say by way of greeting.

"Aren't they?" He opens his arms for me, so I close the gap between us and hug him.

He places a kiss on the side of my head, and when we step back, he smiles down at me.

He's wearing beige pants and a red polo t-shirt, and I know it's a bit darker here, but I can still see the circles around his eyes, and how prominent the creases on his face look. He seems tired, and I don't know if it's because Mom's absence is getting to him, or if it's the elections. Probably both, I'd wager.

"You sure you wanna do this?" I ask him. "You look exhausted, Uncle Chase; you need rest."

"Nonsense. I called you here because I wanted to spend some time with you, and that's exactly what we're going to do." He moves behind me, then pulls a chair out for me.

I can't help but chuckle as I settle down, and when he does the same, I grab the pot and fill our cups with coffee.

"I'm glad you came," he tells me. "I was of the impression that you wouldn't want to see me for a while."

I sigh, then set the pot back in its place. "Make no mistake, I'm still mad at you. And I'm not here for *you* today, but only for the macaroons you promised me. I am too enticed by them for my own good, and you know that as well."

He laughs, and his eyes crinkle around the corners. "Well, I'm glad you're here, regardless of the reason."

I smile, then grab a lemon cookie off one of the plates before biting into it. A chorus of birds' chirping echoes from high above, and I notice a few butterflies flittering around the lawn. Their black wings, dotted with pink, make for a beautiful contrast against the green around me, and when one of them sits atop a patch of grass near me, I notice that its entire body is pink, with spots of black on the side.

"I didn't know we had Pink Rose butterflies here," I tell Uncle Chase, then finish my cookie before grabbing a coconut macaroon.

"Fascinating, aren't they?" he says before polishing off the scone he was holding. "I've seen them quite a few times during my afternoon walks around the estate. I can have one of them caught for you, if you'd like to own it."

"No." I face him so fast, that it makes him chuckle in surprise. "Sorry." I laugh a little, then shake my head. "It's just that I wouldn't want to cage it. It wouldn't be fair to its nature." I glance at the butterfly again, and its velvety wings shine against the sunlight as it takes off after the others.

"Your mother never had an affinity for these things."

I look at Uncle Chase again, and he gestures at the table before us.

"Nor these, for that matter," he adds, grinning to himself.

I finish my macaroon before responding to that. "She always looked at the bigger picture, I suppose, and not the smaller ones that constituted to the entire thing."

He nods. "She did have dreams that were too bold, even for my imagination."

"But you still helped her achieve them."

"Of course I did. She was, and always will be, my family."

I reach out and give one of his hands a squeeze, then grab my cup and lean back in my chair. Taking a sip of the warm, creamy coffee, I try not to moan at its decadent and nutty taste. It's strong, and something I most definitely needed.

"What have you been up to these days?" Uncle Chase asks, then exhales heavily. "I've been so busy that I haven't even checked up on you."

I drink some more of my coffee, then set the cup down. "You're good, don't worry." I swipe a strawberry macaroon off the plate to my right, and then lift a shoulder at my uncle. "I've been thinking of starting a fashion blog. Maybe a YouTube channel, too. I've got so many ideas I wanna let out, and while I'm at it, I can perhaps help people who are looking for fashion advice."

It's not something I've mapped out yet, but I've discussed the possibility of it with Julian. It's the second-best thing to *Lure*, I guess, especially because it'll help me establish myself as a public figure before I can launch my own brand in the future. Well, that's what my end goal is for now, at least.

"That's good, sweet pea," Uncle Chase says, then nods. "I'm looking forward to seeing what you do with the idea."

I smile at him, then pop the last piece of macaroon into my mouth. "It'll take a while for me to arrange and set everything up. But yeah, I'm excited to see where it takes me."

"Your mother would be proud of you," he muses, then sighs.

I scoff, even before I realize I've done it. "She never really cared for my inputs or objectives. She was always too busy doing what she thought was right, and never paid any heed to what I had to say."

Uncle Chase studies me for a few moments, then places his forearms on the table and leans forward. "So, is that why you had her killed?" he asks so casually that it takes me a minute to fully come to terms with the question.

My entire fucking world turns on its axis as I stare at him in shock, and my heart goes out of control as my breathing accelerates.

I open my mouth, then close it. I open it again, then try calming myself down before I can speak. I'm cold – so cold. My hands, my feet. Fucking *everything*.

I realize that my delay in responding to him might come off as suspicious, so I swallow and shake my head, pretending to act confused.

"What are you talking about?" There's a bit of quivering in my voice, but I hope it's not detectable.

Uncle Chase laughs, and it's a crude gesture – something very unlike his usual demeanor. "I'm not stupid, Cignette. You really thought you could get away with having my sister *murdered*? Did you seriously think I was that gullible?" He sneers at me. "I've had people looking into the matter since the day of her *accident*. And everything my team found out, pointed to one thing, and one thing only…" He leans in further, then grits his teeth at me. "*You*."

My hands are shaking, so I clench them into fists on my lap. "Uncle Chase, that's not tru–"

"Oh, just shut up already." He stands, and on instant, the guards around us start closing in on me. They point their guns at me, and one of them grabs me by the arm before hauling me to my feet.

"Don't touch me!" I pull out of his grasp, then glare at my uncle. "And here I thought this was a casual get-together."

"Isn't it, though?" he says coolly.

I hear footsteps, seconds before one of the guards from Mave's team brings him into the lawn. He has a gun pointed at Mave's head, and when I try to go to him, he very subtly shakes his head at me.

My breaths are now frosty from how quickly my heart is beating, and my mouth feels all but grimy from how dry it has suddenly gotten.

Ignoring the guns, I turn to face my uncle, and when he gives me a look of disgust, I clench my hands further and take a step towards him.

"She deserved to die," I say, then blink when my eyes sting. "She deserved every bit of what happened to her."

"She didn't." He gets in my personal space, glowering down at me as I seethe at him. "She *didn't*." His eyes turn misty, and his anger turns to sorrow.

"She laughed at me while her bodyguard tried to *rape* me," I tell him, then swallow against the tightness in my throat. "She laughed, and she clapped. She took pleasure in my pleas for help, not thinking for a *second* that I'm her *daughter*."

He seems taken aback by my confession. But it's only momentary, because his love for his deranged sister soon overpowers any rationality he possesses, and he once again turns into the weasel that he is.

"You could have come to *me*; you could've told me about what she'd done."

I have to laugh at that. "And you'd do what?" I snort. "Numerous times I've come to you, begging you to talk to her; begging you to do something about her behavior. But instead of taking any sort of action against her, all you did was remind me that she's my mother, and then left me to endure her cruelty. But I'd had enough of it. I cowered, I suffered, and I waited, but nothing changed. And so, I did what I had to; I took the power into my own hands." I bring my face close to his. "I fucking *killed* her."

His nostrils flare as he scowls at me. I know he's itching to hit me, and my God, I wanna see him do it. Because at the end of the day, he's just like my mother, isn't he? Spineless. Uncaring.

Self-righteous.

He works his jaw and steps away from me, then nods at his guards. "Take my niece and her dog inside the estate. Make sure they're comfortable while I go fetch the rest of my guests for this…" He clicks his tongue. "What is it that you called it?" He smirks at me, then claps his hands in front of him. "Ah, yes; a *get-together*."

I know who he's talking about, and that does absolutely *nothing* to calm me down. I wish I could warn Dorran somehow, but my phone is in my dress pocket, so I can't possibly call or text him without eating a bullet or two.

I glance at Mave, and he looks just as worried as I feel. But when our eyes meet, he once again shakes his head at me, silently asking me not to do or say anything that might get us in further trouble.

It's too bad I don't always do what I'm told to do.

"If you hurt him," I tell my uncle, "I swear to God that I'll fucking *destroy* you."

He grins, because I've now erased the last bit of uncertainty he must've had by confirming Dorran's involvement in all of this.

He faces his guards and jerks his head towards the estate's doors. "Take them inside. And if they don't comply, beat them into obedience." He bends so that he's eyelevel to me, then smiles when I lift my chin and raise a brow at him. "I've got to go pay a visit to my friendly neighborhood killer," he says to me. "But when I'm back, *sweet pea*, I *will* make you pay for what you've taken from me." He straightens and walks by me, leaving me utterly disarrayed.

65. DORRAN

There's a low hum of engines, followed by stones crunching under tires, which indicates that there are cars in the driveway. I step away from my workstation and look outside, only to curse under my breath when 3 black Nissan Maximas come to a stop in front of *Finesse*.

What the fuck is Chase doing here?

"Ledge?" Jayce says, closing the hood of the Porsche he's fixing.

"I see it."

Alex and Varsha walk over to me, and when I glance at my crew, they seem just as confused by Chase's presence here as I do.

"Stay alert," I tell them, then nod at Jayce. The two of us step outside, just as Chase gets out of one of the cars and greets us both with a clinical smile.

"To what do we owe the pleasure?" I say, squinting a little against the glaring sun.

Jayce is standing to my left, and I can practically feel how agitated he is right now. All I can do is keep a straight face and get whatever this is, over with.

"I've got a job for you," Chase tells us, then stops a short distance from us. "Someone I need you to kill."

"We never discuss work at my garage," I state, then give him a quick once over. "What's changed?" I glance at the guards flanking him. A dozen, perhaps, maybe more. That's an absurd number, even more so than the ones he has in his estate's office, where we usually discuss the kill and its price.

"This is a special case – one that required an unfamiliar meeting spot." He gestures at one of his guards, who pulls a brown envelope from his jacket before handing it to him. Chase in turn offers it to me – his expression perfectly neutral. It's hard to study him like this, because the fucker knows how to reign himself in when he wants to.

I take the envelope from him. My grease-stained fingers imprint themselves onto the paper, but that's the least of my worries. Because when I pull out the photo that's inside the envelope, my entire body paralyzes in place, and my mouth dries up.

It's because the photo I'm holding in my hand right now, is Cignette's. It's not a recent one for sure, but still, it's her. And I'm about to lose my shit because I don't know what the fuck Chase is playing at. He either knows about what really happened with Miranda, or he actually wants Cignette out of his way, for she poses a direct threat to the position and wealth he holds. Either way, the truth will come out, and if not, I'll have to find her and get her the hell away from this asshole.

I loosen my body a little and get ahold of myself before I can accidentally give myself away. Beside me, Jayce tries to do the same.

I look at Chase, then put a fake grin on my face while I wave the photo sideways. "This one'll cost ya big," I say to him, completely indifferent and casual, when in reality, all I wanna do is cut his throat open.

He narrows his eyes at me. "Twice as much as the others, I take it."

I wink at him. "Higher still."

He laughs, then shakes his head. "You're a way better actor than she is," he says, then smirks in a way that's both smooth yet unsettling. "I'm surprised you even lasted this long, given your…affection towards my bitch of a niece."

Literal red flashes before my eyes. I've reduced the space between him and I in all but a heartbeat, and the guards barely have time to draw their weapons by the time I've fisted Chase's collar and pulled him to me. He's slightly shorter than me, so he has to look up at me while I sneer down at him.

"Call her that again, and I'll fucking *end you*," I warn him. "Where is she?"

I was right; he knows about what happened with Miranda. How? I don't exactly know.

He raises a hand towards the guards, asking them to stand down. "Come with me and find out for yourself," he tells me.

I scoff. "I'm not in the mood to play your mind games, Chase. Tell me where my Cignette is, or I'll gut you from the leg up."

He chuckles. "Oh, trust me, I'm not playing any fucking games with you." He grabs the fist I have on his collar, and pulls it off himself. "If you and your crew don't come with me, then you'll get a nice little video on your phone in the next few minutes where my guards are taking their turn fucking *your* Cignette while she screams for them to stop. Isn't that what almost happened with her all those days ago, which eventually led you to kill my sister?"

My eyes burn as I glare at him, and when he grins at me, I grit my teeth and punch him in the jaw, making him stumble backwards.

"You motherfucker!" I move forward, but a couple of his guards hold me back.

"Take your fucking hands off him," Jayce says, then shoves them away from me. He gives me a look full of warning, then turns and hollers Alex and Varsha's names.

"We'll come with you," he says to Chase. "But only if you give us your word that Cignette is okay."

Chase spits blood on the gravel, then snorts at us. "You are in no position to ask things of me. All you need to know is that I have Cignette, and if you don't want my guards to get their eager hands on her, then you'll come with me."

I groan and make to go to him, but Jayce stops me. When I glower at him, he grits his teeth and lifts a brow at me.

"You know how impulsive he is," he says to me. "Don't give him the ammunition he needs to hurt Cigs. Because he *will* have her raped, just to get an upper hand on you. Fucking stay calm and do as he says. It's the only option we've got."

"The 4 of us can take them all," I argue. "You know that, Jay."

"I know, you asshole." He sighs and runs a hand over his head. "But it's not about any of us here, man. It's about *Cignette*. Killing Chase or his goons won't change her fate right now, but doing as he says – that just might."

Varsha and Alex walk outside, and a group of guards immediately surrounds them.

I look at the former, who gives me a barely-detectable nod, letting me know she's informed Solo about what's happened here.

I swallow and try to level my anger, then face Chase again. "Well, let's fucking go, then."

He purses his lips as he looks me up and down. "In just a second." He walks up to me, then bends his knees a little and jabs me in the gut.

I double over, and my breath catches in my throat as a dull ache spreads across my stomach, making it hard for me to draw air in or out of my lungs.

Fucking piece of shit.

If it wasn't for Cignette, he'd be very dead right now.

"Perfect. We can leave now," he all but announces, and his guards start dragging me and the crew towards the waiting cars.

66.
CIGNETTE

"I'm scared," I whisper, then look at Mave. "I'm fucking *terrified*, and I don't like feeling this way – not after everything I've endured to ensure otherwise." My head is fuzzy from thinking of ways I can get myself and the others out of this, and the buzz in my ears, along with the sweat running down my temples and neck, are making me fidgety.

Mave places a hand over mine and gives it a squeeze. "Just breathe, Nettie, and know that I'm here. Whatever Chase is up to, we'll face it together. We've got this."

We're sitting on one of the couches in the foyer, and with each tick of the clock, my anxiety heightens. The guards that are surrounding us are making things worse for me, and I'm *this* close to bolting, and damning the consequences that'll come with it.

The estate's doors open, and I get to my feet almost immediately. Uncle Chase enters the foyer, and the power he exudes with each step he takes, would have made me look at him in admiration once upon a time, but now, all it invokes in me, is hate. Hate that he gets to have this moment, despite being a spineless turd that he is.

I look beyond him, and let go of a relieved breath when I see Dorran. His eyes meet mine, and the way his chest heaves when he exhales, tells me that he, too, is anxious about this.

He shoves the guard next to him and runs to me, and I all but fall into him when he wraps an arm around me and cups the back of my head as he hugs me to him.

"Did they do anything to you?" he asks against my ear. "Tell me you're okay, Cigs."

I hold onto him and sigh against his neck. "I'm fine, I promise."

He pulls back and scans my face. "He knows," he says to me. "I don't know how, but he knows."

"I don't know, either." I swallow. "I'm so scared, Dorran."

"We'll figure it out, sweetheart. We've got no other choice but to."

I'm about to answer, but yelp instead when I'm pulled away from him. He's being dragged away from me as well, towards his crew.

"Don't fucking touch her!" Dorran yells, then shrugs off the guard who's holding him.

The one who still has a tight grip on my arms, lets me go, and Mave pushes him in the shoulder before coming to stand next to me.

"Careful with your hands, Ashton," he tells the guard, who says, "Sorry, boss," and steps away from me.

"Such dramatics, Dorran," Uncle Chase taunts, and takes a seat on the chaise lounge in front of us. "I didn't take you for the romantic type, I really didn't."

There are guns being pointed at the 6 of us from all directions, but still, I manage to get close to Dorran and the crew. Mave joins me.

"Tell me why we're here so that we can be done with this bullshit," Dorran says.

"Oh, but I'm pretty sure you already know why you're here." Uncle Chase leans back on the chaise lounge. "But I'm also sure that you're confused as to how I know about what you did to my sister, so let me give you a quick rundown of things." He grabs a bottle of scotch from the table next to him, then helps himself to a glass full of it.

"My initial doubt seeped in when I reached Miranda's scene of death and found her in her car," he starts, then takes a long pull of his drink. "They said it was an electrical failure that caused the car to burn, but how could that be? My sister always had her car serviced, so something like that could only happen if her car had been tampered with." He glares at Dorran, who remains unaffected as he glares back at him. "The fire department had been successful in dousing the fire on time, so Miranda's body didn't burn off completely. There was enough on it that accurate, *useful* evidence could be gathered from it." He finishes his glass and fills himself another. "The forensic experts informed me that she'd been dead before her car burned down, and that there were signs of assault on her. Her wrist and ankle bones were fractured, probably due to them being tied for a long period of time. Some of her fingernails were missing, and I was told they'd most probably been plucked off her nailbeds." The hold he has on the glass tightens. So does my chest. "And the final bit of information that set things into motion for me, was her broken neck. The experts thought she'd been choked, or that her neck had been twisted by force, causing her cervical vertebra to all but shatter. Learning all of this wasn't easy for me, because no one has ever had the audacity to even *breathe* in Miranda's direction the wrong way without losing their life, so the question I had to ask myself – whilst standing above my sister's victimized body, was: who would be so stupidly bold as to not only *touch* Miranda Adler, but also bring about her end in such a disrespectful, disturbing, and painful manner?" He polishes the scotch and places the glass on the table, then brings his eyes to Dorran again. "And, you see, I didn't have to think too much on it, because the only man impetuous enough to do such a thing, would have to be the Bloody fucking Prince of Riverside. I knew without a doubt it was you, but I needed to know *why*."

"And so, you had me spied on, no doubt," Dorran says matter-of-factly.

"Precisely. My people found you with Cignette, and I was sure she'd hired you to kill Miranda. But now…" He glances between Dorran and I. "I feel like I was wrong; this is something entirely different than her simply paying you to kill my sister, isn't it? The two of you – you're *together*." He scoffs. "Scum attracts scum, I suppose."

"Glad you had the commonsense to figure that out, at least," Dorran remarks.

"Mom deserved to die," I say, repeating myself from earlier. "You had the habit of brushing her immoral behavior under the rug, but it didn't change the fact that she was a mentally unstable woman. Deranged even, given the things she's said and done to me over the years."

Uncle Chase gets to his feet so fast, that it makes me gasp and take a step back. And when he pulls a Glock out from behind him before pointing it at me, I feel my throat close up a little.

"You'll keep that bitch mouth of yours shut, you fucking hear me?" He gets closer to me, and I in turn move back.

"Put the gun down, Chase," Dorran warns, and shifts his body towards mine. "I won't ask again."

"You wouldn't want to, because if you do, I'll blow her fucking head off, and I won't hesitate."

Dorran shifts towards me further, but doesn't do anything.

Uncle Chase grins and looks at me. "I was so proud of you," he hisses. "So proud of the woman I *thought* you were. Beautiful, lively, carefree, charming – those are the terms I've always labeled you with, but I realize now how fucking wrong I was." He snorts and brings the Glock nearer. "You were the greatest thing your mother and I created. At least that's what you were to me – my treasure, my heir; a source of continuation of the Adler line. Miranda didn't match my enthusiasm over the same, but I was so happy when you were born. You were everything to me, up until the moment you decided to take from me what meant the most to me." He sneers down at me, and my insides all but flip.

You know that feeling when it seems like the ground has quite literally slipped from under your feet? Yeah, that's what I'm experiencing right now. Because what Uncle Chase just said – it doesn't make any sense.

"You…" I swallow, then shake my head a little. "What did you just say?"

His laugh is short, menacing. "I'm your daddy, *sweet pea*," he confirms, using the endearment mockingly. "Did you really think your mother had a drunken one-night-stand and ended up pregnant with you?" He chuckles. "Cignette, you're *my* daughter, not a random elite's."

I suddenly can't breathe; I feel like I'm being drowned. Beside me, Dorran has gone rigid, which means that even *he's* shocked by what has just been revealed. Mave and the others remain silent, but the air in the foyer has grown impossibly thick.

"You're lying," I say, then let go of a breath. "You're lying to me."

"I fucked my sister to keep our bloodline secure, Cignette. Call it old-fashioned or corrupted, I don't care. You're my daughter, and that's the truth."

"Why not tell me about it, then?" I sniff, and realize that I'm crying.

"It was an insignificant detail," *my father* tells me. "I didn't think it was necessary for you to know."

"You didn't think it was necessary for me to know…" I chuckle, but there's no humor in it. "And who the fuck gave you the right to decide that, huh? How could you have kept this from me and played pretend for all these years like you weren't hiding *the biggest goddamn fact about me*?" I swipe at my tears and point a finger at him. "You are a selfish, conniving piece of shit, and you deserve a downfall far worse than the one Mom received."

He cups the back of my neck and fists my hair, making me wince. "You are nothing but an ungracious little slut who loves playing the victim whenever it pleases you," he grits out, then pulls at my hair. "You will no–" He stops when Dorran grabs him by the collar and all but hauls him away from me.

There are orders being yelled, and thumps of footsteps getting closer. And then – as if the tides have turned completely – utter havoc ensues, hazing everything around me.

67.
CIGNETTE

The piercing sound of a gun firing meets my ears, just as Varsha yells, "Dorran, no!"

I look towards him, and see that he's barely missed being shot by my dad.

Mave pulls me back, and when I struggle against his hold, he tightens it and pulls me back further.

"Don't try to do anything stupid," he says to me. "Dorran knows what he's doing; I can't fucking let you get hurt."

"I told you not to touch her!" Dorran spits at Dad, then punches him in the gut.

He bends forward, but recovers surprisingly fast.

"Stand the fuck down!" Jayce tells the guards. "Or my brother here will cut the old bastard open before any of you can so much as blink."

They look unsure, but when Dad nods at them, they step back.

"You forget your place, Dorran," he says, then groans and places a hand on his stomach. "You forget who has been providing for you and your *pets* for all these years."

"For airing your dirty laundry so that your manicured fingers remain clean? Trust me, Chase, I *know*." Dorran gets in Dad's face. "But the thing is: Cignette means more to me than you or your money. She completes me. It's something nothing and no one has ever had the power to do."

"She will be the end of you; the end of everything you've created for yourself, and everything that you *are*."

"Oh, Chase." Dorran smiles, then chuckles. "Put me in a fucking grave, and watch how I come back to life with the smallest of breaths she takes in my name. Cignette is my beginning, and if she's to be my end, then I'll go a happy fucking man, I assure you."

Dad gives him a once over, then tilts his head to the side. "Not if I kill her first." He points the Glock at me, and before I know what's happening, he fires it in my direction.

I suck in a breath and wait for the impact, the pain, but it doesn't come. What instead happens is far more agonizing than I could have ever imagined the bullet wound to feel like.

Mave has stepped in front of me, and I watch – completely shell-shocked – as he takes the bullet that was meant for *me*, right in the center of his throat. It exits through the back of his neck, and as a scream rips out of me, he falls onto the floor with a heavy thud.

"Motherfucker!" Dorran yells, and I see a flash as he punches my dad in the jaw, but I'm too broken to do anything but fall on my knees in front of Mave.

In front of his body.

"Mave…" I shake him, but he doesn't respond to me.

He *always* responds to me.

My vision is blurry; I'm trembling from head-to-toe. I want to throw up, but I also need him to fucking answer me.

"Mave, please." I shake him again, then look at his wide-open eyes that are staring into nothingness, and the thick stream of blood that's pooling under him and seeping into the hem of my dress. "*Mave*."

He remains still. So still that it paralyzes me for a minute.

"Mave…" A sob breaks out of me, and it's loud enough that it rattles me and makes my body tremble harder. "Mave, please… Please, please,

please." I shake him yet again, but nothing happens. It doesn't wake him up; it doesn't make him look at me. And that's because he's gone.

Mave is *dead.*

Just like that, he's been taken from me. My constant, my best friend. The man who always listened to me, no matter what. The man who loved me for who I am – flaws and all. Who made me see things I wouldn't have otherwise seen. Who fought for me, and *with* me whenever he thought I was wrong. The man who was my shadow, who always stood behind me, even when I asked him not to. All I would have to do is look over a shoulder, and he'd be there. *He'd be there…*

Not anymore.

I place a hand over his heart, and mine practically breaks when I don't feel a single heartbeat under my palm.

"I love you," I say in between my tears. "I know I've never said it, but I love you, Mave. I always will." I briefly close my eyes when I can't look at him lying here like this. "I'm sorry. I'm so fucking *sorry.*" Knowing that he's dead because of me hurts so much, but I know he wouldn't want me to blame myself, so I have to try not to. And even though I don't deserve a single breath I'm taking right now, I'll keep on taking them, because they are the reason Mave gave up on his. And I can't let his sacrifice go to vain.

Glass smashes somewhere, making me open my eyes. I look ahead, and see that Dorran has tackled my dad on the floor. There are shards of glass and spilled scotch around them, and every time Dad tries to slip away from Dorran, he pulls him back and punches him harder than he did before.

The guards – who only minutes ago were pointing their weapons at me and the others – have now put them down, and are instead looking at Mave with the same amount of pain that I'm feeling. These men may be working for my dad, but they were part of Mave's team. They looked to him for orders, and I'm sure they respected him more than they do my father.

Dorran stands – his arms marred by cuts from the glass – and grabs my dad by the collar before pulling him to his feet. I see that he now has bruises on his face and neck, but they are still nothing compared to what he did to Mave.

"I will take my time with you," Dorran grits out. "Skin you inch by fucking inch until you're begging me to kill you. And you'll see, Chase, just how ruthless I can be when someone messes with me or my family."

"You're a *butcher*," Dad sneers. "Nothing more, nothing less."

Dorran jolts him in a way that makes him stumble. "At least I'm not a petty loner, eh?"

Dad groans, and I notice too late that he's left his Glock on the floor, and is now holding a shard of glass in his hand instead. Before I can open my mouth to warn Dorran, Dad is already raising his arm to slash the shard across Dorran's face.

The latter lets go of a surprised sound as he moves away from my father, and when he touches his hand to his right cheek before pulling it away, I notice that it's stained with blood.

"Ledge!" Jayce reaches Dorran, and while he's busy trying to move Dorran away from my dad, the latter raises his arms and brings the pointed edge of the shard against the side of Jayce's neck.

"No!" I scream, then stumble to my feet.

This can't be happening right now. This can't… It can't.

"Jay, no!" Alex rushes towards his husband, and Jayce falls onto him. He's gurgling blood whilst cupping his wound, and his wide, shocked eyes are glazed. He grabs for Dorran, who has gone so pale that I'm scared he'll pass out.

"Jay…" He kneels at his side and takes his free hand. "Brother."

Varsha and I join them, and Jayce's eyes land on me.

"*Look after him*," he mouths. "*Please*."

I shake my head, and when my tears blur my vision, I swipe at them and move close to him.

"You'll be here to do it yourself, you fucking hear me?" I tell him. "I've already lost one friend today. I can't lose another."

Dorran is silent as he stares at Jayce. There's no expression on his face, but his cheeks are wet with tears. A few of them fall over his bleeding cut, but he doesn't flinch.

Jayce gasps, and the hold he has on his neck loosens. A second later, his arm goes slack, and then his shoulders. His eyelids flutter shut, and his chest stops moving.

"No…" Alex whispers. His breathing is heavy as he jerks his husband. "Fucking no, goddamn it!" He's crying now, and so are Varsha and I. But Dorran – he continues to stare at Jayce.

How can a normal, regular day turn into something so catastrophically wrong? How can you have everything you wanted in one moment, and then have it taken from you in the next? It doesn't make sense.

It doesn't fucking make *sense*.

"Jay." Alex jerks him again, then touches his forehead to Jayce's as he cries harder. "Babe, please don't do this to me. Jay… Baby…"

Varsha wraps an arm around him and holds him close, all the while keeping one of her hands on Jayce's slumped shoulder.

Dad laughs. He's out of breath, but still, he laughs. "Martyrs, these *fools*." He laughs more, then gestures at Mave. "They died protecting those who shouldn't be alive in the first place."

Anger boils in me. So much so that all I can see is his smug face, and how I want to wipe the look of victory off it.

I touch Dorran's thigh, but he remains as is. So, I slip the thing I want from him, from the front pocket of his jeans, and then let him be. My dress tangles with my ankles as I get to my feet, but I manage not to fall. My head is so heavy that I want to sit back down, but I can't – not right now.

Instead, I make my way to my dad while trying to maintain my balance, and the moment he sees me, he stops laughing.

"Before you decide to do something idiotic, know that I have a dozen guards in here that are ready to tear you apart where you stand," he threatens, then grins. "And anyone who tries to save you."

A snort leaves me, and his amusement vanishes. "You really think these men will defend you after you just killed the man they respected and followed?" I blink against the sting in my eyes. "If anything, I'd wager they'll be more than willing to help *me* in tearing *you* apart."

He glances around us, and what he sees makes him go a little pale.

"You think you're so smart and powerful, don't you?" I say to him. "You think that by killing those who meant the most to Dorran and I, you've proven a fucking point?" I step closer to him, knowing he won't answer me. "But all you've done, *Dad*, is written your own death sentence."

He hums. "Have I?" He chuckles, then ends up wincing and grabbing his stomach. "And who, exactly, will carry out this sentence of mine?"

"I'm *so* glad you asked," I tell him, then flick open Dorran's switchblade.

Dad's gaze falls to the weapon in my hand, then comes up to meet mine. Something shifts in him, and despite it being drastic, I can't put a finger on what it is, exactly.

"Do it, then; what the hell are you waiting for, daughter?" There's a readiness in him, in his posture. It's like he was expecting this to happen, or more like, he *wanted* this to happen.

A cry rips out of me as I stab the switchblade right in the middle of his chest.

Dad's eyes widen at the impact, and his sockets start turning red. His face blotches, and there's sweat coating his forehead and neck with how much he's straining himself.

"I wanna count all the things you've done wrong today, but I won't," I say. "And you know why that is?" I twist the blade's handle, and he wheezes against the pain I know I'm causing him. "Because I know for a fact that it'll only make you gloat, even in these final fucking moments of your life."

There's utter silence in the foyer, and it's clear that all eyes are on me right now.

Dad wheezes again, and I see that there's drool dripping out of his mouth and onto his chin.

"Hurts, doesn't it?" I slowly pull the blade out of him, and he tries to stumble away from me. I don't let him, though, and kick him in the balls, which makes him fall onto the chaise lounge behind him.

I step between his spread-out legs, then bend so that our faces are aligned. He seems bewildered and out of it, and his eyes are frantically moving around, but remain unfocused. His breathing has slowed down considerably, and I know I've hit him close to his heart.

"Look at me," I hiss, and when he doesn't, I slap him and yank his chin forward. "Fucking look at me, you asshole. I want you to keep that fading eyesight on me. I want you to know that *I'm* the one who brought you to your goddamn knees; who put a full stop on Chase Adler's ever-going chapter." I push the blade in through the same spot, and smirk when he convulses beneath me. His legs thrash, his mouth opens and closes as he tries to say something, and then finally, mercifully, he stops his protests and goes fully immobile.

Justice should never be expected – either from life, or from the people around you. It's something that needs to be *taken*, be it by force or by practicality. But the thing is: people like my father don't understand rationality. They're so used to getting everything they wish for, that they forget about the inevitable consequences of their actions. They need to be brought down to Earth every once in a while, or perhaps be dragged six feet under.

I scan him from top to bottom, then wipe the switchblade on his t-shirt. “For Mave, and for Jayce. And for letting me be treated like shit by my mother for over two *decades*.” I straighten and step away from his body. “May you rest in fucking *pieces*, Dad,” I say, then turn my back on him.

68.
DORRAN

Jayce is dead. And as much as it hurts to think about it, to let the words play in my head, it won't change the fact that I lost my brother today. The man who understood me better than anyone ever has; the man who protected me so fiercely that in the end, it cost him his life.

A life that was far more valuable than mine.

I'm not someone who dwells on things – or people, for that matter. But Jayce – him and I were bonded. He was an extension of my darkness; my morals. He balanced me out, and I knew that if I needed his advice, or his presence, all I'd have to do is look to the side, and he'd be there to guide me, to stop me if I were about to mess shit up. Not anymore, though, and the pain of that truth is enough to crumple me on the inside. It has petrified me to the point where everything feels constricted, and I don't know how to get rid of the fucking weight of it. Of the guilt and the loss. It's too much; too strong.

A series of gunshots are fired just outside the estate, which startle me out of my trance.

"What the fuck was that?" Varsha asks.

Alex doesn't say anything; he's lost in his own head while he holds Jayce to his chest.

"Let's hope it's Solo," I say, then touch the scar on my right cheek, only to flinch at its tenderness. It's not bleeding as much now, but it burns like a motherfucker.

I move my hand away from my face and turn around, and notice as one of the guards – Maverick had called him Ashton, I believe – pulls Cignette to the side when a bullet somehow ends up hitting the chandelier hanging from the ceiling. He says something to her, then motions for the others to follow him outside. There's yelling, more gunshots, and then, I hear a voice saying, "Maverick is dead. He died protecting the people in this estate. Shooting those who have come to their aid goes against everything he taught us, and everything he stood for. I want you guys to stand down, and if anyone wants to disobey me, they can come forward and let it be known."

Solo is here, then.

The guard's words ignite strong murmuring from those in the garden. I can't hear, or understand, what they're saying, so I instead look at Cignette again.

She's sitting on the floor now, next to Maverick's body. Her hands, and most of her dress, are covered in blood – both Chase and Maverick's. There's color on her cheeks, as if she's flushed or something, and her hair is a sweaty mess around her. She's staring at her hands, and is running the pad of her thumb over my switchblade's handle. I don't remember when or how she took it off me, but then again, I'd been completely out of it when Chase had attacked Jayce, so I wouldn't have known anyway.

The commotion from outside stops. Silence takes over, but it's only brief. I hear footsteps marching up the estate's stairs, and then…

"Dor?"

Varsha lets go of a breath, but it quickly turns into a sob. Alex doesn't so much as react; he remains as is.

Solo all but runs towards me, with Eddie right behind him. There's a guy with them who I haven't seen before, but with the crisp blue suit he's wearing, along with the earpiece on him, and the pistol he's holding, he looks like he could be a security personnel or something.

"Dor?" Solo kneels before me and places a hand on my shoulder. "What the fuck happened here?"

Eddie glances around the foyer with wide eyes and a too-shocked face. "*Holy shit*," he whispers, then pulls his phone out of his leather jacket before putting it to his ear.

"Jayce is dead," I tell Solo, then swallow and look at him. "Chase and Maverick are dead, too."

His face crumples. "Dorran…"

"My brother is dead, Solo," I say out loud for the first time, and it sucks. It fucking *hurts*. It makes me wanna heave, but it also makes me wanna scream until I can't.

Solo's eyes mist over, but he sniffs and glances at Alex and Jayce. The former is crying now, and his tears are painting Jayce's paling cheek.

"I'm so sorry I didn't come sooner," Solo says, then grabs one of Jayce's hands before bowing his head. "Fucking hell, I wish I could kill Chase right now."

"There's unfortunately no chance of that happening, since he's already very dead," Eddie says, then steps closer to us. "And you guys need to get outta here. *Now*."

"I'm not going to leave Jayce here," I tell him.

"I'll get the body to you as soon as I can."

Body…

I'm on my feet so fast that it makes me momentarily dizzy, but I manage to get in Eddie's face without falling on my ass.

"What the fuck did you just call him?" I grit at him.

He frowns, and his expression softens. “I’m sorry; I didn’t mean it like that.” He sighs and touches my arm. “It’s a force of habit, man. Seriously, I’m sorry.”

My throat tightens, but I clear it and give him a curt nod. No use taking my frustration out on him. He’s only trying to help.

I step back, and see that Solo is attempting to pull Cignette away from Maverick. She’s trying to push him off, but he isn’t giving up.

“Just two more minutes,” she’s pleading with him. “Please let me look at him for two more minutes.” She starts crying, and even though I try, I can’t hold my own tears at bay. A few of them drip down to my scar, and to my jaw, and I let them.

How much can a broken human being take before they reach their limit? How much can they push, and push, and push, until they’re tired of it, of losing?

“Grow a fucking pair and come to terms with the fact that he’s gone, kid,” Solo says to Cignette. “Because he really is; Maverick is gone.”

She shoves at his chest – once, twice – and when he takes my switchblade from her before grabbing her wrists, she lets him pull her in for a hug.

“Be strong for him,” he encourages. “Because this is *not* how he’d want you to behave – not for him, at least. And you and I both know that.”

She cries into his shirt, staining it with blood and tears. “He shouldn’t be gone,” she whispers, then shakes her head. “He *can’t* be.”

“You live in a world where you can’t hope for things to always go as planned, kid. That’s your truth – one you gotta know by heart.” He holds her tighter, and I see how much he’s struggling to keep it together.

Watching them like this, I realize that Solo knew before I did that Cignette needed this; needed the reassurance, and the hug. It may not do wonders against what she’s lost, but it’ll help her see that she’s got people on her side who refuse to let her shatter. Solo’s tough love may seem too much for her to handle right now, but I'm sure Cignette will appreciate it in the days to come.

It's a lesson for me, too, to be honest, as bitter as it may taste.

"Solo," comes Eddie's voice.

When Solo looks at him, he jerks his head towards the stranger. "Him and his team have work to do here. We should leave."

"Who are you?" I ask the guy.

"This is Aarav," Eddie answers for him. "He's Roman Washington's head of security."

"Roman Washington?"

"He's Dad's opponent at the elections," Cignette provides, having moved away from Solo.

"I'm sorry, did you just say *Dad*?" Solo says while staring at her, then goes, "Oh my fucking *God*."

Cignette runs the back of her hand under her nose. "Yeah."

Eddie looks like he's done with us, and with everything, but he blinks and pushes his fingers into his hair before gesturing at Aarav.

"Um, so yeah. Roman and Chase are competing for the administrator's seat at the elections, but now that Chase is dead, Roman is most likely to be named Riverside's new Administrator. *Unless* he's challenged by a member of Chase's family," he starts, then nods towards Cignette. "Solo was sure Chase was gonna die today, so him and I struck Roman a deal – one he couldn't, even if he wanted to, refuse."

"What deal?" Cignette asks.

Eddie folds his arms across his chest. "Roman has wanted your…*dad* dead for a while now, but he isn't keen on the idea of getting his hands dirty. Solo and I used that to our advantage and offered him to take the full responsibility of Chase's murder, and in turn, we guaranteed that you will *not* challenge him for the Administrator's seat in next year's election."

"But I don't wanna run for the position anyway."

"That's great and all, but there's still the matter of Chase being dead, isn't it? So, to keep suspicion, and the cops, off our tails, let's let Roman stay under the illusion that you only backed out of the elections because he consented to our term." He glances at Aarav. "You won't tell your boss, right?"

Aarav lifts a shoulder. "I'm sure he'd have agreed to take the credit for Chase's death regardless of what Miss Adler decided."

I shake my head. Fuck, this is too much; my brain can't keep up with this shit.

"I don't understand," I say. "Roman said yes to this just like that? Why would he do that? Wouldn't that disqualify him or, I don't know, *get him arrested*?"

Eddie gives me a tired look. "No, Dorran, it *wouldn't*. And that's because the current sheriff is Roman's man. Roman personally helped him get the promotion, and has assisted him financially on numerous occasions. Letting Roman take the blame for Chase's death works in our favor because he's all but untouchable, so there won't be a case, or any kind of inquiry, and the incident will go down in history as a random, untraceable shootout. The press, the people, the elites – no one will question Roman. And the law?" He chuckles. "He has strings attached way too deep into its crevices for any of us to even *try* to comprehend."

"And yet he lost to Chase during the previous elections," Varsha points out.

"Chase was a people pleaser. The citizens who voted for him were stunned by his charms. Roman, however, is a brute. He works through power, status, and wealth. The citizens of Riverside are too loud, and their voices have always received prominence. But now that Chase is out of the equation, they won't have a choice but to accept Roman as the Administrator."

"And how will this supposed shootout be labeled *untraceable*?" Cignette asks. "There are cameras both inside and outside this property. And the guards? Won't they tell a different story?"

"We killed the ones that were stationed at the gates and the gardens when we got here," Solo tells her. "The ones that were with you were loyal to Maverick, and have agreed to say nothing. They won't be a threat to us."

"The guards we killed will be used as casualties," Aarav says. "My team is currently outside, staging their bodies. The cameras you speak of will be hacked into to show subterfuge, and even though the sheriff won't need any of these *proofs*, we'll set the scene here in such a way that it's believable to his and the deputies' eyes."

Cignette glances at Chase, and then at Aarav. "He wasn't shot to death, though. I stabbed him."

Aarav smirks. "I'll just say that I was feeling rather…*creative* with my methods."

"If the sheriff is, indeed, Roman's guy, why fake shit anyway?" I question.

"Because patriotism and righteousness are things that have a tendency of popping into these lawful bastards' hearts at unreasonable times," Eddie asserts. "So it's good to be prepared."

Silence takes over us all as the weight of everything sets in. And in my state of quiet contemplation, I notice a few people entering the estate.

A deal has been made and things are being done. It's over; it's all fucking *over*. Just like that, it's done. But stuff isn't the same anymore, because *he's* gone and life's still moving forward. The future has already been written, but his – it was taken away from him the moment he decided to step in front of me; to take the brunt of the attack that was meant for *me*.

God, I wanna close my eyes and sleep. For a week, a month, a year – I just wanna fucking zone out. Because staying awake will remind me of what I lost today, and that's a scar that'll forever stay infected, even when it ages. I might fade to nothing one day, but this wound – it won't leave my side, even in the fucking afterlife.

I glance towards Jayce, and see that Varsha and Alex have now moved away from him. A few members of Eddie's team are wrapping him up in a body bag, and as Alex breaks down again, I swallow the painful lump in my throat and force myself to look at Jayce's face right before the bag has been zipped shut over it.

"I'm sorry," I mouth, just as a tear slips past my lips. "I love you, Jayce, and I'm so damn sorry."

69.

CIGNETTE

I can't get the images out of my head – of Riley trying to force himself on me, of Mave's lifeless body bleeding out before me, and of the fear on Jayce's face when he made that request to me before he died. It's a constant loop of nightmares, despite me being fully awake. It incapacitates me, tightens my chest to the point where I can't use my lungs to draw in air. And when I close my eyes, the exact same images come to life. I can suddenly smell Riley's breath as he tries to lean into me. I can feel Mave's ice-cold hands grabbing mine as he looks at me with pain on his ashen face, his throat punctured by a bullet wound. And I can feel the weight of Jayce's final words, and how much they mean, both to him and to Dorran.

Speaking of Dorran…

He's been standing outside in the rain ever since Eddie dropped us at *Finesse* a few minutes ago. I had asked him to come up to his loft, but he'd refused. I had wanted to insist, but I also didn't want to trouble him, so I'd let him be. I know exactly what he's going through right now, and even though leaving him alone has been gnawing at me, I had to do it. I guess it's because I, too, needed some time to myself – to think, to forget, and to push myself to move forward. And so, when I'd entered the loft, I'd all but slumped against the living room wall – knees pressed to my chest, and my arms wrapped around my legs.

I sigh and glance at a piece of tile in the leftmost part of the room. It's beige, untouched and unbroken, and I fucking envy it. The idea of it makes me laugh a little, and I realize that I'm crying.

"Fuck," I breathe, then slide my fingers into my sweaty hair and push them back.

My thoughts go back to Dorran. He's out in the goddamn *rain* – all fucking alone. And I need to be there with him instead of cowering in a corner.

Solo has driven Alex and Varsha to his condo. He wanted Dorran and I to come with, but the former said no to the offer so fast, that you'd think Solo had suggested something outrageous. I don't think I'll ever fully figure him out in this lifetime.

I sniff, swipe my hands over my face, then get to my feet. My entire body feels weighed down, making me groan. I use the floor as a support and haul myself up, then stumble my way towards the small window in the living room. I've left Dorran to himself for long enough.

The day has set, and the grey evening light is casting dull shadows against the street, making the view before me a bit spectral. It's still raining pretty heavily, and there he is – amidst the brutal sheets of downpour – standing right in front of his garage, unmoving; staring at nothing.

I swallow and let go of a breath, in turn fogging the window's glass, then move away from it before making my way out of the loft.

He may not say it, but I know for a fact that Dorran needs me. Whether to simply be by his side and experience the loud silence with him, or to talk to him – he *needs* me. And I'm not at all hesitant to admit that I need him. More than I've ever needed anything in my life so far. No exaggeration.

70.

DORRAN

The only sense of reality I have right now are the fast-falling drops of rain that are all but pelting onto my skin. They are relentless in their approach – biting into the cut on my face – yet somehow, they make me feel…I don't know, grounded, I suppose. Because if it wasn't for the rain, I'd be too far down in my head, and my thoughts would end up pulling me under eventually. But the cold wind is keeping me stable, and the goosebumps it's igniting are reminding me that I'm still alive.

I don't know how I'll move forward without Jayce, and it's because I haven't had to do that for more than half my life. He's just always *been there*, and even though I can't sit on his loss for the rest of my days, I can sure as hell let myself *feel* it. The hole he's left in my goddamn chest will never fill up, but I guess that's how it is when you lose a part of yourself. And that's exactly what Jayce was: a part of me; the other side of the coin.

A reflection of myself.

I bow my head and close my eyes, and try not to shiver when a gust of chilly air swishes past me. I hear soft splashes of water behind me, seconds before I sense her presence. Her warm, steady breaths cut through the cold when she leans in and presses a kiss on the back of my neck, and my body all but folds in on itself at how good that one small gesture felt.

I turn, and there she is – soaking wet, and still, the most beautiful thing I've seen. My twisted fucking addiction; the woman who has all but consumed me inside out.

"Come inside, Dor; it's fucking freezing out here," she says, then pushes away the wet strands of her hair that are sticking to her face.

"In a bit," I tell her, then clear my throat when my voice sounds scratchy to my ears.

Cignette frowns, then steps close to me. "Then I'll stay here with you."

I shake my head. "Go back inside, Cigs. You'll catch a cold."

"You can catch it to, you know? You're not invincible."

I know she said this as a logical response to my comment, but it makes me flinch regardless. It's because she's right; I'm not fucking invincible, and it literally took losing someone important in my life for me to realize that.

"I didn't…" Her brows knit together as she frowns. "I didn't mean for it to come out like that, I swear."

"I know." I swallow and hold her by the waist. "Trust me, I get it."

"I'm so sorry…" she whispers. Her lips part as she sucks in a breath, and then she starts to cry.

"Cigs." I pull her to me, and just looking at the pain, and the utter sadness on her face, makes my own tears fall. Because I can echo what she's going through – the turmoil, the guilt, and the emptiness.

"I've caused nothing but chaos," she says while crying harder. "Loss and sorrow and…*chaos*."

"No." When she looks to the ground and continues to sob, I grab her chin and lift her face. "What happened today was not your fault. Maverick and Jayce's deaths – they're a result of Chase's madness. Me and the crew knew there'd be fatalities the moment we stepped into his estate, and even though I'd hoped nothing would go wrong, it did. But that's not on you, and I don't, not for a second, blame you. And I'm sure Alex and Varsha don't, either. You can't carry the weight of something that wasn't even in your hands to begin with. It's not fair to you."

She shakes her head as if she doesn't believe a word I'm saying. "You and the crew got involved into all of this because of me. If I hadn't come to you after killing Riley, you wouldn't have gone after my mom. She'd still be here, and Dad wouldn't know about us, and Jayce and Mave would still be alive and–"

"Fucking shut up."

The rain has slowed down a little, so I can now see her face with a bit more clarity when she blinks up at me in surprise.

"Putting an end to Miranda is something I'll never regret, and if I could, I'd do it all over again," I tell her honestly. "And Jayce – he died trying to protect *me* today. He took the blow that was meant for *me*. And Mave – he did exactly the same for you. You know why that is?" A fresh stream of tears blurs my vision. "It's because they wanted us to *live*. It's because they knew that it was next to *impossible* for all of us to make it out of that situation unscathed, so they willingly put themselves forward. It was stupid and reckless of them, but still, they did it for us. The least you and I can do, Cigs, is respect their decision by doing what they wanted us to do."

"I don't mean to be a burden to you, not when you're grieving as well. I just…" She looks to the side. "I wish things had been different. I wish I could do something to fix this; to make it better somehow."

"You can't. And I can't, either. They're gone, and we're here, and that's the fucking truth."

Her shoulders shake as she cries, and something in my gut twists.

"Baby…" I cup her jaw. "Look at me."

She doesn't, and keeps her eyes on the street behind me.

"Cignette." I run the pad of my thumb over her cheek. "Look at me, please."

That shifts something in her. She brings her gaze to mine, and when I scan her face – the openness on it – I let go of an exhale and say the words I've known to be true for a while now.

"I love you." I pull her closer to me, and watch as she inhales sharply in return. "I fucking *love* you, Cignette Adler, and I won't be able to do any of it without you. Living, breathing, functioning – none of it. I'll need you by my side every step of the way, so I want you to get a hold of yourself and stop feeling sorry for the both of us. It's not going to help anyone, and it's not the way to honor Jayce and Maverick. So yeah, whether you like it or not, you're stuck with me, and I'm too fucking selfish to let you hurt yourself."

She cups my wrist with one hand, and fists the front of my vest with the other. She looks dazed, almost shocked.

"Say that again," she rasps, then sniffs.

I bend and touch my nose to hers, making sure to keep my eyes on her. "I love you," I repeat myself. "I think I've loved you for a while now, but I kept pushing the thought away in fear of rushing you with it. Every time I'd feel my body buzz in your presence, or feel a welcoming weight on my chest when you were near, I knew; knew what the fuck it meant. And as much as I've loathed the term for the power it holds over us, I can't deny that I feel it for you. I'm in love with you, and it's a thing that'll never go away, because it's instilled into every fiber of my being."

She laughs, and then she cries. She fists my vest tighter, then tilts her head to the side and places a kiss on my lips. "And I love *you*. I've known it since the night you took me to that hill after Varsha killed Gavin. You told me then how love made you weak, but all I could think about was how much stronger I was, simply by knowing I loved you. You help me fly, Dorran, and it's something I'll forever be grateful for."

Hearing her say these things is overwhelming. It's thrilling and terrifying, and I'll never get tired of it, despite knowing that I don't fully deserve it.

"It's all you," I tell her. "It's always been you. Whether it was surviving your mother's cruelty or standing up to her. Whether it was ending Riley's life for his intentions towards you, or killing your father for what he took from you and I, you did it all by yourself, Cignette. And as much as I'd like to take credit for your strength, I won't, because you're a force of nature – one I'm more than happy to stand behind, and not overshadow."

She cups my face and pulls me down to kiss me, and I wrap my arms around her middle and kiss her back.

She tangles her fingers into the hair at the nape of my neck, and my body hums against the pressure. "Promise me that you'll never leave me," she commands in between kisses.

"Never. And if I've ever given you the impression, then I'm sorry." I press her body against mine. We're so close that we're sharing the same breath. It's perfect. It's everything.

"No…" She opens her mouth and kisses me harder, and I can only keep up with her. "I love you, Dorran."

"I love you, Little Swan."

The rain picks up again, but Cignette and I continue to hold onto each other. As long as I have her, and she has me, we can take on anything together. Broken and battered and bruised – she is it for me, and I can only hope that I'm enough for her.

The Flawed Princess and her Bloody Prince – we're a tale not many know about, but maybe one day they will. Maybe someone will write our story onto pages, and if they do, I wonder if it'll resonate with those who read it.

Not every love story is inked in blood, but mine and Cignette's is. And it's okay, because it's *our* misshaped reality – the only one we know.

The only one we'll always know.

EPILOGUE
CIGNETTE

1 year later

I place a hand on top of the gravestone, then settle down next to it. I set the pink rose I'm holding, in front of it, then sniff against the burning sensation in my nose. "Day 365 without you," I start, then swallow. "Still hasn't gotten easy, but I promise you that I'm trying." I glance at the inscription on the gravestone, and read it over and over until it starts to blur and I have no other choice but to look away.

In loving memory of

Maverick Justinian Constance

1982 — 2023

Protector. Friend. Professional eye-roller.

It was today, one year ago, that Dorran lost Jayce, and I lost Mave. The two of us have been taking things slow, and even though it hasn't been an easy process, we're doing our best with it.

I look ahead, squinting against the sunlight, and see that Dorran, Varsha, Alex, and Solo have knelt around Jayce's grave. Dor and Solo seem somber, but Alex and Varsha – they appear completely crestfallen.

Burying Jayce with his family was not an option, since he'd cut ties with them years ago. And, because Mave didn't have a family of his own, him and Jayce were put to rest a few feet from each other.

I sniff again and smile down at the gravestone. "Remember that construction guy I've been telling you about?" I chuckle, then flick a tiny piece of rubble with my forefinger. "I asked him to fix the countertop yesterday because it didn't look the way I wanted it to, and when I turned around, I swear I heard him call me a menace." I laugh, but it turns into a sob. "Fuck, I miss you, Mave." I close my eyes and will for the tears to stop, but they don't. And when a soft, feather-light breeze touches my wet cheek – almost like a caress – I suck in a breath and open my eyes. A chill runs through my very bones, leaving me stunned.

After my dad's death became old news last year, and Roman was named the new Administrator, Dorran and I decided to leave Riverside. Living in the city where we lost all but everything wasn't doing wonders for either of us, so I sold both the Adler estates, and Dorran sold *Finesse*, and we moved to Anaheim, California. And, because Dorran has reopened *Finesse* in Anaheim, Varsha and Alex have joined us.

When I started my YouTube channel just a couple of months ago – dedicating it solely to fashion – I wasn't expecting it to reach an audience so quickly, but it surprisingly has. I continue to gain more and more traction with each video I upload, bringing me one step closer to my ultimate goal of turning myself into a well-known name in the industry before I can start a brand of my own. Getting there will take a while – lots of setups and milestones and competition – but I'm determined, and I believe in myself, so I should be fine.

"Cigs?"

I wipe the tears and snot off my face, then look up. "Alex, hey."

He gives me a small, forlorn smile. "You ready to head out? I kinda wanna leave." His voice cracks, so he blinks and clears his throat.

I get to my feet and dust the mud off my hands and jeans, returning his smile with an understanding one of my own. "Sure, yeah."

He glances at Mave's grave, then brings his gaze to mine. "You okay?"

I push a few errand strands of hair behind my ears. "I think so." I shrug. "Honestly, it's not an answer I've perfected yet, because the question kind of makes me want to scream."

He clicks his tongue. "Fair enough."

"And you?"

He lifts a shoulder and slides his hands into the pockets of his trousers. "I have to be, right? It's how it's supposed to be, after all."

"Not necessarily, no." I notice that his eyes have misted over, so I erase the distance between us and pull him into a hug. "I love you, Alex, and I need you to know that you don't have to be strong if you don't want to be."

He hugs me back and sighs against the side of my neck. "There are days when I feel like I am – strong, I mean. But then there are days when I can't stand his absence. I go mad, and then I just feel…"

"Numb," I provide, then move back to look at him.

"Yeah."

"I wanna say it's all part of the healing process, but you and I both know that's bullshit. Whatever we're experiencing, it just *is*, and it's fucking tough. Exhausting, even"

"I'd probably knee you in the gut if you said that anyway," Alex remarks, and I can't help but laugh at his comment.

Dorran and I's condo is currently under construction, so we've been crashing at the one Varsha and Alex are sharing. There are nights where we reminisce about some of our good memories with Jayce and Mave, and then there are those where we drink ourselves to the point where we don't feel anything at all.

Alex once again clears his throat, then jerks his head to the right. "The others have left, it seems. We should go as well."

I look to the side, and notice that Dorran and the others have indeed left.

I nod at Alex. "You go on ahead; I'll meet you guys in the parking lot."

"You sure?"

I nod again. "Yup."

He gives my arm a quick squeeze, looks at Jayce's grave one last time, then starts walking out of the cemetery.

Once he's gone, I make my way to Jayce, pull another rose out from the back pocket of my jeans, and place it below the gravestone.

"He hates it when I fuss over him," I say, referring to Dorran, "but I *am* taking care of him, I promise. Of all 3 of them." I step back and glance between Mave and Jayce, and then, with a slow exhale, I turn around and head towards the parking lot.

Solo and Dorran are having a conversation when I reach my Cadillac, whereas Alex and Varsha are standing next to Jayce's Jeep, which Alex now drives.

"You kids sure you don't wanna stay a while and have a few drinks with me?" Solo asks.

Dorran shakes his head. "We should get going, but the next time we're here, we'll stay for a round."

Solo ruffles his curls, then gives him a one-armed hug. "I'll take your word for it." He comes around and embraces the rest of us, then gets in his SUV before driving out of the parking lot.

Dorran walks over to me, then runs his long, calloused fingers over the front of my Cadillac. "To think, it all started because of this car," he tells me.

I blink at him. "Huh?"

He looks at me, then chuckles when he sees my confusion. "We met because you brought your Cadillac to *Finesse* over a year ago," he says, and shifts closer to me. "I knew I was done for the moment I saw you, and I was so pissed you were with *Gavin*, of all people."

I laugh a little, and he does the same. "I'm glad he suggested we go to your garage, though. That's the one good thing he did, if nothing else."

He seems contemplative for a moment, but then he just smiles. "True." The sunlight has reached its peak, and makes his midnight-blue eyes appear all but violet. He's a bit flushed from it, too, and the scar on his right cheek – now faded yet still visible – stands out against his complexion, making him look so fucking stunning that I wish I could stop time and just…admire him for a while.

"Hey." He tilts his head to the side. "You okay, sweetheart?"

I swallow and straighten a little. "Yeah." Cupping the side of his face, I rise on my tiptoes and press my lips to his. "You ready to go home?" I ask him.

He grins, and it's such an effortless gesture that it pulls at my eager heartstrings. "Yeah, let's go home," he answers, then kisses me.

Hardships are a part of life. They shape a person, teach them lessons nothing and no one ever can. Every hurdle, downfall, and loss have their value, and only when you've experienced it all, do you realize how precious, and *priceless*, life is. Some get to live it to the fullest, while some don't, so make sure to spend your time loving those who love you, disregarding those who envy you, and forgiving those who have hurt you. Remember: the only way for you is *up*, because darling, for you, even the sky is not the limit.

THE END.

ACKNOWLEDGMENTS

A massive thank you to my darling, Mary Meredith, for polishing this story so that the readers could enjoy it to its fullest.

A heartfelt thank you to my cheer team, aka my besties, Ashleigh Watkins, Emily Kurosawa, Jett, Candice Clark, Toyah O'Garro, Jenna Lockwood, and Garry Michael for lifting me up when I felt like I couldn't go any further during the entire process of writing this book. Thank you for sticking by my side and believing in Dorran and Cignette's story. You made a difference, please know that.

My family – without whom I would still only be dreaming of writing books, of telling stories. Thank you, Mom, Dad, Qadir, and my lovely aunt.

A cuddly thank you to my bunnies: Moon, Snow, Velvet (I miss you), and Coco. You four are my babies, and I'm beyond happy to be your momma. Thank you for the endless cuddles, kisses, and sniffs. Those got me through some of the hard times.

My lovely readers, I love you so much. You've stood by me from the beginning, have given my stories a chance, and for that, I'll forever be in your debt. Thank you – from the very bottom of my dramatic heart.